AN AIR THAT KILLS

A NOVEL

BY

J. J. BOHNAKER

Third Millennium Publishing

A Cooperative of Writers and Resources
On the Internet
http://3mpub.com

ISBN 978-1-947483-06-4
346 pages

Michael McCollum
Proprietor
Third Millennium Publishing
PO Box 14026
Tempe, AZ 85284-0068
mccollum@3mpub.com

11262019

Into my heart an Air That Kills
From yon far country blows
by
A.E. Housman
From
A Shropshire lad

Table of Contents

PROLOGUE

If you drive northwest of Albany for less than an hour, you will find yourself entering the foothills of the brooding Adirondacks. Forests of northern hardwoods mixed with stands of hemlock, spruce and pine dominate the landscape. Dotted here and there amongst the dark forests are isolated cottages and the pastures of small wilderness farms.

Fronting on one of the back-country roads is an abandoned farmhouse. The FOR-SALE sign disappeared long ago leaving only the rotting wood frame and the sign and the house are mostly hidden from curious eyes by the branches of untidy trees and wild bushes. The house was built between the road and the foot of a sharply inclined hill directly behind it and is connected to the outside world by a dirt path ending with a rusty mailbox. The RFD mailman who used to deliver to the house decided it was a strange bunch who lived there, what with two tyrant women running the place, a wandering woodsman, an old derelict hired hand who died mysteriously, and a kidnapped orphan, and then those murders... well, it was no wonder so many strange and terrible things happened as they did.

PART I

THE HERITAGE

CHAPTER 1

As of late, mind tricks were plaguing Matt Barry. He felt strange, erratic; his moods unpredictable. Sometimes it was difficult to focus and he raged at his wife, Lillian, in half sentences: "You... you... if only you... " but couldn't say what he wanted to say; say what he should have said years ago.

He was sitting in the den, *his* den, normally his place of refuge, but now it seemed strange, accusing, almost frightening. He was having scary visions of death; at least he thought it was death; like something or someone hovering around his chair, commanding him to follow; and the big, unliving eyes of the deer heads, usually dark and dull like pecan shells, now had the glow of life and were filled with a mean, unbearable glare that made his skin tingle. The others, birds or beasts hanging in winged death or frozen tension on the den walls, seemed possessed by the same demons. He closed his eyes, to make them go away. They wouldn't.

Matt was normally a quiet man, handsome in a rugged sort of way, not given to great distractions or dramatic moments, but now he knew that something was very wrong with him and his life, that it would have to be changed, corrected, before it was too late. *Something big* had to be done to correct this dirty mess; he didn't need help from a shrink as his cold, calculating wife said. She was so wrong about that, and Joyce too. She just kept posturing, pushing him to do things he just wouldn't do.

The over-sized leather chair, a gift Lillian had given him last year for his 43rd birthday, stuck to his sweaty palms as he got up and walked over to the custom-made cherry wood gun cabinet. His complexion, like his outdoor life, had grown pale and soft after years behind a desk, and now those soft hands passed over the smooth top of the cabinet, searching for the brass key. Unlocking the door, his eyes darted over the exquisite collection of shotguns and rifles: a superb 12 gauge Winchester model 21 side by side double-barrel, a sinuous beauty with the appeal of an ancient Greek Goddess; well-used but gleaming with care; the Browning Midas Grade Special 12 gauge Over and Under, looking delicate and tender from certain overhead angles, massive and dangerous from the side; and the custom built .300 Weatherby Magnum that always reminded him of Great White Hunters and lions padding through the African dust. It was good for lions or for the Kodiak grizzly he hoped to bag someday. There were several other guns of lesser lineage, like a 30/30 Winchester lever action he used for deer; he admired and cared for them all.

He slowly lifted the Browning Midas Special out of the cabinet, one of his favorites with its richly engraved stock and receiver, showing scrolled silver field scenes with gold-inlaid ducks and geese. The heft of it was solid and reassuring. He swung it around and aimed it at the accusing deer heads and then slowly lowering it and with a slight tremble, pushed the thumb lever on the neck of the stock. The action broke open, exposing the brilliantly milled surfaces of the chambers and the deep black emptiness of the barrels. "Yes," he whispered to himself, while inspecting the chambers, "beautiful piece of work," and it brought back the cold, dark waters of the Great Sacandaga Reservoir. When the dry leaves rustled and blew in the fall winds, now rushing down through the Adirondacks, he often went to this lake in the wilderness with his friend, Jack Tooley, for ducks. Jack had a cabin on the eastern shore near the point where the lake split into two arms, and an old Lyman runabout that he used in the warmer seasons to hunt the "Great Northern Pike", as he called it, but now, if the wintry cold or blustery weather had not gripped the lake, would be used on weekends scouring the reedy areas of the southern shores, waiting for the ducks to come in.

Jack had just called him a few weeks back: "Hey Matt, where the hell have you been? Haven't heard from you in months. You're spending too much time in Albany. Well, it's that time again. Ducks. Ducks! Remember? George and Babe are waitin' for you… " George was chocolate and Babe was black; two of the finest Labs he had seen. He loved those dogs, especially after losing Rusty, his golden retriever.

And it was great too that Lillian… well if there was one thing she could do and do it right, she knew how to prepare wild game birds, was something of an expert, learned it from her father, was especially good with beautiful, iridescent Mallard ducks, could tell the young and tender from the old and tough, knew when they needed plucking or skinning, knew... Knew... *Where the hell is that damn Lillian anyway?*

He cradled the Browning in his arm and with some difficulty, opened the drawer of the gun cabinet. Fumbling open a box of # 04 Duck loads, he slid the corrugated shells into the lower and upper chambers and found it very satisfying how the Browning closed again with a solid click, all the parts fitting together as if they were seamless. Then he broke open the action again and removed the shells. *Where is she?*

Once more the leather chair engulfed him and he found his hands running over the fine wooden stock and the engraved receiver. Then he stood up, yawned, and put the gun back in the cabinet. He felt good, reassured that he could own such fine guns and that they were still his. *They were still his, weren't they?*

Lillian was wrong. She was the problem. Always had been. Time passed like this while he tried to deal with other dark, fugitive thoughts. He would take the gun out of the cabinet and then put it back again, each time loading a shell into one or both of the barrels. He trembled again and lost focus and became disoriented. Then, he just sat there with the loaded shotgun, the prize of his collection, across his lap, with his mind reeling: *it's all about Lillian... Lillian!*

His eyes closed, he nervously stroked the hair-trigger. Then Matthew Barry remembered what he was doing and what he had decided and planned, not very long ago. Linda, his daughter, was out as usual and Lillian would be back home very soon. *Lillian!...* He waited.

CHAPTER 2

The wild landscape she loved and knew so well rolled by through the car window, but she stared at it dully; the harsh words hurled at her by Matt over the cabin clouded her view. What should she do? What *could she do about it*? *What was wrong with the sonofabitch anyway!* Her head shook and she grated her teeth. She hated that word, but now it had just forced its way into her head and demanded recognition.She didn't mean it. She *couldn't* have meant it.

The slowly moving car had just entered the foothills of the Adirondacks, leaving the thin woods and rolling green hills of farmland behind. Tall hemlock trees, fat with the year's growth, and undergrowth bushes, fighting for the autumn sunlight, were crowding right down to the road and the forest behind was thick with dark stands of spruce and pine and maple. After some time, the drone of the engine relaxed her, driving out the tension, and her vision began clearing and she was able to take in the moving landscape: hillside pastures of small isolated wilderness farms would come into view. lonely houses stood here and there, almost hidden by the dense trees. *Who would dare live in such isolation?* Yet, in spite of her gloom, living there appealed to her; it always had.

"I like it here," she said faintly to her companion Rosemary, who was driving. "My grandparents had a place up here... "

"What?" The car's little engine, something related to a chainsaw, now spat out its annoyance. "Oh... yes, I remember. I like it, yes, it's nice alright, maybe, in a wild sort of way," the younger woman said. "But it's too damn lonely. I couldn't live up here."

Lillian sighed and stared out the window. Sometimes there was little understanding between them. "I guess there's not many working farms left," she said, ignoring Rosemary's remark. "I see cars and trucks and piles of junk but no sign of animals or any indication that the places are being worked. Some of them look abandoned. My father always said it would be a tough place to farm.

Too many rocks stuck deep in the earth, too many trees killing the light."

"He was right," Rosemary said. "Winters are rough, too. Like living in Alaska or on the North Pole. But Harry claimed the opposite, said the land was good, said it was government policy after the war that's driving those people out."

They were driving north to the summer cabin at Caroga lake, less than an hour's drive from Lillian's home in Johnstown. It was the cabin Matt had sold that morning; they had fought viciously over it and as the argument evolved into its terminal crescendo, he yelled that he needed the money to cover investments that had gone sour. "Just throwing the damn money away," she had cried. "What's wrong with you! Have you lost your mind?" And, before his rage grew physical, she had walked out. Now she needed something to balance that; to see it once more and pick up a few things always left there. Trivial stuff, things that didn't matter at all but now took on a new importance: pots and pans and dishes and bedding and a few other things for cooking and cleaning. *What am I doing?* she thought.

Her daughter's cruel words about her selfishness had cut her the most, Because Lillian hated selling the cabin and It wasn't just a place of recreation for her as Linda said; it was a last connection with her rural roots, roots entwined in her soul. No, it wasn't like a real farm or anything like that, but it had brought the outdoors, the woods and water and animals back into her life and now it was important; important just to see the cabin one last time before letting go. It was her place of memories.

"Rosemary - take that next road to the right," she said, suddenly remembered something. "It's a short cut. I want to see something."

She slowed and turned right up an old narrow road. She kept the speed down; the faded asphalt surface had been etched through by violent Adirondack storms and cracked by the heavy blades of snowplows, giant Rios burdened by the tremendous cover of snow. Ancient trees branched across the road, keeping the sun away. The road looked like it hadn't been used in years.

"Where are we going?" Rosemary asked. "It's lonely back here."

"About another mile or so, not too far."

They stopped in front of an old abandoned farmhouse that sat back from the road, on the slope of a small hill. The house was mostly hidden by the branches of large tamarack trees, branches hanging in long swaying curves. There was a faded. Half-torn "For Sale" sign in front by the road.

"Let's take a look at this place," She said and got out. "I've passed by so many times... I've always wanted to see it."

"What for, Lillian?" Rosemary asked.

She didn't answer but led her up a weedy path to the house. Long ago the covering clapboards had weathered to the color of ruined wine and when she got up close, she could see that many were split and brittle with age.

"It looks old and gone to seed," Rosemary said. "The Weird Sisters could live here."

"Ha. And I suppose," Lillian said, sweeping her arm around, "That this is Birnam wood?"

Rosemary looked around at the trees.

"Just some old boards and weeds," Lillian continued, "Nothing that can't be fixed; replace the boards and clean out the weeds. The Weird Sisters, indeed. Look at this place. Isn't it great? Those tamaracks, so tall, so graceful. At night I'll bet you hear the owls and whippoorwills, just like we did at the cabin."

They looked around the old house, probing and poking as if it were a sick patient. It was a two-story structure with lots of paned windows some of which were broken. They tasted the water from a little spring on the hill above that ran down through a small pipe laid up on a waist-high rock just below the house, with an open faucet on the end. It still worked because people from around knew about the spring water and would come and fill their jugs with it. "Best water around," folks would say, as Lillian later found out.

Walking up a weed-filled tractor road, they found an old barn built into the side of the hill with a sagging roof they hadn't seen from the road.

"It was a dairy farm, that's for sure," Lillian said as she looked through some broken boards into the barn. "Looks like they kept about ten cows." Lillian had been raised on a dairy farm and knew what a cow barn looked like.

The tractor road actually led to the upper side of the barn, to the sliding doors of the hay loft which was the second floor. They had been looking at the lower first floor surrounded with bushes and weeds.

"Damn!" Rosemary said as she started to brush thistle burrs from her slacks. "Look Lillian, your jacket! It's full of burrs! Let's get out of here. I'll bet we walked through poison ivy!"

Lillian frowned and shook her head. They walked back down to the car and looked at the rocky creek that bordered the road. Normally it would be running tall, making lots of watery noises rolling over and around those same rocks, but now it was low water time and the bed was filled with glassy pools reflecting the fall sky overhead.

"Must be a lot of trout in there," Rosemary said. "You know, I think Harry used to come fishing up here? He mentioned a Sand Creek and I think that's what this is, don't you? Look how clean the water is. Not that slimy brown-green it is in town."

Lillian looked up and down the creek. "Why do men fish?" she asked. Rosemary's mouth quivered slightly and she frowned as if remembering something unpleasant and looked at Lillian.

"I... don't know. Why do they?"

"Maybe... . well, nothing... "

When they drove off, Rosemary shook her head. "I don't like that place, Lillian. There's something about it. Gives me the creeps - like something bad has happened there... and may happen again. Why did you want to see it?"

"Why did you say that?"

"Say what? Why did you want to see it?"

"No. That something bad may happen. Why did you say that?"

"Don't get upset, Lillian. It's just a feeling."

"I... wish you hadn't said that."

They continued on in silence, heading north up to the end of the old road.

Finally, Rosemary spoke: "I think Harry was lying about fishing. I think most of the time he was doing something else."

Lillian remained silent.

"Matt likes to hunt, doesn't he?"

"you promised me not to talk about him!"

"I know, don't get excited, but you really need to face up to it."

"I don't know. I don't know him anymore. But, well... yes, he likes to hunt, and you know it. He's crazy about hunting and guns. Sometimes, I can't stand it. I think I hate his guns."

"Just take it easy, Lil. At least he didn't hit you this time."

"I almost wish he had."

Lillian looked at her friend of many years. They didn't always understand each other, but she needed Rosemary, didn't know what she would do without her, especially now. Her fragile world, Matt's world, was tearing apart, casting her and Matt adrift. Without Rosemary, she felt lonely and vulnerable.

"You've been a big help, Rose," she said, touching Rosemary's arm.

Rosemary touched Lillian's hand. "You haven't been able to get him to see a doctor yet, have you," she said.

"No. He just won't go. He says I'm the one that's crazy. And Linda, she... she loves her father so much... takes his part... she says cruel things to me. Like today, about the cabin. God, Rosemary, I don't know what's going to happen if he keeps on like this."

Rosemary squeezed her hand. She had heard it all before. "Well, when we get back, you'd better make up with him," she said.

"You shouldn't let him upset you like this. He's been a pretty good husband so far."

She reached the end of the old road where it rejoined the main highway running north to the cabin at Caroga lake. They rode on, deep in their own thoughts. Lillian wondered what she could possibly say to Matt.

CHAPTER 3

Rosemary dropped Lillian off in front of her house. It was a beautiful large two-story in the wealthy knob Hill section of Johnstown. It was already dark and they had decided to leave the things they'd brought from the cabin in the car. Rosemary would come back over tomorrow to unload.

"Bye, Lil," and she waved goodbye when she saw her unlock the side door and turn on the entrance light. Then Lillian disappeared into the house.

The drive had done her good. Glad she had walked out, she was sure it had given them both the time needed to cool off; she was calm now, and after seeing the cabin again it was certainly not worth so much anger. She would tell Matt that it didn't matter, that she was sorry for flaring up.

The side door opened directly into the kitchen. She flipped the wall switch and the florescent lights hummed into view. Looking at the kitchen, it was clear that it hadn't been used. *Linda must not be home yet.* Then she peered into the unlit hallways and became aware of the quiet and darkness. The hairs on her neck quivered into erectness; she felt the back of her neck tingle. It seemed too quiet; something was not right. Something seemed amiss. Nostrils flared as she sniffed and became aware of a strange smell drifting in on the air from the hallway.

"Matt?" she called out. "Linda? Is anybody here?" She walked into the dining room and turned on the light. The overhead chandelier filled with faux candlesticks holding clear glass bulbs came on, blinding her. "Matt?" she called again and passed from the dining room into the living room. She paused... and heard the hum of silence.

Then out onto the covered porch fronting the house, now sealed up by the winter windows, and Lillian became aware again of a strange presence. She could feel it; it penetrated her mouth, her nostrils, her brain like a living presence; a warning to take care, watch your step. Waves of fear swept over her skin. she couldn't identify it but it was there.

The door to the den was at the far end of the porch and stood open. It was dark inside as she tiptoed in front of the doorway. "Matt?" she called again, her voice trembling. *The light would be on if he were in there*. He was the only one that used that room. It was his sanctuary and she almost never went in. The room was filled with stuffed creatures that she now found repulsive, even frightening: several deer heads with glassy staring eyes; ducks with black beady eyes accusing her of cutting them up, beautiful cock pheasants that looked mean, one pecking at the ground, and strangest of all, a large crow with a blackness that glowed in the lamplight. Lillian wasn't afraid of animals or guns or deer heads, she grew up around them but now... now It all seemed unreal.

She passed the doorway and continued on to the far end of the porch and went down the outside steps. Walking around the house, she looked up at the upstairs windows, saw a light in her bedroom and tried to remember if she had left it on. Maybe Matt was up there and hadn't heard her call. She came back in through the kitchen. Although she had found nothing but the upstairs light, she was still trembling. *Maybe I should go upstairs?* Her mouth was dry, so she drew a glass of water from the faucet and lifted it to her lips. But before she could drink, a strange thought flashed through her mind and she let out a low gasp. The glass slipped from her fingers and shattered when it hit the sink, the shards falling into the sink and to the floor.

"The den," she said under her breath. *How stupid I am. I better check the den again... something is very strange... or maybe someone is in there. Maybe I...*

She ignored the broken glass, kicking it out of the way, and forgot the upstairs light, and walked slowly back to the porch where the weak porch light provided only a yellow-stained darkness. Her neck tingling again as she approached the door to the den. Now that strange smell was wafting stronger as she moved closer and suddenly, seized with fright, her mind filled with a blankness she couldn't comprehend, feeling as if she couldn't see, as if she were blindfolded by the blackest of masks. *God!*

When she flipped the switch on the inside wall of the den, the table lamp illuminated filling the room with light, blinding her further, until her eyes slowly adjusted and when she perceived the raging redness of the blood splattered wall, a scream froze in her throat as she staggered, falling into the room, choking, and then saw what she expected, what she knew all along. It was then that her whole world shattered and she sank to the floor, unconscious.

CHAPTER 4

"God will forgive this man," the Pastor said, on his first visit with Lillian, several weeks later, "for what he has done to you and your children. And you must forgive him too. It will make your own heart shine again." He held her hand while he said these things, squeezing and relaxing with the cadence of his voice, as if he were playing some kind of instrument.

Almost paralyzed with grief, Lillian struggled to hold things together. It would be months before she could confront the reality of Matt's suicide; the awful details of finding him like that, and now her life alone. What should she do? Where could she go? Her soul had been cut in half.

the youngest daughter, Julia, blamed *her* for Matt's death. They were estranged before, but now Lillian felt it was much worse; that the loss of Julia was permanent. And Linda, her oldest, seemed to be harboring some fierce resentment. Rosemary Allen was her only comfort.

Harvey Detriech, the pastor of her church, just made her feel worse. "Can I get Margaret to help you?" he boomed. "Maybe come over during the day to keep you company?"

He was a big man with wavy iron-grey hair and seemed very much unlike a minister. Except for the voice: he spoke in practiced cadences with a resonance that sounded like Johnny Cash. She expected him to break out in a revival hymn at any moment.

Lillian knew Margaret Detriech well and wondered if Margaret knew: the Pastor, it was said, had a keen eye for the ladies. *Why,* she thought with frustration, *is the wife always the last one to know these things?*

"No, no, I'll be alright, reverend," she said, trying to avoid his penetrating stare. "I mostly need to be by myself to work things out. But thanks very much for the kind offer."

The Pastor looked deep into the eyes of this handsome woman. Time had treated her kindly. She had the vivacity of youth coupled with the wisdom that only time can bring and even in her grief, she had a vibrancy; an electricity that penetrated the minister to his bones. She could feel the sweat from his palms and a slight tremble in his fingers. She gently pulled her hand away and moved towards the other end of the couch.

"You sure there's nothing I can do?" he asked. "You can meet me at the church and we'll pray together."

"Thank you reverend, you're very kind," she said, hoping he would leave. "But not just yet."

"Well I'm here. I'm available to comfort you."

"Thank you. I'd just like to be alone for now."

He shrugged, and after a few more unwanted solicitudes, the Pastor left.

* * *

"Didn't Matt leave a Will? Rosemary asked later.

"No. At least we can't find one. I'm afraid he didn't leave much of anything else, either." Lillian had only been vaguely aware of Matt's financial situation. He had kept a tight lid on that kind of information and now the enormity of the consequences of that secrecy was becoming more and more obvious. Her grief was burdened by the anxious wait to reveal the status of his accounts, the foundation for the rest of her life.

Rosemary, her best friend since they were kids, had a cheery disposition which Lillian needed desperately to counter the morbid cynicism of her daughters. A heavyset strawberry blonde with a plain, almost homely face, Rosemary used little makeup; just a touch of rouge here and there to help brighten things up. Yet she was shapely and sensuous and attracted men easily. Two years earlier, she had been widowed by a deadly heart seizure, after 18 years of a rocky, childless marriage to Harry Allen and Lillian helped her through that difficult period. She always helped her; especially when Harry had started his affairs with other women. Now Lillian hoped

Rosemary would be there when she needed her.

"I'm sure, Lil, that everything will be alright," Rosemary said. "Matt was a good man. He wouldn't leave you without the means to live. I just know it."

"I don't know Rose," Lillian said. "This has left me numb. This horrible, awful thing. You just never expect something like this to happen; you don't know what to do. But I got Reed... that lawyer we've been using?" Lillian was again close to tears and her voice cracked. "He's... working on it. We've turned the house upside down, looking for a Will. Matt never talked about it, I mean a Will; I suppose he really didn't make one. I mean, he would have talked to me about it... don't you think?"

Rosemary nodded.

"But I've been saving money, too," she continued. "Money that Matt gave me for other things. I've been saving it secretly; he didn't know. I don't think. I guess I knew, deep down, that something was wrong with us - with our marriage."

"How is your brother and the kids taking it?" Rosemary asked. She hadn't seen them since Matt's funeral.

"I don't know about Robert," Lillian said, a twinge of anger in her voice. "Things were bad enough before this. All we tried to do for him, it just hasn't helped. Did you see how bad he looked at the funeral? I don't know if I'll still be able to give him money."

"Matt never did know, did he?"

"You mean about me giving Robert and Maryann money? No. I don't think so. I was giving them money because I was concerned for Bobby. God, he's only six and those two are alcoholics; they aren't capable of raising a child. But, you know, after all that's happened, I don't really know if Matt knew ... ? I just... can't be sure."

She looked angry and upset and Rosemary embraced her. They sat there awhile, under the portrait of Matt's father, without talking.

"And Linda, Linda too," Lillian continued. "She can't seem to take care of herself. Since her divorce she's been running off with a new man every six months, it seems like. And sometimes she takes up again with that beast she divorced. God... her father was the only thing she respected. She's so down about me, about everything. What will become of her?"

"Maybe you worry too much about your kids," Rosemary said. "Right now, you've got to think of yourself."

"Why did he do it, Rosemary? Why? You know Julia blames me for her father's death?" Lillian continued as if she hadn't heard Rosemary's reply. "She hasn't said as much, but I can tell by the way she's been acting. That Neanderthal she's married to probably put it in her head. Matt couldn't stand him. I can't either. I haven't been to her house since they've been married. But she blames me, Rosemary, she blames me," and tears welled in her eyes.

CHAPTER 5

"Is this Mrs. Barry?" came a deep voice over the phone, later that evening. Lillian shuddered as she recognized it as the police - Lt. Davis.

" Yes," she said, "this is Mrs. Barry," her voice quivering. Davis had been in charge of the investigation of Matt's death, and had not been clearly convinced that it was suicide: the broken glass, the bloodstains on her jacket, her bloody fingerprints on the shotgun stock and the telephone. The police tore the blood-stained room apart, looking for clues. Lt. Davis had been particularly brutal with her during the questioning. The whole scene came back to her, like a dark, recurring nightmare:

She remembered the phone ringing. The loud squawking ring had pulled her out of her swoon, but she was groggy and staggered and fell again touching the pool of blood and the stock of the shotgun and the phone just kept ringing and in desperation, thinking of help, she got up and answered it, but there was no response.

"Ma'am, this is Lt. Davis," the detective continued. "I was in charge of the investigation. Remember me?" came the unwanted voice.

"Oh, yes, Lt. Davis, I remember you."

"Good. I'm calling to ask you to pick up the shotgun and the other things we had to confiscate for the investigation. When can you do that?"

"What? You want me to take back that gun?" The wild scene she had come upon that day flashed into her mind. The blast had thrown Matt out of the chair and splattered blood and bits of flesh everywhere. He'd come to rest across the top of the shotgun, as if he were embracing it. The gun had been covered with blood. When she fainted, she fell into some of the pooling blood. "Look, I don't want that awful thing," she said, on the verge of tears again. "Just keep it. Destroy it if you want."

"Sorry ma'am, can't do that. It's against regulations to keep seized property when the case has been cleared. The coroner has ruled it a suicide," he said, the words dripping with disappointment. "I've got to give it back to you. And we need you to sign a receipt." His voice rang with authority; she knew it would be useless to say no.

"Well I won't come and pick it up," she said now with some authority of her own.

"We'll deliver it, then, ma'am. I'll send someone out with the material this afternoon," and he hung up, without confirming if she would be home.

The thought of the shotgun, its awful bloody presence, returning to the house made her cringe. "Rosemary. That was that – that damn neanderthal, Lt. Davis. They're sending back that shotgun. I can't stand to look at it again. I don't want it in this house. I know you can't stand guns, but take it for me? Take it and burn it or have it destroyed? God, I can't even think of it without shaking all over. If you had seen what it did... to Matt." She started crying again.

The tears worked; Rosemary reluctantly agreed and waited. Lillian left; she couldn't stand to be there when the police came. When they arrived, Rosemary signed the receipt with Lillian's name. The two young rookies didn't know the members of the household. The one in charge, while eyeing her shapely figure, made her examine the serial number on the shotgun to confirm it was the same model they had taken. She hesitated to touch it. There was a tag dangling from the trigger guard. And then she saw the dark brown stains on the barrels. The thought that it was Matt's blood revolted her.

"See, it's a Browning, miss." The rooky in charge said and he showed her the trademark. "I'll bet it's worth a lot of money. Lt. Davis said I should make sure you understand you're getting back the same gun they took." He stood the shotgun in the corner, by the entrance.

When they left, Rosemary still couldn't bring herself to handle the gun. In Lillian's bedroom, she found a bed sheet and carefully wrapped the Browning with it. Carrying it outside, she looked around to make sure that no one would see her, then put it under some rags and boxes in the trunk of her car. She trembled and felt guilty, as if she were doing something evil, like hiding a dead body. *Why had Lillian given her the responsibility for this terrible thing? What would she do with it?* Rosemary had premonitions, something some people said she was gifted with, and her mind filled with thoughts that something bad could come out of this. She shuddered when she closed the trunk.

CHAPTER 6

It was a bleak day in February when John Reed called Lillian from his office. Many months had passed since Matt's death and still the probate had not finished; all his accounts were locked; his bills went unpaid and creditors were becoming nasty.

"I think you should come over," he said. Even over the phone she could detect an air of uneasiness in his voice. "I have some information for you."

"What is it?" she asked, impatiently.

"I think it's better if you come here," he said. "Too hard to explain on the phone. Or I could come over to your place?"

"Well... No, I'll come over there," she said. "It's just so awful out."

"I know. Worst snow storm this year," he said. "But the streets are still open. I don't think you'll have any trouble."

She called a cab; it was too hard to get the car out of the garage. The temperature was hovering around 10 degrees and sinking and a bitter wind was blowing. Fresh snow stood thick in rolling drifts and blew into her face when she stepped into the cab.

After a slow, fifteen-minute ride in the swirling snow they arrived at the two-story brick building just off Main street, near the center of town. When she entered the building, the wind swept wisps of snow into the hallway. She shook her coat and stamped her feet to knock the snow off and to chase the chill from her bones. A door just off the stairway on the second floor displayed a brass sign:

J.J. REED
ATTORNEY-AT-LAW

For all their meetings, she had never been to his office before. They'd met in bank offices, Insurance buildings, real estate offices and her house.

She knocked.

"Lillian? Come in, Come in."

She entered the room. looking around, she stood speechless, thinking this was the wrong place. Enormous piles of paper were everywhere. There were several leather tufted chairs piled full of papers. Mounds were scattered here and there on the threadbare carpet.

Behind a pile of paper on the desk sat a small man with a black mustache. His face appeared pinched and made him look as if he'd been on a hunger strike. An aquiline nose supported a pair of black, plastic frame glasses with thick lenses. He stood up when she entered.

"Come in, come in," he said again. She approached the desk, fearful he would jump at her like one of those jumping spiders. "Sit down, Lillian. How was the drive? are you alright?" he spoke in a thin, high-pitched voice. He motioned to an empty chair in the corner she'd not seen before. She was confused by the mounds of paper and wanted to turn and run, fearing she was in the clutches of some paper maniac. "All this... paper... " she said.

"Go on, Lillian. Just take a seat over there," he replied. "Did Northgate call you back? They should have."

"Northgate? Oh, yes, yes they did," she said. "Thank God that policy is settled. I thought for a while they weren't going to pay."

As she warmed up, a blush fell over her fair complexion. When she unbuttoned her coat, he couldn't help see once again that she was a full-bodied, shapely woman. Although her green eyes revealed a deep sadness, they also displayed a sensuality not lost on the little man. She expertly kept grey from her hair, which now fell in velvety chestnut rolls as she removed her fur pillbox hat. In the dim office light, her face was delicately handsome and bright; her expression one of intelligent curiosity.

"Did you get all the papers I sent?" She asked. "I found more papers in the basement after you left on Wednesday. I meant to bring them with me... but I forgot. They just had to do with the cabin at the lake. Real estate things, I don't think they're important. But tell me... how can you find anything in this... this--"

"Mess?" he responded and laughed. "Ah, you don't know the way of lawyers. You see all these piles of paper?" he pointed around the room, "each pile represents a different case or client. This pile on my desk is all yours! If I had to file these papers, I would not only lose time, I wouldn't be able to find what I need. Now I know exactly where everything is. Well ... almost where everything is. But to answer your question, yes I believe I received everything from you."

She was restless and got up and looked out the window fronting on Main street. Snow was falling thicker now. It was only late morning, yet headlights pierced the falling flakes and cars crawled by slowly; the muffled womp-womp of loose chains against frozen fenders could be heard.

"When can we get this settled? You know I need to make some important decisions depending on what's left in the estate."

"Well Lillian, without a Will... well that complicates everything."

"He was too young to think about a Will. It never really came up between us."

"I've gone through everything here." he pointed to the pile on his desk. "Unfortunately, it seems that for all you may inherit, including the house and car, your net may not be very much. Matt's investments were not doing very well."

"Yes, I know... I know. But surely, he couldn't have been that bad of an investor? He was a trained accountant."

"Well, I can't be sure. That's why I called you. He lost a bundle of money with a shyster real estate company in Florida. It also seems that a lot of capital was used up on one account, and I don't understand it. It's with the First State Bank in Albany. Did you know about that account? "

"First State Bank? Yes. I think that was where he kept the account for Markham and Burge? - his stockbrokers. What don't you understand about it?"

"Markham and Burge had access to the account alright. But they were limited to a $700 a month withdrawal. Matt was depositing around $1500 a month. He also opened the account with a $25000 deposit, but his initial investment with Markham and Burge was only $17000." He pulled some papers from the pile in front of him and studied them for a moment. He walked over to the window and looked at the struggling traffic below. "It is getting bad out there, isn't it?" Then he looked at her. "Lillian, did you know anyone by the name of Hutchins?"

"Hutchins?" Silence followed; the traffic noise seemed to penetrate the room. "No... no, I don't think so. I don't remember any Hutchins."

He walked back over to the desk and picked up some of the papers. "Someone called... Joyce Hutchins also had access to this account. I had it checked and her access was completely legal. She was designated as a private investment counselor. She had a signature card on file. She ... in fact, withdrew all the money that didn't go to Markham and Burge. She also withdrew the other $8000 from the initial deposit."

An icy chill rippled over Lillian's body. "And did she... did she invest that money?" she asked, almost in a whisper.

"I checked with her lawyer and she, in fact, did not know that Matt had designated her as an investment counselor. She claims that-" Reed walked around the pile of papers on the floor, his eyes on the papers he held, as if he were lost.

"What, Reed? For God's sake, what did she claim?" Lillian said, her voice trembling.

"Claimed that ... that Matt gave it to her. He just... gave it to her."

CHAPTER 7

Although she owned a car, Lillian intensely disliked driving. Matt used to drive her everywhere, she remembered, as the dark winter trees flashed by through the train window. Except for occasional trips to the store or to pick up the kids at school. She drove so infrequently, that she often had to rehearse the operation of the car before she started out. she wasn't afraid to drive, it just seemed so unnatural to her.

Only a few weeks had passed since her meeting with Reed. She'd driven to the station to take the local train to Fonda. From there, she was riding the Empire State to Albany and had a coach ticket; she had murder in her heart and wanted people around her. Since that day in Reed's office, when the unbelievable, outrageous infidelities were revealed, she didn't want to be alone. Periods of being alone brought on nothing but depression and black rage. The nearness of strange people helped to keep her alert.

The coach was clean and warm. The mustard-colored seats faced each other and were just big enough for two. Across from her sat a big man in bib overalls and checkered shirt, wearing a Ralston's Feed cap. A woman in a plain dress, unadorned by any jewelry except for a watch, sat next to him. She wore no lipstick or other make-up, except patted little spots of rouge on her pale cheeks. They both looked uneasy, like this was their first time on a train.

Next to her, a heavy foreign-looking woman sat. She had a child on her lap and when she spoke, which at first was little, she had a strong accent. Lillian guessed it was Polish. thankful not to have a chatty woman next to her, she patted the frowning boy on the head.

"Ja. I go to visit the family in New York. I take my nephew here back to home. Ja, Johnny? Isn't dat right?" The boy squirmed and looked as if he would cry. Lillian nodded and smiled.

They rode in silence for a while, each one moving and shaking with the rhythm of the train; the sounds of the wheels mesmerizing. Lillian's mind began to drift.

"I live in Stone 'Rabia, the woman said suddenly, her tongue tripping over the double name, making it into one. "Where do you Live?"

Lillian didn't hear her. Her mind had sunk into the vortex of a deep whirlpool; seeing the woman and the farm couple and the others in the car swirling around her, like a rotating jury panel. They seemed to be pointing fingers at her, accusing her, demanding something. A wave of dizziness rode over her; a sharp pain gripped her gut. She felt faint.

"Where do you live?" the woman said, louder.

"Oh... why yes." Lillian said, reviving. "Yes. Where do I live? Oh, I live in Johnstown." Nausea still gripped her.

"Oh. Dat's nice place. I have friends making gloves dere. Nice place."

It was still deep winter and the Mohawk river bordering the railway was mostly frozen. Long ribbons of freezing black water split the snow-covered river ice. The late afternoon sun glinted off the water, looking like twisted strips of steel. Naked trees lined the snow-covered banks; trees that in the summer, hid the river from view. Now their bare, black branches made Lillian feel cold and uneasy. She turned from the window view, but tried to avoid the eyes of the foreign woman. At that moment, the woman's head was bobbing as if it were on a spring, and once in a while, it would fall over on her shoulder and she would awake with a start. The boy seemed asleep.

Lillian took pills from her purse for the pain in her stomach. When she returned the pillbox, she saw the bright metal gun barrel buried under her cosmetics and it startled her. She had lost focus of her purpose for this trip.

A .32 caliber Beretta was nested in her purse. Matt had given it to her years ago, so she would have a way of defending herself and the kids while he was off on trips. It was a kind of affectation of

Matt's, to suppose that their wealth made them especially vulnerable to burglaries and kidnapping.

She felt the hardness of the gun through the sides of the purse and thought of Joyce Hutchins and remembered her resolve to shoot this woman right through the head; a bullet between the eyes if she could control herself and shoot straight. Then she abruptly put the purse down, between her and the wall of the train. She shouldn't think of *that* now. She had learned from her parents that when you had an unpleasant chore to do, like killing a calf or a pig, you just couldn't think about it or for sure you wouldn't be able to do it. Her father wanted all his children to be able to face the "hard" things in life, and on the farm, butchering was one of them.

She remembered that day when he'd told her it was her time: time to help with the butchering of a calf. The thought of it had made her want to scream; she'd run from the barn and hid.

But he waited until he had her under control and led her to where the calves were penned. On the way, he told her about doing the hard things:

"There are many things in life a person has to do Lillian, and lots of them are hard to do. You can't always expect someone else to do those things for you. The thing is not to think about it. Put it right out of your mind and just go and do it."

Later she learned to do what he said. But that day she'd felt brutalized; she'd felt as if the cruel hammer had crushed into her own skull and she couldn't forget the strange, almost human cry the animal made at that instant.

She again became aware of the clackety-click of the train; the reassuring sound, familiar, stunningly repetitive and it brought her back to the present. The sharp pain was gone.

"Ja, in Stone 'Rabia I work for Brinkman's hotel. You know dis place?" The woman was awake again. Lillian was startled by her question. In fact, she knew the place well. She and Matt used to eat there often. It was deservedly famous up and down this area of the Mohawk for its good food and pleasant atmosphere.

Brinkman's was a large three-story colonial style building. It had a simple lobby with wicker furniture, and each room had two huge sash windows overlooking the beautiful river valley.

"Oh, yes. Well, how long have you worked there? Yes, I know Brinkman's." But as soon as she said that, she knew it was a mistake.

"How long?" The woman seemed confused and squirmed in her seat. She scolded the boy again for moving too much. "How long? Maybe it's not too long? I think maybe ... five years?"

Lillian looked out the window. She'd let herself get drawn into a conversation she didn't want to take place.

"You eat dere? You look like customer for Mr. Brinkman's."

She looked at the woman. She was stocky and pink and had a huge wart on her cheek.

"Yes, but not lately," she said with little enthusiasm. "Not for the past few years."

"You like da food? I help cook." she didn't wait for an answer. "Many big chefs work dere. Mr. Brinkman, he's always dere. He's always checking things, tasting food. He's a good man, Mr. Brinkman. Always gives us left-over food." The boy started squirming and whimpering. He wanted to go to the bathroom.

The woman, still chatting about Brinkman's, took the boy by the hand and finally left Lillian alone. When they were out of sight, Lillian stood up holding onto the seat, feeling dizzy then walked down the swaying car in the opposite direction, feeling nauseous. She was glad the child had interrupted; afraid of too much conversation, of being known, identifiable. And Brinkman's of all places. It really had been one of their favorites. Sometimes they would make the drive on Friday evenings during the glorious days of summer, passing through the rustic country side, smelling the turfy breezes moving across the newly mowed fields. Then they would have a meal you could linger over and maybe even talk about later. Sometimes they would stay the night, making love in one of the grand rooms with a huge bed and overstuffed pillows, and later sit on the covered porch and watch the twinkling lights of barges on the river. Brinkman's sat on the brow of a hill overlooking the Mohawk. But she thought, that was all long before the financial problems;

before this Joyce Hutchins bitch had ripped her life apart.

Suddenly the bouncing train lurched as it slowed and coasted into the West Albany station. The violent motion made her look down at her empty hands; with a shock she realized she had left the purse in the seat. The rolling sounds died away until the screech of metal wheels brought the train to a shuddering halt. When she returned to her seat, she noticed that the farm couple wasn't there; they must have gotten off at Schenectady but she couldn't remember. Her heart sank when she didn't see the purse. A cold sweat broke out as panic swept over her: where was the woman? Could she, would she have taken the purse? Did she see the gun?

At that moment the woman returned with the boy. She saw Lillian standing there looking dazed. "Oh, you get off here? I wonder how long we wait here?" Lillian started to interrupt her when she pointed under the seat: "Don't forget your purse." Lillian saw it now, laying under the seat. It had slipped down between the car wall and the seat edge. She picked it up and said goodbye to the woman and the boy. When she got off the train she was shaking.

Evening was approaching and the temperature started to plunge. She buttoned her coat and walked up to an empty bench at the far end of the platform and sat down. She needed to calm down before going on. After a while, she pulled a piece of paper from her purse, unfolded it and stared at it for several minutes. Written on the paper was:

Joyce Hutchins, 114 Scotland, Albany. WA2-6718

It had been written by Reed, who said he thought it would be a good idea to "talk to this Joyce Hutchins". Talk, indeed, she'd thought at the time. Reed's handwriting brought his presence into her mind. All the smoldering rage against this woman now flared up. Although she resisted it, Hutchins's image jammed its way into her mind. She had the gun in her hand, approaching from behind, a woman with long, loose brown hair. That's what she had seen in one of the photos the detectives she'd hired had given her; a woman with long, loose brown hair and not, she thought with fury, very attractive at all. From their investigation, it was clear that Matt had been living with and supporting this woman for several years. The images continued; she raised the small pistol slowly, trying to aim the shaking Beretta at the center of the head. She remembered in practice shooting sessions with Matt how heavy the hated small gun seemed and how hard it was to hold it steady. And then she pulled the trigger on the wavering pistol and the image disappeared.

She shuddered with the cold. "what am I doing?" she said to herself. *Keep it out. Don't think about it or you'll never do it.* She had conditioned herself to accept the consequences of her plan. No guilt. No fear of prison or even execution. And she wouldn't give herself up, even though she was resigned to being arrested.

She walked down the long platform to the small station house. The cold air had cleared her mind. Suddenly she remembered that she always got sick on trains or planes, and that's what must have caused her dizziness and dazed feeling.

She asked a white-haired man who was sweeping the floor in the vacant station when the next train left for Fonda. He shook his head and pointed to the schedule board on the side wall.

A train should be leaving in two hours. Another would leave three hours later. I'll make the one leaving in two hours.

She didn't take one of the waiting taxis in front of the station, but took a bus to a city square, a ten-minute ride away. From there, she caught a taxi to the 300 block of Scotland Avenue, within walking distance of 114. To her surprise, the cab pulled up in front of a new office complex. She thought it would be a private home area. She walked to the address at 100 Scotland. The building appeared to house a combination of apartments and private offices. It was past six, so most of the offices were closed. When she reached 114, she was shocked to see that it was Joyce Hutchins's office. Reed had given her the office address, not the home address.

The office appeared closed, but there was a light on inside. She debated for a second about waiting for her to leave, in case she was with a client. But then her father's words came rolling through: "Don't think about it; just do it." Her heart skipped a beat when she pushed the buzzer. She'd forgotten whether the gun was loaded or not. Then her mind raced about the safety catch on the pistol. She hadn't used the gun in years.

Through the wavy glass pane in the door, she could see a figure walking towards her. unlatching her purse, she pulled the pistol over the top of her cosmetic bag. Then she held the purse loosely in her left hand with her right ready to seize the gun.

A voice came through the door: “Who is it?”

“Joyce Hutchins? I'm looking for Miss Hutchins.”

“I'm sorry, but we're closed for the day. Can you come back tomorrow? Miss Maclean can help you tomorrow.”

“It's urgent that I see Miss Hutchins. Is that you?”

She saw the figure move to the door. Clicking sounds told her the lock was being opened. Lillian's heart was pounding; she felt that it was going to leap out of her throat. When the door swung open, she faced a small dark-haired woman that looked like one of her former teachers. She knew it wasn't Joyce Hutchins.

“Oh, ... hello,” Lillian stammered. “I would like to see Miss Hutchins please?”

“Well, I'm sorry, but Miss Hutchins is out of town,” the dark-haired woman said. “She went to a meeting in New York. Maybe I can help you... if it's urgent, but if it can wait until tomorrow, Miss Maclean is a partner.”

“Who are you?” Lillian's mind was racing, trying to plan a course to follow.

“I'm the secretary. I was just getting ready to leave.”

“When will she be back?”

“ She should be back by Friday. Two more days.”

“ Two more days? I didn't think... ” Lillian swallowed hard and tried to fight off a mounting panic “I... I--”

“Is something wrong?” the little woman asked in a perturbed tone.

“No... well, yes. Yes. Look... look here. I need you... you give her a message." She looked down at the handbag that was still opened. She wondered why it was open, why it seemed so heavy as if she needed all her strength just to keep it from dropping. Her head whirled like before on the moving train. "Tell her... that Lillian Barry was here. Tell her that I... came... here... to kill her." The woman's eyes flickered in disbelief. "Do you understand?" Lillian choked out the words, her lips trembling, her whole body tingling.

The woman stepped back into the office. "What in God's name... Who are you? What do you want?" her voice was cracking.

"I just told you." Lillian said, regaining some confidence, some control of her voice. "You can tell her that I ... I came... came... came to kill her," and she pulled the gun partway out of the purse so the woman could see it. "I won't come back... I came to kill her, kill... and it's done; it's done! Tell her... tell her *the cat will play while the dog's away.* She's dead! Dead! You hear me! Like my husband, the one she killed."

When the woman saw the gun, she turned deathly pale. She couldn't move; she was frozen in terror. "I... you... what... better leave, or... or I'll call police!" she shrieked, tripping over her words.

"Yes... Don't ... don't you worry, I'm leaving. But remember, remember! I'm Lillian Barry. You just... give her my message."

The woman stood there with her mouth hanging open, watching Lillian walk away. Lillian's legs were like jelly, she worried she would collapse before making it to the end of the hall. but she felt lighter, a great weight lifted from her chest, and that helped keep her moving.

It was over. She had done what she had to do. In her own mind, Joyce Hutchins was dead, with a bullet between her eyes. All the tired jealousy, the awful hate, the unbearable tension, seemed to flow painfully out of her mind.

When she reached Fonda, it was very dark. There were no cars and she stopped and stared at the black waters of the river and wondered what had brought her here; here at this ungodly hour. She felt as empty as she ever felt; It was cold; the sky shrouded in mist made visible by the few lights along the way. She made her way to a black iron bridge crossing the Erie Canal When half way over, she leaned over the cold metal rail and holding it out at arm's length, dropped a lunch bag containing the Beretta into the freezing water. There were no cars crossing so she stared at the swirling lights reflecting off the shifting black mirrors below her and thought of the bag sinking to the bottom. *Would it slide from side to side like sometimes flat rocks would sink in the water when she was a child? Would she not slide, but sink straight to the bottom if she followed it in. Would the water embrace her in its deathly freezing grip, so cold she would lose all feeling before reaching the bottom?*

A car horn blew and when she turned to see, she almost fell, one shoe was hooked on the lower rail. She shook her head, pulled her frozen foot free, and waved. She picked up her purse from the ground where she had set it. The dark figure in the car hesitated, but then seemed to nod and slowly moved on. She also made her way slowly over the bridge, the image of the swirling waters slipping through her mind.

That was close.

Nervous hunger pulled at her; She hadn't eaten all day. She crossed the dark street and went into a well-lit All-Nite diner. It felt safe; the warm lights embraced her, pulling her back to reality.

CHAPTER 8

A week passed, with Lillian waiting for the knock on the door or the phone call. But nothing happened. As more days passed, she assumed that either Joyce Hutchins had no stomach for the fight or her secretary had not given her the message. At least the police weren't after her.

Linda was becoming intolerable, threatening to move back with her ex-husband. Lillian didn't want that to happen; Frank Boyle was dangerous. She felt she soon had to make another dramatic change in their lives to get over this shock. Staying in this house, Matt's house, was no good for her or Linda, even with the den cleaned up, repainted and sealed off. But she couldn't let her strong-willed daughter rule her life either.

Lillian worked hard with Reed to settle the estate. It made her furious when she thought about all the money Matt had given to Hutchins. Reed said she had little legal recourse for regaining that money, but with her persistence, a lawsuit was mounted to declare Matt legally "incompetent" to manage his affairs and that this woman had used an adulterous relationship to illegally obtain the money. She felt that Matt's incompetence could easily be show by his bizarre behavior over the last two years of his life. She told Reed she would sell the house to help pay the bills.

"Well, where are you going?" Rosemary asked when Lillian told her she would be selling the house.

"I'll be moving from Johnstown," she said. " Anyway, there's too many rumors. Too many prying eyes. You lose a lot of friends when your husband commits suicide," she sighed. " And Linda, ... she's too depressed by this place."

Rosemary was over for lunch and she served her a ham and cheese sandwich. "But not far. I mean I'm not running to New York or anything like that."

"I'm glad you're not running off," Rosemary said.

"No, I'm not running. But lately I've been thinking a lot about how I've lived for most of my life. I mean, since I was married." They took a few bites from the sandwiches.

"And what have you determined?"

"Well, you know, Rose, I'm a country kid, like you. I was not at ease at all with the townspeople when we first moved here. I never knew townspeople when I was growing up. To me, they were always something of a mystery. In many ways, I disliked them."

Lillian had been raised, with her two younger sisters and a brother, on her parent's Mohawk valley dairy farm. The parents were religious and strict and insisted on their children using their full names: Lillian, Robert, Elizabeth, Carol. She knew that her father, George Wiggs, had been a good farmer, in that he always managed to pay his bills for sustenance, feed and seed, and most always had a substantial surplus at the end of the year. Lillian and her sisters and brother were well trained in feeding and milking and keeping the barn and milking stalls clean after a herd of three dozen Holsteins. This left the Wiggs family busy from dawn to dusk, in winter as well as summer, with almost no time for play. It was an environment that Lillian had loved.

Rosemary's parents had also been farmers and operated a truck farm just outside of Lewiston. They too, had been good farmers, that is, before they broke up. They'd surrounded themselves with the rich products of their labor: bright strawberries; crunchy potatoes; swollen ears of golden corn; small, velvety cucumbers that would become the finest pickles, and enormous purple cabbages. Throughout the year the house, the root cellar, the woodshed, would be laden with these things, each to its own season.

"Remember when we first went to high school?" Lillian said. "Dad used to drive us kids in every day. But later you and I were the first kids bussed to town to go to school. Remember? I think that's when I first started to dislike them."

"Oh yes. When they first put those busses on it was a real novelty. Later all the farm kids were bussed into town. We got a real nasty reception from those town kids, too. Some of the priggish teachers seemed none too pleased to have to deal with us either."

" And sometimes the older farm boys would go right from cleaning the barn onto the bus," Lillian said. "And their boots still covered with manure. They smelled very much like the horses and cows and pigs they tended to."

"That's when the teachers would throw a fit and very often send the kid back home to clean up or, if it was too late, into outside detention," Rosemary said and laughed.

"Remember Sally Weston?" Lillian asked.

Rosemary nodded. "Uh Huh. She used to be the worst snob of all. She called us the 'hick chicks' and made fun of our clothes."

"We were hicks alright," Lillian said. "And I was proud of it."

"Well, what does this mean? Rosemary said. "Do you feel like you're still a hick? Is that what you're getting at?" They both laughed.

"I guess in college my rustic charms gradually wore off. But I never got over my love for the country or the farm. And it took me a long time to get used to living in Johnstown after college.

"You never told me how that happened? How did you come to live in Johnstown?"

"I met Matt in college remember? His father wanted him to take over that small leather factory he owned in Amsterdam? But Matt hated it and wanted to do something else, so his father sent him up to Utica. That's where I met him. He was finishing a degree in accounting."

Rosemary decided to make another sandwich. Lillian had brought fresh French rolls, her favorite bread. "I guess that's when I was dating Sam, my old boyfriend," she said absently, as she peeled the slices of Swiss cheese apart.

Lillian remembered them fighting over Sam when they were in high school. It was then that she had found that Rosemary had a serious character flaw: she seemed possessed by a strong streak of jealousy, masked by her easy-going outward appearance. She had seen it in school and later on when they were dating. But Lillian could never directly bring that out, out of fear of losing her friendship. She knew that Rosemary was unsure of herself and mostly unaware of her charm. It seemed like she had always been afraid of entering into a relationship with a man; afraid mostly of failure, she guessed. So, it was that most of the affairs Rosemary had accused her husband of having were fictions of her imagination. But none of that had stolen one ounce from her love for Rosemary.

"Well," Lillian continued, putting Sam and Rosemary's jealousy out of her mind, "that was about the time my father died and Mom sold the farm. She was too old to run it and she felt us kids should do something else, just like Dad had felt. That's why he sent me off to college to be a teacher. That's really when I lost all contact with the farm and country life." She went into the next room and retrieved a picture of her parents. It was mounted in a plain wooden frame. Both her parents looked stern and rough in a rural sort of way. She showed the photo to Rosemary.

"If only dad had let me stay on the farm... I asked him, you know to let me stay and help run it. He said farming wasn't something a woman should do. You know Rosemary, they were really much better looking than this photo shows them." She studied the photo for a while. "Matt and I married right after I finished college. His best job offer had been from Conway Foods and that's why we moved to Johnstown.

"You know, I guess I never realized it before, but for all those years that I was married, I really had a secret desire to return to the country, the farm. I mean sometimes you live with some suppressed desire that only manifests itself when something traumatic happens." She looked at the photo again. Her parents were standing in front of the barn she'd been so fond of.

Rosemary looked at Lillian and grinned. "Well that certainly doesn't sound like a farmgirl talking. But I know what you mean. I always wanted to move back, but I guess I never had the courage. Got used to the easy life."

"I guess you could say Rosemary, that I'd like to buy a small farm. Not a big one down in the valley, but maybe something up north. There's lots of cheap farm land up there. Remember that place we stopped to look at?"

Rosemary thought for a minute and then remembered. "You mean that old place I told you I didn't like? Oh, not that place!"

"I Think you'll feel different when you see it again," Lillian said.

"I don't know Lillian. I don't think so. Why do you want to live there? It's so ... isolated."

Rosemary said she had a friend in real estate who sold undeveloped land and farms. "Would you like to talk to him?" She hoped he would show her something else that she liked.

But Lillian knew what she wanted; she needed independence and isolation. When she went to see the agent, she convinced him to show her the old place they had visited in the Adirondack foothills. He was happy to oblige and showed Lillian, Linda and Rosemary the "old Morrison place" as it was called. It was still the same as when they had seen it before. There were 140 acres of scrub pasture, almost gone back to wildwood and an 80-acre woodlot. In years past, 30 acres had been tilled for hay and oats, but now this acreage was overgrown with thorn bush, scrub pine and wild grasses.

"I still don't think so," Rosemary said, after they had looked around. "I don't think you should move up here, Lillian. This place still gives me the chills. It's only ten miles from town, but it might as well be a hundred."

"You don't expect me to live *here*, do you?" Linda said. She was wearing her best Sunday clothes and looked attractive and imposing and entirely out of place in the simple farmhouse. "Where's the goddamn toilet?" she continued. "This is the most godforsaken place I've ever seen. I'll be damned if I'm going to live like one of those dumb backwoods' hicks. They're all ignorant and superstitious. Didn't you learn anything from Dad? How can you think of moving to this place, Ma? Dad would never let us live like this. How can you forget so soon?"

Lillian absorbed the cruel words. She didn't want to hurt her daughter and hadn't told her about her father's dirty tricks. She was continuously being lectured about how "Dad would have done this; how Dad would have done that."

"Well, if you're afraid to live here... you know you can do as you please," Lillian said, throwing down a challenge. It was a gamble; she didn't want to lose Linda and knew she couldn't live in this isolated place alone. But this was the best way to deal with the rebellious Linda. She had always been forward and outspoken; it was one of the things that had endeared Linda to Matt.

In spite of Linda's outburst and Rosemary's efforts, she decided to buy the place, contingent on the probate settlement. The holding company readily agreed; the place had been for sale for almost ten years.

CHAPTER 9

"I'm afraid we got a bad judge, Lillian," Reed said over the phone. She braced herself for bad news. "The judge in Albany threw the lawsuit out," Reed continued. "Said we had no grounds for suing over monies legally received."

"Oh God Reed, what now? I can't let her get away with that."

"Well, we could mount a new lawsuit and hope for another judge. I think this judge was way out of line."

But Lillian felt deceived, and now she couldn't afford to pursue the risky case further. The rejection of the lawsuit opened her wounds afresh; her anger and hatred for Joyce Hutchins returned with renewed force. Her mind flirted with real vengeance and another trip to Albany.

Several days later Reed called again. "Lillian, I've finally got some good news. The probate's settled. Looks like there's going to be enough to give you something. Quite a bit more than I thought."

"Ah, well that's something. Will I have enough to buy the Morrison place?" she asked with her fingers crossed.

"Still want that old place, eh? Yes, I think so Lillian. I think you'll have more than enough."

Lillian smiled and was able, for a while, to forget her problems with Joyce Hutchins. Her house sold quickly. She was anxious to get away from the bitter memories that had invaded her old home. Yet when she finally moved out, she couldn't help feel that another significant part of her life had been lost.

After some substantial but hasty repairs and several weeks of cleaning and painting, she moved into the Morrison place and started what she hoped would be the beginning of a new life.

When she got settled, plans for getting the place in better shape were made. a small dairy farm was her main goal; one that she hoped would be profitable. But to begin, she needed income, so she applied for another teaching position at a small, three room schoolhouse in a nearby village, for the upcoming school year. To take up teaching again seemed hard, but for the first time in more than a year, she felt the faint stirrings of happiness.

* * *

Lillian found it difficult to concentrate on plans for murdering Joyce Hutchins when the old place kept her so busy. She liked the big kitchen that occupied most of the ground floor, with a walk-in pantry and a small bedroom connected to it. The largest stove in the house, the great Merrimac, stood with its massive iron presence at the dead center of the kitchen. Four heavy top plates and a deep grate allowed log-sized chunks to be fed into its burning maw. There was a smaller, pot-bellied cousin in the adjoining parlor. Lillian learned that getting in firewood would be one of her main priorities. The Merrimac served not only for cooking, but was the main source of life-giving heat.

But she had to learn about the primitive rural life all over again. At first, she was appalled by the lack of central heating and running water, meaning no ready hot bath, and then there was the crudities of the outhouse.

"You see, Ma. I told you this was no way to live," Linda said when Lillian complained about the smell in the outhouse. "And I'm moving out as soon as I find someone to share an apartment with me in town."

"I'll just get somebody out here to dig a new pit and cover the old one. Then we'll have a nice, new and clean outhouse," Lillian said. She tried to accept this radical change in her way of living, difficult things that she had forgotten about long ago; It was Linda who continuously threatened to move out.

She didn't want to lose Linda and had planned to make other improvements. "I've found a contractor, Linda, who can build us a bathroom. He's going to build a room on the back of the house and pipe water down from that spring that's up on the hill. He'll install a tub and a sink and a small woodstove to keep us warm and to heat the water for a bath. I need that as well as you."

"Thank God you've come to your senses," said Linda, and flashed a rare smile.

One day shortly after she moved in, she was making her way down the steep path between the barn and the house. Red Brady, the carpenter-repairman she'd hired to bring the sagging barn up to the point where cows could be moved in, had asked for water. As she moved down the path, she noticed a big black car in the road parked behind her car. Then gradually the figure of a woman dressed in a black suit took shape. Her mind reeled: she knew immediately from the pictures that it was Joyce Hutchins. She stopped; speechless, feeling for the purse that had contained the gun. *The gun! Why did I throw it away?* But all she had now was the basket of eggs she'd collected.

"Lillian Barry?" the woman said, looking steadily into Lillian's eyes. She didn't answer. "Yes. You are Lillian Barry, aren't you." Lillian remained frozen, unable to move or speak. The woman opened her purse and drew out a small pistol. She aimed it at Lillian with a trembling hand. All Lillian could think of was how ironical this was; how absurd. *To pull a gun on her?*

Before she could react beyond the gasp she'd let out, the woman spoke: "It's your fault that Matt killed himself," her voice rising in intensity. "It's all your fault. *You* made his life miserable. And you had the nerve to come after me? How could you!" Her voice crackled with anger.

There was no one in the house. Linda was at work and Red was hammering away in the barn. Lillian was dumbfounded by what was happening, but she found herself almost unafraid of the wavering pistol. She could tell by the way that Hutchins was holding it that she had no experience with guns.

"Me! What are you talking about? Who are you?" Her voice was quavering, but she looked steadily at the gun. "Please put that gun down... You don't understand."

"No... you don't understand, " the woman responded. Matt really hated you, you know that? You... you made his life miserable."

"What? You must be crazy. That's a horrible lie," Lillian said. She moved slightly towards the woman.

"That's close enough ... Don't you try anything or you'll be sorry."

"It's a lie," Lillian shouted again. "He loved me... I loved him. Where did you get these lies from? Your own black heart?" Lillian moved again and Hutchins waved the gun menacingly.

"Sit down, over there," she said, pointing the gun in the direction she wanted Lillian to move, a spot on the front lawn. "I'm going to make you understand. They aren't lies." She looked steadily at the anger and fear twisting Lillian's face. "You really don't know, do you? You think I'm the source of all your troubles? Couldn't you tell what was wrong between you and Matt? What kind of woman are you?"

The words burned into Lillian's heart. She was sitting on the grass, with her legs folded underneath her. She breathed heavily and with each breath, sucked in a new kind of anger, an anger which seemed unreasonable to her, a confused anger. she did not understand. "Me?" she shouted "I think the question is what kind of woman are you! You, the golden whore, you took advantage of him, of us. You--"

"Shut up!" Hutchins yelled, "and listen. Matt wanted desperately to get away from you. He wanted a divorce. But you know what? He was a coward... he was afraid of you... afraid to tell you the truth."

Lillian blinked in the bright sun. Her fingers dug into the earth. "I don't believe you. Your making this up to justify your own disgusting self. I--"

"You don't believe me?" Hutchins interrupted. "Well, I knew you wouldn't. But I brought proof. That's why I'm here, to give you this proof. I want you to know what you did." Lillian's eyes flashed in surprise

"What I did?"

"Yes. What *you* did." She waved the gun threateningly again.

"Stay where you are." She stepped back to where she had dropped the purse. While watching Lillian and holding the gun pointed in her direction, but wobbling and moving around in all directions, she fished out white envelopes from the purse. She walked up to Lillian, removed the rubber band holding them together and dropped them on the ground close to Lillian's feet.

"I could have mailed them to you," she said, "But I needed to know who you are; to see this woman that came to Albany to kill me."

Lillian sat without moving. she stared at the envelopes on the ground. She could see no marks - they seemed to be just plain envelopes.

"Those are letters Matt sent to me while he was living with you. I want you to read them. Go on - pick one up - any one. Open the envelope and read it - aloud." She waved the gun at Lillian.

A great fear seized Lillian's heart. She wasn't much afraid of the gun. She was convinced that Hutchins wouldn't use it. She was afraid of the letters and the ring of truth, the undeniable conviction, in Hutchins' voice.

"I won't do it," she said. Hutchins waved the gun again.

"Do it - now!"

Lillian hesitated. The sun had rolled itself into high noon and she felt its warmth on her head and on the hand now moving slowly towards one of the envelopes. She didn't want the hand to move; it seemed to have a life of its own. What could be in those letters, she thought. What could be on those simple pieces of paper that gave this woman such confidence, such certainty? Just as the hand was about to touch one of the envelopes, she recovered her will and quickly withdrew it.

"No, I won't!" she said, and stood up to get further from the envelopes.

That move left Joyce Hutchins confused and slowly she let her gun hand drop to her side.

"I see," she said, some of the strength gone out of her voice. "

But you must know. Just remember this, Matt wanted a divorce. If you don't read those letters, you will never know the truth. I want you to know the truth." She walked over and picked up one of the envelopes. "I don't want you coming to Albany again to kill me." She looked at Lillian without moving for a few seconds. Then she lowered the gun slowly to the ground and left it next to the purse. "Don't make me pick that up again," she said.

She opened the envelope and slowly withdrew a sheet of paper. Lillian could see a copy of Matt's large scrawled handwriting. She was sure it was his... Hutchins unfolded the paper. Lillian's heart began to beat faster.

"No! I don't want to hear it!" she shouted and put her hands over her ears.

"Don't be so foolish," Hutchins said as she searched for a passage to read. "Here. Here is the end of one of his letters," she shouted and started to read:

> *"... I haven't been able to sleep at nights. Lillian makes me feel so guilty, I don't sleep in bed anymore. I've moved into my den; I sleep on the couch. All that's left in the den is this couch, a chair, and the gun cabinet. "Please help me Joyce. I want to get away from Lillian."*

Hearing these awful words, in spite of her hands covering her ears, Lillian slowly dropped them to her side.

Hutchins continued:

> *"She lies to me about Robert. She's helping him, but won't talk to me about it, because she knows I think she's wrong. She's just making her brother more helpless, more dependent on her."*

She stopped reading and stared coldly at Lillian, questions burning in her eyes. Then she continued:

> *"She doesn't love or respect me at all. She treats me badly; she is very cruel. But I don't want to hurt her and the kids. That's*

why I haven't asked for the divorce yet. Forgive me, Joyce. I know you want me to tell her and I will. I just need to get things settled first. I'll be coming to Albany soon. I need you. I wish I could keep writing this forever."

She stopped reading, stopped before the passionately worded endearments of the closing. She let the paper fall from her hand. It caught a slight breeze and floated towards the house. "There's much more... about you and Robert and others. You'd better read them."

She picked up the gun and put it in her purse. Lillian was frozen and white. "You won't be coming to Albany again, will you?" she asked.

Without waiting for an answer, Joyce Hutchins walked down the path to her car and drove away.

Lillian didn't hear the car; the grinding starter, the nervous quick warm-up revolutions of the engine; the crunching gravel of the car making a U-Turn and then pulling away. She was enveloped in silence, even though the wind sighed through the soft, feathery limbs of the Tamarack trees; even though the stream was playing its watery melody; even though the birds were scratching and squabbling, pecking and flying. Lillian heard nothing: Her total being was focused on the letter, now dancing lightly like a fallen feather away from the house. But it was not the silence of fear. It was the silence of numbness.

She watched the letter flip over and over and then stop, like a tired runner; and then lift again on a short breeze and start over again. Soon it would be gone, a small gust would carry it down to the curve in the road. For some time, she was unable to move, but before the letter disappeared, something in the recesses of her consciousness brought life to her limbs and made her run to retrieve the wayward note.

She caught the letter and held it between the tips of her fingers like it was something dirty or diseased and then picked up the other envelopes. Then she picked up the basket of eggs. She didn't remember dropping them, but they were mostly broken and oozing through the basket.

She walked blindly into the house, threw the basket of eggs down into the trash box and put the letters in a drawer in her bedroom; she could not bear to look at them. She didn't want to see that nightmarish handwriting again.

She slowly eased herself into the rocker in the kitchen and tried to make sense out of what had just happened. *Matt hated her?* The words grated; they turned and twisted in her mind. The vision of Hutchins reading those words made her cringe in disgust. How could this have happened? Wasn't this all upside down? What had she done?

For the first time since finding out about Matt's affair, bewilderment replaced the bitterness she had known. But she couldn't look at the letters; at least not yet, she wasn't ready, she was too numb; too bedeviled by her rival.

"Everything's just about done, Miss Lillian," Red said, after he knocked and came through the front door. "Say, you're looking poorly. Is everything alright?"

She nodded her head. Very slowly, the sounds of the world returned to her ears.

CHAPTER 10

For days thereafter, the words of Joyce Hutchins burned deep into her brain. Especially the words "She's just making her brother more helpless, more dependent on her." They seemed a terrible indictment of all she had tried to do for Robert. She hadn't seen him or her nephew Bobby since the funeral. Now, she felt, she must see them to reassure herself.

But she was shocked the day she walked into the hot, stuffy apartment at midday and found Bobby sleeping fitfully on a mattress soaked with urine; with roaches scattering over the bed and over the smoke-soaked walls. She stifled a scream; the roaches terrified her; she looked for a chair to jump on, but there were none. She just stood there and shuddered. Powerful, overwhelming smells, coupled with body odors and alcoholic vapors drifted up from the two parents on the floor; it made her heart sick.

She hadn't seen Bobby since Matt's death: she had been too preoccupied with her own misery. He looked filthy and, she thought, too thin, although later she realized her imagination had been running wild. He moaned when she lifted him from the bed.

"Aunt Lilly?... what do you want?" the boy said with sleep still in his voice. He was startled and frightened.

"Bobby! Oh, Bobby. Just look at you. I want to take you out of here. I want you to come home with me. Would you like that?" It was an uncontrolled impulse: she had planned nothing.

Bobby didn't answer, but looked wide-eyed, as if afraid to think about it. But then he seemed to understand what she had asked him. "Take me? Maybe... I don't... don't...know."

Daylight streamed through the dirty window shade, casting a yellow hue on everything. The parents slept on in a deep alcoholic stupor. They were laying almost naked on a mattress on the floor. An empty gin bottle lay next to the mattress. Ashtrays filled with stale butts repulsed her. *Surely, they would burn this awful place down; that they would all be consumed in fire.*

She took the trembling boy into the bathroom and stripped him of his filthy underwear and washed him in the sink. She ransacked the drawers in the bedroom, but could find no clean underwear, only dirty clothes and roaches. She cursed at the dresser and the roaches then dressed him in his street clothes.

She took the boy back into the bedroom and shook Robert by the shoulder, shook him violently to break him out of the powerful drugged sleep. She loved her brother, but, at that moment, she could have killed him. He stirred slowly to life.

"I'm taking Bobby with me," she said. He rolled over and looked up at her, his large blue eyes sunken and glazed, lips cracked and tinged brown with nicotine, skin varnished with filth. His week-old beard was matted with drool. He tried to speak and coughed; the hacking cough of a huge tobacco hangover.

"Lilly? What?... are you... doing... what are you saying? Take Bobby? What? Take Bobby? No... you can't," he croaked "Maryann... she won't like that." He started to stir himself from the bed. Lillian stepped back. "Why did you come here, Goddamit. Leave us alone... please."

"Robert, if someone reports you to the state welfare people, they will take Bobby away," she said, her mouth trembling with disgust. "I can't leave him here any longer. Look at you! Look at this place! My God... what, what are you doing to yourself and this child. Why did you ever marry that disgusting... you are disgusting! Both of you."

She felt Bobby's trembling hand tighten in hers; she sighed deeply and tried to calm herself. Suddenly his father tried to grab the boy, but his efforts were too clumsy and Lillian easily pulled him away. She moved towards the door. "Bobby wants to go," she said, calmly. Robert struggled to get to his feet. Maryann started to stir. "He'll be at my house. When you sober up, maybe we can talk." She opened the door to leave.

"Bobby. Don't go with her," he shouted. "Bobby. You stay here, you hear?" His voice cracked with a hoarseness that made him almost unintelligible. He was on his knees, trying to balance himself, but he couldn't get up. Maryann was beginning to sit up and moan, when Lillian closed the door and walked down the dingy stairs with Bobby and they stepped into the fresh air outside and she felt a tremendous rush of relief, like she had just stepped out of hell.

* * *

Robert never came over to her house, as she suspected he wouldn't, but they had met at Hill's diner for lunch, several times after that. Since they both had no phone, she wrote him notes and then left them in his mail box.

The first time he'd met her for lunch was almost a month after she had taken Bobby.

"We want you to bring Bobby back, Lil. We ain't waitin' anymore," he said.

"I'll bring him back when you straighten out your life. Not until then."

"We ain't goin' to wait, you know," he said with little conviction. He looked much better. He had clean, although rumpled clothes, clothes that had been washed and bleached but never, ever ironed. He was shaved and his face was a bit cleaner, but he still had the unmistakable signs of the alcoholic: the rheumy eyes, the nicotine stains, the trembling hands.

She took an envelope out of her purse and handed it to him "Here. There's a hundred dollars in there. Don't spend it on gin, dammit."

They had other meetings and he always demanded that she return Bobby and she said she would when he sobered up and moved out of that pigpen. She would give him more money, usually a hundred dollars if she had it. He always came for that reason and she felt like she was paying him for Bobby; she knew he felt like he was selling him.

Bobby adapted well and loved the freedom of a child's life on the farm.

"Aunt Lilly, when's my daddy coming to get me?" he asked her, after he'd been there for a few weeks.

"Your Daddy loves you very much. He'll be here in a while, Bobby. Don't worry, he'll be here for you soon."

"I hope he doesn't come, " he said, surprising her. "I like it here with you."

"Don't you miss your Mommy?

"Ah, no. 'Cause sometimes she scares me. And she sleeps too much, sometimes."

Lillian knew she could never let him go back to that terrible place again, unless there was a drastic change in Robert.

CHAPTER 11

One night, after every one was asleep, she found herself pacing her small bedroom. It was the letters that Hutchins woman had brought. they were sitting in a drawer next to her head when she slept, and sitting on her mind like a horrible cancer. Yet she had found no courage to read them. After pacing and trying to read something else for hours her mind still couldn't shake them off. Finally, she took one of the envelopes out of the drawer from underneath the family bible where she'd kept them hidden. Her hand trembled as she removed the letter from the envelope. As the paper unfolded, she could see the opening: *My Dearest Love,* and she cried out and flung it back in the drawer again. She wanted to destroy them, all of them, but couldn't. She knew she would have to read them. To understand this part of her life that now seemed like a wasteland, a dark mystery that was now an obsession, a searching for understanding of the last few years of her married life, the period that seemed to have gone haywire, she now understood there was more amiss than she had realized. When they didn't talk, when Matt seemed strange and sometimes aloof, she'd thought it was just the symptoms of an aging relationship. She'd seen similar symptoms in her parent's life. But now she understood that Matt had been sorely depressed and that depression made everything different and had been the probable final cause of his suicide. But where had it started? With their worn-out relationship? Or with the financial problems? Or with their kids and particularly, her brother Robert? And what had she done to contribute to this deterioration? What had she done?

She took the letters out of the drawer again. She was determined to read them. She picked up the first one and skipping the salutation, she read on. It was dated October 16, 1949:

> *"I miss you so much. I can't stand this being separated forced to meeting through the mail. I love you.*
>
> *"My situation is getting worse. I'm selling off everything.*

I don't think that Lillian knows the trouble I'm in. If I told her she would never understand. She would only get angry, like she always does.

"I've had to cut way back on the money I'm giving her. She knows something is wrong. She's been giving Robert large sums of money- she thinks I don't know. But Robert's wife tells me everything. Everything."

So that's how he knew about me giving Robert money... She wanted to choke this Maryann. This creature that Robert had married. She read on, about his need to divorce her, his need to get away. The letter continued:

"I know you want me to tell Lillian about us; to get a divorce. I just haven't been able to yet. I just can't face her yet. And now with all my problems. What will Lillian do?"

The letter ended with him declaring a deep, passionate love for Joyce and of his determination to get a divorce and be with her.

Tears welled in Lillian's eyes but she cursed loudly and fought them back. Instead, she smoldered in bitterness at Matt and the deception he had played on her. She'd been the fool, thinking that their marriage was worth something.

She dropped that letter and now more calmly read the other two. They said much the same things. That she was cruel. That she shared most the blame for Roberts alcoholism. That Maryann had told him everything. That Lillian was always angry. And then they talked about his love for Joyce and about meetings and liaisons, one that apparently took place under her very nose, right in Johnstown.

She dropped the letters and sat on the bed, searching her mind, thinking about those cruel, incredible words. What had she done to cause Matt to say those terrible things, all untrue? Why hadn't she seen the signs? And she had no idea that he had been talking to Maryann. When had he done that? She sighed and then tried not to cry and tried to shake the awful questions from her mind.

But the reading had been good for her, like lancing an ugly boil.

The pus and bitterness had drained away. She lay back in the bed, feeling sad yet strangely better. The reading had purged her mind of damning speculations and of thinking of Joyce Hutchins and her ridiculous indignation. Of Matt's cheap infidelities. And Matt's senile accusations convinced her that he had sunk into a deep psychosis.

After a while, she got up and gathered up the letters from the floor where they had scattered. she went into the dark kitchen and lifted the heavy lid on the Merrimac. The cooking fire had died now, but she saw the faint glow of some dying embers. She dropped the damnable letters on top and waited. After a few seconds, they started to smoke and curl like living things and she savored the moment when they flared up into flame and then turned to a black crisp, and crumbled into white ash and disappeared forever in the bowels of the stove.

CHAPTER 12

"I know I don't look like much, ma'am," the man said, standing in the doorway with a week's growth of beard, an old pin-striped suit that hadn't been cleaned in years, and a greasy old sweat-stained fedora on his head, "but I do need the work and I really do know a lot about farmin'. That's what you're a-doin' here, ain't it?" His long bony fingers were brown with nicotine stains and he gave off a faint, musty odor, like old rotting rags in a damp cellar. He looked like an urban bum rather than a farmhand.

Against her better judgement, she let him in. Lillian always knew that a hired hand would be needed, but she was reluctant to look for one and had put it off as long as she could. Then this man, Fred Haynes, came knocking at the door.

"Have you farmed before?" she asked. "Did you have your own place? Where are you from?"

She offered him a seat on one of the hard kitchen chairs.

He sighed deeply and sat down. "Yes, ma'am, my folks, why they were from Ohio," he said slowly, in a thin, nervous voice. "They had a small place there, near about Kanduski, as I recall." At that point, he seemed to lapse into a reverie.

"And?"

"Well, my Pa's brother, why he had a place close by here, in Cherry Valley. Had a nice dairy operation there. Then, back in '35, I believe it was, why he up and died and left the whole place to my Pa. That's when they moved there, to Cherry Valley that is, and I moved with them." He was making his hands into fists, stretching his fingers slowly, like a person with arthritis. He fell silent again.

"And?" Lillian could see she had to prompt him.

" I was about, oh, 35, or 41, hard to remember. You see ma'am, I'm only about 58 years old, even though I know I look a lot older.

But I got gassed real bad, in the war, ma'am, and wounded in the leg to boot. And I ain't been right since, I mean as how I look. And ma'am, government pays me a disability check, every month, but it ain't enough for a bird to live on. I mean, you can see that, can't you?" Now his hands were shaking. he fumbled around with his shirt pocket and brought out a pack of matches. Then he fumbled in the rest of his pockets, turning the jacket pockets inside-out.

"You were in the first world war?" she asked, not quite sure which war he was talking about.

"That's right, ma'am. That was the big war, you know." He continued to fumble in his pockets. "Say, ma'am, you, ah, wouldn't have a smoke by any chance? Think I left all mine at home."

She shook her head.

He sighed again. "Yes, I um, spent most of about six months up in Belgium, 'fore we were hit with the gas. I was bein' drug back to the dead wagon when a shell exploded and got me in the leg. Course, they thought I was already dead from the gas, so nobody tended my wound till I came around. When I saw I was in the wagon with all those dead soldiers, why I let out a warhoop that the devil could hear."

Now she was interested in his story. "Did they take care of your wound, then?"

"Oh Yeah, they did that. But I near bled to death. They sent me back to a hospital, where I spent most of a year, trying to get my organs all corrected again. Gas does terrible things to a body, ma'am. But," he quickly added, "doesn't bother me much anymore. I'm real good with my hands, ma'am, and I know a lot about dairyin'."

She tried to get back to the business at hand. "What about your folk's place in Cherry Valley?"

"Oh, that... well, it was a good place ma'am and my Pa made a good livin' there. And since I was what they call a disabled veteran, my Pa said I should stay there and help him with the farm. Said it would be mine when he passed on."

"And?"

"My Ma an' Pa died, let's see, about, oh, it must be six years now. First my Ma died, after havin' dizzy spells for a time. Pa put her in the hospital, but they said they couldn't do nothin' for her. Told Pa she was full of the cancer. They sent her home and she died about a month later. My Pa, he cried a lot. Then he got sick, and about three months later, he told me from his bed that he was a-dyin' too, and that he was real sorry. Didn't know what he was sorry about till after he died and the bank up and takes over the farm. I've been workin' for other folks ever since."

Lillian knew in her bones that the story was at least mostly true, so she hired him. That next week, when he showed up for work, she bought him some new work pants and blue cotton shirts and made him scrub up, which he didn't like one bit. He refused to wear the railroad cap she'd bought; said he thought he'd just keep the hat he had, but he thanked her very much. Fred wouldn't go anywhere without his greasy fedora covering the few hairs on his bald head. He'd brought a small cardboard suitcase and she moved him up to the attic room. Fred was thin and wiry and not very big, so she gave him the furniture she'd bought for Linda when she was a child. It seemed to fit Fred just right. And after a few weeks, Linda got used to the hard, reddened face, sunken mouth and fierce beak of a nose, and stopped annoying her mother for giving away her furniture to a "bowery bum" as she put it.

Fred worked hard at first. He helped her to cut the wood and fill the woodshed for the winter and get the two heifers Lillian had bought fed and the barn cleaned. But after a few months, his "war sickness" seemed to bother him more and Lillian didn't drive him too hard. When she allowed, he would sit on the porch, in front of the woodshed, with his legs crossed, occasionally switching one for the other. He would hunch over forward in the chair and stare blankly at the woods across the road. Smoke was always curling up from a cigarette stuffed between his fingers. Fred's mind mostly matched his stare, but once in a while an old memory would pop in and float around in his head until he smiled faintly or would let out a slow... "Damn."

She watched him sometimes, through the kitchen window and tried to guess what he was thinking. She thought he'd been ruined by the war. And now, the same society that had sent him to war rejected him. He was feeble before his time and seemed to lack all interest in the future, except for food and drink. And, oh yes, those damned cigarettes. Sometimes these thoughts made her shiver; sometimes she could see Robert sitting there in Fred's place.

CHAPTER 13

The first year had been a hard struggle, trying to hold the place together, coping with everyone's criticism and their reluctance to get their hands dirty. She also found it impossible to fill the woodshed before the heavy snows fell in November.

When Able Grisinski, her neighbor down the road, offered to help, she accepted. He came over as often as he could, but he told her he was short-handed himself.

"Got two boys fightin' in Korea," he said. "Pete, he's twenty-two, why they drafted him. And then his younger brother, Paul went and enlisted to help his brother." Able was a big man and had lived in the area all his life. "All I got left to help me is John here, my twelve-year-old." John, a handsome boy with freckles, blushed.

Able had the biggest dairy farm in the area. He'd been the first to make Lillian feel welcome. Able said he and his wife were living on edge, with every radio newscast and the once-a-week headlines he read. Still, Able and John managed to cut up several cords for her.

She'd been forced to buy firewood by early February, an expense she needed to eliminate. And now, with her first two Jersey cows about to freshen, she needed Fred full-time just to tend the animals. Linda still lived with her, in spite of her outspoken dislike for the place, although the new bathroom had calmed her a lot. She helped a little around the house, but had a fierce dislike of anything to do with cows or barns. Lillian laughed when Linda complained that everything "smelled of cowshit". But she was happy that Linda had a full time clerking job in town. It kept her out of trouble.

It was at this point that a stranger knocked on her door. She'd been at her desk in the kitchen, working on some papers for the school Shakespeare festival, when the loud knock sounded. She jumped and looked out the kitchen window; no one had knocked like that since Fred came calling. She saw the stranger standing there, dressed in a red-checkered shirt, heavy gray wool pants with suspenders, and rugged-looking lace-up leather boots. He held a blue watch-cap in his hand.

She went quietly to the pantry, a small walk-in room, covered by a printed draw-curtain. She kept a .30 caliber rifle standing in a dark corner of the cupboard. It had belonged to her father and he had trained her well in its use. But It wasn't loaded and she didn't have time to get the shells from the bedroom drawer where she'd hid them. She didn't want Bobby to get his hands on them.

A second, louder knock resounded through the kitchen.

"Miss Wiggs-Barry?" the man called out. "You in there? My name is Harold Sims. They told me over at Peck's store that you might be needin' some help puttin' up wood for the winter? Miss Wiggs? Anyone home?"

She had mentioned to Maynard Peck that she was looking for help. Relieved, she stood the gun against the wall and opened the door.

She saw a powerful looking man of medium height, with rugged, weatherbeaten features, plain but not unhandsome. It was the face of a man who'd spent most of his time in the wind and the arctic cold and the sun. A wing of straight, black hair fell over his right eye. He was showing a thin, but full beard.

"Yes, I'm Wiggs," she said, and stared at him. She was impressed by his rugged handsomeness, so different from Matt. "And... and I did mention to Maynard that I'd be looking for help in October to get the firewood in. Is that what you do?"

"Oh, yes, that's what I do." He stood there, nervous, looking embarrassed by the presence of this handsome woman. He didn't extend his hand. He wasn't used to dealing with a woman. "I... I'm a contractor. Cut timber up north for Pearson's sawmill and Lake's, up in Speculator. Right now, I'm cuttin' firewood for the folks around here. Maynard said I should come over and check."

She was staring at him, making him lower his eyes. "Umm... Well, yes, that's good," she said. "Because I might be, ah, needing some help getting that wood in. If this winter's going to be much like the last, I'll probably need another five or more cords, I think. Woodshed's big enough to hold it. I've already got a couple of cords in there."

She told him where the woodlot was and after some further talk, he quoted a price for doing the work. She agreed to let him know in a week. She wanted to find out a little about him before she let him work on her property.

"I'll come back next week then? Well, I'll come back, I think. It's just that I can't promise I'll still be available. I mean, I might find some work in the meantime. And I just can't afford not to take it. But - I'll be back."

* * *

She chose to take a chance and wait. But she really wanted him to come back. Later, at the store, Maynard told her that Harold Sims lived in a cabin about five miles from his store, due north. Said he didn't know much about him, but folks around seemed to like him well enough.

"Think he's originally from Fonda, from what folks say," Maynard told her. She noticed that Maynard always qualified everything he said by claiming it was all what "folks say" or thought. He usually made this statement while scratching his bald head.

"Yup. That's true." Ira Smith said. He was sitting on an empty nail keg that Maynard kept in the corner for that purpose. "Came up this a-way about, let's see, six years ago. Yup." Ira sucked on his pipe and blew out a great billow of smoke. His white hair had a strange blue tint from the florescent light overhead. "that's when I first saw him around these parts." Lillian was surprised that old Ira had spoken. He was usually silent when she was in the store, and he was usually there, sort of a permanent living fixture that Maynard had installed.

Lillian found that Maynard Peck's store was a general meeting place for most all the people that lived within a 5 - mile radius. He sold on credit and kept all his accounts with a thick mechanical lead pencil his father had given him. He seemed to be the clearing center of all local news and gossip, a kind of rural message center.

He knew just about everything about everybody. People came to him not only for kerosene, salami, lo and hi-test gas, margarine and six-penny nails, but also for advice on how to cope with the outside world.

During her rounds, it wasn't unusual to see four or five men from the surrounding farms and homesteads hanging around Maynard's until he closed around ten. And some of them would help Maynard once in a while, especially when he had to go to the front of the store to pump gas. But Maynard chose to do most things himself and usually politely declined offers of help. His store wasn't very large, being about the size of good-sized living room, but it was complicated by the variety of goods he carried. His gas pumps were Flying A powered pumps, with both regular and hi-test available, but the kerosene was kept in a 50-gallon drum and he had to pump it by hand. She thought it wonderful that he sold beans and pickles and flour from big barrels, just like a century before. But he also had a modern cold meat case where he kept porkchops and small steaks, rolls of salami, baloney and pressed ham. When Lillian discovered that sometimes he would slice up a half-pound of baloney on the deli slicing machine right after he pumped a gallon of kerosene, she didn't complain. She knew that most folks didn't complain much about the strange flavors; they all knew he was just too busy.

When Lillian had first come to the store, all conversation usually stopped. But after a while, when she started dressing less sophisticated and introduced herself as Lillian Wiggs, and started asking for advice on setting up her farm, they warmed up and began for a while, to treat her almost like a regular.

Lillian liked Maynard; liked his consistency; his seeming permanence in her new and ever-changing world. Maynard was a short stocky man and he always wore a full-length work-stained blue apron. When it was cold, he wore a deer hunter's red cap, with the ear flaps turned up on the outside. In warmer weather, he would sport a green eye shade, his bald head projecting above the eyeshade like a cue ball. He had run the store for 16 years now and had no plans to retire, although he was eligible for social security.

"Frankly Mrs. Wiggs-Barry, I think Harold Sims will do you a good job. That's what most folks around here would say. I guess I can say I wouldn't hesitate to hire him and most the folks around here would hire him too. I think you can bank on Harold Sims," Maynard concluded. "And say, you bein' a teacher an all, did you hear the news today?" Maynard's was one of the few places around that was "electrified", since he was close to a cross roads where power lines had been run. He had a 12-inch RCA console television in his apartment over the store and became a ready source of surprise news announcements, news from the outside world. "Ol' Eisenhower said that if he gets elected, he would personally go to Korea, and stop everyone from guessin' about what the government should do about the Korean war. What's goin' to be the outcome of all this? Eh, Mrs. Wiggs-Barry?"

"Maynard, Please, please, everyone here, can you just call me Lillian or just plain Wiggs? She looked around and Ira and two other men seemed to be nodding yes.

"Well, Eisenhower promised to end this war one way or the other," she said. "I guess that means, if he gets elected, he'll use whatever force is necessary. I think the Chinese feel that he'd use the bomb. He's another general, after all, just like McArthur. What do you think?"

Maynard squinted his eyes. "Think it's a damn shame that a real hero like McArthur got put down by Truman like that. I agreed with McArthur; always thought we should 'a A-bombed those Red Rats. Maybe Ike will finish the job." Everyone in the store chimed in their agreement. When Lillian left, they were in a heated debate on how to get McArthur back in control.

CHAPTER 14

"We can go ahead with the cutting," Lillian said to Harold, standing in the doorway of her kitchen. "I've decided I can afford it."

Harold had showed up when he said he would. "Well, you won't be sorry ma'am," he said. "We'll cut them into fourteen to sixteen-inch lengths, if that's alright." He showed her a sample stick he had with him.

"That's fine," she said. "Will you be needing me to come up to the woodlot?"

"I don't see any need for it, Miss Wiggs. We'll pick out only dead trees, or mostly dead, I guess. We'll try to use anything that's already down."

"Anything you need?" she asked.

"No, I've got everything I need. But, oh yes, we'll be using that buck saw you've got behind the barn. I checked it out and I think I can get that old Fordson engine to run. Is that alright?"

"I'd be obliged to you if you got that engine working," she said. "Fred's been bucking wood with an old hand bucksaw. He can't get much done that way." She smiled. She was happy with the arrangement. "Would you like some coffee?" she asked.

"Thanks, ma'am, but my helper is waitin' in the truck. I think we best get started."

Harold had all his equipment loaded in the back of the old International truck. There was a big red two-man McCullough chain saw, a pair of Peaveys, a two-man crosscut saw, two one-man crosscut saws, A pair of awesome double-bladed axes, log chains and Cant hooks, a 5-gallon can of gasoline and three quarts of two-cycle oil, splitting wedges, two sledge hammers, a splitting axe, two 50 foot lengths of frayed and stained 1-inch hemp rope, topping harnesses, a set of three-inch block and tackle , rusting chains, cables and hooks, and six peanut butter and jelly sandwiches inside a battered tool box. He had a thermos of coffee on the front seat next to Junior.

"Well, Junior, we got to find us some nice dead trees," he said as they bounced their way up to the woodlot. "We're goin' to need about five full cords. That's a lot, but she wants to make sure she won't run out." When he reached the edge of the lot, he shut down the truck engine. "What do you think, Junior?"

Junior, a strapping boy of 17, got down from the truck. He'd been helping Harold for several years now and seemed to have a keen eye for finding just the right stand for cutting. "looks good," he said, as he looked over the woodlot. "There ought to be plenty a' dead ones in there."

Junior helped Harold unload the heavy McCullough, and then fueled it up. It was a wet, misty day; they threw a tarp over the chainsaw and then set out to locate trees to cut. Except for the chattering whistle of a red squirrel and the squawking of a bluejay, whose sounds echoed through the deep silence, the only sound was the crunching of twigs under their heavy boots. Junior pointed through the damp mist to some fallen trees. "There's some oak layin' there. we can make a good cord or two."

They found some rock elm, some maple and beech. "This is an old woodlot," Harold said. "Hasn't been cut over much." Still, Harold was surprised to find small patches of the wood where no cutting had been done at all. The few trees in those patches were the proud, old, patriarchs of the woods. "We won't do any cuttin' here," he said when they found a stand of ancient, living maples. Harold was always happy to find places like that and he hoped he could come back later and see these silent, primitive giants again.

When they finished surveying, they retrieved the chainsaw and started to cut. The big red McCullough howled with its sputtering, disagreeable tremolo rolling throughout the woodlot for most of the day. This was followed by the thud of axes trimming the branches then the chainsaw again cutting the heavy trunks into logs.

Most of the trees selected were two feet or less in diameter, but one particular old dead Maple measured almost four feet. It was a hard tree to fell and Harold reckoned that it would give them almost half the wood they needed. Cutting that tree was almost the end for the McCullough as it coughed and spit and howled its way through the dry, dense heart.

Harold always hesitated about cutting old trees like that. The tree was mostly dead, yet still lived: there were a few, last red leaves near the top. Most of the huge lower limbs had died long ago. Harold suspected that the wood would be hollow and with some rot throughout but was surprised when they cut it into logs, to find it otherwise. When they finished trimming it out, Junior took off his cap and wiped the sweat from his brow. "That was a tough mother," he said. They sat on the trunk to take a break and Harold lit a cigarette.

"You know, that lady there, that Miss Wiggs? She's real pretty," Junior said.

"I didn't know you noticed," Harold said.

"Well, didn't you see that? Don't you think she's pretty?"

Harold and Junior worked at the job for two weeks and Lillian was getting used to his coming and going. When he announced that they probably would finish up the next day, she was disappointed. "You'll come for supper, then," she said hopefully. "You and Junior? To celebrate a job well done. Tomorrow night? Will that be Ok?"

Junior's words came back, and he agreed. "That's real nice of you, Miss Wiggs," he said shyly. "Be glad to. And by the way, we've cut enough wood to carry you well into next year. And I've got some logs from an old maple that I think you can sell for lumber." Harold had found that the rot he'd seen at work in the lower end of the trunk of the old maple didn't travel far. "That wood is clear and straight-grained and could be quarter-sawn into fine maple boards."

When Preston's sawmill offered her enough money for the maple logs so she could pay most of Harold's charges, she was happy. It was the first time she'd made any income from her land.

CHAPTER 15

Lillian had by this time shed much of her town veneer. When she was young, she had always been at home in the kitchen; her mother had taught her to be an outstanding cook. It was a skill she had little use for with Matt, but now it would be useful once more.

She gathered her courage and for the first time since she was a young girl, decided to butcher two hens for roasting. "I want you to help me," she told Linda and Bobby.

"Have you lost your mind?" Linda said.

"No," Lillian said, "it will do you good. You'll learn something important. Sometimes you've got to learn how to do things for yourself."

She had forgotten about butchering and marveled at the amount of time it took: first there was the killing itself; she lopped off the heads with a sharp hatchet.

"God don't do that! "Linda screamed when she brought the blade down on the first hen. She and Bobby both yelled and ran into the house. Lillian had to drag them back out again. The wildly flopping headless hen frightened them both and Linda groaned. "That's so cruel," she said. "how can you do that?"

Then she showed them how to pluck the feathers, with boiling water poured over the limp bodies.

"I hate that horrible smell," Linda said. "What is it?"

"That's wet feathers," Lillian said. "I don't like it either."

Bobby had stayed hidden until the bodies stopped flopping. Then he returned and helped her with the feather plucking, although he didn't seem eager to do it.

Later, there was the gutting, with the new smell of hot steaming guts which the two learners didn't like at all. The shiny red and blue tubing, covered with thick lumps of yellow fat, was pulled loose and dropped into a pan. “You have to do it just right,” she told Bobby, showing him how to stick his hand into the slithering mess, without breaking the sac containing the bitter bile. “You take out the heart, gizzard and livers,” she said and then showed them how to separate the parts. “You feed the rest of this to the pigs.”

“Disgusting,” Linda said. “The whole thing is totally vile and disgusting. I'd never eat chicken again if I had to do that.”

“Anyway, you've really learned something, Linda,” Lillian said, when they were finished. “And you too, Bobby.”

“Like what? I don't know what I learned except that I would rather do anything else than do *that*,” Linda said.

Lillian laughed. “Well, you stayed, didn't you? And now, at least you know how to do it; you know what it's all about.”

Later she had Bobby and Linda dig some potatoes from Rosemary's garden. She had given Rosemary a plot of the rich soil behind the barn for a vegetable garden. Rosemary still loved to have her vegetable patch and was amazed at how well potatoes and red cabbages grew in the Adirondack soil.

“So, Bobby, you go to school here at Wickersville?” Harold asked, later that evening. He and Bobby were sitting at the kitchen table waiting for Fred; Lillian had gone to call him. Junior hadn’t been able to come.

Bobby was a curious, energetic boy, with a big mop of light brown hair.

“Uh huh, that's where I go.”

“Well, do you like it there?”

“Umm... it's ok.” Bobby was helping himself to the mashed potatoes. “Sometimes I don't like it though.”

“What don't you like?” Harold asked, just to be polite. Harold never had liked school himself.

“Don't know. Just don't like school much. Sometimes, some of the kids are mean. Rather be here helpin' my Aunt Lilly.” He scooped a spoonful of mashed potatoes into his mouth. “Did you like school?" he suddenly asked.

Harold was surprised by the question. He didn't really know how to answer the boy. The truth wouldn't be helpful.

"Sometimes I liked it. Sometimes."

Bobby passed the mashed potatoes to Harold. Harold put them down on the table, waiting for the others.

"I know... that's what I mean." Bobby said.

Fred and Lillian came into the kitchen. Fred seemed to be having a hard time walking.

"Linda's out tonight, so she won't be joining us." Lillian said as she sat down at the end of the table across from Harold. Bobby sat across from Fred. Earlier, she'd lit the lamp on the kitchen table; it was her biggest lamp and when the wick was turned up, it cast shadows around the room. After sitting, she noticed that the lamp cast shadows up against the surrounding walls like some spectral projector, making the atmosphere gloomy. To brighten the place up, she lit the lamp on her work table in the far corner of the kitchen. That provided the cheeriness she was looking for; the ghostly shadows were gone. She was still learning how to live without electricity.

"It's my war wound," Fred said to no one in particular, after he'd sat down. "Sometimes it hurts real bad."

"Oh... I didn't know you were wounded," Harold said. His mouth watered with the mild aroma from the faint traces of wood smoke combined with the smell of the roast chicken. Lillian passed the platter of chicken

"Got shot in the leg," Bobby said. "Ain't that true, Mister Haynes? Bobby had a hard time keeping his energy under control. Lillian looked at Bobby, annoyed by his words.

Fred looked at the boy with a weariness and a shrug. He looked bleary-eyed and seemed to sway in his chair.

"Isn't that true," Lillian said.

"Got gassed too, by god," Fred said.

"Wars were really bad in those days, eh Fred? I can't imagine going through a gas attack," Harold said while serving himself.

"Oh, it was bad... oh, really bad in them days," Fred said. "I remember when the heinies... well when we were drivin' them across the border up in Belgium, that's when we got hit by the gas. Came on in with the artillery."

"Really, can't we talk about something else; something more pleasant," Lillian interrupted, looking sharply at Fred. She didn't think it was good for him to dwell on bad experiences, as he so often did.

Fred grunted and slid a chicken thigh off the serving plate and onto his lap. When he tried to pick it up, it slipped out of his hands onto the floor. The cat, Blackie, that Lillian had forgotten to put out was on the thigh in no time and Lillian chased the lucky animal outside.

When everyone's plate was full, except for Bobby who kept eating, Lillian said that she was very happy that they could all be there together and she thanked God for their company and these blessings. She never said formal grace at the table, but always slipped God in somehow.

They all enjoyed the food, in spite of Fred, who kept dropping things on himself and the floor. When he dropped a glass on the floor, Lillian knew that somehow, he'd gotten hold of some liquor. She lost her temper: "You shouldn't be drinking Fred." she said. "I don't want you drinking in my house." She looked at him with fire in her eyes. Harold lowered his head a little.

"It's my sickness Miss Lilly, sometimes a drink or two helps makes the hurtin' bearable. I'll allow as maybe it's not right as far as it goes for you."

"I won't put up with it, Fred. Just remember that." But she dropped it there and they enjoyed the remainder of the meal without interruption.

"This whipped cream is just great," Harold said, a little nervously, when Lillian had served the pie. "The pie too." He smiled at Lillian. "A great meal, Miss Wiggs. Can't thank you enough."

She wanted to know more about him, but he said so little. She tried to ease it out of him. "Have you always lived up north of Maynard's store?" she asked, while clearing the table.

"No. haven't always lived there. But mostly, I guess." He took a sip of coffee. "You know that back woodlot of yours has some real nice timber in it," he said trying to change the subject. "And talk about berry patches. I'm surprised you don't have every bear in the country down here. There's a patch where some of those bushes must be, oh, eight, ten foot high. Way over my head."

"Funny, I don't remember that place," Lillian said. "Bobby do you go there to pick berries?" The mention of bears and the remoteness of the berry patch had her concerned.

"Sometimes it's spooky in them berry patches," Bobby said. "But I ain't afraid."

"But I'm *not* afraid," Lillian said.

"Nope. And I'm *not* afraid, either," Bobby said. "But I've seen a funny looking man in the woods."

"What?" Lillian said. "A strange man?"

"Yes ma'am. He's an old man with a white beard."

"My God. What's he doing in my woods," she said.

"Bobby, how was this man dressed?" Harold asked.

"Well, he had a green hat with a feather in it."

"Did he wear a fur vest?" Harold asked.

"Uh huh. Looked like some kind of animal," Bobby said.

"Did he talk to you?" Lillian asked.

"No. He just waved and went by."

"I think I know who it was," Harold said. "And there's nothing to be concerned about. I think it's old Charlie Stout. He's a hermit, but he's harmless. He used to live in town, but after he got out of the service, he took to living in the woods. He couldn't stand people no more."

"Do you know him well?"

"I can't say I know him well. But he does come by the cabin to trade for salt or sugar sometimes. He seems like a kindly fella. Just wants to be left alone."

"Still makes me nervous," Lillian said. "knowing that he's prowling around in the woods."

"Well, I'd rest easy about that, Miss Wiggs. He belongs in the woods. I really think it's just the opposite. If Bobby got in trouble and old Charlie was around, he'd likely be his rescuer."

"Well you stay away from there from now on," she said to Bobby, smiling. "There's plenty of berries in the woods nearby."

"It is a good ways up there," Harold said. He knew there were creatures in the woods that could harm the boy. He'd seen them around his cabin. "But it's too bad about all that scrub brush growing in the old pastures," he continued. "Looks kind of wild, I guess. I mean those patches of alder and locust and scrub pine make the place look abandoned. Too bad we can't get the hardwoods to grow there."

"I'll get those pastures back in shape," Lillian said. "We're going to clear the brush and cut down those wild saplings. I intend to farm this place." She said with a smile.

Harold raised his eyebrows. "Farm... here? You mean to make a living at it? Don't think anyone made much of a go of it here. I thought you were teaching school?"

"Oh, yes, I am. But I'm going to make a go of it, as you say, here as well. Between Fred and Bobby and myself, we'll do... maybe with some contract work, once in a while."

"What about the neighbors?" Harold asked. "Do they think--" At that point, Fred stood up and, and after attempting to say something to Harold, slumped back into his chair. Then, while everyone looked at him in amazement, he fell sound asleep, threatening at any moment to fall out of the chair.

Lillian grabbed him to keep him from falling and shook him to wake him up. "Legs gave out," he said, when he came out of his sleep, his voice sheepish. "Think I better lay down. It's this war wound--"

Lillian and Harold helped Fred up to the second floor, although he protested. "I can make it myself," he kept muttering. They couldn't get him up into the attic room, so he went into Linda's room. "You'll have to move later, Fred," Lillian said. "I mean, before Linda comes home. If she finds you laying on her bed, she'll be furious."

"Don't you worry, Miss Lilly," Fred said. "As soon as I get rested, I'll be getting on up there. Just don't you worry."

When they came back down, Bobby had moved to the parlor, with school books spread on the parlor table. He was plunking notes on the piano.

"Miss Wiggs, this has been a very nice evening," Harold said. I really enjoyed your food. And the company. I'll be finished splitting tomorrow. Wish... I wish." He stopped talking and shook his head.

"What Harold? What do you wish?" she asked.

"Well... I wish we could do this again. I know it's a lot of work for you, but--"

"Yes Harold. We can do it again. But only on the condition that you stop calling me "Miss Wiggs."

He smiled and nodded. "Will Fred be Ok? It's great that you put up with him like that. Is he really sick like he says or--"

" Is it drink? well, he did get hurt during the war, that's for sure. I guess it's a combination of both, although this is only the second time that Fred has done this to me. I don't know how he manages to sneak a bottle into his room. He was embarrassed tonight, I could tell." She paused while Harold lit a cigarette.

"I feel for him," she continued. "You know, Fred is one of those people who is always a victim. They believe too much in the government, in other people, and in the goodness... of God."

"What do you mean?" Harold asked.

"Well, when things go wrong, and nobody seems to give a damn, some people are surprised and hurt... I guess that's what I mean." She was silent for a minute. "And I don't think that anyone has paid attention to Fred Haynes for years," she continued. "I think his imagination has just got a hold on him. He'll be alright."

Harold nodded and walked down the dark path towards his truck. "Nite," he called back. "Goodnight... Lillian." His voice carried back through the still night.

She stood on the porch and watched him leave. The dampness of the coming night, a dampness that would soon turn to frost, made her pull the sweater tighter around her. But for all the cold and dampness, a warmth dwelt inside her that had been missing since long before Matt's death.

CHAPTER 16

Harold surveyed a new section of Lillian's woodlot and found several more hardwood trees that could be sold for profit. When he told her, she smiled and began to associate him with good news.

"But don't clear cut it," she said. "Linda tells me there's a family of raccoons living up there. I know they can be a pest and most people would ask you to shoot them, but for now, it pleases me to know they live on my land. Besides, there's lots of bobcat and fox to keep them in check."

Harold nodded in agreement. He had seen some clear-cutting up north near Speculator. "If only more of the farmers around here felt like you, there would be more hope for the Adirondacks," Harold said.

"Don't blame the farmers," Lillian said quickly. "Most of them here in the park can barely make it... most have had to sell out, just like this place. I don't think a new field has been cleared up here for the last fifty years. In fact, it's just the opposite: most farms are turning back to wilderness. Just look at this place."

"And that makes a good point. I don't mean to harp on this Lillian, but I don't see why you want to farm it up here. There's no electricity and there's so much good land down around the river."

"You're right, I know. But that land is being taken over by those big dairies and they have driven the price of land out of sight. Only a big operation can compete, with the market price of milk today. My parents used to keep thirty head on their farm. We thought that was big then. Now Bullocks owns that land and most of the farms that were around us. Bullocks has over 500 milkers now, and keeps growing. That's not what I want. I really think this is one of the few places around where a small farm can survive, if you're careful with costs and make yourself different."

Harold listened, but he didn't agree. His own trade in lumber was up against it, but nothing as bad as small farming. And he could never be a farmer; he had no calling for it and wanted none. He went into lumbering because he wanted to be outside; he could never work in an office or factory. And he enjoyed the freedom of being a contractor and not being tied down by daily routines, especially those found on a farm.

Harold had been raised in town where he finished high school, so he already had that built-in prejudice about small farmers: they were ignorant, backward people that badly needed educating and cleaning up although he never felt that he was any better than they were and he never expressed those feelings to anyone else. He still couldn't see how she could make the farm pay for itself up here.

But it wasn't really his business yet. He was growing fond of Lillian and enjoyed her cooking, but he had made no moves yet, no commitments. And he felt that Lillian was smart enough to do anything she wanted to, even if he didn't understand it.

She agreed to cutting five more trees. That next Saturday, Harold went up to the woodlot in his old ford pickup to select the trees and do some further surveying. He was alone that day. There were still parts of the woodlot he hadn't seen yet. He used the old tractor road that ran behind the barn.

When he got to the log trail he'd used for snaking the logs down to the back of the barn, he shut off the truck engine and waited. After a while, his hearing tuned to the sounds of the woods in the noon-day warmth. In the Indian-summer weather, the hazy air pulsated, a kind of heat rhythm played by the late season insects. Chipmunks, sensing his presence, let out their bird-call squeals, warning every creature in the wood lot. A lone crow, roosting on the bare branch of a big pine that bordered the lot, peppered the air with its staccato cry, acknowledging the chipmunk's alarm. From deep in the woods, arguing jays and red squirrels punctuated the other sounds.

Harold left the truck and walked back to the northwest end of the lot where he knew there were a few of the better trees. It was the opposite end from where he had cut earlier. He breathed deeply and filled his lungs with the warmth and emptiness of the woods. It smelled of wild things and of the north, of spruce and pine and wild blueberries; a place unused and clean, touched lightly by the hand of man. The scars of past cuttings were veiled by wildflowers and giant ferns and blue-green mosses.

When he reached the area of the big trees, he saw a movement, a flash of white that caught his eye. He crouched down, hoping to see a deer. He was surprised to hear a voice call:

"Harold?" Linda's voice was clear and she stepped out from the shadows of the trees.

"Linda! Hello. What are you doing way up here?" Lillian had introduced him to Linda weeks before and he had thought her very pretty; but in following encounters, her brashness had bothered him. Her tongue was caustic and foul words came too easily. He felt like she'd been challenging him all the time, as if he were an intruder. He mistrusted her.

"Hello Harold. I might ask you the same thing... but I already know why you're up here." She walked up close to him. She looked very pretty in the dim forest light; a tall, robust woman, with long, brown hair and a light, rosy complexion, marred only by a faint scar across her left cheek. Her dark eyes were large and penetrating, but her left eye was slightly askew, looking outward. She avoided looking at people directly and that always gave her that far-away look and a false air of shyness.

"Hmm, yes, I guess you do know why I'm here," he said.

"Well, this is my favorite place on this poor farm... my secret garden. Did you ever read that in school?"

"No. Don't know what it is. Why do you call it your secret garden?"

"Because there is a wild garden up here and only I really know about it. No one else comes here... that is, until you started cutting. I want you to see it. C'mon, I'll show you."

Harold looked around at the surrounding woods. "Better not," he said. "Gotta do this survey for Lillian."

"All work and no play?" she said. "Don't you ever screw around? It'll only take a minute and maybe you can do what it is you need to do on the way. C'mon. I won't bite you."

Harold tossed his head, reluctant to follow her and yet feeling like he should. She took off and saw that he shrugged and followed. She led him through the big trees to the far corner of the woodlot. They came to a clearing. In the center was a small clear, pond. A stand of cattails stood on one side, and on the other, banks of water lilies had taken hold. All of this was surrounded with wildflowers and what appeared to be trimmed grass.

"It's a... a nice place," he said, looking around. "Yes, you're right. It does look like a garden."

"Yes. And it's all natural. You see, the deer keep the flowers and grass chewed down over there." She pointed to the other side of the pond. "You can see their path, there, over there." A well-worn, narrow path came out of the woods on the opposite side of the pond. "And the coon family comes here to fish. The water is filled with fat minnows. They fish over there, where that brook enters the pond. Do you see it?"

"Oh, Yeh," Harold said. It was the first time he had seen Linda in such a happy mood. He was feeling less tense. "Where does it run out?" he asked.

"It doesn't. I think it must just seep back into the ground. The brook comes from over there, on old Able Grisinski 's place."

At the upper end of the pond, well back from the water, was a large granite boulder, with its lower half buried deep in the earth. Lying just behind it was an old fallen beech.

"I didn't know you liked this kind of place," Harold said.

"There's lots about me you don't know," Linda said, nodding her head. "I don't like livin' here much, and I sure as hell don't like farming. But I like the quiet of the woods. I come here to think and write poetry."

"Think? Poetry? You write Poetry?" Harold said. He didn't believe her.

She laughed at his questions. He saw how pretty she looked when he laughed or smiled. It was far different then the sneers and frowns she'd given him before. She seemed like a different person.

She sat down on the grass next to the beech log. She stretched an arm backward over the large trunk, her sweater unbuttoned, thrusting her breasts tight against the low-cut blouse. "You know, there are hardly any black flies or mosquitoes here? It's really clean... come on Harold sit down for a minute. See how nice it is just to sit here. Just for a minute."

He looked at her, trying to keep his eyes off the mounds of breasts. "Better not, " he said.

"Why not, Harold, are you afraid of me?"

"Hmm. Not much afraid," he said. "I'm up here to get some work done." Although he turned to look at the trees, his eyes kept drifting to the alluring curves and his blood began to race. Her eyes looked past him dreamily and seemed to urge him to sit down. But he remained standing against the beech log only a few feet from her. He braced his arms back to the log and stood there without words.

"Don't cut up here Harold." she said, looking up at him. "I don't want this place destroyed."

He saw that the biggest, oldest trees were around the border of the place she'd discovered. "No, I wouldn't touch them," he said, glad to find something to talk about. "Lillian wouldn't want me to, anyway. Does she know this pond is here?"

"Sure. I told her about it. You know, before she bought this place, she walked it from one end to the other. Maybe she saw it then. But she never told me."

Harold didn't like dealing with women. He knew he was being awkward with her. He wanted to leave but his feet felt glued to the ground.

She talked about the farm and Lillian's intentions and they found that they had something close to an understanding on the subject. While they were talking, Linda was moving, wiggling, pretending to adjust and brush her skirt and just managing to show more thigh while sliding closer to Harold. Soon, he could smell the perfumed airs and musky odors of her body and a stirring took place he had no power to control. Her closeness, the breasts, the thighs, the smells, the warm air and the surrounding Eden caused him to break out into a sweat. She eased him down into a rolling embrace and kissed him although he was clumsy and rough. She made it a long, hard kiss. Then she was on top of him. He was clumsy getting her clothes pulled aside or off; getting his suspenders down. They kept wrapping around his arms, frustrating his attempts to get ready. But she seemed to know what to do and helped bring him to bear. Soon he was making crude love to this woman he had been wary of. A savage impatience he'd not known in a long time drove him, and her passion was wild and indulgent. After a feverish and sometimes brutish coupling, they lay exhausted in the shafts of light penetrating to the grassy floor. With their strength drained, they put their backs against the beech log and bathed in the piggish sweat of their lovemaking.

Linda smiled and nodded her head, her eyes focused on the clouds over his head. She seemed to be holding a conversation with herself. He worried about that smile; it was the one that had made him uneasy. He felt a trickle of blood running down his chin into his beard.

Without speaking they let their bodies restore themselves; recharge all the nerve cells; create the new energy required for more mundane functions, or even perhaps another go at it... but then Linda stood up and Harold fumbled to button up. She dressed in front of him, then wiped some drops of blood from his lip.

She said: "That was good, Harold. Real good." She laughed when he sighed and looked away. She slipped her blouse over her head and pulled it down slowly. "You better finish what you were doing. What did you call it? A survey? "

Harold continued fumbling with his clothes without speaking. As she turned to leave, she added: "Oh. One other thing. Please do me a big favor? Stay away from my mother? You wouldn't want her *now,* would you?" And then, like an Adirondack deer, she was gone.

CHAPTER 17

He was too embarrassed to see Lillian that day or the next and, in fact, did not go back to Lillian's house for weeks. He was afraid to see Linda again. He asked himself if he was afraid of Linda or was he afraid of her mother?

He found work in Pearson's mill, cutting slab-wood. He didn't like the job; it was tough, dirty work and he had to be at work by dawn each morning. But it kept him away from Lillian's. His equipment sat idle at the cabin and his horses, a team of Belgians, stayed stabled over at Cool's farm.

A month passed like this when he found a letter in his mailbox. It was from Lillian.

"Dear Harold,

Where have you gone off to? I've been waiting for you to come back. It's past time for cutting those trees and I need your advice on some other things. Please come over. We miss you."

He didn't reply and a week later he found a note on his door. She told him she'd dropped by to see him and really needed someone to cut the trees. She reminded him that he had promised to do so.

He had wanted to go after the letter arrived, but he was stopped by a black mood that had replaced the embarrassment, and he had been drinking again. The note found him feeling better and sober.

"I had to take a job at the mill," he told her, when they finally met again. "I needed the money. But I'm finished now." She shook her head in understanding. "Where's Linda?" he asked tensely.

"She quit her job and went to New York. God knows why. Her ex lives there, you know. And he's threatened her. Said he'd beat the hell out of her if she ever came back. But she knows him, knows what she's up against. That's how she got that scar on her cheek." Lillian paused, watching for Harold's reaction.

"Her husband did that?" he asked.

"Yes. I'm afraid he's not a very nice person. Dangerous, in fact. Thank God she's divorced." She was silent for a moment, thinking about how much she disliked Frank Boyle.

"Oh yes," she said, returning to the present, "Linda told me she met you up in the woods when you were here last. Showed you that special place of hers."

Harold's body twitched. "Um huh, yes, that she did," he said. "Uh, nice place." His gut trembled. "Well, I'll get started on cuttin' those trees next Monday, if that's alright," he said nervously.

"That'll be fine," she said. "That'll be just fine."

After the trees were cut and sold, Harold started helping Lillian with some things that needed fixing around the old place. "There's an awful lot of work for such a small farm," he told her one day after making some new fence posts. "Seems like there's always something that needs to be done. Fred doesn't seem to be able to handle it all."

"Fred's been sick lately," she replied. "Cold weather makes him feel worse. Right now, I think he's got the flu or a bad cold." She secretly thanked God that Fred was living there since Linda had left.

"That's too bad. I'm free for a while, I guess. I can help you with those cows you just bought. I have to warn you though, I don't know much about milking cows."

"You don't have to do that Harold," she said. "In fact, I was just going to ask you if any of your helpers would be available? I'd be willing to take one on until Fred feels better."

"I don't think so Lillian," Harold replied. "They're all in school except Junior Dixon, and he's staying at his uncle's place over in Stone Arabia for a while. Look, I don't mind helping out until Fred comes around."

"I appreciate it Harold. I'm working on some milk samples for a creamery right now, and I sure could use some help. Teaching takes up all my time."

Harold felt closer than ever to Lillian. And though he still didn't like the farm work much, especially working in the barn with the pungent smells of manure and urine lacing the air, he found that Lillian made it all seem different somehow. To her it was like some kind of mission; a primitive technical challenge. He tried to understand this challenge, although he was still convinced that farming would never work in that area. But he was beginning to see Lillian with new eyes.

CHAPTER 18

In the spring, Lillian decided it was time to start on rebuilding the barn.

"But why, Lillian?" Harold asked when she told him about her plans and asked him if he would do the job. "Why put so much money into that old barn?" They were eating hot dogs in the outdoor pavilion at the Caroga Lake Amusement Park. The winter had been mild and that spring had been unusually warm, and the operators decided to open the picnic pavilion and the big carousel a month early. The carousel was housed in a glassed-in pavilion with stained-glass windows around the top. Lillian thought it was one of the nicest carousels she had ever seen anywhere. "I think you're just wasting your money," Harold continued. "And I hate to see you do that."

"Have you checked the barn, Harold? " she asked. "I know it looks bad on the outside, but if you'll look at the structure, you'll see my point. Here, look, you see this pavilion?" and she pointed at the massive beams overhead. "The barn is built post and beam, that's what Able told me, and this pavilion is built the same way. I think you'll find it worth fixing."

It was just before sunset on a Saturday night and they were having a dance at Moody's Dance Hall, across the walkway from the pavilion. Lillian decided to bring Bobby to the Amusement Park to ride the carousel and eat hotdogs. He'd seemed listless lately and was having a hard time with his school work. She thought getting out would help. She'd invited Fred and Harold and Rosemary along for the outing. Rosemary had been by at the house that Saturday doing the spring work in her vegetable garden.

Bobby had been playing around the rental boathouse, watching the people work on the row boats and paddle boats. When they'd left, he'd moved to the beach, bordering one end of the pavilion. He was looking for rocks to skim off the water. But there were no rocks in the white sand, just small pebbles.

"Remember, Lillian, the Morrisons quit your place," Harold said. "They couldn't keep it going and their kids didn't want any part of it. They all went off to Schenectady to work in the GE plant and their kids went to school in Utica, just like you. I just don't see why you want to put money into farming that place. It's a nice place to live, but farming?"

Bobby returned from the beach. "Can I have another hotdog?" he asked, sitting down next to Rosemary.

Rosemary seemed fidgety and jumped up. "I'll get the hot dogs for Bobby," she said.

Fred looked at her and smiled. "I could sure use another one. Is that Ok?"

Then Harold jumped in. "They sure are good. Would you get me another one too, Rosemary?"

Rosemary threaded her way down the path where the closed booths were. In June, they would open and offer anyone willing to put up 15 cents, a chance to win a prize. She remembered how often she'd tried to win a doll at the milkbottle booth, but could never knock down the three bottles with three balls. After a while, she came to realize that the balls were too soft and the bottles too heavy for most people; it would take the pitch of a Yankee to knock them down.

She came to the muscleman hammer and bell where so much male strutting took place during the summer mating season. It was silent now, and alone. With canvas wrapped around its base, it looked remarkably timid, like it was afraid that some brute was going to strike it. She remembered when her Harry had sweated down the hammer without ever ringing the bell. He didn't seem to be able to get the sliding weight even half way up the scale. And Harry had nice muscles in his arms; she'd always admired and touched them, making him feel good. But in the end, they'd told lies about his weak and feeble heart.

She crossed the dirt road that ran around the perimeter of the east end of the lake to the open hot dog stand. There was a line of people, mostly from Moody's Dance Hall, waiting to buy hot dogs or sodas or Svenson's ice cream, and she mingled in the line waiting under the glowing neon lights with the usual fleets of darting bugs.

Music from Moody's drifted over on a breeze, a country western band cranking out old-time fiddling and the nasal booming of an amplified square dance caller. Between square dances, twanging electric guitars filled the air. From the other direction, pavilion organ music came from the wheeling carousel. Grilling hot dogs added their pungent smell to the surrounding pine and hemlock woods. Rosemary watched the people standing around others in line, already licking the rich ice cream cones or munching down hot dogs, waiting to get back to Moody's for more dancing. The girls from town were dressed something like she was, outfitted in smart blouses, filled by stretched bras and tight-fitting slacks topping a pair of penny loafers or low-heeled patent leather shoes.

Most of the country girls, especially those that lived on farms, looked much older, much more like their mothers. They wore just a little make-up; a light touch of old rouge to hide winter pallor and a faint trace of lipstick. They never did their eyes. But their common print dresses clung to their bodies and were more sensual then the tight-fitting slacks of the town girls.

The women chatted, while the young girls looked around in anticipation. The men grunted and ate hot dogs. It was a happy crowd and suddenly Rosemary felt lonely.

"You dancin' over at Moody's?" a voice behind her asked.

She turned and saw a nice-looking man about her age, waiting behind her in the line. His hair was streaked with gray and was combed back with a curly, wavy sweep on the sides.

"Hi. My name is Warren Stacey. And you know what? I'm short a dance partner tonight. Wondered if you wouldn't like to dance?"

She smiled and turned away without answering. That was because she wanted to say yes, by all means, she would like very much to dance. But she couldn't bring herself to say yes. Just like she couldn't acknowledge her growing attraction to Harold. The reason why she had to go get the hot dogs: she was staring at him too much. And she knew he'd noticed her stares. But she didn't know what answer, if any, lay in his eyes.

"I... really can't." she finally said, looking halfway back at him. "I'm with some other people. But thanks for asking." The man shrugged. "Well, that's my bad luck," he said.

When she turned back a minute later, he was gone.

She returned to Lillian's table with the hot dogs, eating a cup of Svenson's ice cream and resolved to ignore Harold. They were having a discussion about the farm.

"Well, that took some time. Bobby's already had two more rides on the carousel. " Lillian looked at Rosemary with a question on her face.

"You mean the merry-go-round? And there's quite a line waiting for hot dogs. Moody's must be packed tonight." Rosemary said. She sat down next to Bobby.

" Is that Svenson's ice cream?" Lillian asked.

"Oh, yes. Everybody's eating it. It's really good."

"Can I have one of those?" Bobby asked as he started eating the hot dog.

"Maybe later," Lillian said. "That ice cream... Svenson is using the milk from my Jerseys... at least he's testing it for a new brand of supreme he wants to introduce."

"I didn't know you were selling milk already," Harold said.

"Well, I'm not. I've been giving Svenson's the milk free. I have to get inspected by the county agent before I can sell, at least to be legal. But listen, everyone. Let me tell you about my plans for the farm. Maybe you won't think I'm too crazy... "

"Not crazy, Lillian." Harold said and smiled. "We never thought you were crazy... only crazy about farming."

"And that's it, isn't it? I am crazy about dairy farming. I know it seems that most farmers around here would give their eye teeth to get off the farm; I know it's hard; It's seven days a week; it's morning, noon and night, and it doesn't pay much. Most small dairymen can't even break even. I know all these things, yet I still want to do it."

The others searched for some response. Bobby fidgeted. He was about to eat the last bite of the hot dog. When no one spoke, Bobby said: "Well, I like farmin' too."

"Good for you, Bobby," Rosemary said. "I like farming too."

" Well, he inherits that from his grandpa," Lillian continued. It's my Dad's fault. He loved dairying so much. He gave that love to both of us."

"Well, what about breaking even?" Harold asked, as he swallowed a bite of hot dog. "You mentioned something about small farmers not being able to break even. Do you have any plans to break even? I mean, that's what I'm getting at when I say you shouldn't farm that place."

"Well, I do have plans. But it's nothing magic." She stopped talking for a while. She'd noticed Rosemary staring at Harold and Harold fidgeting under that stare.

Bobby was squirming on the bench. "Can I go down to the boat house again?" he asked.

Lillian looked across the lake. The night had come on and lights were lit in some of the cabins around the lake. She could almost see the place where she and Matt had had their cabin; the place where they had spent some good times. It was on the far side of the lake nestled in hardwoods and hemlocks. They also had a small dock where Matt kept his runabout. A twinge of nostalgia gripped her heart, but she shook it off. She knew the image of Joyce Hutchins would pry its way into her mind.

"It's too dark, Bobby. Wait and I'll get you some of that ice cream. Wouldn't you like to ride on the, uh, merry-go-round again?" Lillian asked. Then she realized she was trying to buy the child off. It was supposed to be his outing.

Bobby shook his head. He was dizzy from riding. "I'm tired," he said, annoyed. "Can we go home... please? I'm really tired."

Bobby was tired she knew, and bored with her talk of farms and farmers, her rural geography lessons.

Shortly after, they left the pavilion. Rosemary looked wistfully at Moody's dancehall. Saturday night was just beginning there. The music seemed louder than before. Lillian drove the Buick down the back roads to the what she called the Sand lake house.

When Bobby was asleep in the back seat, Lillian spoke in a very low voice:

"I'm going to specialize in champion Jerseys," she explained, looking at Harold. "Like I said, I've been negotiating with Svenson's. Old Mr. Svenson, that's Bill Svenson?" Harold nodded that he understood. He knew about Svenson's Creamery. "Well, he wants to start a new super premium ice cream line, mostly because I suggested it, with 18 percent butterfat." She continued. "And he'll pay premium for Grade A milk from champion registered Jerseys. They can't get that from the Co-op. That's all blended and from mostly standard Holstein stock."

"Uh, Lil I would slow down if I were you," Harold said. She noticed he was bracing himself against the dashboard. "Lots of deer on the roads at night."

She slowed down when she saw the speedometer touching 65. "I didn't realize." She said.

"But I still don't understand," Harold continued. "Why does it matter? I mean, what's the big difference between Jersey milk and Holstein?"

"Jersey milk is richer, creamier, rich in butterfat," she said, warming up to one of her favorite subjects. "And Jerseys seem to thrive up here in these northern pastures. Something in the grass they really like. That gives their milk a special flavor. And that's what makes the big difference. Flavor. Svenson knows that great milk flavor makes great ice cream. Now he's testing the milk from my Jerseys for that flavor." Lillian smiled. "I already know he's going to like it."

Bobby was still asleep between Fred and Rosemary in the back seat. They rode on in silence.

"I guess I'll take that contract to rebuild your barn, Lillian," Harold said. "Sounds like you know what you're doing."

Those were the words that she had been waiting for. "That's great, Harold," she said. "You won't regret it, I promise. Now I can concentrate on building the herd."

Fred perked up again. "How many cows you figger' on havin'?" he asked.

"About twelve, total Fred. We won't get too big. Ten might even be enough. Mr. Svenson thinks he'll start with about 300 gallons of the premium ice cream a week and gradually build up. He'll buy all the production I can put out."

Fred shook his head. "Ten? Twelve?" He was taking care of four now. "Isn't twelve too many? How will I do it?" he mumbled under his breath so no none could hear him.

"What did you say, Fred?" she asked. But he had dozed off again as the car rolled down the narrow road.

* * *

That night Rosemary stayed over at Lillian's place. It was too late, too dark to drive home. Lillian was glad Rosemary stayed; she had something needling her mind, something she had to ask Rosemary about Harold.

"Svenson, Svenson. Why do I remember something about him?" Rosemary asked, thinking about the conversation they just had in the car. She was changing into a night robe that Lillian had loaned her.

"With good reason. My family used to be friends of the Svenson's. My dad sold milk to them before he joined the co-op."

"Isn't he the one that uh, wanted to marry you?... I thought you told me that once." Rosemary sat down on her side of the bed.

"See... I knew you'd remember." Lillian put down the mirror she was using to apply her night cream. She looked at Rosemary. "You know, he asked my father for my hand in marriage. That was just before I went off to college. I was only 18 and my father said he was too old for me." She sat down on the bed next to Rosemary. "It's funny, isn't it? The way someone's decision can change your whole life?"

"You mean you would have married him?" Rosemary asked.

"I liked him a lot." Lillian said. "He was a good-looking man, and he came from a farm background. We understood each other. I think he was only 30 years old then, and still a bachelor." She took Rosemary's hand in hers. "Yes. I do believe I would have married him."

"Wow... , I didn't know. Can I ask you a question?"

"Why not?"

"Is this why he's offering you such a good deal on the milk?"

"Oh, maybe, Rosemary, maybe. I can tell you that he still has an eye for me. I try not to encourage anything because he's married, and ... now he *really* is too old for me." She got up and picked up the mirror and looked at herself. She looked at the forming signs of age on her neck and face. "It's funny, how after all these years-- " She put the mirror down. "But he really is looking for someone to supply the special milk he wants. I just happen to have what he wants."

Rosemary seemed loss in thought. Lillian said: "Now, can I ask you something?"

"Sure." Rosemary said with a puzzled look.

"I noticed at the pavilion that you seemed to have ... eyes for Harold."

Rosemary stiffened; her face flushed. She got up from the bed without saying anything and walked to the door facing the darkened rooms just outside.

Lillian said, " I didn't mean that you--"

"Was it that obvious?" Rosemary interrupted. She turned to face Lillian, her arms crossed.

Lillian saw a bewildered, angry look in Rosemary's face. The one she had seen before during her fits of jealousy. "I'm afraid it was," she said mildly, hoping to defuse an explosive situation. But her voice carried a certain tone, a subtle inflection that betrayed her caution.

"And so what?" Rosemary demanded. "Are you saying that I did something wrong?"

"Oh, no, Rosemary, no," Lillian said quickly. "I... I shouldn't have said anything. You didn't do anything wrong. Nothing."

"Are you interested in Harold?" Rosemary said, a wild look flickering over her face.

"Oh, Rose," Lillian said, and sat down on the bed. "Let's not make a mistake about men again. Let's not get upset over this. We've both been hurt too much."

Rosemary nodded her head. "Well, anyway, are you?" she demanded.

Lillian searched Rosemary's face, trying to gauge her answer. "Yes. In a way, I guess I am," she said, her voice trembling. "But I'm not falling in love, if that's what you mean."

Rosemary turned back to face the door. "But you need him, don't you? I mean you need his help?"

Lillian was silent, focusing on her hands now rubbing nervously together in her lap. " Do I?" she finally said. "Sometimes I feel lonely out here. But that doesn't mean anything. He's just a friend, a contractor I use sometimes. It hasn't gone beyond that."

"I guess I *knew* that. I haven't seen anything. You don't have any real claim on him, do you?" She turned back towards Lillian.

"No, I don't," she said. "So far there's nothing between us. Maybe never will be. God. I'm so afraid of men now."

Rosemary saw tears welling in Lillian's eyes. "I'm sorry, Lillian," she said. "I didn't mean to act so huffy."

Lillian slowly got to her feet and they embraced until Lillian was calm again. Then they both sat for a while, silent, fidgeting with cosmetics and other things.

"How's your garden doing, Rose," Lillian said, breaking the silence. "Are you going to plant your Scarlett Ohara's again this year?"

Rosemary dropped the cosmetic tube in her hand and looked

at Lillian. "Yes, Lillian," she said, her face more relaxed. "You know I always plant my Scarlett Ohara's when I have a garden. I'm going to try some Ruby Reds too." Then, after some further talk about the cabbages and the garden, they both went to bed.

But as the full moon rolled over the wooded hills and then sank behind the dark horizon, they both remained wide awake.

CHAPTER 19

Rosemary continued to come over to tend her garden, insuring that each seedling was planted just to the right depth, especially the Scarlett Ohara and Ruby Red cabbages. The incident between the two women seemed to be buried.

Harold had already sized the replanking and roofing needs of the barn. He'd made arrangements with Pearson's to have the boards cut and delivered from some local second-growth spruce. He knew it was not very resistant to decay and was soft and had low durability but it was cheap and available and with a good coat of paint or preservative, it would last well enough.

Lillian let Harold select the lumber for the siding and the roof, but she wanted to buy the paint and tools and other things that they needed. She let the kids go early from school one afternoon and had Harold drive her to town in his old truck. She went to Jordan's hardware in Fort Plain. Jordan's was the biggest hardware retailer between Schenectady and Utica.

After pricing the paints and comparing durability versus price, she decided on a good whitewash for the siding.

"Whitewash?" Harold asked, puzzled. "Nobody around *here* uses whitewash. Most every barn is painted red... "

"I know Harold. But we don't have to do what everybody else does, do we? I want a different style barn, like they have in French Canada or Norway or Sweden or Germany. I think mine will look good with whitewash."

She got the good kind made of slaked lime with casein added for binding and calcimine and gypsum for a deeper pigment. It was the kind her father had used on his barns. It was cheap, easy to put on and seemed almost as durable as paint.

She bought thirty pounds of 6 and 8 penny nails and twenty pounds of roofing nails, 16 gallons of whitewash (by Harold's calculations) another good carpenter's hammer, a nail puller, two utility chisels, five 4-inch paint brushes and some empty gallon buckets. She looked at a good extension ladder but Harold said he could make one just as good, and for nothing. She had all that loaded on the truck and then they went over to Boylston's Ford and Equipment Company to look at a new Ford tractor with hay mower and rake and field plow and cultivator attachments, a used John Deere manure spreader, Cory's stainless-steel hooded milk pails and cans and other items that interested her.

"Harold, these are the things that The Morrisons needed to make the farm work, especially a tractor," she said. "But they probably couldn't afford it."

"Probably so, Lillian. I never saw a tractor over there."

"Well Able told me that they had tried to work the place with a team of horses, she said. " Now I love horses, but it's slow going with a team. Too much backbreaking work for drivers and caretakers. And they need regular feeding and watering and brushing and shoeing. And there is hay to get in and oats to keep rats out of; and manure to clean out, and the horses get sore feet and toothaches and infected eyes and ears and colds and--"

"Whoa there, Lillian," Harold said. "I know what you mean. Where did you learn all that? "

"My father had a team; I used to help care for them."

Harold smiled and nodded; he kept his own team. "For logging, they're worth it," he said. "Horses can snag out a log from places where a tractor could never get into. But I thought you *liked* the primitive life, Lillian," and he laughed.

She laughed too. "Now a tractor doesn't need any of this," she explained. "A tractor doesn't need sex or hay or oats and doesn't get sick, at least not very often, or bite and fight. There's no harness and no manure to deal with. Just a little oil and gas." she said. "That's all. There is a limit to my yearning for the primitive life, Harold. There is definitely a limit. I think a tractor is needed on any kind of a farm."

"Well, I'm mighty glad to hear you say that Lillian. Puts me at least a little at ease." And he laughed merrily at Lillian's light-hearted attempt to entertain him.

"But I've never seen anyone so fired-up about farming as you are Lillian. You make it seem like a vacation or something that everyone should want to do. And yet it's the meanest, most back-breaking work I've ever laid a hand to. How do you figure that?"

She laughed and said: "Oh Harold, how you talk! My, you jabber off at the mouth. Backbreaking work! And you a logger! How can you carry on like that?"

This exchange had been refreshing for both of them. If there was one thing she wanted, it was to lighten up. But it was hard to do; it was not in their makeup. And she found there was something about living in the north woods that lent a serious purpose to every move; that created an economy of mood and intention and reduced human intercourse to a minimal state. It was as if the dark trees and deep winters had decreed that no foolishness would be tolerated; only the serious would survive.

She made a price list of the things they'd seen at Boyleston's that she thought she might consider buying, and then they walked back to the truck. "you think it's strange that I like farming so much," she said. "you know, for all these years I've been afraid to be myself. I loved the farm when I was a girl. I wanted to stay and help my father, but he wouldn't hear of it. He said we needed to get educated; to be somebody, to do something exciting, something that didn't require so much risk and hard work. He sent me off to school; that changed my whole life."

"Didn't you want to go to school?" Harold asked. They were nearing the parking lot where they'd left the truck. The lot was filled with huge Caterpillar construction equipment, waiting to start work on the new highway that was to go all the way to Buffalo. "I guess I just assumed that all girls wanted to go to school." Harold continued.

"No. Not really. But you're right in a way. All us girls were expected to go to school. Mostly to become teachers." They reached the truck and got in. She had something else on her mind. "Say Harold. It's getting late. Can I talk you into joining me for a bite to eat? I don't feel up to cooking."

"As a matter of fact, I was just going to ask you the same thing," he said, glad that she had broken the ice. "How about a burger over at the Hut?"

"That would be great, Harold, but look. I would really like to go to the Hillside Tavern. Would you mind going there? At least this one time? I used to go there a lot and I just feel like doing it again. It's on our way home... almost." She looked at him till he had to turn away.

Harold hesitated for a bit. "Don't know the place, Lillian," he finally said, "but I'll go if it pleases you. It's just that-- "

"Harold, before you say another word, this is my treat. It's just a small payment for you taking me around today." She'd guessed that Harold didn't have much money with him.

"Ok, Lil," he sighed. "I guess I'll let you treat this once. But it's my turn next time. Ok?" He felt a little better. "Uh, it's not a fancy place, is it? We bein' dressed in our best work clothes, that is."

"No problem. I'm sure they'll let us in." She was anxious to see the Hillside again. It scared her to visit places where she had spent so much time with Matt, yet she didn't want things from her past to always stand against her as forbidden fruit. Maybe she could fill these places with new memories to drive out the old ones; the ones best forgotten. But while she was out to build a new memory bank, she was also working to get Harold's attention.

The Hillside Tavern was located in an historical farm house that had been reconstructed. Some important personages had stayed there during the American Revolution. It was the site of the battle of Stone Arabia, where one of the Tory regiments had been defeated. The entrance was through a small room housing the bar and some Early American tables and chairs. The entrance was always filled with a lively crowd, mostly diners waiting for a table in the dining room.

The main dining room was decorated with paintings of colonial scenes. At one end, there was a great stone fireplace. It wasn't lit that evening because of the heat. Instead, each table had a small oil lamp or candle lit. The dark wood tables were covered with starched table clothes topped with settings of expensive silverware gleaming in the flickering lamp light.

As they took their table, Harold rolled his eyes when he thought she wasn't looking. When the waitress came to their table, Harold ordered a chicken fried steak and a beer and Lillian, a New York cut and a dry martini.

Although she didn't show it, Lillian felt uncomfortable, because of the memories. And then she thought she recognized one of the waitresses: a short grey-haired woman. Barbara, she thought she remembered. But the waitress made no sign that she recognized Lillian, and she wondered why. Was it because the waitress thought she was there with her lover?

"This is the first time I've been here since I moved," she said, after the drinks were served. "It hasn't changed at all, at least not that I can see." The familiar clink of ice cubes and the soft lighting helped relax her. She sipped her drink and watched the old waitress serve a couple on the other side of the room.

"Really?" Harold said, uneasily. "Its uh, kind of a nice place. But I'm glad everybody isn't wearing a tie. I feel just a little outta place in here."

She laughed. She felt that he would have to learn how to deal with it. "It's Ok Harold. Look. Most people are dressed like we are."

Harold looked around. In truth, he didn't see anybody dressed much like him.

"So, you went to college but you really didn't like it?" He asked, sipping his beer.

"Oh, I liked college alright. I just wanted to study something else. I did manage to take chemistry and two courses in dairy science while I was there. My father never knew about it. They were elective courses, but only the chemistry counted towards my degree." The Martini tasted good, but she was not used to drinking any alcohol and her head began to feel light. After her first healthy sip, she drank in very tiny sips.

"Did you like those dairy courses?" He asked.

"Yes, I really liked them. But I never realized how hard they would be. Mostly complicated chemical analysis of milk and studies of bacteria and cattle diseases. I really learned a lot."

Harold toyed with his almost empty glass. "Maybe that's what makes the difference," he said.

"What kind of a difference?" she asked.

"Well, just maybe now, an education makes a difference. It makes farming seem like somethin' it really isn't. I mean, like the way you think about it."

"You mean you don't think I see farming as it really is? "

"Would you like another drink?" the waitress asked, interrupting.

The waitress was pretty: red hair and cool green eyes; a pale complexion dotted with freckles. Her apron was starched and fit tight around her robust body. Lillian noted that she was young, and attractive in a country sort of way. Lillian swore she was making eyes at Harold. He seemed to be unable to speak, and smiled and nodded yes to her request, but Lillian declined. Harold asked where the restrooms were.

When he came back, a fresh beer was at the table.

"I think you're right, Harold." Lillian said.

"Right about... what?" Harold asked cautiously.

"Right about education making a difference. It's really about more than education though. It's really about money. About having it or not having it."

The waitress came up with the serving tray.

"This looks good," Harold said, avoiding the waitress but eyeing and enjoying the aroma of Lillian's sizzling steak.

Lillian smiled and buttered a slice of bread and the steaming potato. "So, what do you think, Harold?" Do you agree that it's money that makes the difference?

"You mean like not having enough money to see you through a bad year?"

"Well yes, something like that." Lillian said. "It's like any business. If you don't have enough capital, you're not likely to last. But I meant more about something like the culture of poverty."

Harold took a bite of his steak and then put down his fork and looked at her. "Culture of what?" he asked.

"Poverty. Being poor. You know what I mean. A lifestyle based on being perpetually poor. The average farmer around where we live is dirt poor. They farm because they can't do anything else. No education; they don't have the money for it. No way to get money. No way out. So, they farm, it's the only thing they can do. It's hard dirty work and that's how they look. Poor and dirty and ignorant."

The Hillside was busy that evening. The scurrying of waitresses and bus-boys and the coming and going of customers and the crashing of gathered plates and silverware made Lillian think of how much she used to enjoy coming here. "Isn't it wonderful here, Harold?" she blurted out, unable to contain her enthusiasm.

"Umm, yes, it is." He said. But she saw that he still looked uneasy. "So, you're sayin' that your farm will be a lot different than this uh, poverty-type farm you just spoke about? But isn't it all the same, Lil? I mean the cows have got to be milked; the barn's got to be cleaned... . and manure ... uh, cow manure, well it's just about pretty much the same everywhere."

"No Harold, everything's not the same. I'll never be running at the margins where everyone is too exhausted to look after their own needs." She laid down her fork. "There has to be a little time for baths; time for movies at the Rivoli; for eating in places like this; for books and reading. The poor farmer can't afford these things, as basic as they are." She picked up her fork again and started waving it around. "They are luxuries for him. He's working day and night just to keep the bank from taking the place from him. It's real tough when you're trying to farm your way out of debt. Do you see what I mean?"

Harold seemed to be enjoying his food until she said that and he laid down his fork. "Well, what you say seems to make sense, I guess, and it is different if you're not hard-up for money, but most farmers around here don’t care much about goin’ to the Rivoli or reading books, or taking baths or eatin’ here, for that matter, even if they did have money.”

This tit for tat made them fall silent and they busied themselves finishing the meal. They were hungry; they hadn't eaten since breakfast.

Lillian thought that maybe she was pushing too hard but noticed that Harold was sneaking glances at her while he ate. She thought that was a good sign.

After the dishes had been taken away and coffee served, Lillian said: “It's been a nice day Harold,” and she impulsively put her hand over his. “I'm glad you brought me to town.

Harold looked surprised. She smiled at him; the smile that lets you know that it's alright; that this should be expected. It could have been just a sign of thankfulness.

“Yes, yes, it's been a… been a good day for sure, Lillian. I'm glad, glad you asked me to town with you.”

The bill came and Lillian paid. She felt her quest for new memories had worked.

She also knew that she had no need to come back again.

CHAPTER 20

When they left it was dark. Harold was driving the old International, a truck which made any notion of rolling romance entirely impractical. The gear shift stuck up from the middle of the floor, springing out of the metal plates like a giraffe's neck. He doubled clutched it through a series of seemingly magical shifts, swinging through arcs of several feet, with each change accompanied by a crashing, grinding sound. Lillian tried to move more towards him, towards the middle of the torn seat, but he kept crashing into her knees with the gear shift. Finally, when they crossed Stony Creek, he had clear sailing and let the old International scream along at 35 miles an hour. The transmission and engine set up a chorus of roaring, grinding and whining and blue, oily smoke came up through the floorboards and went out through the open windows. Their hair streamed and fluttered in the warm oily, breeze. The truck tried to steer itself and it took all of Harold's strength to keep it on the road.

They rode without speaking; a conversation was impossible above that mechanical din. As they neared her house, Lillian knew that she was losing an opportunity; perhaps a moment that could never be recaptured.

"Harold," she suddenly yelled over the engines roar. "Let's go over to your place. I've never been there, you know? I'd really like to see your cabin."

For a moment, Harold wasn't sure that he'd heard correctly.

"My place?" he yelled.

"Yes," she replied.

"But it... it's not ready. I didn't expect no visitors."

"So what?" she shot back. "Let's go!"

Harold seemed puzzled, confused. But then he continued on past her house until it was too late to stop. Lillian smiled.

They drove along a lonely dirt road lined on both sides by thick, dark woods. He drove slower now, maneuvering around ruts and holes caused by rain, the headlights bouncing off large trees that came right to the edge of the road. The truck jolted crazily on the rough surface and Lillian found herself bouncing to where her head almost hit the roof. Occasionally, animal eyes shined menacingly in the truck's headlight glare; pairs of eyes that seemed to be disembodied; then they would disappear. Lillian didn't like them.

"You live quite a ways back," she chattered through the clamoring din. Harold nodded though he didn't understand what she was saying. The lights rolled over a clearing on the left and Harold swung onto a small dirt track that led up to the cabin. He pulled alongside the wall and shut down the mechanical dragon. The engine belched and coughed for several seconds before wheezing to a halt.

The sudden silence was overwhelming, and Harold sat in the truck, stone-faced, waiting. "It's awful quiet," she finally said. "Kinda' spooky. I thought it was quiet at my place, but here you can *feel* the silence."

"It's just that the noise from this old truck has scared everything off," he said. "You wait, in a minute all them crickets 'll be singing again. And then the owls will hoot and the wild dogs will howl--"

"Wild dogs?"

"Well, some say they're really part coyote or maybe wolf. But I've seen 'em and they look more like wild dogs to me."

"Are they dangerous?"

"Naw. At least I've never heard of no one being hurt. Course none of us spend much time in the woods after dark. That's when they're most active." He sat there looking through the windshield.

Lillian knew she had to make a move. She struggled with the door handle and opened the door, stepping out into the unsettling quiet. Harold took courage and opened his door. After a few nervous paces, she could see the cabin walls clearly; they were made from logs. There was a porch covering the front.

She followed Harold up the side steps. She could just make out that there was a large window on the wall fronting on the porch. Next to the window was a screen door. Harold opened the screen door and lifted the latch on the door behind. There was no key. The door could be latched from the inside but usually was left unlocked.

"Wait here a minute," he said and walked into the dark interior, leaving Lillian alone. Lillian waited a few seconds which seemed much longer to her, when she thought she heard a twig snap from the woods behind her. She turned and looked at the small clearing in front of the cabin, lit up by the newly risen moon. It was all surrounded by the dark impenetrable woods. She swore she saw a shadow moving close to the trees. She felt the back of her neck tingling with fear and a chill passed through her body. She stifled a moan and quickly stepped into the cabin. Harold was just lighting a kerosene lamp and the light slowly came up. "Come on in," he said. Lillian closed the door, grateful to be inside.

"Harold. I think I just saw one of those wild dogs outside," she said, shaking slightly. Harold looked at her; there was fear in her face. He turned the lamp back down and stepped over to the window. He saw a shadow race across the clearing and dash into the woods.

"Think it's a fox. Or a coon," he lied, seeing that she was nervous. "I get them around here a lot. Haven't seen any dogs around here lately. Don't worry Lil. I'm sorry if I scared you with that talk about wild dogs." He turned the lamp up again. "Here Lil, come and sit down over here." He pointed to an old faded and scratched leather chair by a small stone fireplace. "Ain't nothing around here to be afraid of."

Harold had first moved out to the cabin when he had worked a cutting contract in the surrounding woods. It was old then and had been vacant for years. He'd bought the cabin and rebuilt it himself. The log walls were basically sound and only needed some insect damage cut out and filled. He refinished the logs on the inside and oiled them, replaced the roof and built the porch on the front.

The surrounding land was primitive and remote, even though

no more than fifteen miles from town. There was no chance of electric power or telephones ever being connected here. The well was his only luxury. But he wanted the solitude of the North woods and the nearness of all the wild animals.

Harold killed several deer every year to keep himself in meat. There had been illegal salt licks put out before his arrival, probably by the previous owners of the cabin. He always found deer hanging around these old licks and by taking a stand by their trails leading to and from the licks, he could take all the deer he needed. He butchered the deer and stashed the meat in a cold locker buried deep in the snow. In warmer weather he smoked the meat first or gave some to poor farmers in the nearby valley.

From the beginning, he had some trouble with the wild dogs. Most of the locals called them coy-dogs, because they believed they were a cross between a dog and a coyote. Harold said they were too big for that and thought more likely there were some wolf genes surviving in the packs that hung out around his cabin. He just called them wild dogs.

Killing and cleaning the deer and other animals gave the dogs a keen interest in Harold's activities. Whenever he gutted a deer, always some distance from the cabin, the dogs would have the place cleaned up within a day. He was mostly poaching, so he welcomed this service that eliminated the evidence; otherwise he would have to bury the remains. He thought he could keep the dogs under control, if need be, with a shot over their heads now and then. But he misjudged their needs.

When he built the stable for the horses, he never gave the dogs much thought. He wanted the horses nearby because he could hitch them to a work wagon and drive them straight to the logging site. One of his helpers would bring over the truck.

It didn't take long for the dogs to sense that all that horseflesh was being kept in the small stable. There was little or no chance of them killing one of the big horses and they were not hungry enough to try an attack. But the smell of the horseflesh was irresistible to the dogs, and they hung around the stables after dark, usually showing up after midnight. At first, they stayed a good distance from the stable, but gradually, they overcame their fears and started crowding around the small building. This spooked the horses and they would rear and thrash their giant hooves into the feed boxes and hay mangers and stood a good chance of splitting a hoof or worse, breaking a leg. Harold had to do something.

At first, he thought he could drive the dogs off by chasing them with a torch and shooting over their heads. But that did little to dissuade them from hanging around for the potential of such a huge, tasty meal. Finally, he took to shooting them. He killed several and found that the other dogs would drag off the dead ones before morning. Within a few days they would be back, with new dogs replacing the ones he'd killed and others to enlarge the size of the pack. It was as if they were daring him to try and stop them. After one particularly bad night, when the horses almost broke a hole through the wall, he knew he would have to move them. The next day he stabled them at Cool's farm. And after a while, when the smell of horseflesh had faded, the dogs stopped hanging around the stable. But he would still see them at times, slinking across the clearing around the cabin. That's what Lillian had seen, just a few moments before.

Lillian sat down and let the moment of fear pass. Harold lit a second lamp which cheered things up. When she gained her composure, she looked around her, into what was truly a male domain. The logs had been flattened on the inside and oiled and the wood surface had turned a soft gray. The chinking between the logs was plastered over leaving rows of yellowing white striping. There was a deer head over the fireplace and some mounted animals on shelves attached to the wall. Underneath the deer head, mounted on turned-up deer hooves was an old shotgun and a rifle. They looked well-used; the stocks on both of them were scratched and dull. He was so different from Matt, she thought. Matt used to spend hours fondling and polishing his locked-up guns.

The cabin seemed large in the dim light, but had only a single L-shaped room. A small bed with a varnished maple headboard and a small matching chest of drawers was against the side wall. Harold had already noted that he *had* made the bed that morning.

He brought a small wooden ladder-back chair from the kitchen located on the opposite side of the cabin.

"Ain't much to look at," he said as he sat across from her.

" It's really nice," she said. "I like it. Can I look around? Do you mind?"

He showed her around the cabin and she thought it showed real warmth. There was a shelf next to the bed that had several books on it. She leafed through an old, large sized edition of James Fenimore Cooper's Leatherstocking tales with full-color illustrations of Iroquois and Huron Indians, and The Deerslayer and tales of the beautiful lakes of the region.

"Harold. These are wonderful books. I didn't know you were interested in reading."

"Not much interested, really." He replied. " But I like his books a lot. My Highschool teacher got me interested." He looked at the book that Lillian was holding. "Those were my mother's books."

She saw some paperback classics by Hawthorne and Poe and some back issues of Fur-Fish & Game. "This is a nice cabin, Harold. It's so... warm. You must really like it." She went back to the chair and sat down. There was a low maplewood table in front of the chair and a side table where a lamp sat. That was the only furniture.

"Would you like some water? I've got some of your Jersey milk, but it must be sour by now. Best milk around, remember?" He laughed.

"How about your horses, Harold? Don't you have to feed them. Remember what I said before?" and she smiled.

"Well, aren't you the one for remembering things. But they're not here, you see. I've got them over at Buddy Cool's place. They get out and exercise over there. I only keep them here sometimes when I'm working them."

It was a cozy cabin, but not really a good place to start a love affair, since everything was designed to accommodate one person. Harold didn't account for guests. But they talked into the night and

Lillian gradually overcame the natural obstacles and Harold's shyness and wound up in the only place that could almost accommodate two people: the bed.

He'd never had a woman in his cabin before, never mind making love to a woman he thought was only a dream. He was clumsy as always and cautious, almost afraid, but fell under the spell of Lillian's mature lovemaking. Her kisses were passionate and wet, yet soft and tender. She didn't push him, but guided him as he was unable to unbutton the front of her dress with his calloused fingers and failed altogether to unhook her bra. She finished the undressing and tried to make him feel comfortable in bed with her. And then she used her patient approach to satisfy their animal needs.

"I'm so happy, Harold," she whispered later. Harold sighed and nodded. Then they lingered in each other's arms, although Harold kept uncoupling their embrace because he kept fidgeting with his suspenders.

"I best be going, " she said, finally. "It's late and Fred and Bobby will be wondering."

They dressed and Harold drove back to her place. Lillian felt lighter and happier than she had in years. Even the shining eyes along the road failed to dampen her spirits.

But Harold, after unloading the materials they had bought that day, was nervous and cautious about his joy and felt confused. He found himself thinking about Linda. He was, in fact, shocked at himself. "What have I done?" he said aloud, as he drove back to the cabin.

CHAPTER 21

The barn restoration was going just as Lillian had planned, with Fred helping Harold. They removed small sections of the wall at a time, wrenching out the rotting rusty nails and pulling the splintered boards free from the framing posts. The posts were still strong and solid.

The rotting tin roofing and planking was pulled from the rafters. When it had been removed, the exposed rafters were seen to be mostly in good condition.

It was delicate work on the high rafters. Harold didn't trust the old rusted tin and planking and started stripping it off from the eaves upward. They used a kind of scaffolding to work their way up the rafters. Fred had a hard time climbing up the ladder Harold had built.

"It ain't safe up here. This damn roof is too rotten and wobbly," Fred said when he finally made it to the edge of the roof.

"You be real careful, Fred," Harold said. "If you feel you can't handle it, don't come up."

But Fred stayed on and gradually, the new planking was put down and the first of the new tin panels were laid over it. Then Harold and Fred started on the walls and the new boards were nailed up to the posts and the walls went steadily up. The barn went gradually from looking like a forlorn derelict about to collapse to a building with a feeling of freshness and renewed vitality. As Lillian suspected, it revitalized everything and everybody on the farm.

"Only a week or so, left Lillian," Harold said, after unloading the final truckload of roofing tin. "Are you going ahead with pouring the concrete floor?"

" Yes. It looks so good now, I've got to finish it. The cement floor will bring us up to code and will make it a lot easier to keep clean. I'm going to have a small silo put up, too. We'll put it up front, so you can see it right off when you come up here. We'll show off, just like the big boys in the valley." She grinned.

* * *

"Fred's dead!" Bobby shouted as he came running down to the road where they were unloading the tin, his face flush with excitement. "He musta' fell off the roof. He's on the ground, dead!"

"What? What are you saying!" Lillian cried. "Fred fell off the roof?"

They ran up the roadway to the barn. It was a golden August afternoon, a bit hot, with a haze of dust in the air. They arrived with sweat streaking from their faces and found Fred lying crumpled with his face down in the dirt. Lillian walked up to him saying "Oh God... Oh God," over and over under her breath.

They were afraid to touch him. Harold felt for a pulse. "I think he's still alive. Should we roll him over?" Harold asked. "I think we should."

"Thank God he's alive, but what if his back's broken?" She asked. "He looks... broken. Like something is broken."

They couldn't leave him like that so they rolled him carefully on his back. He moaned, but still seemed to be unconscious.

"Fred. Fred. Please wake up... come out of it." She shook him slightly. Suddenly his arm shot up and his hand hit Lillian hard in the face. Harold was listening at Fred's chest when his hand shot up.

"What... what's goin' on," Fred rasped feebly. He opened his eyes and then closed them again.

"Thank God, Fred. Fred? Fred?" She shook him again; he was dropping off into unconsciousness again. When he didn't respond, she asked Bobby for his shirt. She put it under his head. Then she wiped the blood that was coming from his mouth.

He seemed to come to and then would lapse into unconsciousness again. "He's delirious," Harold said. "I'll bet he's got a concussion. We better keep him warm or he'll go into shock." Bobby ran to the house to get a blanket.

"Harold. You better run over to the store and call the town hospital." Lillian said. "Have them send an ambulance. I think it's best."

It took almost an hour for the ambulance to arrive. They had been on another call. Fred was starting to turn blue and shiver. But he'd been able to talk a little.

"Slid... off the roof, Miss Lil. Couldn't stop... went right over the edge. couldn't stop... too slippery. "Tell my Pa, will you, Mis Lil? Tell him I tried real hard... Just kept sliding. Tell him, will you Miss Lil?" She was cradling his head in her lap. Tears welled up in her eyes.

"Fred, you're going to be alright. They're taking you to the hospital now. You'll be Ok." He was unconscious again.

After five days in the hospital, Fred gave up. Lillian and Harold were devastated. Sheriff Gates came around and questioned them about the accident, and seemed satisfied with their explanation. Harold told him that he had told Fred not to go on the roof alone. He said that Fred was mumbling something about people always telling him what to do when he left for the barn. He said that Fred was stubborn and would do what he wanted to. When they asked questions about Fred's personal life, she realized she knew nothing other than what he'd told her on the first day when she interviewed him. She went through his few belongings and found little except his driver's license which had expired years ago, a birth certificate and some old letters and photos from his mother. One showed Fred in uniform. She knew he was a veteran of the First World War. But she couldn't find any discharge papers.

At first she was going to have Fred buried in the nearby cemetery, but after talking with the local VFW, she realized he was entitled to be buried with military honors in a national cemetery. She worked hard with the VA to get all the paper work in, but it was too late to get all the records she needed to get him moved and buried in time. But then she got the VFW to agree to give him a Veteran's burial with honors in the local cemetery. It was the best she could do with such little time.

The day of Fred's funeral, it was overcast and drizzling. She'd got Able Grisinski and his wife to come out, even though she was deathly sick, and Maynard Peck and his wife and old man Smith and a few of the other store regulars, when she'd told them that he'd been a war hero. The VFW had called the personnel records section in St Louis and after a few inquiries into the archives in Washington, they found he had been awarded the Purple Heart and the Silver Star. They were there too; twelve people from the VFW and they'd donated an American flag to be draped on his coffin. During the service, after the minister committed his soul to heaven, Jacob Herkheimer from the VFW read a nice eulogy based on the heroic actions of the troops of the First World War and the particular heroics of Fred that they had to imagine. Then they played taps and rolled up the flag regulation style and gave it to Lillian.

"The sad thing is I don't think he ever knew." she told Harold and Rosemary when they were leaving the gravesite. "I mean, I don't think they ever told him he'd been awarded those medals. He always thought they didn't know or care about what he'd done. I wish we'd listened to him now. He always wanted to talk with us. I just thought he was exaggerating everything to get out of work." She thanked everyone for coming and invited them to her house for food.

She had his gravestone made with a special inscription under his name:

FIRST WORLD WAR VETERAN
AWARDED
SILVER STAR/PURPLE HEART

After some weeks, all his records arrived from the archives in Washington. The medals were included in the package. She had the medals mounted and framed, along with his discharge papers and hung them on the wall in the parlor. She would keep them until relatives could be found; relatives who cared. She locked his clothes and other belongings in his suitcase and stored it in his attic room. But she hung his battered fedora from one of the coat pegs in the kitchen. It was there to stay.

CHAPTER 22

Fred's accident brought Lillian and Harold together like nothing else could have. But it was some weeks before they could continue working on the barn.

"It's not our fault, Harold." she said, as she looked at the half- finished barn. She had asked him to start work on the barn again, but Harold was having a hard time coming to terms with Fred's death.

"We could of prevented it, " he said. "At least, I could of." He kicked his boot in the dirt. "Maybe you should of tore that old barn down."

" It's not the barn's fault, Harold. It's nobody's fault. We've got to get on with our lives."

"I know. But Fred helped me with every part of the rebuilding. I feel him around every time I go up there." Harold felt nervous; he kept hearing Fred's voice.

"Maybe we should hire someone else to help you," Lillian said. "I think that would help."

Harold remained inconsolable for the next few days, then, feeling obliged to Lillian, he started working again. He found one of his part time helpers. They finished in two weeks.

"The barn looks wonderful," Lillian said, drinking in the sight of the new walls coated with whitewash and the shiny tin roof reflecting the sun. "I never believed it could look this good."

Lillian had a new cement floor poured and Fred Simmons built her a nice new silo. It was still just a small barn, but somehow now it took on the dimensions of something far beyond its utilitarian purpose.

"You know, even the cows seem happier," she said when they started milking on the new floor.

"And Fred would be proud of it," Harold said.

* * *

Because of Fred's loss, Harold felt obligated that year to help Lillian with the farm.

"What about your timber contracts?" she asked, when he told her his intentions. They were having breakfast in the kitchen.

"Not much doing right now, Lillian," he said. "Best I can get at the moment is some work at the sawmills. The big guys are getting most of the cutting contracts."

"I don't want you to lose out on account of me," she said and served him more coffee.

"Not losing much, Lillian. I'll keep helping till we find a hand. Maybe you'll have to take on a kid like Junior."

"No. I really don't want someone that young," she said. "I'd worry too much about Bobby."

Harold worked on the farm throughout the winter into the spring. They had no luck finding a hired hand. Then Harold invited Lillian and Bobby to the 21st annual Sand lake volunteer Fire Department Memorial Day picnic.

By now, Lillian knew that Harold would never propose on his own. And Rosemary was still around, still tending to her garden. So, at the picnic, in the warming sunshine of the spring afternoon, surrounded by steaming pots of clams and corn and chili and grilling hot dogs, she sent Bobby on a pony ride and took him aside to a picnic table, with two plates of steamer clams and said:

"Harold, we need each other. We should get married."

Harold remained speechless for a minute and then said: "I guess you're right, Lillian. We best get married and get it over with." He was fooling with his steamers and spilled some on the table.

"Oh Harold. You big ape. Yes, I will. I will," and she leaned over the clams and kissed him.

"There's just one thing, Lillian. I ain't staying at this farming thing. I'm keeping my cabin and my business. Ok?"

"Of course. I don't want you to be a farmer. I want you to stay as you are."

"Then I think we can get hitched."

"There's one other thing Harold," she said. "I'm still going to build up the herd. I want that contract with Svenson's. I need you to help me for a while... till we hire someone. Can you do that?"

"Sure," he said, and they both ate the steamers, waiting for Bobby to finish his ride.

They had a small private ceremony with only a few friends invited. Rosemary had a bad case of the flu, she said, and couldn't make it.

CHAPTER 23

Except for those few, they told no one else about the marriage, not even Harold's mother. Harold told Lillian he was afraid of her disapproval. When he'd told her earlier that he was kind of sweet on Lillian and she discovered that Lillian was an older woman, she had been unhappy.

But a few weeks after the ceremony, Harold wanted to explain about his marriage to his mother. Since it was an accomplished fact, he thought she would accept it. He seldom visited her, not because they didn't get along, but because of the black memories of his father that would be revived. The house she continued to live in stood as a constant reminder of his tortured youth and his mother's torment.

Harold had a rough life as a child, up to the time he was a teenager. He'd been beaten by his drunken father and was terrorized when he had to watch his father rip the clothes off his mother and rape and beat her mercilessly. Both of them suffered terribly at the hands of this man, who was moderate and kind when sober, but would go into a beastly rage when drunk.

When Harold had begged her to leave his father, she would cry and say that it was not possible. Where would she go? What would they do? She had been raised an orphan and she hadn't seen her only brother in years. Besides, she believed he would kill both of them if she did that.

His mother had done everything she could to keep Harold from drinking. She feared drink, knowing the pain it had brought them. She feared that Harold might inherit the same evil moods.

He announced his upcoming visit by mail; she was to expect him on a Tuesday a day that fell three weeks after the marriage. When he arrived, she was ready for him.

"Harold," she said. "you have been away too long." Her smile was, as always, very warm. She had always been a handsome woman with deep-set eyes and Harold felt that on this day she looked particularly attractive.

"I know, Ma," he said. "But it's a long way to my cabin and I've--I've been busy. And how have you been?"

"I've been Ok, fair," she responded. "But I probably should say great rather than fair, now that Mr. King has taken such a positive interest in me."

"Mr. King? You mean our old neighbor?" One of the few pleasant memories Harold had of his childhood here was his friendly association with Mr. King.

"Yes, the same," she said. "His wife died awhile back, oh, I'd say about two years ago. We--- well we're kinda' keeping company now. What do you think of your old mother now?" and she laughed lightly.

He could see the happiness in her face. "I think that's fine, Ma. I'm glad you have someone like that." He looked around the sitting room where they were and tried to suppress the bad memories it evoked. "Have you been gettin' my money orders?" he asked. He'd been sending her a money order for one hundred dollars every month.

"Yes, Harold, God bless you. It's such a help to me."

They talked for a while about Harold's affairs at his cabin, avoiding painful discussions. Finally, Harold determined to get the difficult announcement over with.

"Ma, I know you're not going to be too happy about this, but I got to tell you. I married Lillian Wiggs a couple of weeks ago." He watched his mother's reaction.

She didn't move; the smile slowly faded from her face. She looked at him stonily: "You mean *you* married that... older woman?"

"She ain't that much older, Ma. And she really looks a lot younger than me."

"Well!" she said with an air of indignation, staring out the window. "Well!" she said again, with no apparent intention of saying anything else.

“I'm sorry Ma, I didn't tell you before. But I just knew you wouldn't approve.” He looked closely at her when she didn't answer. The late afternoon light fell gently through the window. She remained silent, sitting rigidly and staring blankly at the window. He could see tears welling in her eyes. When she continued not to speak, he knew it would be better if he left.

“ I'm sorry if you feel bad about this. Really, I am. I hope you'll get over this bad feelin'. I want you to get to know Lillian. I know you'll like her.” He asked her if she was Ok and she nodded yes. Then he said he had to leave.

“Are you sure you're Ok? Is Mr. King coming over? I don't want to leave you feelin' like this.”

The last question broke her silence. “Yes,” she said, “You can leave. He'll be here,” and she sighed. Without knowing what other course` he could pursue, Harold left. He thought that she would never accept Lillian.

But two weeks later he got a letter from her at the cabin mailbox. She wrote that she was well and that Mr. King was providing a steady, helping hand. She mentioned nothing of the day of his visit or the marriage, but said that she would be glad to see Lillian anytime he cared to bring her over.

CHAPTER 24

Towards the end of the summer, Lillian invited the Svenson's out to inspect the new barn. She wanted a contract before the next winter set in. William Svenson came, but his son Bill jr, stayed away. Lillian had sensed that Bill jr was reluctant to meet with her and she wondered if William had told him about them.

She hadn't been exactly honest with Rosemary about her first meeting with William. As soon as William saw her (for the first time since she had been packed off to school almost 30 years ago), he fell in love with her all over again. But he was already married and had been for 25 years; he had three grown children and his oldest son was his business partner. When he surprised her by embracing her in his office, she surprised herself by letting him kiss her fully.

"We mustn't do this William," she said. "It's horribly wrong. It's unfair to your whole family." She told him they would have to control themselves or she wouldn't come back. He promised her he would, although she could see the love in his eyes.

She hadn't expected this to happen; not the embrace; not the kiss. Now she felt that maybe she had made a mistake coming to him, but she desperately wanted that contract for her milk.

"When you went away, Lil, I thought my life was over. It took a long time for me to get over that. When you walked in just now, I thought you were... just coming back to me. Everything else in between just dropped out of my mind."

" Oh, William. My father was cruel to do what he did to us," she said, "But he was a good man and thought he was doing best. But it's over now. It's over. That was almost 30 years ago."

William came out to the farm alone that day, and she felt like she was playing with fire. She'd hoped that the son would be with him. The invitation was on a Saturday, the day she knew that Harold would be off to town to buy some supplies and Bobby would be home.

"Haven't been up this way for quite a while," he said when Lillian greeted him on the front porch. He was tall and the lines of middle age were sagging into those of old age making his complexion gnarled and burly with thin crimson-blue veins splotching his cheeks. His white hair stuck out like straw beneath the rim of the green felt Tyrol hat he always wore. Yet he was still handsome and at a distance, looked much younger than his age. He'd injured his leg in a farm accident and seemed to lean backwards when he walked in a kind of sliding gait; he always seemed to be walking uphill. "Beautiful country up here," he said. "You can smell the pines from a way's off."

After meeting Bobby and having a too polite cup of coffee in the kitchen, Lillian took him up to see the barn. She made Bobby go with them. "Now I want you to take Mr. Svenson on a tour, Bobby. Show him the new barn and the cows." Bobby seemed pleased with his new importance.

"It's up to Grade A standards," she told him on the way up. "The barn is probably 75 years old. Built post and beam." She pointed them out to William when they were on the upper ground level. The new wood and nails and whitewash and wood preservative gave the barn a fresh smell of something new and growing.

"Nice, " he said. "It's real nice. Looks a lot like a small version of your Dad's. My family's always had nice barns. I always liked a good barn. Best place on the farm." She smiled; she'd known that he felt that way.

"Yes, William. I feel the same way," she said. "I guess it runs in the family. My Dad had a big barn, with a silo towering over the roof and a fancy side building to hold all that farm equipment he'd bought." She looked at his pale blue eyes and thought about how much they reminded her of Matt. "Do you remember?"

"Oh yes. And I remember how clean you and your family kept that place. Why you could invite guests for dinner into that barn." He grinned at her.

“Well, this one is small,” she said, “but it's perfect for my purpose. I'm going to run ten to twelve head here as I told you. This barn is perfect for that size herd.”

“Nice the way it's built into the side of the hill, just like some of those banked barns I've seen.” he said. “Keeps the frost out of the milking area.”

“Show him where the cows are,” she told Bobby. They took him down to the lower level where the cows were kept. She was relieved that he'd made no attempts to pursue the events of their earlier meeting.

“These are my first four head,” William. The cows stood with their tails toward the stanchions, facing the new center walkway, which was sparkling clean. She had lead halters on them with the rope leads tied to cement blocks, she'd put there just for this occasion. The animals didn't mind the switch, they were show animals and used to being fussed over.

He grunted in approval when he saw the cows. She had them in prime show condition; they were some of the finest Jerseys he'd seen. Each animal wore a silver chain around the horns, draping a medallion on its forehead. Their large, lovely udders would make any dairyman's heart beat with joy. They all had classic fawn coats with white faces and the large eyes for that breed.

After putting on his glasses, William read the medallion on the first cow, which was the finest animal of the herd. It read:”Sophies Princess 1631351---- Flora, AJCC Excellent.”

“I want to introduce you to Flora,” Lillian said.” American Jersey Cattle Club premium member.” She patted Flora on the flanks. The cow looked as regal as a bovine could. “She's the class triple A champion... Gold Medal winner. Best cream in the world comes from Flora. That's the milk sample I brought you.”

“That's from Flora? I'll say. That's the best cream ever. Silky smooth, full of flavor. I made a test run and it's like you said, makes true super premium ice cream. You can't make ice cream like that with milk from the co-op.” He petted her flank and she mooed.

Bobby showed William the other three animals, also registered champions. They were almost equally as impressive as Flora.

The barn was spotless. The stone milkhouse, in which she had redone the floor and tanks in the interior, smelled new and she had sample milk cans in the ice-cold spring water.

"Notice that you don't have electric power up here, Lillian. How long can you keep the milk without refrigeration?"

"Feel that water, William. It's from a deep well; spring fed we believe. Ice cold, all summer long. But then, I'll also get ice delivered in the summer. I put that big ice chest over there in the corner to keep it frozen for a week. The whole milk house is below the hill level and stays in the shade all summer. The stone wall makes for perfect insulation; seems to stay at about 70 degrees inside, all year round, at least until it gets very cold." She pointed out the thermometers she had installed to keep a measure of the air and water temperature. "But I shouldn't be keeping the milk more than a day before delivery."

William felt the icy water and examined the stainless-steel ice chest. "Nice, Lillian. You're doing a lot without electricity. But mark my words, there'll come a time when you won't be able to do without it. I expect they'll be runnin' power lines out here soon."

She was silent for a moment, thinking of her response. "I expect they will," she said. "But you know, I've learned to do without. I lived with it for so many years, such a luxury; I know what you mean. But I'm going to do without as long as I can. I know everyone thinks it's a wonderful thing. Maybe. But there's this thing about electric power; it changes everything. Now I know that it not only gives you the power to run refrigerators and televisions and lights and milk houses, It also changes the way you look at things, including yourself."

He thought for a moment about what she'd said. "That's mighty interesting Lillian. But what on earth *do* you mean?"

"Well, up here I've found there's a kind of timelessness that you don't find easily anymore. Everyplace else seems to be growing, changing; progress they say. It's mostly electric power that allows this to happen. And changes and progress will be coming faster and faster. It's power, William. Electric power."

"Probably so. But Timelessness, Lil? Timelessness? What are you getting at?"

Bobby had lost interest. "Aunt Lilly, can I go to the house?" he asked. When she hesitated, he said he had to go to the bathroom, and so she let him go.

"It's not easy to explain, William. It's in the big rocks, and some of the very old trees." She looked around at the horizon. "You see, nothing much changes around here except the seasons. You can expect to see the same thing here next year that you see today. Or saw ten years ago. And the rocks, especially the big ones, they hold all those ancient memories within them, if you don't disturb them." They started back down to the house. "But this is my own personal philosophy... I'm getting carried away. All this must sound pretty silly to you William?"

"No, not at all. I... believe you."

She smiled. "Thanks, William. But do you think I'm strange?" They stopped walking and he looked at her. Listening to her talk had sent memories coursing like electric currents through his mind. Time seemed to have collapsed again. "Silly? Strange? Lillian, I... I'm ... God I'm still crazy about you. I think that's a kind of timelessness too. I guess I'm like one of your rocks... holding ancient memories. But don't worry, I won't lose control again." She put her finger on his lips. But he continued: "Forgive me, Lillian. I'm just a foolish old man, with a heart that never mended. Listening to you now just made me remember, but I won't ... won't break my word."

Lillian took his hands in hers and they felt cold, like the ice water in the milkhouse. For once, she seemed to have no words. Her thoughts were confused, twisted in tangled emotions. "William. I'm sorry. I've made a terrible mistake. I should not have come to you. I'm sorry." He squeezed her hands. The faint trace of a smile appeared on his face.

"No, Lillian. After all, you have nothing to be sorry for. I'm just being foolish, I'll get over it. He freed his hand and lightly touched her cheek with his finger. "I cherished seeing you again. At least I have that. I'll always cherish that. You see, you actually have made me a happier man." He heaved a deep sigh and smiled. "I'm Ok now. Look. I have the contract in the car. It's just a simple agreement so that you can bank on us buying your milk. Let's go down to the house and sign it."

"William," she said. "Are you sure?" Her face radiating her smile. He nodded. "You don't know how happy you've made me."

CHAPTER 25

With the contract signed and plans underway to visit breeding farms and livestock shows to enlarge the herd with heifers or mature champion cows, she was able once more to turn her attention to her fallen brother.

Although she had never mentioned it to Harold or anyone else, she had always believed that with some luck, she might get Robert to move to the farm. It made little sense on the surface, yet she needed something to believe in; some spark of hope for her brother

She knew he could never move in with her, so she had been thinking about building a small cottage. A small Island had been formed by the creek, across the road from the house. It seemed an ideal place for such a cottage.

"Well, I don't see how building him a place out here will do much good," Harold said, when she told him about her plans. "Will he ever live in it? Does he want to live out here? How about his wife? Have you talked to them yet?"

"No. I haven't. I haven't." She bristled under his probing questions. "I can't talk to him about it, he would never agree. I have to build the house first. I think I can convince him that it's good for him to live out here; that a good house may just cure him. Maybe, just maybe, he can convince *her*."

"Doesn't make much sense Lillian," he retorted. "You'll be using up a lot of your reserves, just to build that place. And he probably won't move in anyway."

"Well, I could always sell it."

"What? In today's market? No one's buying out here now. You know that. You got this place dirt cheap, didn't you? It was on the market for what? five, ten years?"

"I know Harold. But... well, look. It's just something I feel I have to do. He won't get into a recovery program, and as long as they live in that hellhole, I can't do anything for them. I won't even tell him that I'm building the place. I'll just get it built and then I'll get him out here. Maybe just a short stay at first, maybe just for a day. At least I'll be able to help him with them close by like that."

"I don't think so," Harold said, with anger building in his voice. After his childhood experiences, Harold couldn't stand to deal with an alcoholic, and he thought Robert should stop taking advantage of his sister. "I don't think you should do it," he continued. "Why are you helping him so much and interfering with his life? It's really a little stupid Lillian. You're usually so smart about everything else."

Lillian flushed crimson with Harold's tart words. Bitter memories of Matt raging at her over helping Robert flooded through her mind. But she tried to hold the thin, fragile line. "Harold. Please. Let's not fight over this. Please," she said, her voice rising. "Maybe it is stupid. Maybe it isn't a solution at all. But it's something I have to try."

Harold shrugged. "Well, I don't know. We didn't talk about this before we got married. Never knew you had planned such a thing. But, let me ask you: what about Bobby? Have you thought about that, the situation you'll be making? After all, you did kidnap him, didn't you?"

Her heart skipped a beat. The word "kidnap" angered her. She had kept that part of it buried in the back of her mind and had never considered Bobby as a part of this problem. What if Robert came out just to snatch Bobby back? He wanted him back. But that could never be. He belonged with her. Never, she resolved, never would she give him up.

"I don't want to talk about it anymore," she said, angrily. She didn't want anyone upsetting her plans. "I've got to go to town. I need new filters--"

* * *

Harold left the house in disgust. It was the first night that he spent in his cabin since they were married. Before he went to the cabin, he went to the Pine Knot tavern and played some Hank Snow records on the juke box and drank more than he should have. It was the fear he constantly lived with; his dislike of anyone drunk and yet he drank himself. But he went back to Lillian's house the next day.

"What happened?" she asked the next morning.

He sighed. "I'm sorry Lillian. I just... Oh, I guess I just needed to check things out at the cabin. I stayed there last night."

"Everything Ok?"

"Uh huh. Everything's Ok."

"Can you put the hay down for the cows? I've already milked, but I'm running late."

"Sure. I'll put the hay down."

She left without kissing him goodbye.

When Bob Ellison came out to look at the site and give her an estimate, she tried to involve Harold, but he refused to have anything to do with it. Alone, she selected a one-bedroom bungalow from the plans that Ellison showed her. It was the most economical he had to offer. The building site she chose was on the little island across from the house. It had good walking access to the road, a well, and some large maples to provide protection from storms and the sun. A slight slope provided good drainage. Ellison said she'd made a good choice. He said he thought that if he started immediately, he could have the foundation in before winter set in. Then he could finish with the building in the spring. She said that would probably be OK.

" Moving into it when it's done?" He asked, when they had come to an agreement on an estimated cost. They were sitting in the parlor at the round table. "You know," he said, before she could answer, "I can tear this old place down for you when you're ready to move. Wouldn't charge you anything if you'll let me have the lumber I can salvage." He smiled at her.

"I'll... let you know," she said.

When he left, she walked around and looked over the old house. Somehow, she had grown used to its look of decay and failed to remember that it was still in sore need of attention. She had patches over patches over holes; new clapboards spliced in pieces to some of the older, rotting boards; chinking stuffed up between the clapboards where the shrunken boards had separated from each other, leaving gaps to the outside. The tin roof was rusted through in places and full of leaking patches. The inside wasn't in much better condition and much of her furniture had been spotted by leaks.

"What am I thinking?" she asked herself aloud. "With everything else going on, I've completely forgotten you." She often talked to the house as if it were a person. "No. I've got to do something for you."

CHAPTER 26

With the cottage plans taken care of and Harold feeling better about it, at least, seeming willing to accept it, she went to visit her brother once more before leaving on her trip.

She went crazy with fury when he told her that Maryann was pregnant again.

"How could you? How could you! Are you trying to kill me?" she shouted in the diner. The other patrons stared, some angry at the interruption, others embarrassed for her.

"What have I done to you, Robert, that you treat me like this? What have I done!"

"What have you done? You know damn well what you've done. You're the one that's doin' everything, aren't you?" He started to stand. "Keep your goddam money," he said. "I don't want to see you anymore." and he left her at the table and walked out.

But she knew he would be back. He always came back.

Finally, she was glad to be off on the trip. She wanted to forget what Robert had told her. There were several county fairs that year that interested her; a two week's leave of absence from the school became necessary. More importantly, she wanted to visit some of the breeding and consignment farms for Jersey cattle, even though the big sales were done in the early summer. She travelled in the aging Buick, first to Springfield, Ohio to visit the Chester Folck consignment sales farm. It was a two-day drive and would be the second time she'd made the trip. From there, she would swing down through Pennsylvania and visit a cousin in Chester and the local county fair; then on to Lincroft, New Jersey to visit the Marlu farm, where she'd bought the first two cows. She spent the first night in a small motel just outside of Dunkirk, N.Y. and experienced the first set of raised eyebrows when it was known that she was travelling alone. It was something she knew would happen and just had to get used to it.

The next day she visited a nearby breeder's farm famous for champion Guernseys. It was owned by John Gasparelli; she'd first met him at the state fair the year before. He had been nice to her and seemed to respect her work. He had invited her to stop by to see his operation.

"John, next to Jerseys, Guernseys are my favorite breed," she said.

"They're closely related," he said. "As you well know." He was clearly delighted to see Lillian. "How is your herd coming?"

"Slow, but steady. My champion cows are really producing great milk. But they've been producing bull calves too. I've had to sell them off."

"Seems like that always happens when you're trying to build a herd," he said. "So, you're out to buy a few more head?"

"Yes. But from what I've read, I doubt if I can afford mature champions again."

"Hmm. Say, I may have just what you need," he said. "I made a lot buy a few weeks ago and wound up with two nice Jersey heifers. Why don't you take a look at them?"

They were from champion stock, just what she wanted. Their papers were sound. When John said he'd let her have them at cost, she made a deal.

"One of my trucks will be going your way in about a month. Will that be Ok? No charge for delivery."

"Well that's just great, John," she said, happy with his offer.

They went up to the house to sign the papers. John showed her his private library. He had dozens of books and manuscripts about the life and times of Guernsey and Jersey cattle breeders going back to the tenth century. She was fascinated by these masterpieces of breeding lore. One document in particular, about the origins of Jersey cattle, captured her attention.

"Here, sit down there at that desk and read it," he said. "I have to step out for a minute. I'll be right back."

Lillian was completely engrossed in the old manuscript when she began to feel uncomfortable. Something told her that someone else was in the small room with her. She turned and saw a tall, dark woman in the doorway, shrouded by the light behind her.

"Who are you?" the woman asked in a demanding voice.

"Hello. I'm sorry... you startled me."

The woman just stared at Lillian.

"I'm Lillian Sims... a friend of John's?"

"What do you want?" the woman asked.

"John... John asked me to look at some of these documents."

"He's my husband," the woman said. "Where is he?" She started walking towards Lillian.

Lillian saw black, piercing eyes in the face of the dark woman. Her hair was black, long and streaked with gray. She had a sharp nose and a ruddy complexion.

"I don't know," Lillian said. "He left me here and went out. He said he'd be right back."

"Lillian Sims?" the woman said. "He's mentioned you, I think. What are you doing here?"

"I'm... I'm on a buying trip. I'm buying cows."

"Oh, you're *that* one. The woman who runs her own farm? He told me about you."

"Yes. I'm that Lillian." she extended her hand to the woman, but Mrs. Gasparelli made no move to respond.

"Why are you here?" she said. "Who told you to come here?"

"I told you. I stopped to see some cows."

"Why are you in this business," she said angrily. "Why don't you stick with women's work. Why are you out cavorting with these men?"

Lillian was shocked into silence, but then responded.

"Cavorting? I'm not cavorting, Mrs. Gasparelli. This *is* my work." Lillian decided it was best to leave. She put down the manuscript, picked up her purse and walked around the woman towards the door. She could see the woman's face twisting in anger and kept her eyes locked on her. She was prepared to defend herself.

At that moment, John walked in. "Oh, hello Sarah," he said. "Have you two introduced yourselves?"

"I was just leaving, John," Lillian said, and walked out of the room.

"Don't leave just yet," John said. "Wait for me outside."

He met her at her car, a minute later.

"I'm really sorry," he said. "I didn't expect her back so soon. Was she very angry? She's very jealous--"

"I understand, John," Lillian interrupted. "I'd best be going."

"Well, those cows will be on their way within a month. Thanks for stopping by. It was great to see you again."

Sarah came to the doorway. She stood there with her arms crossed.

Lillian waved goodbye. She promised herself to remember she was a woman and be more careful in the future.

She travelled on to Springfield, and visited other breeder's farms she'd found through the consignment houses. As she engaged the owners in technical livestock discussions, it became clear again that she was the only woman in this environment actively acting as a participant. All other woman were wives like Sarah, or companions and most displayed some hostility to her. But she was generally accepted by the men as some kind of female oddball, and several made passes at her. She put them off and moved confidently amongst the buyers, those who called themselves "dairymen", with a sure knowledge of her breed. And she knew after all this, that she was as much a "Dairyman" as any of them. It was in her blood.

CHAPTER 27

While Lillian travelled, Harold managed the farm and kept searching for a steady hired hand. It was something she'd asked him not to do until she got back from the trip. But he thought he would be doing a good turn. When he couldn't find anyone suitable, he decided to take on one of his part time helpers. Even though she had said no, he felt that Junior would make a good hand. He was now over 18, a big lad and very strong. The army hadn't taken Junior in the draft because he couldn't pass the basic psychology tests. But Harold felt sure that if Lillian would give him a chance, she would agree that he would make a good hand. He went out to Junior's house to talk with him and his widowed mother, Edna.

"Well, what will he be doing, Harold?" his mother asked him. She was a small, fragile looking woman.

"Just a farm hand. Anything needin' doing, really."

"Well, you've used him before. You know what he's like. You know he needs watchin' sometimes."

"I've never had problems with Junior ma'am. He always does as he's told," he said.

Junior sat at the table between them, jerking his head from one to the other as they talked. His mother put her hand over his.

"Well, he's a good boy," she said. "Just needs a little watchin', that's all. I'm mighty obliged to you for hiring him Harold."

When Harold had used him to help with cutting trees, he found him to be a good worker. Harold had been amazed that Junior could work all day, in the hottest of weather, and never ask for water. Further, Junior lived with his mother and didn't need to stay at Lillian's place. He had his own car to get back and forth. But every one said that the way he drove, someday he would kill himself with it.

Junior wasn't very handsome. His teeth were bucked and crooked and seemed to be covered with a brown-green moss. No one had been able to get him to brush his teeth. His nose was twisted slightly, having been broken when he was 12. It was rumored that he'd come home one day after picking berries at Lowrey's farm, with his nose flopping on his face. He'd told his mother he couldn't remember how it had happened. When she'd questioned the Lowery people, no one could offer a clue about his strange condition.

But Junior wasn't enough help, so Harold also used Bobby. He'd learned how to milk and was beginning to develop enough strength to milk one cow. He seemed to enjoy the work. The milking wasn't bad, but it was tiring and tedious to Harold because of Lillian's milking rules. She had shown them the method for washing the udders, rinsing, then rinsing the teats with an antiseptic solution. Only after thorough drying (always with clean towels), could the milking begin, but only after the milker thoroughly washed and dried his own hands. And there were many other tidy rules she had given them. But Bobby had learned to do all this with pleasure, except for the hooded pails which made milking seem more like target practice. He liked milking because Lillian made it seem so important.

Junior had worked on other dairy farms and seemed mystified when Harold showed him how to milk using Lillian's rules. He slapped his leg and hooted when Harold showed him how she wanted the udders and teats washed and dried.

"This some kind of cow beauty parlor?" he said and laughed at that thought until he got Harold laughing too.

"But listen Junior, don't say a word about that to Miss Lillian," Harold told him through his laughter. "It's best to hold your tongue on this subject when Lillian gets back or you won't be working here very long."

But the more Harold thought about Junior's comment the more he laughed. "Maybe we should put a sign down by the road," he said through fits of laughter, "with a picture of cow's teats on it and sayin," and he had to stop to get his breath, "Lillian's Cow

Beauty Parlor: Udders groomed, tails curled and teats massaged." They both roared until tears came into their eyes.

But through it all, through Junior's crazy humor and the sometimes-strange behavior of Bobby, Harold seemed to have a handle on things and thought that Lillian would be pleased with his efforts when she got back.

CHAPTER 28

Although bitter about Lillian's marriage, Rosemary kept working her garden. She had felt cheated by Lillian's move; she hadn't expected it so quickly. And she resented her own lack of commitment to break Lillian's grip on Harold; she knew she had made no real effort to attract Harold's attention. But gradually, through casual contact, she'd renewed her relationship with Lillian, although both women were keenly aware of the new thorn between them.

Rosemary grew peas and carrots and broccoli and heads of iceberg lettuce and good potatoes and leafy crowns of cabbage. It was time to pull up the purple heads of the Scarlett Ohara and Ruby Red cabbages that she had so carefully nurtured since early that spring. The cabbages had reddish blue leaves that stood up to her waist and looked purple in the sunlight. They'd thrived and grown huge in the black soil behind the barn. Her mother, from a German background, had grown those same cabbages to make red cabbage and pork for the family; they had all loved it. Rosemary carried on this tradition.

Harold happened to be in the barn one day when he noticed her struggling with the cabbages and offered help. The cabbages were heavy and the roots deep. She was surprised to see him.

"Thanks, Harold, but I think I can manage. I think these are," and she grunted with the effort to pull one up, "the biggest damn cabbages I've ever seen."

"Yes, they are big. Here, let me help you. No charge."

They pulled the cabbages out by the roots and hung them upside down in the root cellar under Lillian's kitchen. And after much close contact from working in the soil side by side, with hands and arms and hips often touching, Harold found himself strongly attracted by Rosemary's powerful sexuality. Rosemary didn't realize, at first, that she was attracting him so. But Harold managed to hold himself together.

"I'm goin' down to the road, Rosemary," he said, trembling when she touched his hand. "Bobby should be here soon. Rosemary, maybe we shouldn't... ah, we shouldn't--"

"We shouldn't what?' Rosemary asked, now realizing that she had some effect on him. "Is something wrong?"

"Oh, no... no, no. I was just thinking, cabbages and stuff, you know." He was red.

Rosemary looked into Harold's eyes, forcing him to look away. "I'm really thankful for your help Harold," she said, "these cabbages are really heavy. I'll leave the few that are left here in the garden. And I'll try not to bother you again."

But she couldn't abandon her garden. She also couldn't shake Harold out of her mind.

The next day she was back, trying to dislodge a rock the size of two footballs. She'd wanted to move the rock for some time; it was in the way of her little cultivator. She had dug around the rock and was trying to pry it loose with a crowbar.

Harold came home early that day to work on the harness that hung in the barn. But he saw Rosemary working again and watched her, unnoticed. He had been thinking about her in spite of his resolve. When he saw her struggling with the rock, he called out to her: "Hello, Rosemary." She was startled by his voice.

She dropped the heavy crowbar and stretched her back to get it straightened out. "I must look awful," she said, looking at the dirt on her clothes.

"No. You look like you could use a hand," Harold said, a slight tremble in his voice.

"Oh, thanks, Harold, but I'll manage. This rock an me have been goin' around for months now. We're almost old friends."

Harold laughed uneasily. "Well, it's time I got acquainted with that rock," he said. He took the crowbar from her and dug around the rock with the tip, trying to get a grip under it. It was deeply lodged in the ground and held there by the forces of time. Once he got the blade to grip, he tried to lever it out, but it seemed like he didn't have the strength to get it loose. She reached down to help him. When the rock was almost pried free, the blade slipped, the rock fell back and they both tumbled to the ground.

They lay there for a moment laughing and then Harold rolled closer to her and breathed of her sweat and she came close to him and they kissed, their passions flaring up. Then suddenly, Rosemary pulled away.

"Oh, no Harold, god. I've wanted that from the day I met you. But this is wrong. Lillian is ... is," but she couldn't finish and Harold pulled her to him and looking into her eyes, said: "Rosemary, I know what you're going to say. And I know it's wrong. But... I, God, I'm sorry but... I, I better... leave. I'll move the rock tomorrow."

Rosemary sighed an OK. "I'll put that... crowbar back in the barn."

* * *

Bobby had cut school that day, the third day in a row, and came home early. He had spent most of the day in the woods, trying to figure out what to do. He'd walked in the barn, deep in thought about the great mess he was in, really afraid that someone might see or hear him. He was careful not to make noise and sat down by the wall looking over the haymow. But then he heard voices and groans and other noises coming from the haymow and he ducked and when he was sure they were not coming towards him, he peeked over the low wall that sided the mow. Something seemed to be moving around in the hay but he couldn't see what it was because it was almost covered with hay. He thought he recognized a man, but he couldn't make out the other one, except he could tell by the noises that she was a lady. Just as he was beginning to get a good look, the man turned his head towards him and he quickly ducked. He didn't see much, but it looked like Uncle Harold. Everything went quiet.

"Someone's in the barn," Harold whispered to Rosemary. "I think it's Bobby. Stay here and I'll go after him." Rosemary gasped and put her fingers over her mouth. Harold struggled with his clothes and finally crept up to the wall. When he looked over, there was no one there. He muttered a low curse and then motioned for Rosemary to join him. Together, they searched around the barn and the house. Bobby was gone. Afraid to be seen together at Lillian's house; afraid because of the burden of guilt they now shared, they drove over to his cabin.

"What are we going to do Harold?" she asked. "This is terrible. I feel so... so lousy."

"I know, Rosemary," he said, fear in his voice. "But we didn't plan to do this, did we?" He embraced her, seeing the tears in her eyes. "I guess we just lost control... "

"I guess so, but what are we going to do now?" Rosemary pleaded again.

"I don't know Rosemary. I just don't know. But I'll find Bobby and have a talk with him. I'm not sure what he saw. I just don't want Lillian to find out that way."

They embraced once more and Rosemary sighed. Harold shakily resolved to find a solution to their fearful dilemma. She left and Harold returned to Lillian's to wait for Bobby.

When he pulled up to the house, he saw a strange car parked in front. He could see an attractive young woman standing on the path leading to the house.

"Hello," she said. "I'm Miss Ellison. "Do you live here? I'm looking for Mrs. Sims, Bobby's grandmother?"

"I'm Harold Sims, Lillian's husband," he said. "She's not his grandmother, she's his aunt. She's out of town right now. Can I do something?"

She sighed. "Well, I'm Bobby's teacher. I really need to talk with you or her about something... that's happened to Bobby at school. It's, well, it's important."

She looked concerned. He invited her into the house. Bobby had not returned yet.

CHAPTER 29

Lillian was surprised at how quickly the miles slipped away under the Buick and at how relaxed she felt to be on the road. It was a kind of freedom she had never know before; this new life had given it to her. Nevertheless, she had left Springfield much later than she'd wanted to and the traffic was heavy on Pennsylvania route 30, so she knew she wouldn't make Chester before dark.

She was thinking about Harold and Bobby. She was pleased with the way Harold was taking to Bobby. If Harold had any jobs, he would take Bobby along on his days off from school and teach him about lumbering. At first, Lillian objected that it was too dangerous, but Bobby insisted and she was persuaded by Harold's assurances, to let him go. Harold was teaching him how to handle the horses and how to drive the Ford tractor she'd bought. But he kept the boy away from the axes and saws and especially from his John Deere tractor.

She had Linda on her mind, too. Linda wrote about every three months, insisting that she would return soon. She was living with her ex-husband again, that was for sure. Lillian was tempted to drive into Manhattan to see if Linda was alright but she knew that would only cause her more trouble.

Thoughts of her other daughter, Julia, also tugged at her mind. Julia had become estranged from her and had acted hateful at Matt's funeral. It was another dark spot in her life that she hoped she could clean up someday. Where was Julia now, she wondered. How was she doing? Could they ever come together again?

She spotted a likely motel just outside of Chambersburg called the “Trail Blazer”. She stopped; she was tired and it was almost dark. It was a Mom and Pop place with phony western decor. But it seemed clean; she found she could tell something about these small places by the smell of disinfectant in the front office: the stronger the smell, the dirtier the place. This one had no smell and seemed bright and cheery.

"Pop" was a man closing on ripe maturity, but she saw him really look her over when she checked in. He was thin, with high, bony cheeks, laced with purplish veins. After she signed the register, he licked his dry lips and offered to show her a room. "We got several real nice rooms, lady," he said as he started to get some keys from the rack. He turned the ledger. "Uh... Mrs. Sims? Maybe you should let me show you a couple. Then you can pick the one you like the best. They're real nice." His eyes burned like hot coals into her skin.

"Oh, no, no need to bother. I'll just take that key you have there. That I'll be fine. My husband will be along shortly."

"Oh. Then you'll be needing a double. Didn't know there was two of you." He harrumphed and smiled at her as if they had a shared secret. When she left, he concentrated on her curving buttocks shifting against the tight slacks. Somehow, she knew his eyes were firmly fixed on her and it made her stomach tingle. She pulled the windbreaker tighter around her. she knew this was also part of the new freedom she felt as a woman alone. The man licked his lips again and after she left, he went back to watching the comedy hour on the tiny TV.

The room was like any other small motel room with a motel-only phone and a portable radio screwed down to the Formica table top. She looked in the small dresser mirror and saw that she was really frazzled from the drive; there had been more big truck traffic than she'd expected. She slumped in a small overstuffed chair, dirty and spotted by a thousand other guests, and thumbed through the local paper, put in the room as a "courtesy copy". It was dated October 6, 1952, already two weeks old. There was still some daylight and she wanted to kill time before getting ready to go eat. She gazed uneasily at the big headlines:

REDS DRIVE HARD AGAINST 7th MARINE DIVISION

There was a brown coffee stain right on the story. She threw the paper down in disgust. The Korean war was a sore point with her. Old Mr. Henderson, the mailman, had lost a son as had the

Smiths. And Able was on edge for his two sons. It seemed that every other family had a son over there, wounded, killed, or about to be. It was a miserable conflict that nobody understood, least of all the U.S. government.

It was a warm, Indian summer evening and she dozed for a while, thinking of the farm and things she had seen at the breeder's farms. A few cows had interested her in Springfield, but she would have to wait for the spring auction sale. It was dismal to find that the price of champions had almost doubled since she'd bought her first four cows.

Would Harold be holding up or would he be ready to flee when she got back? And thoughts of William and the contract she had with Svenson's Dairy made her smile. She was getting a dollar fifty more per hundredweight than she would from the co-op and he picked up and washed and returned her milk cans. He'd told her that his super premium ice cream was great, thanks to her milk, and was selling very well.

Finally, her mind stopped wandering and light sleep overtook her. In what seemed a short while later, the sound of the newspaper rustling woke her and she jumped up with a start. The luminous hands on the table clock read 12:30 A.M. She couldn't believe she'd slept that long. She had turned off the table lamp when she put the paper down in her lap intending to take a few minutes nap. Now it was dark inside the room. Suddenly, the back of her neck tingled as she *felt* the presence of someone else in the room. Who? Sleepiness still fogged her brain; her vision was blurry. Then she noticed that the front door was ajar, some of the outside neon light was filtering in. Who? She became aware of a darkness, a shadow moving across the floor. Her heart pounded fiercely. "Who's there!" she yelled desperately. The shadow moved towards the door. The door swung open and quickly closed again. "Who's There? she yelled again and then there was a loud bang that made her jump in fright. She stepped back and stumbled into the chair. "Goddamit, keep it down in there!" came resounding through the wall from the next room.

She was terrified now, sure that the shadow was still in the room. Then she remembered the table lamp. She fumbled and turned the tiny knob at the base of the lamp. The room flooded with the white glare from the lamp and she squeezed her eyelids together, the glare shattering her vision. Nothing moved. She sat frozen in the chair for moments that seemed unending. But all was quiet--no movement--nobody. When she could see, she slowly slid from the chair and cautiously peeked under the bed. But there was no one. Then she got up and switched on the light over the bed. She checked the closet. She now was certain the room was empty. She moved to the door and closed it quietly and locked it. Then she moved the curtain and looked outside. Nothing moved. With the lights off, she slowly opened the door and looked up and down the covered walkway. It was deserted. She closed the door and locked and bolted it. Then she turned on the light and sat back in the chair. Suddenly a chill gripped her and she pulled on the windbreaker. Who? The question rolled over and over again in her mind. After a while the terror subsided and she lay back in the chair. Resting with her jacket on, she slept fitfully until dawn.

When she woke up, she opened the window curtains and daylight filled the room. Slowly, the events of the preceding night came back to her. *She hadn't locked the door. She fell asleep in a dark room with the door unlocked. Of all the dumb things.* She was sure someone had been in the room. The manager's face flashed into her mind.

She got her suitcase out of the car, took a shower and changed clothes. Then she went to the front office to check out. She decided to tell them what happened. If the motel manager were there, she was very interested to see his reaction to her story.

"Hope you enjoyed your stay," he said as he tore off a copy of her bill and laid it on the counter. His tone was much more business-like than it had been the day before. A fat woman was sitting at the desk, working on some papers.

"Well, I didn't enjoy my stay." she said.

"What was wrong?" he asked. His eyebrows arched in surprise.

"Someone broke into my room... in the middle of the night."

"What?" the man and woman said almost simultaneously. The

woman stood up and looked suspiciously at the man.

"Yes. Someone was in my room. I don't know what they were after. I must have scared them off before they could do anything." She looked accusingly at the man.

The man looked keenly interested but unperturbed. "Well. I'll be," he said. "Are you alright? How did they get in? Do you want us to call the police?"

She told them what had happened and said no to the police. She didn't know what else she could do. She was beginning to feel uneasy; to believe that maybe she had dreamt it.

Then something flashed in her mind and suddenly she knew the man had been in her room.

"It was you, wasn't it," Lillian said looking steadily at the man. "You were in my room last night."

"Wait just a minute there ... where'd you get that idea? I wasn't anywhere near--"

"Oh yes you were. I recognize this newspaper." She pointed to the paper laying on the counter next to her bill.

"What? Newspaper?" the man squeaked. he grabbed the paper and put it under the counter. "That's a laugh. We got dozens of these papers--"

"Shut up, George, you jackass!" his wife yelled. "Look, lady," she said, turning to face Lillian. "I don't know what your problem is, but I think it best if we just drop this."

"Drop It?" Lillian said in a rising voice. "Are you just going to let it go at that? Drop it?"

"Yes, drop it," the woman said, her face turning red. "We'll refund your room costs for the inconvenience."

"Inconvenience?"

"Wait a minute Hilda," the man said to his wife. "I don't--"

"Shut up, you jackass!" she yelled. She was getting some money from a drawer under the counter.

"Here lady," she said to Lillian. "Just take this and please go."

Lillian could detect pleading in her voice. She looked at the bills in her hand, then at the ashen face of the man. He made her feel sick and weak. "Keep your money," she said. "You're going to need it." She shook her head in disgust and left.

She wanted to go straight to the police. She knew it was the same newspaper. She recognized the coffee stain. It was in exactly the same place. He must have been picking up the paper when she woke up. What in God's name was he trying to do? Then, thinking about it, she realized she had no real evidence.

After she drove for a while, the sickness passed and the tenseness in her neck eased. She decided to skip the police. It was good to be on the road. She was glad to be away from that awful place: she remembered the manger when she'd checked in: there had been a meanness and an uneasiness revealed in his eyes. She shuddered when she realized his wife must have known what he was up to.

* * *

Back at the motel, George was silent as his wife unleashed a tongue-lashing: "You almost blew it George! God, we've been so careful and you didn't keep an eye on him? You know it was Tim, he brought the newspaper from that room. We're going to have to watch Timmy better. He's roamin' the rooms again."

Tim was their twelve-year old boy. The doctor had said he was "kind of autistic" or maybe had "real mental" problems and said he would be better off in an institution. The couple had been trying to deal with this burden for years. Hilda was terrified of losing her son.

CHAPTER 30

When Miss Ellison asked to speak with Harold about Bobby, he wasn't sure what to expect. He asked her if whatever it was couldn't wait until Lillian got back.

"Well, I was hoping to speak with his Grandmother," she said. "But it's important, so I better tell you."

"Oh, well she is his aunt." He offered her a seat in the parlor.

"Sorry. OK. Is Bobby here?" she asked.

"No. He was here earlier," Harold said. "He's out somewhere in the fields now. He should be here soon."

"Well, I'm glad about that. I mean, that he's here." She took a deep breath. "You see, he hasn't been to school in three days."

"What?" Harold said, puzzled by her words. "But how can that be? I've sent him every day."

"Well, that's a relief," she said, studying the man sitting across from her. She didn't know what she was looking for except that she wanted the truth. "I thought maybe you were keeping him home. Then he must get off the bus and cut out before we meet in class. Does he come home during the day?"

Harold reddened thinking about what had happened between him and Rosemary in the barn that day. "Ah, no. At least I don't think so. But I'm very seldom here all day. But what... . what do you think he's up to?"

"Well, it's a sordid business, Mr. Sims," she said, shifting her weight nervously in the chair. "You know, I do my best in that little school house and yet there are somethings that go on... I can't do everything." Harold nodded, but he understood nothing.

"My younger kids, especially the ones in grades three and four, have been acting strange lately. For a while, I guess. I couldn't put my finger on it. The kids started staying out too long. They were sick or so they said." She paused and looked at Harold as if she were going to cry. "And their school work fell off. They seemed to be afraid of something. Of course, Bobby's in that group."

He offered her a drink of water and she accepted. "Nothing was going on in school, I was there all the time." she continued. "But Monday, after I left for home, I turned around and went back. I had forgotten some papers I needed to take home. It was a beautiful day, so I parked below the hill and walked up to the schoolhouse." She sipped some of the water and sighed. "Before I got to the school, I saw some kids off in the woods on the side of the road. I could tell they were up to something so I... well, I guess I sneaked up on them. They were so occupied with what they were doing, they didn't even see me. What I saw... " she put the glass down. Her hand was shaking. "What I saw, I couldn't believe. Three of my older girls, seventh and eighth graders, were surrounding Bobby and a little girl, a third grader I won't name for now. The little girl was being held down by one of the big girls, with her dress pulled up. The other two girls were laughing and pulling Bobby's pants down and pushing him towards the little girl."

"What? " Harold looked at the teacher. "What?" He was shocked and embarrassed by what he'd heard. She seemed sincere enough. "Are you sure?" he said, trying not to believe what he'd heard. "Are you sure *that's* what they were doing?"

"Oh yes, I'm sure. And when they finally saw me, they scattered. I helped the two kids to get dressed again. They said the big girls were forcing them to... , well, sort of act like they were grownups. They said they were making other kids do it too. It was pure bullying. I could see the fear in their faces."

Harold thought for a moment. The scene she described seemed incredible, like it was invented. Here was a young, impressionable woman. Maybe she saw the kids playing their usual pranks. But he'd never heard of this before. "Sounds like kid's stuff to me," he said, nervously.

"Oh, no, Mr. Sims. No sir. I can assure you this was not just kid's stuff," she said with her eyes narrowed. "And I believe that's why Bobby hasn't come to school for three days. I believe he's ashamed and afraid."

Harold shook his head. "It's hard to believe. But... what do you think we should do?"

"I want you to know that I've been to the parents of those girls," she said, trying to reassure him. "Right now, I'm not sure that was the best thing to do. But I couldn't let them get away with that, now could I?"

Harold nodded agreement, although he wasn't sure.

"The thing is, the girls were laying for me. They must have gotten together and concocted some story before I came over. And when I brought it up to the parents, each girl claimed she had nothing to do with it; that they had just come upon the two kids in the woods. Each one said it was Bobby that did it, and they were just trying to help the little girl. Mr. Sims, the sad thing is that the parents believed them. But I'll tell you right now, they're lying. I saw enough to convince me of that."

"Well, good lord, what now?" Harold just wished it would go away.

"Well, I told the parents that this behavior should not go unpunished and that I was going to recommend a suspension for the girls for bullying and bad behavior. I felt something had to be done. But the parents said that if I did that, they would go to the board and tell them their story. And you know what? If the board believes them, Bobby may be permanently suspended, expelled, and I... I may get fired." Now the teacher was wringing her hands. "Isn't that awful? How can people lie and be so vicious?"

Harold now felt the full impact of her words. "Oh, what a mess this is," he said, his concern now apparent. "You didn't recommend the suspension, did you?"

She shook her head. "No. Not yet. Look. Those girls may have the upper hand at the moment, but don't believe for a minute that they aren't scared." Her voice was beginning to quaver. "They're afraid some of the other kids may talk, too. Right now, it's my word and the little girl and Bobby's against those three girls. But I don't want to take a chance; I don't want to get Bobby hurt." She stood up and started pacing the floor. "So. I'll keep quiet, if that's what you think best. For Bobby's sake. I've asked for an assistant to supervise the grounds until the kids get on the bus. I've also asked for the bus to get there earlier. They had a 45-minute wait before."

"Well, maybe you've got it under control," Harold said, now becoming upset about what she had said. "But I'd really like to go knock their heads together."

"Well, we must be careful. I feel awful about the poor kids who were the victims of these hooligans. But they could wind up getting hurt even more if we're not careful. That's why I hope you can get Bobby to come back to school. I've got to get things back to normal."

"I can get Bobby back to school, alright. I'll take him myself for a while. But I don't know about everything gettin' back to normal though. Have you talked to the parents of the little girl?"

She sighed deeply. "Well, no. To tell the truth, I'm very much afraid to. If they get into a huff over this, it could blow the whole thing wide open. I mean, suppose they believe the girls?"

"And not believe their own child?" Harold asked.

"The little girl said the big girls made them take their clothes off, and I know that's true. But people have a way of making little children say what they want them to say. Fear can make a child forget, or remember things that never happened. We best be very careful with this, Mr. Sims." She thanked him and started to leave. "Oh, one other thing. Would you mind telling me about Bobby? I mean who his parents are? I don't mean to be prying, but there are so many rumors out there."

"Rumors?" Harold asked. "Rumors about what?"

"Well, one of the older girl's mothers said that Bobby was a kidnapped orphan from a home for ... for mentally retarded? She said he could be dangerous. Of course, I didn't believe a word she said."

"Well, of all the ... damned nonsense I've ever heard." Now Harold got up and paced around. "His parents live right here in Johnstown. They just... well they decided to let him stay with his aunt for a while. He likes living out here in the country much better than town. That's all there is to it. Now those people ought to be put away for telling vicious lies."

"Well, thanks for telling me. Now at least I know the truth."

"Who are these people? I'd like to set them straight." Harold's anger began to show.

"Mr. Sims, I really think it's best if we stay away from those people for now. I mean, Bobby may turn out to be the real victim if we aren't careful. If you confront them, they for sure will take that contrived story to the board. And I can tell you that there's a person on that board, a Mrs. Grubbs, who'd like to see me get into trouble. I think it's best to just try to get him back in school. You should tell him that he will not be bothered again by those girls. I can promise you that."

When she left, Harold was confused and really didn't know what to do. But, for the moment, she was probably right. Better to let it alone for the time being. And it was still another week before Lillian would be back.

* * *

Bobby came home just at dark. He was holding Blackie in his arms. He tried to go right to his room. When Harold stopped him, he'd looked at Harold with a wild stare.

"Hi Bobby. You're real late." he said in a friendly voice. "I was beginning to worry about you. Are you alright?"

"Uh huh."

"Where have you been?"

"Just walkin'."

"Just walkin'?"

"Uh huh."

Harold scratched his head. "Well look. I got some of them good ham sandwiches you like from the Red Mill. And a big dill pickle. And potato chips. Like to eat?"

Bobby put the cat down. “Can you give Blackie some milk?” Then he sat down at the kitchen table and wolfed down the sandwich and pickle and potato chips and a coke Harold had also brought.

“Bobby, your teacher was here today. She said you haven't been to school in three days. She told me what happened with the big girls an' all. Now I don't think any of this is your fault. But I do want to know: Is all that true?”

Bobby's face reddened. “Please don't tell Aunt Lilly. Please?”

“Bobby, I just want to help you. Don't be afraid. Now, did those girls undress you like Miss Ellison says?”

His eyes opened wide. He nodded his head.

“Are you afraid to go back to school because of them?”

He nodded his head again.

“Well Bobby, Miss Ellison is going to punish those girls and she said she won't let them ever do that again. And I'm takin' you directly to school; then I'll pick you up after school. Will that be OK?”

“I'm scared of them, uncle Harold. Them girls is witches.”

“That’s bad English, Bobby.”

“No it ain’t, it’s the truth.”

“Don't be silly, Bobby. Where did you ever get that idea?”

“They told me so their ‘selves. Said they were real witches. And that if I ever told what they were doin', they'd dry up my... thing, and it would fall off like a dead leaf.”

“Dead leaf? Oh, God. Fall off? What do they... ? That's a bad lot isn't it?” Harold was up, pacing around. “Don't you worry about them anymore. We know about them now. They're just trying to scare you with that witch business. Now, can you tell me who they are? What's the name of these witches?”

“Oh, no. They'd kill me for sure! I can't tell uncle Harold.” Bobby started for his room.

“Wait, Bobby. OK. You don't have to tell me their names. But I want to ask you something else. I saw you in the barn... today." Bobby looked frightened.

"What were you doing there?"

"Nuthin'."

"Did you see me or anybody else?"

"Didn't see nuthin'."

"Are you sure? I mean, you must of seen somethin'?"

He nodded his head in long, slow shakes.

"Well, did you hear anything?"

Bobby looked at Harold and grimaced. "Well, I guess I heard somethin'."

"Well, what was it?"

Bobby hesitated for a minute. He rolled his eyes and looked around the room. Then he said: "Think it must a been rats. Rats in the hay."

"Are you sure it was rats?"

"Uh huh. It coulda been somethin' else, maybe. But anyways, it sounded to me like a whole bunch of rats thrashin' around."

CHAPTER 31

Lillian made the special auction at the Marlu farm as planned. On all her stops she had met the important people, both in breeding and farming. She was carefully listening and learning a lot about the business. Some buyers treated the pedigreed cattle as if they were fine furniture or paintings and they bid up the price so that she couldn't afford to stay with them. She could no longer afford the tested champions she had bought before, so she bid on the untested daughters instead. It was still in the spirit of her agreement with Svenson and she could always replace any undesirable daughter. In this way, she bought four nice looking two-year olds at auction at Marlu. She was happy that her trip had been a success.

The next morning, she drove home, a day earlier than planned. Her journey had proven itself; she had accomplished most of her needs. She went back through Pennsylvania and took the road north to Binghamton and continued up through Cooperstown. As she travelled, she could see the coldness of the land growing around her. The Pennsylvania countryside had been still green and warm, but as she neared the Adirondacks, mostly naked trees appeared and the dark green spruce of winter showed its face. Still she was glad to be home and she thought of Bobby and Harold, and felt the anxiousness of the weary home-bound traveler.

When she arrived home, there was no greeting and except for the cat, Blackie, waiting on the porch, the house was empty. The cat rubbed happily on her leg, a rare show of affection. Bobby would be at school, she remembered and Harold could be anywhere. It was cold inside and she lit a fire in the Merrimac and cheered herself by walking through each room and seeing that everything was the same and after satisfying herself this way, she changed into work clothes, a denim mackinaw and barn boots, and walked up to see her cattle. Blackie followed her. The sun slanted down on the horizon as the cool, dry afternoon started the descent into darkness; everything seemed lovely to her, especially the regal pine and spruce that now ruled over the edge of the wood, over the big oak and maple and birch that now stood mostly naked, surrounded in disgrace by their fallen leaves.

The white barn fit well into the cool landscape. She found the cows in the barnyard, already gathering in from the fields for milking, rarely needing someone to go fetch them. Her fence line needed mending; the stones had fallen in places and where there was post and barbed wire, much of the fence had rusted and the posts had rotted away. But her cows never strayed and were always back in time for milking and they looked lovely and came to her as she walked in the yard. She hugged each one and put her arm around their necks and stroked them. They seemed happy to see her.

"Hello-oo... there. What do you want?" a strange voice bellowed from the barn.

She jumped back, startled. Nothing could be seen in the gathering shadows. "Who's there?" she yelled noticing her voice was shrill.

"I say, what do you want? This here's private property," the voice growled.

"Where are you? I can't see you."

A figure stepped out of the darkness behind the open barn doors. It was the figure of a big man dressed in a checkered wool shirt and hunters cap with one ear flap curled down. He was slowly walking towards her carrying a manure fork with the tines pointed towards her.

"Who are you? This is my place... I'm Lillian... Lillian Sims," she yelled.

The man stopped and stuck the tines of the fork in the ground, gripping the handle tightly. He seemed to be chewing on her words. The cows tossed their heads and moved back towards the gate.

"Aunt Lilly!" Bobby came running up the hill. "You're home."

She turned and walked towards him and he embraced her legs.

"I'm so glad you're home. It's been awful without you."

"Oh Bobby, Bobby, it's so good to see you." and she bent down and kissed him. After they hugged, she said: "Bobby, do you know who that man is?" she turned and looked at him.

Bobby looked around her. "Oh, him? You know him, that's just Junior. He works here now. Uncle Harold brought him here."

"Junior? He works here?" She looked at him steadily as if she were watching some strange bird, and then waved. He grinned and walked over towards her. Now that she could see him better, it was clear that it was, indeed, Junior.

"I'm Junior Dixon ma'am, " he said. "We met before, remember?" She could see his filthy teeth and fully recognized who he was.

She went into the barn and saw that he had been forking the manure into the wagon, probably several days' worth, from the way things looked.

"Well, keep at it Junior. This place is a mess."

Harold was waiting in the kitchen. He had had a few beers. He hadn't expected her a day early and had been shocked when he saw her car.

He said: "Back early?" and made no attempt to kiss or embrace her.

" Yes," she replied, wondering about his cool greeting. "I came back early. Got everything done and I missed everyone... How is everything?

"Fine. And you? How was your trip? Any problems?" The questions seemed forced; she thought he seemed nervous.

"No. Everything went smooth as they say. How's the milking going?"

"Ok... Ok. We're still getting the milk down to the truck stand on time." He steadied himself on the wall by the door.

Junior walked in and stood grinning in the doorway. "Finished the milkin' and cleanin' the barn," he said. "Everything's done."

"Oh, Lillian, this is Junior Dixon. Remember, he helped me cut wood? I hired him to take ... well kind of, to take Fred's place."

Lillian looked sharply at Harold. She'd told him to wait until she got back. "Oh? Is he using Fred's room?"

"No, he's still living with his mom. I picked him up today because his car's broke down. He won't be stayin' here." He pulled a cigarette from the pack in his pocket and lit it with a shaking hand. The short silence magnified the tension in the air. "Look, I got to run him on home now," he said, and looked directly at Lillian for the first time. She was silent.

Harold left with Junior. She worked off her disappointment by pulling some corn and potatoes from the storage bin. She peeled the potatoes and shucked the corn and cooked a simple supper of scalloped potatoes and corn roasted over the wood coals. She got Bobby fed and then read to him for a while and played five games of checkers. He wanted to play monopoly, but she was too tired for such things. When Bobby was ready, she sent him to brush his teeth. Then she took one of the kerosene lamps and led him through flickering shadows up the narrow stairs to his room. Pausing for a minute in the hall, she looked up at the trap door to Fred's old room. Then she went in the bedroom and lit the lamp on his dresser and waited while he changed into his pajamas. The bed was heaped with a thick comforter; the nights were getting cold. When he crawled in bed, she pulled the comforter up, and sat at the foot.

"Do you think Fred will come down from his room tonight?" he asked.

"No Bobby, I wish you wouldn't think about Fred. I don't think Fred is here. He's in... heaven, I suppose."

He'd told her that Fred had visited him in his room during the night while she was gone. He didn't claim to have seen him, but only that the old rocker was moving and creaking like someone was sitting in it. He could see it by the moonlight that filtered through the window.

And before she'd left on the trip, both her and Harold heard noises coming from upstairs like someone walking around. Fred had made those same noises when he was living there. The house creaked with any movement, including the wind. And that was what Harold claimed it was, although on the nights they had heard the noise, there was no wind. When she pointed this out to him, he just shrugged and said that it had to be something like the wind.

And now Bobby was afraid to sleep alone in his room. But she didn't want to give in to the idea of a ghost. If she did, she was afraid they would have to move.

"There's nothing to be afraid of Bobby," she said. "I'm home now. I'll be right here." and she waited for him to fall asleep.

Going down stairs again, she looked up at the trap door to Fred's room. She might just go in there in the morning and take out some of the things that were stored, including Fred's old suitcase.

The table was cleared and the dishes washed; she sat in the kitchen rocker. Junior Dixon was going to be a problem, for sure. His mother, Edna was a teacher also and she had met Edna a while back at a teacher's conference in Johnstown on teaching in rural schools. They'd discussed the unique problems of one-room schoolhouses and they both seemed to be of the same mind on the subject. She seemed to be a lonely woman and had found in Lillian a receptive ear. Her difficulties with her son, Junior became a serious part of their conversation.

"He's just so unpredictable," she'd told her. "One day, he seems almost normal and the next he'll be uncontrollable. Sometimes he does things that... well he can hurt himself. I have to watch him all the time. But he does need to get out and work. He's too restless at home and I think that makes him worse. But nobody will give him a real job, except for cleaning yards or something like that."

"Have you tried any treatments?" Lillian asked.

"You mean a doctor? Or counseling? When we saw he couldn't progress in school, not beyond the fourth or fifth grade, we did consult a doctor. They tested him for some time and decided he was mentally incapacitated ... meaning retarded. But they said that sometimes he had the mind of a six year old, sometimes a twelve year old, and sometimes he showed indications of being normal.

That's what makes everything so difficult."

Lillian remembered how sorry she'd felt for Edna. But now her concern was about bearing that weight on her farm. Farming was a dangerous business; farm accidents were as common as car accidents and just as fatal. Adding Junior to that mix was unsettling.

She heard creaking coming from the stairs and her skin tingled with fright. She went to the stairs on tiptoes and saw Bobby, white as a sheet. "Aunt Lilly, I can't... " and he cried.

"It's Ok, Bobby, it's Ok." she said. "You can sleep down here. With me. I didn't mean to frighten you... "

And they stayed up and played more checkers waiting for Harold but when the mantle clock struck twelve, they went to bed. Harold came in much later and slept on the couch in the parlor. She'd heard him but said nothing. He was acting very strange, she thought. Maybe she shouldn't have come back a day early.

CHAPTER 32

The next morning she said nothing at first about Harold's indifferent behavior the night before. But she did bring up the problem of Junior.

"I don't think we should have him as a hired hand," she said. "I'm worried about him hurting himself and Bobby."

"Why? What do you think he's going to do? " Harold always protected Junior. "I tell you, Lillian, everyone's against him. All the other kids call him an idiot. Yes, he's not all there, sometimes," he said, his voice rising, "but he's a good worker and has a good character. I've used him on many a job and have no regrets. I think you're wrong."

She sighed. "You're probably right, Harold. I do feel sorry for Junior, and it probably is the right thing to do, but Bobby--" Bobby came in at that moment and she let the conversation drop. When he went back outside, she continued: "I just don't think I want to take that risk."

"There is no risk Lillian. I've used him around all kinds of dangerous equipment. He does exactly what I tell him to do. I'll guarantee it."

"Well... I'll think about it Harold."

"Think about it? What is there to think about?" Now his head was throbbing from the previous night. "Is it because I've made a decision without consulting you?"

"What's wrong with you Harold? What is it? Why are you so upset?"

"You... You go off to buy those fancy-assed cows of yours and leave us here alone. I hire a good hand and you come back and start giving orders again, changing everything." He rubbed his throbbing forehead. "That's what's wrong."

She didn't want to argue with him, but now she was upset. "There's another thing, Harold, since we're talking about things that are wrong. I think you were drinking yesterday. I don't want you in this house when you've been drinking." His face fell and he blinked. "You can go to your cabin," she continued. "I don't want you around Bobby when you're like that."

Harold was stunned. He looked at her in disbelief. "Lillian," he said. "You can't mean that. You don't understand, I wasn't drinking, not hardly at all. You, you just can't throw me out like that."

"I'm not throwing you out, Harold. I... I Oh, God, never mind. I'm going up to the barn." She started out the door. "I guess we can give Junior a try," she said and left him standing in the kitchen.

She walked up to the barn with quick, nervous steps. She had been upset by Harold's strange attitude. What was wrong, she wondered, with this green, untempered relationship? Why was it falling apart so soon?

* * *

Harold was hurt and resolved to get out and away. He stayed at the cabin for days, cooling off, trying to work off his sharp disappointment over her reaction to Junior, his drinking, and his own guilt. He didn't want to get drawn too deep into a hole over Junior and Bobby. But he found that everything about Lillian left him feeling unsure of himself, and that it really had always been like that.

CHAPTER 33

The day after they'd argued over Junior, Linda suddenly reappeared. She was wearing expensive clothes, but looked beat-up and worn out. Her face was thin and drawn and bruised, her eyes were puffed. She had aged.

“You went back to Frank, didn't you?” Lillian said, her voice cold and angry. “I hate that man. He beats the hell out of you, forces you into bed and you still go back to him. My God, Linda.” But she knew that Linda asked for it; no one made her stay with him. Only when she got bloodied enough or Frank threw her out for another woman, would she leave him and come back home. Not crawling back; not humbled; never. Lillian could see that even now she sported her bruises like war wounds, like little purple hearts.

“You're right, “ Linda said, matter-of-factly, after embracing her mother. “He's a dirty bastard. I hope his balls fall off.”

“Linda!”

“Sorry, Ma. That's the way he talks.” She put her suitcase down at the foot of the stairs. “But how are you, Mom?” Lillian knew she called her “Mom” when she was looking for a favor or feeling vulnerable. “I hope my room is clean. I mean not full of batshit, like the last time I came home. “Oooh,” she squealed. “I can't stand those nasty creatures.”

Lillian smiled. “Yes,” she said. “Your room is clean.”

There were no explanations. No remorse. But even though her words were still harsh, Lillian detected something new in Linda’s voice.

Harold learned about Linda's return at the General Store. She'd been up to Peck's buying things and the word got around quickly. He feared Linda and their dark secret and decided to move back to Lillian's right away.

CHAPTER 34

Within a month of Lillian's return, the new members of her herd arrived. That would put at least eight milkers on line by early next year; enough she hoped, to start paying most of the bills. It was a day of celebration and Lillian made a special spaghetti dinner. She invited the Svenson's to see the new cows. Again, only William showed up.

The barn seemed bigger and modern now with five head on each side in the milking area, separated by the new concrete strip. The lack of electricity was unnoticeable; the barn seemed to create its own energy.

"Be up to full production soon Lilly," William said. "Now how are you going to get those champions sired? You going for that new artificial insemination system that everyone's pushin'?" William was much more subdued, now that he knew about Lillian's marriage.

Lillian looked at William in mock disbelief. "Me? A.I.? My cows deserve better than that." She served him a plate of spaghetti. "I thought I told you about Able's bull? He has a champion sire... and I can walk my cows over there; it's only a mile or so."

"Able kept that Jersey bull?" William asked. He had known Able for quite a while. He helped himself to some of the Italian sauce with porkchops, one of Lillian's specialties.

"Yes. Able had a mind to build a Jersey herd, but he changed to Holsteins when he saw the production rates. But he liked that Jersey bull and kept him. He makes good money from sire fees but won't let them use him for AI."

"I hear that Able's son Pete is coming back to the states." William said. "That must be a big load off his mind. And Lena's too. Now he's only got the younger one over there... what's his name? Paul?"

"Yes. Maybe Lena will revive a bit," Lillian said. "She's been doing poorly lately."

Harold said little throughout the conversation. Linda spent her time glaring at him across the table. They'd hardly spoken a word since he returned. Lillian could see the dislike Linda showed for Harold and wondered where it came from.

"We finally got the new water tank finished, William," Harold said, to ease the tension. "Built it to the design you suggested. Want to see it? After we finish eating, I'll show it to you."

They were sitting outside on the front lawn, down by the road, where it was level. Lillian had Harold and Bobby and Junior move the kitchen table and chairs outside. It was a beautiful Indian summer day, with low scudding clouds letting the warmth of the sun come through.

Everyone enjoyed Lillian's spaghetti and the vanilla frosted cake she'd baked with a brown cow sculptured on the icing. The special dinner had been a success.

Later that evening, Harold approached Lillian with a difficult subject. "Lillian. I meant to tell you sooner, but with all that's happened, I clean forgot," he said.

"What is it Harold? Can't be much if it's that easy to forget."

"The electrification folks were out here while you were on your trip. Said they would be here in two months. That's just about next week. They'll wire the house and the barn and it's mostly free. What a relief that's going to be."

Lillian couldn't believe what she'd heard. She stared at Harold stonily. "Did you... sign us up?" she asked, her voice barely a whisper.

"Sure. Otherwise we'd have to wait for the next go around. Might be another year or two. Maybe never."

Lillian was trying to recover from the shock. She couldn't find anything to say. But she knew she was set against it. She felt as if Harold had betrayed her and she said almost nothing to him for the rest of the night. They'd had heated discussions about this before.

The next morning found her in Johnstown to meet the rural electrification program people. After some jockeying with clerks and secretaries, she met with the man that supervised the Fulton County program. They all seemed nice and were eager to help, but the man was astounded when she made her request.

"Let's see. Do I understand that you *don't* want us to hook you up?" He was scratching his head through the short crewcut.

"Yes. That is what I want."

"But this is... practically free. We have everything set up and ready. Won't take long at all. We'll wire your house and the barn with a minimum inconvenience." His tone was almost pleading.

"I don't want the house and barn wired." she said.

"Well. I'll be shot for a bear! If that ain't something to believe in. I've heard it all now. We get people poundin' on our desks every day because they ain't hooked up yet and here you go askin' for a pass-up. Why, for heaven's sake?"

"I've got my reasons. I really need for you to take me off that list."

"Hmm. Well, I never run into this before. I'm going to have to check this out with the county manager. Never had this happen before." He took his glasses off and looked at her.

"What is there to check?" she asked with impatience. "I don't want to be hooked up, period. That's all there is to it. Just take me off your schedule."

He put his glasses back on. "Uh, sure. I can do that. But first I got to talk to the boss." There were lots of people in the office, just as he said, demanding to get on the hook up schedule. The woman behind her looked at her as if she were crazy.

"Look. Could you come back ... let's say, later this afternoon," he said. "I should have something for you by then."

Lillian left the office and went to a diner for a cup of coffee. Was she crazy? Harold had brought up all the points for getting hooked up. With the addition to the herd, hand milking time would increase to more than two hours. It was only her and Bobby and Junior and rarely, Harold. Harold pointed out that two milking machines would get the job done in less than half the time with only one person. And that when she got up to ten head, she would need two hired hands if she didn't get electric power.

But she'd just put everything together without power. So far, she had overcome all the obstacles. And now, with the expanded herd, she wanted to run the farm without power to prove her point. To her, hand milking was the most intimate contact humankind had with animals. This established a bond with the animal that her whole vision of farming was built on.

But deep down she had doubts; she may be deluding herself. Maybe she was putting the farm at stake for some idealistic dream, one that no one else seemed to share with her.

Later that day the manager presented her with a piece of paper to sign. She had gotten her request.

"Can't tell you when we'll be around to hook up again," he said. "Maybe quite a while. This program is about to end."

She felt dizzy when she left the office.

CHAPTER 35

When she got home, she busied herself preparing supper. Harold was staying home that evening and she felt guilty about what she had done. Keeping busy, she felt, would help avoid any stray questions from Harold about the electrical hook-up. Linda very seldom sat down to supper with Lillian and Bobby and Harold; she usually ate later and to keep the peace, volunteered to do the dishes. But she was meeting a friend that evening and decided to ignore Harold and eat early.

When they were seated and eating, Lillian decided to steer the conversation at the table.

"Harold, have you seen Rosemary lately?" she asked. " I haven't seen her since---"

Harold turned red, although in the pale light of the kerosene lamps, it went unnoticed, and he dropped his fork. "Uh, ah, why no," he interrupted. "I mean... yes, oh, no. No, I mean I haven't," he said, shaking his head.

"--since I returned from the trip," Lillian continued. "Now, Bobby, where are *you* going?"

"I uh, have to go to the bathroom," he said.

"Bobby, why can't you do that before you sit down to supper?" Lillian asked.

"Uh, yes ma'am. I'll be... be more careful next time, " and he left the table and disappeared.

"Harold, what's wrong with you? You look like you've just been bitten by a snake," Lillian said.

Harold seemed to be closely examining the food on his plate. "Oh, it's nothing, really. I was just thinking... about when we were going to get hooked-up."

"Are we getting hooked-up?" Linda asked.

Lillian didn't say anything.

"Yes," Harold replied, to keep the conversation moving in that direction. "Ain't that true, Lillian?"

"I guess so. But tell me Harold, how's that--"

"Oh, thank God," Linda said. "Now we can live like civilized people again."

"How's that casserole?" Lillian said, ignoring Linda's outburst.

Harold didn't answer. He seemed to be deep in thought.

"It's real good, Ma," Linda said, unsure of what was happening.

"Harold?" Lillian said.

"Oh, yes, everything is good," Harold replied absently.

"Well, I think it's strange that Rosemary has stayed away so long. She was working her garden before I left; now it looks abandoned."

"Maybe you should go see her," Linda said.

"You're right, Linda. As soon as I get a chance, I'll run over to Fultonville and see her."

"I'm sure she's alright," Harold said. "I've got to get some things from the cabin. "I'll be right back."

* * *

"Sometimes I don't think I understand him," Lillian said after he left.

"Why do you stay with him, " Linda asked. "He's no good. He's as bad as Frank."

"How can you say that, Linda?' she asked, disturbed by the words.

"Well, he's drinking again, isn't he? You shouldn't of married him."

"Why not, Linda? He wasn't drinking when I married him."

"How could you forget Dad so easily? I never understood that."

“I didn't forget your father,” Lillian said. She had never told Linda about Matt's infidelities. She was afraid of what it would do to her. “And besides, it's been a long time now.”

“Well, you should of never married that goddam Harold.”

“Linda!”

“Sorry, Ma,” she said, shaking her head. “I should learn to keep my mouth shut. Look, I'll do the dishes before I leave,”and she started picking up the dishes from the table.

CHAPTER 36

JUNIOR FLIES

One day, Junior took the John Deere with a wagon back to the woodlot. He and Bobby went to clean up left over cuttings for firewood. It was a clear day and the hill next to the woodlot was still free of snow and almost perfect, he thought, for free rolling. Before loading the wagon, he unhitched it from the John Deere. Junior loved to fly.

"Get off, Bobby. I'm gonna' fly down the hill before we load up," he said. Junior knew that Bobby should never be with him when he was flying. Harold had told him never to drive fast when Bobby was on the tractor or in the wagon and Lillian had already yelled at him for driving the tractors too fast around the barnyard.

Bobby was impressed by Junior's daring. He seemed to be afraid of nothing. And Bobby had been watching him operate the John Deere; he wanted to learn. "I wanna' go with you," he said.

"No, Bobby. Harold and Miss Lillian would get mad. You ain't supposed to be goin' fast. Now get off and wait for me up here. I'll tell you some more about how to drive it when I'm done."

Bobby jumped down and watched Junior set up the tractor, getting ready for flight. After he'd thrown the throttle lever back and forth a few times to rev the engine, he released the tractor brake and slowly started down the hill in gear. As he picked up speed, he pulled the shift to neutral and threw the throttle lever to full power; now the full take off was in motion. The tractor continued to pick up speed; Junior struggled to keep the bouncing machine from careening sideways into a rollover. But what Junior lacked mentally, he had physically: the eyes of a raptor and a perfect sense of balance when it came to machines. The John Deere rolled out smoothly at the bottom of the hill; a perfect flight. He stood up on the tractor and waved up to Bobby. Bobby was waving back. Then he drove back up the hill.

"Wish I had a better runway Bobby. Wouldn't bounce so much then."

"When Can I try it?" Bobby asked, enthused by Junior's success.

Junior thought for a moment. But then his memory clicked in and he said: "You ain't ready for flyin' yet Bobby. You gotta' be older, like me." They finished collecting the wood and returned to the barn; Junior slowed down more and more as he approached the barnyard. He knew that was where Harold always caught him.

The next day, Junior was putting in new posts for the fence up near the woodlot. Harold had dropped him off early in the day and then taken the tractor, with a load of wood, back to the barn. Later, when he had almost finished for the day, Junior looked towards the barn, which was a great distance off. He saw something unusual in his line of sight; something big and black, shimmering in the waning daylight. Probably Harold working, he thought. He worked for a while longer, burying the last fence post for that day, and then picking up his axe, he went to find out what it was that he'd seen. When he got close enough, he could see it was the John Deere laying on its side. Then he found Bobby, with his legs caught under the rear wheel. He was unconscious although Junior, his mind filled with terror, thought he was dead. He tried to pull Bobby out from under the wheels, but he couldn't. Fuel was spilling from the engine onto the ground and running towards Bobby. The day was ending and it was getting cold. Junior took off his heavy outer shirt and covered the boy with it. Then, terrified by what had happened, he panicked and ran down towards the barn.

When Lillian came home from school that day, Linda wasn't home yet and Bobby wasn't in the house. She knew he was there because he'd left a dirty milk glass on the table. It wasn't unusual, he would often be out in the woods or fields or up in the barn. But later, when Harold came back from town and it was time for milking, she asked him if he'd seen Bobby anywhere.

"Haven't seen him," Harold said. "Must be up in the woods."

"Well, it's getting late," she said. "Maybe we should go look for him."

At that moment, Junior came running into the barn, gasping for breath. "Come quick," he yelled to them both. "Bobby's been hurt. He's under the tractor."

"Oh God!" Lillian screamed and without a further word, she and Harold ran up the road following Junior.

Harold arrived with Junior and when he checked, he found that the boy was still breathing. "He's alive!" he said to Lillian as she came running up out of breath. They tried to wake him, but he didn't respond. Junior and Harold tried lifting the wheel while Lillian tried to pull him free. But they couldn't get a good enough grip to lift it.

Harold panicked and said: "I'm goin' to get the other tractor and some chains and we'll try to lift it up. We got to hurry; it'll be dark soon." He took off running towards the barn.

"Harold, shouldn't we call the ambulance?" she yelled after him.

Harold stopped and turned. "No, Lillian," he said. "Remember how long they took for Fred? It's best we take him in." And he was off again.

"Miss Lillian, let me get something," Junior said, and he was off up the road. Lillian was left alone with cold fear shaking her body. Bobby lay still, his face chalky white. Lillian had his head cupped in her hands. She let out a wail of grief, afraid she was going to lose him. Then she cried: "Junior. That damn Junior!"

He returned quickly carrying two thick boughs on his shoulders. He quickly dug trenches under the wheel's rim and then stuck one bough under each side of the wheel with Bobby in between. Then he said. "Miss Lillian, when I lift on these, you try to pull Bobby out." He straddled the boy and bent down so he could use his leg muscles and strained with all his might on the two levers resting on his shoulders. He managed to lift the wheel just enough so she could pull Bobby free. She gently embraced the boy, and tried to revive him. One of his legs was twisted and bleeding. When he didn't respond, she picked him up in her arms. Then she turned a fierce gaze on Junior.

"Junior, you damn fool, you're finished here," she told him through tears as she started for the house. "I want you to leave today."

Junior stared at her, his eyes moving wildly. His head started jerking in short spasms to one side. "No, Miss Lillian, ... not me," was all he could say.

Lillian stared at him with angry eyes. "How could you... how could you? Look what you've done. You could have killed him." and Junior sank down on his knees.

"No, Miss Lillian, No," he said once more, holding his hand up as if to stop her words. His head was now jerking violently. Just then Harold came up the road with the Ford. He took the boy in his arms and started for the house. With the anxiety of the moment, Junior kneeling in the dust didn't register with him. He yelled back at him: "Junior -go over to Peck's and call the hospital in Johnstown. Tell them we're bringing Bobby in. Tell them what happened," and he and Lillian disappeared down the hill.

They took Bobby directly to the emergency room at the hospital. He revived a short while later, but was unable to speak and the doctors didn't want him to talk. They said he'd suffered a concussion but they thought he would recover. They wanted to keep him for three to five days for observation. He also had a badly broken leg and a deep puncture wound in the other leg. Lillian thanked God that he wasn't any worse.

* * *

When Junior came home that day, his mother noticed his strange behavior. The head jerking occurred, she remembered, whenever he was in a situation he couldn't handle. She hadn't seen it in a long time. She wondered that he hadn't killed himself driving home. He seemed to have regressed to his lowest stage of maturity as he sat silent and sullen at supper that night.

"Tell me what's wrong, son, " she said several times. But he couldn't be encouraged to talk. She felt bewildered.

When they came home and Harold found out that Lillian had

fired Junior, he was upset. "We don't even know what happened, Lillian. How could you do such a thing?"

"Harold! You know how reckless he was with that tractor! How many times did I tell him not to drive so crazy? He could have killed Bobby, you know."

When he saw how angry she was, Harold shook his head. "Well, I think we should of waited until Bobby comes home. Maybe it was just an accident that could of happened to anyone--"

"I don't think so Harold," she interrupted. "You're always making excuses for him. How else could you turn that tractor over on its side, except by crazy driving?"

Harold knew she was right about the tractor turning over, but just couldn't believe that Junior would have driven like that with Bobby aboard. Not after he told him he wouldn't.

When Junior refused to leave for work the next day, and his behavior hadn't improved, his mother decided she'd better talk with the Sims that evening. She asked her neighbor, Mr. Potts, to drive her over.

Lillian told Mrs. Dixon what had happened with a firm voice and said she was sorry, but she just had to let Junior go.

"I've always been afraid of this," Edna Dixon said, with a deep sigh. "He doesn't seem to have the same sense of danger that the rest of us have. That's why he needs special supervision. I'm very sorry Mrs. Sims." She started to sob. "I pray that Bobby will be alright."

Lillian, who in desperation over Bobby had been cold with Edna Dixon, now went over and embraced her.

"It was unfortunate," she said. "I am really sorry, Edna, I had to let him go."

"Did you... did you yell at him? Or did you tell him he'd done something bad? I ask that only because I need to know why he's behaving the way he is."

"I'm sorry to say that yes, I did tell him that he was a fool and that he was finished here; that he had almost killed Bobby."

Edna Dixon sighed. “Well that explains his behavior.” She was quiet for a moment. “I know I shouldn't be asking you this,” she continued, “But do you think... would you consider coming to see him? You see, he's in a state of shock. He won't talk, won't eat, his body is shaking in spasms. If you would maybe tell him you forgive him?”

“But I can't,” Lillian said, her anger returning. “That's too much to ask. Bobby really could have been killed. Junior *has* to learn. He never will if we keep forgiving him.”

“I know. I just thought--” she was unable to finish. She got up to leave. “Again, I'm very sorry, Mrs. Sims. I'll pray for Bobby.” And she left quickly. Mr. Potts took her home.

When Bobby came home everything seemed new to him. He was so glad to see the farm once more; to be out of the stuffy hospital. He was excited about the attention his new cast and crutch were bringing, even though there was some pain. After a few days, when he got to where he could maneuver with the crutch just as well as he had without it, he was allowed to go to school again where his celebrity status soared. Everyone wanted to sign his cast; he felt like a movie star. When he seemed to be recovered, Harold talked with him about the accident.

“You see what happens Bobby when someone fools around with that tractor,” he said with a stern look. “You two shouldn't a been joy-riding on the tractor. And just because Junior wants to do it doesn't mean you should. Now, can you tell me what happened?”

Bobby shook his head. He hadn't thought about the accident. “But we wasn't joy-riding,” he said.

“Well, then how did the tractor turn over?” Harold asked, his eyes narrowing.

“I don't know,” Bobby replied, shaking his head slowly. “I don't remember. Uncle Harold, where's Junior?” He just realized that he hadn't seen Junior since his return home. He thought Junior could help him answer these questions.

“Junior won't be comin' here anymore,” Harold said, his head bowed. “He's finished working here,” he said.

"Why Uncle Harold?"

"Well, your aunt is pretty mad at him for drivin' so wild. She's told him not to be drivin' that tractor so fast."

Later, Bobby thought about what Harold said and tried to focus on the day of the accident. He walked up to the barn, having fun with his crutch in the light snow that had fallen. He wanted to see the John Deere again, to see if he could remember. The tractor was parked in the shed. When he came up close to it and saw the controls and the steering wheel, everything that had happened started coming back to him. He had come home early from school that day and found the tractor parked in the field, where Harold had left it after unhooking the wagon. *He* had started the tractor and put it in gear! Then he remembered he was going too fast and running off the road and rolling across the field and trying to turn the wheel again to get back to the road. He remembered the terrifying bouncing and losing control, the wheel being pulled out of his hands when he hit a rock and the tractor tipping over. Junior hadn't been driving at all! A wave of numbness passed from his head down through his neck and shoulders and into his stomach. He felt like vomiting.

"Bobby, why aren't you eating?" Lillian asked at supper that night. The day had been cold; real winter was setting in and Bobby usually had a strong appetite for the pot roast.

Harold wasn't home yet. Bobby felt his failed courage returning, and keeping this secret was unbearable.

"Aunt lilly," he said, in a trembling voice, "Junior wasn't drivin' that tractor."

"What?" she said.

"No. I was drivin' it alone."

"Bobby? You... you were driving? But--." She looked at him in shock with her hands opened as if she were in prayer.

"Yes ma'am," he said, with his head bowed almost to the table. "I just remembered it. Couldn't remember before. Junior wasn't even there."

"But Junior was there when we found you... but, Oh God, what have I done now?" she said.

She'd been trying to keep a vision out of her mind since the accident, but now it came blazing through her defenses: Junior, kneeling in the dust, his face framed with fear, holding his hand up against her words; "No, Miss Lillian. No. Not me." The words burned in her mind. She felt as bad as she had ever felt. "Oh God, Bobby, what have I done?" she said again.

Lillian thrashed her soul that night for her unforgivable behavior. Visions of her mother and father came to her, with Junior and Harold at their side. She needed to repair her wrongs. Since Harold came home late and she thought he had been drinking, she didn't tell him anything until breakfast. Normally she wouldn't even make him breakfast when he came home late like that, but this morning she got up extra early and made him pancakes and eggs and bacon and fresh baked bread and coffee as strong as he liked it. Harold was puzzled, but, as usual, he failed to give it any significance. He had spent the previous evening at Rosemary's.

"Nice breakfast," he told Lillian, after he'd eaten a few mouthfuls, but he ate on in silence. Lillian was silent too as she ate and Bobby had run up to the barn. After a while the noise of the forks scraping plates became too irritating, and finally Harold said: "What's wrong Lillian? You're awful quiet this mornin'."

"Wrong?" she said, looking away from him. "No, there's nothing wrong. Is there something wrong with the breakfast?"

"Oh, no, it's real good," he said, puzzled.

They continued to eat in silence. "More coffee, Harold?" Lillian said when they had finished. She was picking up the plates and clearing the table.

"No thanks. I'll finish up in the barn Lillian. Then I'm going over to Prestons... see if they got anything lined up for me yet. I'll try to get home to help with the chores tonight." He put on his jacket and hat and headed for the barn. Lillian cursed and ran out after him.

"Harold, wait. There is something, something I have to tell you. I made a bad mistake about Junior. You were right."

"What? What do you mean?"

"Bobby told me. He said he was driving the tractor, not Junior. And he was alone."

"Well, Lillian! You see what jumping to --" Then he fell silent. "Well, what do you think we should do?"

"Well, I've got to tell Junior how sorry I am, don't I? Got to get him back to work, too. Can you help me with that Harold? You know him so well."

"Sure, I'll help. Just hope it isn't too late."

"Too late? Too late for what?"

He sighed. "Well, with Junior, you never know."

When they went to see Junior, he was pallid and specter thin. His mother looked haggard and forlorn; she thought he was going to die. She said he still refused to talk and was living off soda pop, the only thing he would touch.

"Junior," Lillian said gently, "I know this accident wasn't your fault." He looked at her, cowering in fear. "I'm sorry, very sorry I blamed you. Bobby is Ok and he wants you to come back to the farm. Junior? See, Harold is here. He wants you back too."

He didn't appear to understand at first and his head continued to jerk. But the gentleness of her voice and the reassuring touch of her hand on his shoulder seemed to gradually ease the tension in his face.

Lillian repeated her apology, but the boy remained silent. But after several successive visits, his mother reported he had started eating again. Then he finally said: "You mean... I can come back?" and when Lillian and Harold said yes, he smiled and the head jerking stopped.

Edna Dixon embraced Lillian and said: "Thank God and thank you for forgiving him. I'm sure he won't ever do that again."

PART II

STORM WARNINGS

CHAPTER 1

It was a bad winter. Anyone who could read the signs knew it would be. The cows refused to stray far from the barnyard. The Eighty-six-year-old widow Grayson's right leg was hurting much more than usual. Maynard said that right after pig butchering, folks were saying that their lard set up much thicker than usual.

Lillian looked through the kitchen window at the thick, heavy flakes falling from the leaden sky overhead. She had never seen so much snow. The flakes turned a brilliant gold when the rotating yellow light on the state truck cab glowed in her direction. The big Rio truck was almost hidden behind the huge vampire wings of the snowplow, a ton of predatory-looking cold steel. Sticking out above the main wing, was a flying wing that could be folded flat against the side of the truck. The men operating the plow looked tiny inside the big cab and were almost hidden by the falling snow. The flying wing on the side they were plowing was extended, knocking the tops off the towering banks of snow. They had to make several passes to move the mountainous piles off to the sides. With each pass, the snow became more compressed until finally, even the giant of a truck could move it no more.

The plow had stopped in front of the house. It was still early afternoon, yet it was almost dark. Lillian served Stan Wick and PeeWee Walters hot coffee and homemade muffins with honey.

“We'll plow up your drive a bit, Miss Lillian,” Stan said.

“Those banks must be gettin' to about eight feet or more. We'll break through the bank that's a-frontin' on your drive, so's you can get your vehicles out.”

“Sure could use a refill, Miss Lillian,” PeeWee said. He was a small, wiry man and took his nickname with pleasure. “It's colder n' a bear's behind out there.” She served them both another cup. “Muffins' mighty good, Miss Lillian. Mighty good,” they both agreed.

"If'n this keeps up, I expect we'll be out plowin' most of the night," Stan said. He was a big grizzly of a man with a full brown-gray beard. He drove the truck. "Can't let it get ahead of us. This is gonna be a big one, I tell ya."

"Can you keep the road open?" Lillian asked, surprised at the concern in their voices.

"Yep," PeeWee said. "Problem may be we can't open it wide enough for two vehicles to pass each other without gettin' into the banks. You got a good full set 'a chains? Not none a them wraparounds. They ain't worth a damn."

"Yes. And Harold put on snow tires." Lillian said. "I've never seen it snow this hard."

"Well I guess I have," Stan said. "I guess most of us livin' up here have seen some pretty big snowstorms, ain't that the truth, PeeWee?" PeeWee nodded. "But they ain't coming like they used to." Stan continued. "Not lIke it used to be in the forties when I was just a-learnin' to drive a rig like this."

They finished the coffee and put on their wool caps, heavy jackets and thick gloves. They'd left a pool of water around the chair where they'd hung them.

"Thanks Miss Lillian. Sure does a soul good to be able to get outta that storm for a spell," Stan said. "We'll most likely be back this way tomorrow, dependin' on how bad it gets. You gonna' be alright?"

"Oh yes, I'm sure. Harold has that big truck and the tractor has a plow. We should be alright."

The next day it snowed harder and a strong wind blew up. The snow gathered into deep swirling drifts. The local school systems shut down. Linda decided to stay in town with a friend until the storm blew over. It would be too hard to get to work.

"Harold," Lillian said, "if this keeps up, we won't be able to get to the barn. We've got to keep a path opened."

"Don't worry," Harold said. "I'll plow down the road. But I can't bring the tractor over the hill down the path to the house. Too steep.

Maybe we can shovel that out. But I've got snowshoes over at the cabin. I'll bring them over."

Harold brought the snowshoes and taught Lillian and Junior how to use them. She was clumsy on them and fell many times, but she was amazed at how she could walk right over the drifts. Junior couldn't seem to get the hang of it, but falling made him roll in fits of laughter. And the snow and wind continued and the temperature plummeted.

"It's a good thing that barn sits out of the wind," Harold said. "But the temperature is still goin' down pretty quick, Lillian. It's just above forty degrees in there. I don't know how much cold the cows can take."

"What can we do, Harold?" Lillian asked. "There must be something we can do."

"We can still get the cows out in the barnyard for a short spell each day. That 'll give them some light and fresh air and keeps them moving. Long as I can keep it plowed out."

But then the snow and cold became too intense and they kept the cattle inside. The cows began to get sluggish with the constant dark and cold; they ate less and started to dry up. Milk production sank quickly. They put a kerosene heater in the milkhouse to keep the spring from freezing, but they didn't dare put one in the barn. Junior was having a hard time getting to Lillian's every day. Sometimes he wouldn't get there until noon.

"Junior, you better stay over here until this storm blows over," Lillian told him. "We really need you to stay here."

"Sorry, Miss Lillian," Junior said. "Can't stay. My mom's alone and she's scared a' this storm. I better be home at night."

This answer made new pangs of guilt stab at Lillian. She remembered her actions during the tractor accident.

* * *

"Damn," Harold swore, when the thermometer dropped below 40 degrees in the barn. "Lillian, have you heard anything from the REP?."

"The REP?"

"Yes. They should have been by here a month ago," Harold said. "If we were hooked up, we could get light in here and electric heaters to keep the temperature up in the barn."

"No. No," Lillian said, "I haven't heard anything from them."

"Wonder what happened. Damn bad management, I guess. It better warm up soon. I don't like the way the cows are actin'"

Distant memories of hard winters on her parent's farm made her recall how bad hard weather could be for a farmer. All those years of soft town living; of being out of touch with nature had made her forget. Weather was a primal force up here; much more than just an inconvenience. It could be deadly. "If this storm continues," she said aloud to herself, "my cattle will surely die." She knew they were not toughened to these conditions like some of the common Holsteins were. But she allowed that times would be tough now for any breed.

She prayed for the snow and cold to stop; for the sun to reappear. And she cursed herself for her idyllic, wasteful dreams. Harold was right. With electricity things would be much safer. Much easier. The cattle could have light and some heat. And now even the old house was freezing with all its drafts and snow and ice creeping in upon the inside walls. One morning Bobby woke up with a strange feeling of warmth. His eyes opened in amazement when he saw his comforter covered with an inch thick layer of snow. After that they all slept in the kitchen or the parlor, as close to the hot stoves as possible. But they found that as the house froze and the cracks filled with snow, it became easier to keep warm. It was acting like an igloo.

"Lillian, that new Ford tractor of yours would be ideal for driving in the snow," Harold said. "Why in the hell didn't I tell you to buy the plow for it?"

But it was Harold's old John Deere Model B tractor that gave them comfort, the same one that Bobby had rolled over. It was tall and skinny and they had to put chains on the big wheels and be careful on a slope so as not to turn it over, but it was tough and powerful. And with the hand-made plow attachment hung on it, they were able to keep the barn doors clear of the huge snow drifts that mounded liked glazed pyramids in front. And the huffing, chugging two-cylinder engine brought some life to the otherwise frozen silence.

One blustery day it was so cold in the open shed where they kept the tractors, that she couldn't get the engine to turn over. "This bastardly weather is going to kill us all," she screamed in frustration and threw the can of Wilson's udder balm she'd been carrying at the tractor. The barn doors had to be cleared of snow by the tractor plow and opened to get the manure out. Finally, Junior was able to turn over the John Deere's engine with the hand crank after Harold warmed the crankcase with the kerosene heater.

"Lillian, I'm afraid that concrete floor is too cold, too damp," Harold said. "We got to put down a lot more hay and straw. And change it every day, maybe change it twice a day. It's real dry comin' out of the mow, but it gets damp on that concrete right away."

"Harold, we're running low on hay. Didn't you know?"

"Running low? Damn, I guess I haven't noticed. How about straw?"

"We still have lots of straw," Lillian said. "We better keep the hay for feed."

Later Harold was stuffing canvas and rags around the windows when he saw a heifer go down.

"Get up, girl," he said, and pulled on her neck and head.

But she wouldn't budge and just laid her head down on the straw. Short puffs of breath were coming from her nostrils. He went down to the house to get Lillian.

"One of the heifers is down," he said. "You best get some of them hot water bottles up there right away. I'm goin' over to Pecks to phone the vet."

"Which one Harold? Which one is it?"

"I think it's the one you call... Marylou?"

"Oh, God. Harold, can you get to Pecks?"

"I loaded that old truck with sand. I should be able to."

Doc Farley Mckuen struggled through the snow drifts that day in response to their call, but he was unable to save the heifer.

"You've got to get some heat in this barn or they're all going to die," the vet said. "And It's best if you let them loose in the barn. They'll find the warmest place and then they'll keep each other warm. It's hard on milking and cleanup, but it might just hold them till this storm lets up." they pulled the dead heifer behind the barn and buried her deep in the snow. The vet said she was still good to eat, but Lillian refused to do it. She said there was no place to butcher it in this weather. And she really couldn't bring herself to eat Marylou.

"That's the fifth animal down this week," Farley said. "Worst cold we've had in years."

The vet's warnings made Lillian panic. She believed that the worst would yet happen. They turned the cows loose and they all moved to the back of the barn, where there was no concrete floor. And they huddled together and seemed to improve. They were eating more and some milk could be stripped from their shrunken udders.

They decided to run up both the Ford and the John Deere engines outside until they were hot and then move the tractors into the barn and turn them off. She was amazed at how quickly the engines cooled, but the temperature inside the barn did rise a few degrees. Harold made big canvas flaps with his harness repair tools and covered the barn doors to keep in the heat when they took the tractors back out to warm the engines again.

They pondered connecting a flexible pipe to the exhaust pipes and running the exhaust outside the barn so they could keep the engines running in the barn. Harold went to Peck's and called the vet and asked him about that.

"What's that you say? Run the engines in the barn? Flexible exhaust pipes? Well, now that's a great idea... if you want to get out of the dairy business quickly. Hell no, don't you even think of it. The slightest leak and all them cows 'll be dead." The vet's opinion confirmed what Harold and Lillian had already believed. But they were desperate for solutions.

They struggled for three more days and nights. Finally, the storm blew itself out. The sun came out one day, a dull, weak imitation of its former self, but the radiant, joyful sun nevertheless. Lillian thanked God for letting her little farm pull through this awful time. And the next day the sun shone again and the huge icicles started to melt and there was a sense of renewal in the air; another second chance as Maynard said.

Lillian fully understood now what was meant when they said that farming up here was a real gamble: the winter storms could quickly kill your livestock. Lillian shook off the sense of despair that had gripped her during the storm; survival now seemed possible. Yet the experience had marred her dream and she resolved to reconsider the electric power option.

Shortly after the storm had passed Harold greeted her unhappily when she came home from school. It was a dark, brooding day with low, hovering clouds, pregnant with snow.

"How could you, Lillian? How could you?"

"What's wrong now Harold?" she asked, her mood matching the weather.

"What's wrong? I think you're wrong, Lillian. Wrong again. Why on earth did you ask the REP to bypass us?"

"How did you find that out?"

"I went down to the office today to see what was up; to see why they hadn't connected us. They told me you had signed a bypass order. I can't believe you Lillian."

She looked into his dark eyes and could see nothing there. No feeling. No understanding. She took off her heavy coat and swept the snow off her boots out on the porch.

When he saw she wasn't going to answer him, he asked again, but with less anger. "Maybe I'm missing something, Lillian. I'd just like to know why?"

She started busying herself with preparing supper. "I don't think you'd understand, Harold."

"Try me."

She sighed. "I've said it all before, Harold. But I'll say it once more. This place is part of a dream for me. It's a dream I've always had but never fully understood. You know, like having a really satisfying dream, but when you're awake you just can't grasp what it was all about? Well, when I bought this place, I finally realized what my dream was all about. It was to do something like this; to live like this. And part of it is the natural beauty and basic honesty of everything here." She went to the sink and started pumping water. The pump whooshed and squeaked as the suction pulled up the stream of cold water. "I'm just afraid that connecting up will change everything here. The dream will be destroyed."

He drummed on the table with his fingers. "I don't know much about dreams," he said. "But I guess there's dreams and then, up here, there's reality. The storm we just had was, to me, reality. And maybe, just maybe because of your dream, you could of lost everything. Don't you think that's too much to pay for a dream?"

She looked at him and sighed. "Yes Harold. It is too much too pay." She lifted the lids on the Merrimac and stirred the coals. "But what is reality Harold? Isn't it too, just an illusion? Must we only live with reality. Aren't dreams real?" She was tired of Harold's cold, unimaginative practicality.

"Dreams real? What do you mean Lillian?"

She shook her head. "Oh, nothing." She put a pot of water to boil on the stove. "But you're right Harold. I mean about the electric program and getting hooked up. "

He looked at her, hoping he understood. "Well, now you've seen how bad it gets. A body needs all the help it can get to survive in this place." He smiled faintly. "Here, now here's a new application for a hook-up, Lillian. I brought it from the office today. You best put it in."

He was trying to be helpful, she knew. And he had been critical for their survival during the storm crisis. Yet he was no longer much of a husband. Since she had returned from her trip, her bed had remained cold. Harold's drinking was on the rise. He was coming in later every night and leaving early in the morning. She was tired of battling with him over his late coming and drinking. The nights of enjoying each other's company and making love seemed to be over.

Lillian resolved to confront Harold about his unacceptable ways but before she could, news came out of Peck's that Paul Grisinski had been killed in combat.

CHAPTER 2

The deep snowless cold matched the sadness of the small rural community of friends that knew Able Grisinski's family. The death of "that nice quiet boy" shook everyone's faith in themselves and in the government. They kept hearing reports from the radio and newspapers and TV that Washington said the war would end soon, that there was nothing really going on at the front. And now this; the unimaginable, the unacceptable, happens.

After the funeral, Lillian and Harold went to Able's house where the people had gathered. Food prepared by neighbors, including Lillian, was served. Everyone tried to cheer up and small, uneasy jokes about farming circulated around the kitchen and parlor where they gathered. Lena was deathly ill but made a brief appearance.

"I want to thank everyone for coming," she said, her voice cracking. "Paul was a wonderful son." Then she retired, not to be seen again.

Lillian and Harold joined Able in the kitchen with Maynard Peck and other local neighbors. Able wanted to stay out of the parlor where his relatives had gathered. Lillian found him in deep despair. He was angry with himself.

Able was a few years younger than Lillian. He was a big man with a reddish complexion, and a tough, bulldog appearance, yet he appeared good-looking because he was usually smiling.

Able didn't rage against the war, against the government, or against the enemy: he raged only against himself.

"Able, I know how you must feel. But you can't blame yourself. Paul had to live his own life. He was a brave young man."

"I know, I know," Able said. "But everything is just upside down right now. I can't think about nothing except that he would be alive right now if I had just forbid him to go. I wasn't strong enough. He would have been unhappy, but alive."

She comforted him the best she could, but thought it best not to be drawn too deeply into his anguish.

Then Lillian left Able and Harold and went into the parlor to pay her respects. Able's son, Pete, sat in a far corner in an overstuffed chair, looking forlorn. Able said that Pete blamed himself for Paul's death. The younger son, John, was in and out, handling the farm chores that still had to be done.

In spite of the jokes, the relatives seemed, by nature, a cheerless lot. Lillian was making the rounds, introducing herself, when she noticed a fat woman, seated across the room, making a commotion. Several people stood around, trying to calm her.

"Who is that?" Lillian asked a friendly grey-haired woman who had introduced herself as Able's cousin.

"That's Edith, Able's sister," she replied. "The funeral must of stirred her up. Epileptic, you know."

Lillian watched as Able's sister emitted a loud groan and tried to stand up. The people tried to keep her seated, but she managed to get loose and rolled onto the floor. She started thrashing violently and a blanket Lillian had thought was part of her dress, came flying off. They tried to calm her on the floor.

"Oh Lord," one of the older women said, "Please drive Satan from poor Edith's body," and she held tightly to Edith's hand. When the fit subsided a bit, they carried her to a bedroom in the back of the house. The woman who had been praying, cried. It had been a hard time for them all.

CHAPTER 3

A week later, Able stopped by Lillian's place. "Lillian," he said, " you need that Jersey bull of mine. I'll sell him to you for a hundred dollars."

She was puzzled by the offer. "Why that's giving him away Able. Why do you want to get rid of him?"

"Got to sell out, Lillian. Selling everything."

Lillian was shocked. Able was her nearest and dearest neighbor. Someone with a deep interest in farming like her. "Able, what happened?" she said. "I can't believe it."

"Can't do it no more Lillian. Everything's against me." Able seemed dazed. "You see, Pete, why he's gone and re-enlisted for six years."

"Re-enlisted?" she asked, surprised.

He sighed. "Yup. And it's all clear now. Pete let himself be drafted in the first place 'cause he wanted to get away from the farm. He never was like Paul, you know. He always was wanting to do something besides farmin'."

"I'm really sorry to hear that Able," she said. "You never know these days, do you. Here, sit and have a cup of coffee. I still have some from breakfast."

He sat down and took some coffee. "Yeh. And I tried to change his mind, but I shouldn't have. You know, some are just not cut out for farmin'. Anyway, without my two older boys, I can't operate. Me and John can't handle it."

She sat down at the table. "Able, this seems to be happening to all the small farmers like us. Staying in business depends on the family staying together, but families are splitting up. All these wars seem to have a lot to do with it. And without everyone pitching in, you just can't make a go of it."

Able nodded agreement. "And John, well he's growing up too.

No telling where his interests may lie. I won't make the same mistake with him I made with Pete. I'll send him to school, if that's what he wants. Won't put no pressure on him to stay on the farm."

"Can't you hire help?" But she already knew the answer to that question and answered it herself. "Never works, does it."

Able shook his head.

"What will you do, Able?" she asked. "Won't you stay here?"

"Figure I gotta sell, Lillian," he said, with a hoarseness in his voice. He kept his eyes focused on his coffee cup. "With Lena so sick and John maybe fixing to leave, I don't know. That's a mighty big place for a body to live alone, Lillian. Mighty big. But damn, it's my home. Been in my family for a long time. Can't think about livin' someplace else. Leastwise, not yet."

Lillian knew that Able had just started rebuilding his herd. He had been planning on Pete coming home and with his place being hooked up to electric power, he had added milking machines and upgraded the barn. Then he'd bought a new Farmall tractor and wagons to replace the aging equipment he had.

"Able, if you want to keep that farm, we'll help you," she said with some enthusiasm, grasping for any solution at all. "Everything we have, and I'll allow it isn't much, but it's there for you to use. We've got two tractors and really don't need them both. Harold isn't cutting much anymore. Maybe if you get rid of some of that new equipment, you can make it with a smaller herd?" She sounded desperate. Able had been a tremendous help for her.

Able looked at her and then shook his head. "Thanks, Lillian. That's mighty kind of you. I'll think on it. But I'll keep that bull for you in any case."

CHAPTER 4

Harold was desperate. His clumsiness and inability to have some kind of normal relationship with Lillian had driven him to start seeing Rosemary again. She made him feel good; took away his depression. At first, he was cautious and parked around the block from her house.

Rosemary realized that Harold was becoming an important part of her life. She was also beginning to feel strongly that Lillian had cheated her; had moved on Harold without giving her a chance.

"Harold, did you love Lillian when you married her?" she asked him.

Harold looked at her, puzzled. "Don't know about love, Rosemary, maybe I thought I was in love... maybe."

"What do you feel for me? Is it love?"

"I like you Rosemary. I like being near you."

"But is it love? Or... do I just take the place of Lillian?"

"No Rosemary, no. I don't think of Lillian when I'm with you."

They were drinking coffee in Rosemary's kitchen. She poured him a fresh cup.

"Are you going to keep seeing me?" she asked.

"Rosemary, you know I like being here."

"Harold, please, please. Are you going to leave Lillian? Are you going to stay with me?" She was desperate to get him to do something to make their affair more solid, more legitimate.

He looked at her. "We'll see, I guess," he said.

"Well, we just can't keep sneaking around like this," she said.

"We'll see."

But when he kept coming back, Rosemary felt surer of herself. She told him he must make the break with Lillian. But Harold insisted on waiting. He didn't want to move to Fultonville; it was too far from the cabin; too far from everything he liked. And Rosemary was beginning to show a side he didn't like. She wanted him to make a complete break with his former life.

She wanted him to get a job.

"It's a factory mechanic's job," she said. "You'd fix things when they broke. The man who has the job now is retiring; moving out. My cousin, Ed Giles, is the supervisor there and I know I can get you on. You can learn how to fix that stuff, I'm sure." She had everything planned. "And after we tell Lillian, you can move in here." Rosemary wouldn't consider living in Harold's cabin in the wilderness. She also told him to sell his horses. And she wanted him to sell his logging equipment and the cabin. But Harold said no.

"I really don't want that job, Rosemary," he told her. "First off, I don't know how to fix all that stuff, as you say, and I ain't about to learn. And I ain't selling my logging equipment. I expect to be getting a contract soon. I was talking to Preston's the other day and--."

"I know, I know," she said, desperate that she couldn't change him. "What *do* you want to do Harold? We can't go on like this. We've got to tell Lillian and then what are you going to do? Obviously, you can't continue to stay with her." Harold didn't answer.

And their passion gradually cooled as he relentlessly resisted Rosemary's ever increasing plans and conditions. Now their discussions were turning into arguments. Harold became disillusioned.

CHAPTER 5

Spring arrived late that year, and the cottage was finished except for some interior work and painting. It was too wet from frequent rains to paint and the builder said he would wait for it to dry up. Lillian thought the little cottage was perfect; it seemed to fit right into the natural magic of the small island and the rest of the farm.

The cattle recovered from the killing air of winter, but milk production was still off and she knew she would have to wait until calving before it would pick up again. She registered the herd with the Herd Improvement Association and started keeping records on each cow. This was done mostly as a check on her own husbandry and out of love for her cattle.

She'd made several attempts to visit Rosemary, but the snow and ice had made it too dangerous. Now she was desperate to see her friend again.

Robert was closer and the road was better. She met with him whenever she could; that is whenever she had money to give him. Nothing had changed. If anything, he looked more consumed than before. "You don't look well," she said, at their last meeting. He was gaunt and his skin had a yellow cast to it. His hands were beyond trembling, they were starting to shake.

"Don't feel very hot, either," he said with a stringy voice. "Seem to have a tough case of the flu. Fever... stomach, you know."

She wondered how germs could live in the volatile brew flowing in his veins. "Maybe you should see a doctor," she said.

He shrugged and smiled "You know, it's Maryann I'm worried about. She's not carrying the baby well. She's been bleedin' a lot lately."

"And you haven't seen the doctor?"

"Well no. We don't have the money. You know that. And she

won't go to no charity clinic." He was quiet for a minute, examining his coffee cup. "She wouldn't go anyway, even if we had the money."

"Why not?"

He folded his arms and sat back in the booth, without looking directly at her. "Do we have to go through this every time we meet? Can't you understand what taking Bobby away from us meant to her?" His features hardened into a frown. "I mean you might as well tell her to her face that she was a failure as a mother."

"And so she is. I took Bobby because you both were incapable of giving him the care and love he needed," she said, her eyes blazing angrily. "And you know that. Don't try to blame everything on me. But what's that got to do with her bleeding?"

"She just doesn't care. I think she's really depressed."

"Well that's absurd," she said, frustrated by the constant whining. "I'm going to make an appointment with a doctor for her... and you're going to take her. I'll pay for whatever care she needs. But you tell her it's your decision. Maybe that way she'll go."

"Well, I'll try," he said, trying to steady the coffee cup. "She's gettin' pretty weak. Maybe she will go."

"Why didn't you tell me this sooner? How can you take it so casually?"

"First off," he said, looking at her directly for the first time, "you don't have a phone. I don't have a car, and there aren't any busses out to your place. Second, I have fought with her to get her to see a doctor. But she's set in her ways. She says it'll all pass. But I can see there's more to it than she thinks."

* * *

What he didn't tell Lillian was that she wouldn't see the doctors because she told him they made her feel like a low-life for her drinking; she couldn't hide the signs of alcoholism. They told her that she should have never got pregnant: that her heavy drinking could damage the child's health. She told Robert that even when they didn't say something, she knew what they were thinking: that she had been the cause of her husband's downfall. But Robert knew that wasn't really true; It was he who had brought her down.

Before marrying, Maryann had been a pretty red-haired girl. She was healthy then and had clear skin and a most remarkable and beautiful mouth. And when he came back from the war, broken in mind and spirit, and now a heavy drinker, she thought she could cure him: Robert, so fragile, so hopeless, so unable to deal with his experiences. He had depended on her for strength, but she'd not enough strength to handle the heavy burdens he bore and she too had fallen under his weaknesses. She'd learned to swill gin, so they could stay together. They'd both become dissolute and alcoholic, unable to keep promises made. The constant drinking took its toll; her health failed, her complexion turned red and rough and her hair faded. She lost her looks, no one would say she was pretty anymore.

Lillian, out of ignorance, had shared Matt's perspective and that caused her dislike for Maryann. But now, knowing about the bleeding, it made her feel concerned, regardless of her other feelings.

"Here, take this," Lillian said." I'll call and make an appointment for Maryann on an emergency basis." She had scribbled the name and phone number of a doctor she would call. He was lighting another cigarette and she found it irritating to watch him smoke so much. She noticed that their surly waitress seemed to be smoldering in a corner of the little diner. "Tomorrow, you call that number and find out when your appointment is. And don't forget!"

"I won't, he rasped and started coughing. "But I'll try to get her to go," he repeated. "Oh... and that place you're building out on your farm? I know about that place... know why you're building it. I ain't movin' in there... she would never agree to that. Couldn't live out there no way."

She was shocked by this unexpected attack on her secret plans for the cottage. "How... how did you find out?" she asked. "What makes you think... "

"Oh, I know alright. And I just heard it goin' around."

"Going around where?"

"No place in particular. Word just gets out."

She sorted the facts: only Linda and Harold and Rosemary knew that the cottage had anything to do with her brother. Even the builder didn't know she was building it for him. But Harold never went near Robert. She couldn't see any reason for Rosemary to talk to her brother about the cottage. So that left Linda as the most likely one. She still visited her uncle on certain occasions, like for his birthday. "Linda told you, didn't she?"

"I'm not saying anyone told me. And what if she did?"

"Oh, nothing. It's not important." She didn't want the discussion to break down over who told him. But it was important to her. If Linda told him, then it was just a niece telling her uncle some news about something important to him. But if it were Harold, it could mean that he was trying to undo her efforts to get Robert to move out to the cottage.

The diner was busy and the frowning waitress came over and asked if they wanted the check, but Lillian ordered another coffee. "People are waiting for tables, you know," the unhappy blonde said. Lillian just stared at her and she left.

"Robert. That's going to be a nice cottage," she said, while watching the waitress. She was talking with another and pointing to their table. "And it won't cost you a cent. It's new. It's clean. Not like that terrible place you live in now. It could change your whole life. I just want to help you and Maryann."

Robert shook his head. "How? By trying to control our lives?" He shook another cigarette out of his pack and lit it. The one he had been smoking was still burning in the ashtray. "It won't work I tell you. She'll never agree to that. Wouldn't it be a lot cheaper to just give me the money for my rent? That would be a help. No, I'll not move out there."

* * *

Maryann never kept the appointment that Lillian had made. She didn't want to face any strange doctor. And two weeks later she was rushed to the hospital, hemorrhaging. They stopped it, but the forced withdrawal from gin and cigarettes made her worse. Within three days of entering the hospital she started with violent seizures and during one particularly strong one, she aborted their second son. When she died later from severe hemorrhaging, the contractor was putting the finishing touches on the interior of the cottage. Before Lillian could do anything, her brother disappeared.

CHAPTER 6

Lillian returned from work at school a few days later, preoccupied with thoughts of Robert, to find Glenda Ellison waiting for her on the porch.

"Oh, I'm so glad I caught you," Glenda said. She sounded desperate, as if Lillian could help solve some great problem for her. Lillian knew Glenda from teacher's conferences they'd attended together.

"I hope Bobby's not in trouble?" Lillian said, only half serious with her question.

"I'm sorry to say it could be big trouble, Mrs. Sims. Those girls are at it again, and I've got to do something, and quick." Her voice was agitated.

"What girls? What are you talking about?" The air of concern coming from Glenda Ellison worried her. Harold had told her nothing about the problem with the girls and Bobby's truancy.

"You don't know? Your husband didn't tell you?" Her eyes opened wide.

"No," Lillian said meekly, as if she had done something wrong.

Glenda Ellison sighed. "I better come in," she said. "This could take a while." She told Lillian about the same bizarre incidents she had related to Harold last fall. She was careful in reconstructing the story to be accurate and in many instances had to pause to think, to be sure she was right.

"Oh, God," Lillian said when she had finished. "This is the worst teacher nightmare come true. And my own nephew is involved."

"I didn't report the girl's actions," Glenda repeated, "because of Bobby. And I am concerned for myself, too. But those girls are brazen. Now that the weather's nice they're doing it again and I can't protect myself or Bobby anymore." She seemed exhausted by her decision.

"Is it the same as before?" Lillian asked.

"Almost. They were just getting the two little ones to take off their clothes." She was wringing her hands; squeezing them until they were bloodless.

"Glenda, what do you think they can do?" she asked. "Go to the Board with that story? Or have they changed the story from Bobby to this new boy?"

"No, no. They won't change the story. Remember, they have their parents convinced that it was Bobby. Creating a new culprit would raise a lot of suspicion." She shook her head, as if desperate for words. "It's the way they looked at me when I caught them this time. They didn't scatter and run like the first time." She closed her eyes and grimaced when she recalled the details.

"What did they do?" Lillian asked, her concern mounting.

"I caught them in back of the school this time. They looked at me in a most peculiar way, especially the one I think is the leader, Sally Rigger. If eyes could kill, I would be dead now."

"Did they threaten you with harm?"

"Oh no. They're much to clever for that. This Sally Rigger threatened me with going to the school board. She said I was harassing them to protect certain bad boys and the school board would certainly dismiss me. I really believe she was negotiating with me to leave them be; to let them continue what they were doing." She shook her head in disbelief.

"You're right. That *is* brazen." Like most teachers, Lillian had a few difficult kids in her classes and knew where to draw the line. "I wouldn't hesitate to turn them in. You've got to get them under control."

"Yes. But you see, I thought it was under control. After I went to their parents, I thought those girls would be afraid to do anything again. And your husband; he agreed to let it go, rather than jeopardize Bobby." She rested her elbow on the round table, dropping her forehead on the heel of her hand. "Do you think then, that I should go to the board?" She was pleading for support.

"Definitely." Although Lillian was concerned for Bobby, she had the will to do something. "But first we need to visit the parents of those girls again. They can't all be so easily fooled. There has to be a key to this. Who are these people, anyway?"

"I'm not so sure they are fooled," Glenda said. "At least not Sally's mother. These are strange people; strange indeed. Let's see; there's Sally Rigger of course, and her mother; there's Hannah Green, she lives with her aunt and uncle, the Baumanns, and--"

" I know of the Baumanns," Lillian interrupted. "At least mister Baumann. I've seen him come into Peck's store. Lots of talk about that strange gentleman, I'm afraid."

"Yes. They're immigrants from Holland, I think." She paused to think about the strange couple she'd met. "But I'm not really sure. At least the house was clean when I went to see them. That's more than I can say for the other two." She shook her head. "But they got very upset when I suggested that Hannah was involved in this affair."

Glenda asked for some water and they moved from the parlor to the kitchen. "And of course, there's Susan Slovochek," she continued. "She's twelve, but she's, well, she's well developed and has the body of a sixteen-year-old. She lives with her parents. They have a small farm near the school. Kind of a seedy bunch, seven kids, I think. But they were friendlier then the others. They said it must all be some kind of mistake."

"I know the Slovocheks," Lillian said. "I met them at the county fair."

"Umm, that's good that you know some of these people. Have you ever met Mildred Rigger? That's Sally's mother."

"No. Never met her, and I'll confess, I never heard of them either. Do they live close by?"

"Not too far, but it's hard to find. You go up Sand Lake road about four miles and then turn off to the left and go up a dirt road about two miles. A little house deep in the woods. Mrs. Rigger is very strange."

"How so?" Lillian asked.

"Well, when I visited them, I couldn't believe the squalor they live in. Things were all over like they had just been thrown there; garbage, bones, clothes, pans and god knows what else. But more than that, there were signs of occult activities in that house."

"Occult?" Lillian said. "That is strange. What did you see?"

"I'm not very familiar with these things," Glenda said, "but there were strange symbols painted on the inside walls of the house. The kind that you see in these horoscopes they print in the newspaper? I remember some star-shaped things and a divided circle with symbols inside the circle. There were more, but I can't describe them. But this Mildred Rigger was about as cold and unfriendly and ugly as a person can get. When I tried to tell her what I'd seen, she repeated Sally's story about Bobby and demanded that I leave. She said I was trespassing and that they would go to the board if I didn't get out. She was quite--- quite horrible."

"That sounds frightening," Lillian said.

"Oh, it was. And Sally Rigger is just a skinny twelve-year-old with stringy blonde hair. Who would ever think she would do something like this? I think her mother is a bad influence. From the way they act, I think Sally is leading the other two girls by the nose. She moved here just last year and has been trouble ever since."

"We better go talk with the parents of Hannah and Susan," Lillian said. "Maybe we can stop this before it gets out of control."

CHAPTER 7

Lillian visited the Baumann's and although at first, they were hostile, her calm, reassuring ways at least got them to listen.

"It's a wicked thing that's going on at school, Mrs. Baumann," Lillian said. "We must do everything we can to stop it. We can only do that if we find out the real truth."

"I believe Hannah is telling the truth," Mrs. Baumann said.

"Yes, I understand that," Lillian replied. "But Miss Ellison and Bobby are telling the truth, too. So, there must be something else to this, some other kind of truth. For Hannah's sake and Bobby's sake, will you help me find it?"

"How can I help?"

"First you must believe that Miss Ellison is telling the truth. If you let me talk to Hannah? Maybe I can--"

"No, I cannot do that."

Lillian left the interview disappointed, but hoped she had planted some seed of doubt.

But the accusation against Bobby was made nevertheless after Miss Ellison made her report and requested a suspension for the three girls. Bobby was temporarily suspended because of the insistence of one board member, while the remaining nervous board members considered the conflicting charges. It was agreed to keep it quiet until the board could make some resolution.

But Hannah's aunt did become concerned and suspicious. She could sense a change in Hannah's behavior, something she had been noticing for some time now. And the words of Miss Ellison and Mrs. Sims seemed to ring with the truth.

"That Bobby deserves punishment," Hannah said to her aunt after the first hearing.

"Yes, he does," she replied. "He should be taken from class

until he knows good from wrong behavior. His father... bad upbringing, no doubt."

Hannah looked at her aunt with burning eyes. "I think it should be worse. I think he should be made to suffer pain," Hannah replied. "Sally said they should use pliers to pull out his fingernails and twist off... his..." She grimaced and stopped short of saying "nuts", that strange, forbidden word Sally had used so many times.

"What... What did you say, young lady?" the aunt asked. Her smile disappeared and her grey eyes flared and narrowed.

"Oh, nothing... I mean, just that he should be hurt."

Aunt Katy, as Hannah called her, saw a glow in Hannah's eyes she had never seen before. It frightened her and caused her to reconsider Miss Ellison's words. Besides, she had seen that awful Sally Rigger girl at the hearing. She decided to find out more about Hannah's new friends.

She made a visit to Sally Rigger's mother. The mother had not shown up at the hearing, but had sent a signed note. Mr. Baumann drove her out to the small house, late one afternoon. "We should not get involved " he'd said before they left. "I warn you, it could be bad for us."

The sun was still in the tree tops when they arrived at the old house hidden back in the woods. Mr. Baumann stayed in the car. When Hannah's aunt approached the house, the trees thickened and seemed to envelop the house and the sky darkened. The closer she got to the house, the darker it became. When she knocked on the door, a chill went through her bones.

No one answered her knock, which she thought was loud enough in that still evening air. She moved over and looked through a dirty window by the side of the door. An old woman was standing against the dim glow from a kerosene lamp. She looked frightful and appeared to be frozen, in some kind of trance. Her long grey hair was askew in every direction and her dress was unbuttoned halfway down the front, at times exposing her sagging, flat breasts. She looked directly at the window but seemed to see nothing. Hannah's aunt stepped over to the door and after hesitating, knocked again.

She was frightened but determined to gain something from this trip. There was a rattling and crashing from within making her jump and she stepped back and almost fell off the low porch. She shook herself and regained her wits and then looked through the small window again.

The fire was pouring out of the woodstove. The top plates were off and it seemed that the stove had been violently stoked. The woman stood with the iron poker in her hand, facing the wall, the tip of the poker glowing red. Symbols on the wall blazed in the firelight and the woman took the poker and waved it around in front of the figures on the wall. This frightened her so that she ran back up the path to the car.

"I say to you Frank, there is something very strange going on in that house," she said in short breaths." When that woman didn't show up at the hearing, I was thinking something was wrong. Why would she just send a note with her daughter? Now she is just jumping around like a crazy woman in there. She is half naked. No one answers the door."

"I say to you: we should not get involved," he said. "If she is crazy and naked and jumping around, that is her business." She could see his furrowed brow in the light from the instruments.

"Oh, no Frank. Not only her business. Something is wrong with Hannah. I think this woman and her daughter are maybe the cause. We must find what this is about."

But questioning Hannah that evening only brought out more vivid signs of her new churlishness. Mr. Baumann saw this in Hannah for the first time and he and Mrs. Baumann became very concerned. They were now convinced she was lying.

The Baumanns were Roman Catholic; something they tried to keep very quiet. It was one of the reasons for Mr. Baumann's strange behavior. There were no Catholics in the area and certainly no catholic church. They seldom went to church, but when a special catholic feast day occurred, they drove all the way to Amsterdam to attend Mass. And now, since they had no one else to turn to, they decided to ask for advice from the Monsignor of the church. He listened carefully and then decided they should put Hannah under the charge of a certain priest well versed in these affairs.

After several forced interviews, Hannah became more subdued, especially after her uncle forbid her to be with Sally Rigger. Finally, she broke down and told of her part in the school scandal.

"Why, Hannah, why did you do this thing?" her aunt asked.

Hannah squirmed under the question. "I guess I believed what Sally told us," she said. "She told us that parents and teachers were liars; that they never told the truth."

"Why did you believe her?" she asked.

""I don't know... she has a power to make you believe things. She said things like parents lied especially about... sex, and gave lots of examples of how they lie."

"What kind of examples?"

"Well, like the lie about the stork bringing babies. Things like that. She said grown-ups lie all the time about sex. She said they always do it and then pretend they don't."

"Oh, Hannah, Hannah. What kind of things are you getting into?" She shook her head in disgust.

"I'm sorry aunt Katy. I didn't know what I was doing. Sally told us it was right to teach the little ones the truth about sex. That's why we did it, aunt Katy. I'm really sorry.

* * *

Susan Slovochek also began to feel pressure after Miss Ellison's second visit, accompanied by Lillian. She'd trapped herself with several lies. She was also tired of being told what to do by Sally Rigger.

Under further questioning by her father, she admitted her part in the affair. Eventually both girls admitted that Sally had been the leader; had shown them what to do. But Sally never admitted anything.

The two girls were suspended from school until further notice.

Sally was expelled. Mildred Rigger was visited by a state child welfare officer, who was shocked by the conditions she saw in the house. But she was afraid of Mildred Rigger and went to get help. Before they could do anything, Sally and her mother disappeared.

The Baumann's came under such fierce criticism from the local people because of Hannah's role in the incident, that they too were forced to move out of the area. Only Susan survived because her parents were well liked by the locals.

Shortly thereafter, the little school was shut down and the building put up for sale. The students were bussed to other townships where there were at least three separate grade rooms. Miss Ellison was reassigned to a new school district. Bobby was, at last, exonerated. He had been glad to get out of that school.

CHAPTER 8

Lillian braced herself and turned in a new application for power. But it seemed like it would be more than a year before they would come out. The man explained that the program was virtually finished and there were only a few people left to complete the most remote installations up north of her.

Harold was no longer helping much and when Linda saw the desperation and worry in her mother's face, she decided to help in the barn. She still hated the smell of cow manure and the animals themselves, but she started to learn how to milk. It was still disgusting to her, but she'd run out of arguments against the farm. Her mother's determination could not be overcome; she would sacrifice almost anything.

Lillian showed her how to milk. "You lightly pull and lightly squeeze at the same time," she said, showing her the hand grip. "You never want to jerk or use too much pressure or you'll hurt her and she won't let down."

Linda finally got the courage to try. Lillian gave her the gentlest cow, flora. Linda grasped the two teats as if they were tractor levers and gently squeezed, but nothing happened. The cow moved her feet uneasily. Then after a few more pulls, Linda gradually squeezed harder and the prize Jersey kicked the milk pail out from between her legs and she screamed and fell backwards off the milking stool. "Idiot cow!" she screamed, with her legs kicking up in the air. "Who do you think you are?" The cow mooed. Lillian and Junior were holding their sides, trying to stop the laughing pains. Linda tried again and the cow kicked a second time. Linda stormed out of the barn cursing the cow and farms in general. She went down to the house and sulked in the kitchen.

When Harold came in a little later, she was still furious. "Why the hell aren't you helping my mother run this damn farm. You're eating here, aren't you? You're sleeping here? At least, sometimes.

You should get your ass up there in the barn and help out." Her eyes were blazing.

"Whoa," he said. What's gotten into you? Who turned you on?" He was turning red.

"I'll tell you who turned me on. I can't believe you, you bastard. After screwing me, you go and marry my mother." It had slipped out in this blaze of fury. This thing that she always wanted to say but always felt the fear that doing so would hurt her mother. "Now I have to live with that the rest of my life. What kind of man are you?"

"You! You should talk. You and your ways. You're the one that did everything! You made me."

"Made you? Ah. You're ready to drop your pants for any skirt that you see! I've seen you looking at Rosemary like you'd like to have her if you could." Harold winced at the mention of Rosemary. It stopped his retort cold. "You better start helping around here or *get* out." Her eyes were filled with fury. "That's all I've got to say to you." She flew out of the house and into her car and drove off. She was angry but glad she had finally had it out with him.

Harold's stomach knotted up; he knew he had been tiptoeing on a very thin tightrope. Linda's outburst frightened him and he felt he was about to fall. Harold left the house for his cabin. He was afraid he would be unable to face Lillian; he would go to see Rosemary later.

CHAPTER 9

Rosemary's continued absence was like a needle in Lillian's side. She was at odds to explain it except for Harold. Had she misunderstood her old friend? Had it been more than just a passing fancy; more than just a desire for companionship? Had Rosemary been in love with Harold?

She missed their days together, their shared history and intimacies; the deep knowledge of each other's philosophies and desires. When she went to the root cellar to fetch potatoes or other wintering vegetables, she would see Rosemary's dark red cabbages, still hanging upside down by their roots, still seemingly fresh and pungent. The root cellar was small; only a little deeper than a grave and ten feet wide and the cabbages occupied a good part of it. Then one day it struck her as a good excuse: Take a couple of the cabbage heads to Rosemary. She picked the nicest heads from the cellar and was surprised at their heaviness. She put them in an old Purina feed sack and tied the top with a string.

Harold wasn't home, although he'd been staying home lately a bit more than usual. She thought he was probably staying at the cabin. It was Saturday and Linda had already left to do shopping in town. After her morning chores were done, Lillian changed to plain brown wool pants and a heavy cotton blouse. She put on her black Navy pea coat, and examined herself in the bedroom mirror. It was her plain outfit, the one she wore when she wanted her country heritage to show through. It would be appropriate for this visit to Rosemary's.

She loaded the heavy cabbages in the trunk of the Buick and left Bobby and Junior to finish cleaning the barn. She was no longer afraid of Junior's wild and unpredictable ways. The accident seemed to have changed him.

The roads were clear and salt had melted the ice and snow down to the asphalt in many places. It was still bitterly cold at night and everything that melted during the day, froze solid again at night.

She drove slowly on the alternating patches of ice and water and slush, the wetness softly glistening in the weak sunlight of early spring. The slow progress and lack of traffic on the roads gave her time to think about her upcoming visit. Would bringing Rosemary some of her own cabbages seem silly? Would it matter? Wasn't their friendship more important than the slight she felt; the tiny strokes of anger that galled her because Rosemary had stayed away so long?

As she drove south, the dark forests of spruce and hemlock receded and now clean farm pastures came up to the road's edge. And she saw that the barns and silos grew in size as she reached south for Fultonville where Rosemary had moved last spring. And she knew that these farms rarely experienced the killing cold of her Adirondack farm and that if she lived down here, her life would be much easier, but she didn't want an easier life; there was a wild spirit in her farm that she cherished; It was a special place where she felt she belonged.

On her way she passed the old round barn on the Fletcher place. He'd kept a herd of thirty head, but wasn't big enough to compete with the big farms around him. When his wife ran off with the farm equipment salesman and his boys left, he moved to town and put the place up for sale. The realtor's sign had sat forlornly down at the end of the drive for several years now. She wondered if anyone would have the courage to buy it and try to farm the place.

Before she crossed the bridge over the old Eire canal into Fultonville, she thought about the Svenson creamery that was just a few miles down the road on the north side of the canal. She wanted to visit, but she feared raising William's passions once more. And she also thought it would be just an excuse to delay her meeting with Rosemary. So, she crossed the bridge and drove up Main to Elm street, where Rosemary lived. The tension mounted in her limbs and she gripped the steering wheel so tightly that she had difficulty staying in her lane on the narrow bridge.

Rosemary had inherited the house from her uncle. It was a house she had always loved much more than her own, even though it was no bigger. When she found she had inherited the place, she sold her old house and moved from Johnstown. Lillian remembered when she and Harold had moved some of Rosemary's furniture and things. Although it was a lot of work, they'd had much fun, too, and she remembered their light heartedness and laughter. It was still a time when laughter came easily between them.

She turned right on Elm and thought it was aptly named for the great trees that stood stark and naked on both sides of the street. A few cars were parked in front of the houses where the melting snowbanks had been dug out to make room. Other cars were parked in the shoveled-out driveways. The dark trunks of the trees stood out against the brilliance of the melting snow on the lawns and the white and yellow clapboard houses that lined the street.

As she slowly rolled down towards Rosemary's house, sliding over crusty ice that remained frozen because of the shade, a vision came her way. It was of dancing colors of grey rubber against faded sheets of blue, of rusted metal and dulled chrome, of cracked sparkling glass and rough-edged boards. The vision resolved itself into vague shapes like wheels and fenders and windows and slid around her; enveloping her so that she could hardly see. Her stomach flopped violently, and her lungs felt like she was breathing fire. She accelerated the Buick blindly, forgetting the melting ice and sunken snowbanks, to get past the choking, sucking image that was twisting her gut. Reaching the end of Elm street, she slid around the turn going south and headed quickly down the road back towards the canal. When she crossed the bridge again, she felt weak. She pulled off the road and parked the car. She felt she was going to throw up. After taking several deep breaths to clear her head, her uneasy stomach settled. The trembling stopped and she felt better. Then the cause of her sickness came into full recognition: Harold's old International was parked in Rosemary's driveway.

She sat there for a while, stunned, tears streaking down her cheeks. Then with fury, she remembered Rosemary's cabbages. She got out of the car and took the burlap bag full of cabbages out of her trunk. She walked back to the middle of the bridge. With a struggle, she slung the heavy bundle over the side and dropped it into the river below. It made a big splash and the current carried the widening ripples and the bag under the bridge.

She ignored the stares of a passing driver, a middle-aged man who couldn't ignore her. There was no traffic at that moment so he stopped and rolled down the window. “Is anything wrong?” he said. “Can I help you?”

She stared at him coldly. “No,” she said. “Nothing's wrong. I'm alright. It was just some old cabbages, anyway. Nothing more.”

He stared at her for a minute with questioning eyes and then gave a half wave with his right hand and slowly moved on. He kept looking up into the rear-view mirror as he moved across the bridge. She wondered what he would tell people about what he had seen. Would he tell the police? Would they dredge the bottom of the canal looking for something sinister in the burlap bag? Would he have her traced? She really didn't care. She was too weak to care.

CHAPTER 10

Lena Grisinski finally succumbed to her illness. In the latter stages, it was recognized as cancer and that fact cast a pale of gloom over the entire family. But her death came, in a way, as a relief to Able, because she had suffered so much.

Lillian, still smarting over Rosemary, now felt bad for Able who had suffered so many losses in the last few months. But at the same time that Lena passed on, another death had an even greater impact on her. She was shocked when Bill Svenson Jr. came out to talk with her.

"Mrs. Sims, We need to talk," young William told her, in his best matter-of-fact voice. He was standing on the porch steps. He declined her invitation to come into the house. She had never met him before and decided then that she didn't like him. He was pale and blonde and had aluminum-blue eyes and was dressed in a striped business suit. She believed he had never been on a farm.

"My father died last week. He had a heart attack."

She was shocked by his cold announcement. She stood there for a moment, unable to say anything. "I'm sorry," she finally said, with trembling lips. "Oh, I'm so sorry." and she cried. "He was a good friend---a good man."

"Yes, he was," he said, after a while. "But I didn't come out here for sympathy." Once more she was surprised and shocked by the icy tone in his voice and she tried to get her sobbing under control. He seemed to be waiting for her to stop crying and stared at her as if annoyed.

"What's wrong?" she finally managed to say.

"I know about that meeting you had with my father when you first came to see him," he said.

"Meeting? When I first came--?"

"Yes. Don't you remember? I have an office next door. I happened to open the door and saw you two embracing and kissing." Lillian had been taken off guard. She was embarrassed by his accusing tone and penetrating eyes. " Oh. I'm so sorry. That must have been awful for you, but it wasn't what you think. I know it must have not looked good, but we, we were just good friends and so happy to see each other."

"I don't think so," he said dryly.

"But it's true. I knew your father before he married... before you were born."

"I know. He finally told me."

"You talked to him about me... about us?"

"Yes. I told him what I had seen and asked for an explanation," he said haughtily.

"And?" Lillian was apprehensive. Why had she allowed that to happen?

"Look. I don't really want to discuss this. What I came to tell you is that *I* now run the creamery. I won't be renewing the contract my father had with you. It expires in two months." The words took Lillian's breath away.

"But Why?" she exclaimed with a trembling voice. "My herd is very special. Your father built his super premium ice cream on that milk." She knew she was pleading.

"Look. Mrs. Sims? I agreed with him on that in the beginning? But no more. We just don't need your milk anymore." He was being firm and businesslike.

"But why, for heaven's sake? Isn't the ice cream selling?" He stared at her, looking for some revelation of understanding. "You just don't know, do you?" he said, his voice shaking slightly.

"What do you mean? Know what?" she asked.

"That he was in love with you? That he fell into some kind of melancholy despair and six months after your meeting with him, my mother left him?" His eyes were filled with anger. "You see, he was no longer a husband to her. He was just brooding over you."

"But... I didn't know." She was trembling.

"I think you did," he said.

"But that's not true. I mean, I knew he was -- " She was getting confused. She believed that they had settled the feelings between them. Now she knew that she had been believing what she wanted to believe. "Maybe... I guess I didn't realize... I didn't understand."

"I still think you did," he said angrily and left her in a terrible state of grief.

CHAPTER 11

After the sounds of his car disappeared around the bend, she climbed the hill in back of the barn to the wooden bench she had Fred build. The bench was placed between two beech trees for shade in the summer and provided a view of her entire domain. She came here when she wanted to think or just be free from all the niggling complications of everyday life. She looked at the barn and fields and hills, and the dark, surrounding forest and tears came to her eyes. Her body trembled with grief and anger and she wasn't sure which emotion had the greater grip. Much time passed before she could control the flow of tears.

The cows were grazing in the field near the barn and she noticed how clear and clean the field was. When she first saw those fields, they were covered with wild brush and stringy saplings that had almost swallowed the succulent grasses with their deadly shade. Harold and Fred had worked hard to clear those fields. And she saw the barn roof standing proud and sharp against the horizon and again thought of the two men that had rebuilt it. She could almost see Fred hammering away at the walls. Off in the distance to the southeast, she could see a small leg of the creek, like a shining silver band through the blue mist. And she saw the rusting roof of the house she loved and parts of the unfinished cottage through the budding trees. "Will I lose it all?" she said aloud to the wind.

The young man had been cruel; he'd told her nothing. When did William die? Where was he buried? She would have to check the back issues of the newspaper. It hurt her to think that she had something to do with making William unhappy and with destroying his family, and perhaps, even with his dying.

She was deep in these thoughts when she noticed a movement down on the road. She recognized Harold's truck as it wound its way towards the house. In a flash the truck and Rosemary's house come back to her and the awful reality she had put out of her mind until now, returned. She ran down to the house.

When Harold arrived, she was waiting for him in front.

"Hi Lillian, he said, trying to be cheerful. "Sorry I'm late. I just bought some new milk filters in town. I knew we were low."

She hadn't seen Harold since her trip to Fultonville earlier in the week. She assumed he had been with Rosemary all that time.

"Harold, I want you to pack your things and leave. I put everything that belongs to you in the woodshed. I don't want you here anymore." She said this a with crisp intensity coloring her words but without any real anger showing through. She had rehearsed this moment in her mind.

Harold looked at her and blinked. "What?" he said, with an astonished voice. He immediately believed that Linda had talked with her mother.

"You understood what I said. I want you out of here." Her voice was still calm, although she was beginning to feel weak.

Harold had a wild look on his face. "Lillian. Look. It wasn't what you think. It really wasn't my fault. You can't believe *everything* that Linda says." He sounded desperate.

Suddenly Lillian's self-composure fell apart and her voice became shrill. "Linda?" she said with a grimace twisting her face. "Linda?" And suddenly she exploded. "Linda?"

Harold stood speechless. "What the hell are you trying to say?" she shouted.

Harold was in a panic. He failed to take the cue. "It was nothing, Lillian, " he blurted out. "Really. And it happened before we were married. I swear to you Linda and I haven't... haven't--", and words failed him.

Now all the calm went out of Lillian as the meaning of Harold's incoherent speech sank in. "You... miserable... snake. I know you're seeing... Rosemary!" she hissed, the anger running spittle to the corners of her mouth. "But I don't know what you're doing with Linda." Her mind filled with new sordid possibilities. "My God!" Are you screwing my daughter too?" Her eyes were blazing with fury.

“Get out. Get out, you scum!” She ran in the house and he called after her. “Lillian... Lillian.” She grabbed the rifle from the cupboard.

“listen to me!” he cried.

She ran out and leveled the rifle at him. She forgot it wasn't loaded. “Get out before I kill you right here!” she yelled. She was crying and waving the gun crazily. Harold was seized with the fear of possible sudden death and he ran back to the truck. “You're crazy,” he shouted as he got in the truck and took off.

CHAPTER 12

The day when Lillian passed Rosemary's house, Harold and Rosemary were having their final argument over her. It ended with Harold leaving with no intention of coming back.

At first, Rosemary was deeply saddened by her failure to keep Harold's love. Then her sadness turned into a gnawing anger. After a few days of misery, when she felt that Harold really wasn't coming back, she tried to look for work. Staying home alone was too much for her. But when she went out to apply for jobs, she found herself faced with questions she couldn't answer, asked by people she disliked. She had no skills; nothing to offer.

After a few tough interviews resulting in no offer, she decided to give it up. She didn't need the money. She stayed home again and her dark moods deepened; the anger gnawing at her soul. She would work in her yard and then clean the house furiously, but when she rested, she would think of Harold. She was obsessed by Harold; the longer he stayed away the more she wanted him. When she went for walks, she would see him in the street; see his truck in her driveway.

The days passed and little things began to snap and pop in Rosemary's head as her obsession turned into a black fury. She was beginning to believe that Lillian had stolen Harold from her and fierce jealousy wrapped its black thoughts around her heart. She blamed Lillian for the new levels of misery she now suffered and after several nights of nightmarish sleep with dreams of Harold's lost embrace, she decided something must be done. Visions of that night when she stayed at Lillian's and tried to get her to understand her feelings for Harold had come back to her. Lillian had shown no understanding; no compassion for her or Harold. Lillian had been stupidly selfish, Rosemary thought, and wanted him only to help her with her miserable farm. And when Harold continued to stay away, Rosemary's jealous hatred surfaced in a resolution: she must get rid of Lillian.

But Rosemary was confused by this new idea: she didn't know

how to get rid of someone. She wrestled with ideas and developed fantastic scenarios, but in the end, found them beyond her comprehension.

Before she could think of anything worth developing into a plan, she couldn't stand not seeing Harold and overcoming her wounded pride, she drove out to his cabin. The thought of seeing him again thrilled her and temporarily displaced her jealousy. As she drove, she planned the words for a reconciliation; what she would say; how she would say it. She prayed he would be there.

When she knocked on the door, there was no response. His truck was parked by the cabin so he must be there, she thought. She knocked again, this time louder. A groan came from within. "Harold. Harold. It's me, Rosemary," she yelled. Another groan came from within, and a short while later, Harold appeared at the door, holding it opened a crack.

"Rosemary, for Chris' sakes, what are you doing here?" he asked. He looked and sounded like he was suffering from a bad hangover.

"I want to talk to you Harold. I want to set things straight between us. Can I come in?" she said with hope in her heart.

He remained quiet for a minute, looking at her through the narrow opening. He squinted his eyes against the light. "Rosemary, why did you come here? You know there's nothin' to set straight," he said. "It's got to be finished between us. Please go away," and he closed the door in her face.

"Harold! Harold!" She banged desperately on the door.

"Go away, Rosemary. Goddamit, leave me alone. You've caused me enough trouble." he yelled from within.

She banged on the door again and shouted his name but there was no response. She tried the door but it was latched. "It's that damn Lillian, isn't it? You went back to her didn't you, you two-timing bastard." Anger blinded her. "I'll kill you. I'll kill you both," she shouted. Then she gave up and went back in tears to her car.

CHAPTER 13

Lillian couldn't bear to talk with Linda about Harold. She was emotionally shattered. Her anger for Rosemary and Harold had been smothered by the confusion over Linda and the visit from William's son. And when Linda came home from work that day, Lillian found it hard to even look at her. Linda sensed that something was wrong.

"Where is Harold," she'd asked, suspecting that the strange treatment she was receiving from her mother had something to do with him. Lillian was busy, getting ready to go to the barn. She was crashing milk pails together that she had brought to the house to wash.

"Harold?" She crashed the pails together. "No Harold," and she crashed them together again. "He won't be here. I'm going up to milk." She started for the door.

"Wait. What's wrong, Ma? You look like you could kill someone. Are you pissed at me? What's goin' on?" Linda's concern mounted as her mother stomped out the door.

"Nothing wrong!" Lillian shouted back at her, her eyes blazing.

"Wait a minute!" Linda yelled back. "I know damn well there's something up. I'm entitled to know what it is."

"Oh, yes, you're entitled alright. You should damn well know what's up." Lillian's anger broke through. "How could you? You and Harold... my own daughter." She looked at Linda with an air of disbelief mixed with anger.

"Oh... damn. Did he tell you that? I, I wanted to tell you, but it... was just... too hard."

"I'll bet it was, " Lillian said bitterly.

"Yes, Ma. But it's not what you think. Not at all. Harold and I made love long before you decided you wanted him. I mean, I didn't think he was right for you in the first place. I didn't think he would be good for you. And I didn't think you would want him."

Lillian stifled the sharp reply she was forming. Linda's words were getting through.

"You can't blame me, Ma. I mean, I didn't think the son-of-a - bitch would still go ahead and marry you? What kind of a man does that?" Lillian remained silent. She started to walk up the hill.

"Please Ma, don't hate me for his mistakes," Linda called after her and tears formed in her eyes. Lillian hadn't seen her cry since she was a Child. Her anger for Linda started to evaporate. "I really tried to warn you about him, don't you remember?" Linda said through her sobs.

"Oh, Linda. I... I guess we have both been used. Now I know why you disliked him so much. I've been such a fool." She thought about all the signs Linda had been showing her and the many times she had advised her to leave him. Her need for Harold's help had driven her to accept him without question, without the reassurances she had needed with someone like Fred. Asking Maynard was all show. She blushed when she thought of what a fool she had been.

They went together to the barn and worked hard in the earthy, warm environment of large animals and hay and straw and their bitterness with each other dissipated. But Lillian said nothing to Linda about Harold and Rosemary.

When she came home the next day there was a note on her front door from Peck's store. She had a telegram. She went to pick it up and found it was from her sister living in Tucson:

"Robert here, stop. Everything fine, stop. Letter on the way, stop."

She read it several times and wanted to cry. Her emotions were being torn apart; she was happy and miserable at the same time. After holding the telegram for some time, she became calm.

She hadn't heard from her sister since last Christmas, when she got the usual perfunctory note with the Christmas card. Carol Wiggs remained a spinster and had moved to Arizona ten years earlier. She'd taken to the southwest desert like a saguaro cactus.

The letter arrived a few days later. She tore it open and read:

> *"I'm writing to let you know the good news. Robert is here! He has moved out here. He's looking as well as can be expected, and I really think this may be a new beginning for him. Somehow, when you said he was missing, I knew he would show up again. I'm glad he came here, away from his bad memories. I think he's cut out his drinking (not really sure. I don't want to raise any false hopes). But if that's true, maybe I can get him a job with my company as a courier. He asked me to write to you, to let you know he is okay and to tell Bobby he loves him and will come to get him as soon as he is well. He also asked if you couldn't send him some money. Anyway, I have high hopes that he's going to be fine, and you should rest easier about that."*
>
> *Much Love,*
> *Carol.*

Lillian's was greatly relieved. She knew her sister had a good heart and would do her best for their brother. But with the relief came anxiety. *He would come and get Bobby? Not on your life.* But, as she thought about it, it seemed to her that this living with Carol was the best of all possible solutions, one that she herself would never have thought of. He needed to stay in Tucson.

CHAPTER 14

Finally resolving the issue with Harold and her mother lifted a great burden off Linda's mind. She was surprised and happy with her mother's quick understanding, which made her think that something, some key ingredient was missing. And another unexpected event would bring her even closer to her mother.

Linda usually ate her lunch during the week at the Bassett Luncheonette, a small place with Formica tables and chrome and plastic chairs. She sometimes brought a sandwich in a bag; the Bassett didn't mind brown-baggers as long as they bought a drink from their soda fountain, even if it was only something as simple as a small glass of cherry coke.

Sheila, a co-worker, usually joined her on these lunch-hour outings; it was only a short walk from the dingy brown-brick factory building where they worked. The factory, the Ideal Canvas Company, made canvas products for the US Army. They made tents and duffle bags and backpacks and many other things and were doing well in the government contracting business.

One day she was working on a coffee ice cream soda, sucking bottom through a straw, delighted with all the noise she was making, when a strange woman walked up to her table. She seemed vaguely familiar, yet she didn't recognize her.

“Hello, Linda, “ the woman said. “Remember me?”

She was small and had dull brown hair cut short. Her clothes were the cheap hand-me-down variety and looked worn and shabby. Linda looked at the strange woman with a puzzled frown, when suddenly it came to her:

“Julia? My God, is it you?” she said, standing up and tentatively moving to embrace her. “What... What... Oh, never mind.” she held Julia's rough hands and stepped back. “It's so good to see you! God it's been a long time.” She thought she could detect pain in Julia's eyes. "Here have a seat," and they both sat down. Linda was out of breath and out of words; she was completely astonished by her younger sister's sudden appearance.

Sheila introduced herself to Julia, who appeared uncomfortable and nervous with her two new companions. Her hands remained in her lap and she was visibly trembling. She glanced constantly at the door, as if to insure a means of escape. After some further small talk, Julia said with a shaking voice:

"Linda please. I need to talk to you in private." She looked at Sheila. "Would you mind, Sheila? We'll move to another table?" Sheila said: "Oh, I understand. Look, it's almost time to get back to the office, so I'll leave you two alone." She stood up and fumbled through her purse for some change. "Nice to meet you, Julia. I'll see you in a while, Linda," and she left.

Julia sat silent for a while like she was trying to think of something. "Want a soda or something to drink?" Linda asked, to start up the conversation again. She was concerned by her sister's appearance and hoped there wasn't something seriously wrong. She hadn't seen her in over three years; they never were very close.

"No thanks, Linda," she replied. "But I do need some time to talk to you." She moved her eyes from the table to Linda. "Would you believe I've been trying to find out where you worked for a couple of months? I managed to track down Rosemary in Fultonville. She told me you had left New York and were working here at Ideal. Then the guard told me you usually ate here. I didn't want to bother you at work." her voice was calmer but sounded weary.

"Is something wrong Julia? You look so--."

"So worn out?" Julia interrupted.

"I guess I'd have to say yes, worn out."

"Well, I am kind of tired and I am in trouble. Not police trouble, mind you," she quickly added, "nothing like that. But trouble enough. That's why I need to talk to you. Can I meet you here after work? Say about six?"

"Six? Sure Julia. I can even be here by five-thirty, if you want."

"I can't get back here till about six. That'll be fine. Is that Ok?"

"Sure. Sure, it is."

"I'm really sorry to put you out like this," she said, keeping her eyes lowered as if they could reveal some secret she wanted to remain unknown. "But I'll leave you with some good news before you go back to work... so's you don't fret all afternoon about my problems. You have a new nephew, little Andy." And she smiled for the first time.

A big grin spread over Linda's face and her eyebrows went up. "A nephew? You're finally a mom? Oh, that is great news. How old is he? Who does he look like? "

Julia laughed at Linda's enthusiasm. "He's a little over a year old. And he looks like his father, I guess. But he has your eyes, I think."

"Oh, when can I see him?"

"Soon. Very soon," Julia said. Linda sensed that the conversation was coming to a close. Julia stood up and started to leave.

"That's just great," Linda said. "I can't wait to hear more about little Andy." She stood up to leave. "Are you Ok? Do you need a ride?"

Julia picked up her purse and looked around the luncheonette as if searching for someone.

"No," she replied. "But please remember, at six? I may be a little late. Please wait?"

All that afternoon Linda was preoccupied with thoughts of her sister; her sad looks and her shabby appearance. She knew something was wrong. She tried to recall her past to help enlighten the present. She remembered that Julia had eloped with her high school sweetheart, Duane Lippers. That happened right after she graduated from high school. She'd been driven to it, Linda guessed, by her father's dislike for Duane. He was rebellious and rude and drove an old Indian motorcycle. Matt could just never see Duane as part of the family. When he tried to send Julia off to college in Utica in her mother's footsteps, she ran off with Duane instead. The family ties disintegrated after that, in spite of Lillian's efforts to patch things up. Julia was afraid of her father and could never overcome her hurt. She thought her mother was overbearing and pretentious and had much to do with her father's opinion of Duane. When Lillian's attempts at reconciliation were interpreted as an attempt to get her to leave Duane, the family breakup was complete.

Then Linda thought about how both of them had been sorry disappointments to their parents. Her own folly with her husband Frank; She knew that their rocky affair was not all Frank's fault, and finally, Julia and Duane. Then there was her mother's younger brother, Robert, and Maryann and all the grief that relationship had brought to her, especially with Maryann's death. But Linda now admitted to herself that she had been wrong and her parents right about Frank and, she thought, about Maryann. She was not so sensitive as Julia; She had never felt any deep resentment towards her parents for disliking Frank. But Julia was hurt easily, she remembered, and vowed to be careful with what she said later when they met.

After meeting with Linda, Julia had walked around the block to where her friend Mary Simpson waited.

"Did you find her?" Mary asked as Julia got into the car.

It was a nice spring day, with just a little bite of cold in the air and Mary had rolled down the windows. ,

"Yes, yes I did. Thanks so much for driving me here, Mary."

Julia and Mary worked for a glove factory a little less than three miles from the Bassett luncheonette. She wouldn't ask Mary to drive her here again; she would walk back after work closed at 5:30. If she walked fast, she knew she could make it by something close to six.

For now, she was anxious to get back to her job, although she felt hopeless about it. Her supervisor, Mike Malvino, had told her the day before that if she didn't get her production up to minimum by the end of next week, she would be let go. She'd been there for almost three months and still was unable to stretch and cure her minimum of four dozen pairs of woolen gloves an hour.

It was grinding, senseless work. Standing all day in front of the red-hot sizing irons, she pulled the damp woolen gloves to size. In her haste to make her quota, she had developed horrible burns all over her hands. The burns were slowing her down. After she returned to work that day, Mike told her she was flirting with sure dismissal. Miserable, she told Mary she didn't need a ride home that afternoon and after work, started her walk back to the luncheonette.

She followed the creek since it was the shortest route to the luncheonette. Even though she'd inhaled the foul vapors of the creek all day at work, an occasional light breeze would bring a chemical stench, like burning gunpowder and sulphur combined, that made her turn her head.

She arrived at the luncheonette a little after six. Linda was waiting outside.

"Let's go to McCoy's Pharmacy," Linda said. "They have booths over there; it's more private. Where's your car?"

"I don't have a car, Linda."

"Oh... Ok. Come with me." She drove over to McCoy's and parked close to the entrance. They took a booth in the back and ordered coffee.

"Are you hungry?" Linda asked.

Julia had skipped lunch to see Linda. The walk had burned off any reserve calories. But she had no desire for food. "I think I'll wait. How about you?"

Linda ordered a tuna sandwich. She said they could split it.

"Linda, let me get this out," she said, with her hands in her lap. "It's hard enough to say without dillying around. The thing is, I need some money. I really need to borrow some money."

Linda saw that her sister was trembling. "Money?" she said, surprised. "I've only got a little."

Julia sighed. She had suspected her sister wouldn't have any extra money. "Can't you borrow some from Ma?" Julia asked timidly.

"I don't know," Linda replied. "Can you tell me what's wrong? Maybe I can find a way to help."

Julia seemed lost for words. She started to sob. She kept her hands clasped tightly in her lap, which Linda began to notice. It gave her a strange, nun-like appearance.

Linda was shaken; she had never seen her sister cry like this. Julia had always been a quiet girl, but she also had always managed to keep up a brave front and never let her true feelings show. "Please tell me what's wrong Julia. Really, maybe I can help."

"Oh God. It's all so stupid," Julia sobbed. "And I have no one to blame but me."

"Why don't you start at the beginning?" Linda urged.

"Well, I guess it all started when Andy was born," she said, between sobs. "Duane never wanted children you know. He was furious when he found out I was pregnant. He wanted me to get an abortion, which I absolutely refused to do. I wanted a baby so badly."

"What did he do?" Linda asked.

"About three months after Andy was born, he lit out. It was incredible. No warning. Nothing. " She was sobbing less now as the painful memories returned. "One day, Duane just didn't come home from work. I thought he was out drinking with some of his friends. But when he didn't come home by dawn, I knew something was wrong. I went to the Police and made a missing person's report. I thought he might be hurt; in an accident or something. But later… I found most of his clothes were missing! And the savings account had been cleaned out. He withdrew it all!" She shouted the last words with such force that the people in the next booth stared at them; she didn't care. "He took it all Linda. Took the car and the guns and tools and everything of any value. The bastard left me and Andy with nothing but the goddam beat-up furniture. And the place we were living in was rented. I haven't seen him since. It's been well over a year now."

"Oh Julia, I'm so sorry. What a rotten thing to do." She reached across the table as if to comfort her by touching her hand, but Julia's hands remained firmly in her lap.

"After he'd run out on me, I was scared," she continued. "I tried to get my old job back at Erhardt's, you know the frozen food plant?" Linda nodded. "But they weren't hiring... in fact, they told me they were laying off. Even worse, I couldn't find a baby sitter for Andy. Seems nobody wanted to care for a baby in diapers. And I kept looking for Duane. I went to see his father; I thought maybe Duane had told him something. But ever since Duane's mother died, his dad hasn't been fit to talk to. Drunk most of the time." She stopped talking and sipped her coffee. Linda hadn't touched her sandwich.

"I needed to pay the rent and buy food," she continued. "I'd been selling off the furniture, so I asked the old man if I could borrow some money? You know, I don't even think he understood that Duane had left me. He was no help. Believe me Linda, I was scared, scared for my poor Andy.

"I finally got a job in Longhouse's, waiting tables. They let me work split shifts so I didn't have to leave Andy very long. But I couldn't make it on tips. Then the landlord threw us out when I got three months behind on the rent. At least he said he was sorry. That's when I moved here to town to the Creek settlement. Only place I can afford."

"That's where uncle Robert lived." Linda said.

"Yes, not very nice, is it? Rats and cockroaches everywhere. And later, when I saw that I'd brought Andy to this kind of life, I thought seriously of putting him up for adoption. He's such a pretty baby the agency said they would take him right away. He still wasn't a year old yet. When I saw how much they wanted to get their hands on him, I changed my mind. I was really there just to check the possibilities. So, I thought I'd wait and see if things improved. In the meantime, I'd found a job and a place to board Andy during the day."

"Why didn't you go to Ma for help? " Linda said.

"Ma doesn't exist for me, Linda. After Dad committed suicide, I had no use for her. And I thought you were in New York."

Linda said nothing, although she was upset by Julia's incriminating tone about her mother. But she didn't want to upset the delicate relationship that was unfolding by arguing.

"I looked up an old friend of mine, from high school, Mary Simpson, remember her?" she asked Linda.

"No. No, not really."

"Well, she got me a job, God bless her, at the glove factory where she worked. That's where I'm working now. And she knew of a couple that would take care of a baby. That was my lifesaver."

McCoy's started to fill up with kids coming from a high school basketball game. Linda was glad for the noise they made.

"But I'm not doing well at the job, Linda," she continued. "I'm doing piece work and I can't make the minimum quota."

Linda was familiar with most of the glove factory jobs. "What do you do?" she asked.

"I'm a finisher," Julia replied. "I do glove sizing and cure. I stretch the gloves on the irons. It's just that... well, I'm all thumbs. I can't get the four dozen an hour. "

"Is that a reasonable quota? " Linda asked.

"Well I was told that the man who had the job before me could do eight dozen an hour, easy. Seems incredible to me. Here, look at my hands and you'll see what I mean about being all thumbs." She lifted her hands out of her lap and turned them slowly in front of Linda. They were swollen and badly burned and had infections where she had burned herself over other burns, some of which she had done just a few hours ago.

"Oh God, Julia. That's awful! No wonder you can't make the quota. No one could with hands like that. You need to see a doctor." Tears came to Linda's eyes to see her sister in such pain.

Julia looked straight at Linda. "You won't tell Ma, will you? I don't want you to tell her. I have no use for her, you know." She returned her hands to her lap.

"Oh, Julia, now's not the time for such bitter words. You need help. Thank God you came to see me." Linda dried her tears.

Julia sighed. "They came to my apartment last Monday and

said I'd have to move out if I didn't pay the rent by next Monday." She sighed again. "Of course, I'm behind on rent again. Then, a few days ago, my supervisor told me that if I didn't make the quota by the end of the week, I would be finished. My training period is over. I just got desperate. I didn't want to bother you... I--"

"Bother?" Linda interrupted. "I only wish you had come sooner. I'm family you know. And so's Ma. We're not going to let you alone to fight these things."

Julia's eyes flared. "I told you, I don't want Ma to know." Linda just looked at her.

They finished the coffee. The sandwich remained uneaten. "Can you take me home now?" Julia asked. "I need to pick up Andy on the way. Is that Ok?"

"Ok? That's great. Today I got to see my little sister again and now, a new nephew!"

Linda drove the few miles to the house where Andy boarded during the day.

"It's the Chesnutts," Julia said on the way. "They, er she, Mrs. Chesnutt, that is, takes in children; mostly from working mothers like me. Mr. Chesnutt has an office in his house. He's a, I don't know exactly. They... they're a peculiar couple. Don't have any children of their own that I know of. But they've been real nice to me. And they love Andy."

Linda accompanied Julia to the front door. The small house was on the outskirts of town on a quiet street lined with big trees, still bare from the hard winter past. A wooden sign on the lawn read:

J. Chesnutt, Esq.
Record keeping - Notary Public
8AM. - 5PM.

Mrs. Chesnutt came to the door. An enormous woman with a black dress and a long necklace of fake pearls; she had the girth and huge smile of a small whale. Linda's hand was lost in Mrs. Chesnutts voluminous flesh when they shook hands. "Welcome my dear. It's so nice to meet Mrs. Lippers' sister," she boomed in basso soprano.

"Come in. Come in."

Linda and Julia walked into the small parlor, fitted with what appeared to be antique furniture. But Linda saw later that it was really just threadbare and not antique at all. Two small children were sitting at a tiny wooden table in the corner, playing tea time. Next to them was a play pen with a blonde, curly headed boy. It was Andy, playing quietly by himself. Mrs. Chesnutt walked slowly over to the play pen with a pronounced waddle. "Here's Andy," she said, as she swept him up in her huge arms. He giggled and seemed to be happily enveloped in the mountains of flesh. Julia took Andy from Mrs. Chesnutt and turned towards Linda.

"Look Andy! Here's your aunt Linda." Linda reached for the small child. His hair hung in long curls and he had a cherubic smile. He reached out to Linda.

"Oh, Andy. It's so nice to meet you," and she kissed him and took him in her arms. She thought he was truly a beautiful child. "Well, Mrs... uh, what did you say your last name was?" asked Mrs. Chesnutt of Linda.

"Oh, I'm sorry," Linda replied. It's Boyle. Linda Boyle."

"Well, Mrs. Boyle, please have a seat. Mrs. Lippers, see that your sister takes a seat. I'll have some tea ready in a minute. Water's already hot."

"Oh, no thanks Mrs. Chesnutt," Julia said, still standing. "We just had coffee."

"Nonsense!" replied Mrs. Chesnutt. "I have some nice fudge brownies. Tea will do you good. Besides, I want Chesnutt to meet you're r lovely sister. CHESSS--NUTTTT," she bellowed, before either of them could reply.

"Yes dear," came a squeaky reply from another room. In a moment a small, bald headed man emerged into the hallway. He wore wire glasses, a wrinkled jacket and a frumpy tie. "Yes dear," he said again.

"I want you to meet Mrs. Boyle," said Mrs. Chesnutt. "She's Mrs. Lippers' sister. Came to visit us for a while."

"Delighted, delighted," said the little man, and he extended his bony hand. "Come, sit down and tell us all about yourself."

Linda and Julia both sat down. Mrs. Chesnutt disappeared into her kitchen. Andy played on the floor next to the chairs. The other children were still busy playing tea time, obviously used to people coming and going.

"Did you see my sign outside?" asked Mr. Chesnutt. "I'm a Notary Public. I get to sign a lot of important documents. I have hundreds of clients who use my service." He started to fiddle with the twisted knot in his tie. "Some big names in town, too. Do you need anything notarized, Mrs… uh, what did you say your name was?"

"Boyle. Linda Boyle."

"Yes, Mrs. Boyle. Well, do you need anything notarized?"

"Not at the moment," Linda said.

"Not at the moment," he repeated. "Well, if you ever need a notary, Mrs. Boyle, why I'm one of the best. I'd be happy to be of service."

"Well, thank you, Mr. Chesnutt, I'll certainly keep that in mind."

"My wife cares for children during the day, you know," he said, smiling broadly, displaying a perfect set of false teeth. "Just like Andy here. She's very good at it. She takes them up to five or six years old." He seemed to be getting more excited as he talked. "She makes them behave but keeps them happy at the same time." He laughed, sounding like a squeaky toy. "Now, what exactly is it that you do, Mrs. Boyle?"

At that moment, Mrs. Chesnutt waddled in, bearing a wooden tray with a small jar, pink glass cups and saucers, and a china pot of tea. In the middle was a large plate heaped with fudge brownies.

She put the tray down on a small coffee table and picked up the small jar. "Here, Mrs. Lippers. This is the salve I told you I would make for those hands. You must use it! I would ask for different work If I were you."

"Oh, thank you, Mrs. Chesnutt. You're very kind," Julia replied, taking the small jar.

Mrs. Chesnutt daintily served the tea in the tiny cups and passed them around. Mr. Chesnutt explained how he had become a notary and elaborated on the various important documents he had notarized, and described all the important businesses he kept records for and how valuable and important were the business secrets in his possession. When he finally stopped to sip some tea, Mrs. Chesnutt took that as a sign for her turn.

"I have seven clients right now," she said. "But I can take up to ten, when Mr. Chesnutt isn't too busy. Do you have any children, Mrs. Boyle?" She reached for some brownies.

"No, I don't have any, " Linda replied.

"No," she repeated. "Well, I can tell you a lot about children. If you plan to have any, that is, you can come to me for advice. You can see I have plenty of experience," and she took more brownies. "Have some, Mrs. Boyle, Mrs. Lippers," she said and handed them the plate. "Now, what is it that you do, Mrs. Boyle?"

"Could you pass those brownies?" asked Mr. Chesnutt. "Mrs. Chesnutt makes the most delicious brownies, wouldn't you say?" He looked to Linda for confirmation. She plunked hers in her mouth; she hadn't tried them yet.

"My, yes," she said. "They are delicious."

"We have very limited resources," said Mrs. Chesnutt, "so I make everything I can. But we do try to keep up appearances though. I belong to the Historical Society, you know. They only like people with a good appearance." She wiggled in her chair and put on a haughty expression, lifting her nose high in the air. And then she started to laugh. Her whole body shook when she laughed; then Mr. Chesnutt started to laugh with her until it was catching and Julia and Linda and the children started to laugh; and they all laughed until they had to hold their sides.

It was only the arrival of another couple that broke their interesting visit; they came for the two children.

"They're something, aren't they?" Julia said, when they were back in the car. She held Andy on her lap.

"I'll say. They're so open... so unusual and so generous. They kept me entertained."

Linda parked the car in front of the dingy apartment complex where Julia lived. She had the same kind of apartment that Robert had, but after entering, Linda noticed an enormous difference. This place was very clean, and it seemed like another world. "Wow, Julia, I didn't expect your apartment to look ... so nice," she said.

"It was a wreck when I moved in," Julia said. "I scrubbed and scraped and painted, just to get rid of the vermin. I can't live in filth like you say uncle Robert did. There's no need for that."

"It's so open, too," Linda said.

"You mean empty, Don't you?" Linda laughed. "I took an unfurnished place. It's cheaper and I couldn't see paying for that wrecked furniture. As you can see, I only have a few pieces of my own furniture left."

"Well, I think that's part of the charm," Linda said. She played with Andy while Julia prepared some food for the boy. He was quiet but very friendly. He hadn't cried once since she first met him, but was full of friendly chuckles and other sounds.

"Want some spaghetti, Linda?" Julia called from the kitchen. "I've got some leftovers from yesterday."

When they finished eating and Andy went to sleep, Linda and Julia talked into the night.

"Julia, you need to stop working those irons. Tomorrow, you should ask your boss for another job. Tell him you can't work those irons with your hands like that. Hasn't he seen them?"

"I don't know. But he'll never agree. I'm sure he just wants to get rid of me."

"Then quit. And do it tomorrow. Don't work those irons anymore. I may be able to get you on at Ideal. If not, I know Rosemary's cousin, Ed. He's a supervisor at Walmitt's factory. In the meantime, I'll get you some money to live on. Don't worry. I'll be back here tomorrow after work. Just don't worry." She embraced Julia for the first time. "God, it's good to see you again. And that Andy!" She felt very high. It was a small miracle.

When Linda got home, her mother was already asleep. She couldn't keep this secret very long she knew. And that new grandchild... Lillian would be in heaven... and somehow, she needed to borrow some money for Julia.

As of late, Linda was gaining more respect for her mother. Although she seemed too serious and sometimes cold, Linda now had a clearer understanding of the trials her mother had been through and of her unusual strength in the face of tragedy, her selflessness towards family members and towards others like her neighbors. She thought of how unjust Julia had been to her mother and she wanted to change all that. It wouldn't be easy; she felt that Julia was capable of holding a grudge for a very long time.

CHAPTER 15

Able Grisinski's farm was very impressive; it looked much like the mountain valley farms one sees in paintings of Austria or Switzerland. The house and barns sat in open rolling fields, surrounded by steeply rising hills covered with forests of pine and spruce. The fields were for the most part, natural, having been created by ancient glaciers. They made excellent pasture and held two primitive ponds which lent their beauty to the sub-alpine landscape. The ponds were a haven for wildfowl and were protected from the grazing cattle by wide banks of cattails edging around them.

Able thought for sure it would be easy to sell.

Able and his brother John and sister Edith had inherited these three hundred acres from his father, who had inherited it from his father and so forth until one reaches back to 1814, when the first ancestor built a cabin on this tract of wilderness.

Only a few weeks had passed since Lena's funeral, and Able started looking in earnest for a buyer for his farm.

"How can you, Able?" Lillian asked, when he told her of his plans to sell. He said he wanted to contract with the realtors in Johnstown, but hadn't made a final decision yet. "How can you stand to do it? What will you do?"

Able looked miserable. "Well, I was just waiting for Lena to go, you know. I've already sold forty head to the auction boys. John and I can barely keep up with what's left." He nodded at John who was sitting next to Bobby at the kitchen table. They were eating a late breakfast that Able and John had prepared. "The real estate man said I ought to keep the place operational. Said it might be easier to sell."

Because his problems had been so pressing, she had mentioned nothing of her own difficulties. But now she wanted to tell him. She thought it may make him forget some of his own

troubles. "I'm not doing very well either, Able," she said. "Svenson's will end my contract in a few days. And Harold is gone. He never helped much, except for getting in the wood. But with him gone and maybe Junior leaving, I can't handle even what little I've got. Bobby and I just can't handle it."

Bobby said he thought he could do it if they had to.

"What happened with Svenson's? And Harold? What on earth is going on, Lillian?" Able asked. He was completely surprised by what she had told him.

"Well, Svenson Senior died about six weeks ago." she said. "I thought maybe you'd read about it in the papers or heard it from Maynard. He was the one I knew well; I had all my dealings with him. Now, I don't seem to get on well with his son. He'll be the new owner of the creamery. Came out special to tell me he wasn't going to renew the contract."

"I'll be damned. Sounds like a real *nice* person. Did he give you a reason?" Able stroked his chin in thought.

"Yes. But I'd rather not go into that right now. It's a long, complicated story. And Harold and I are getting a divorce. It just didn't work." Now she was the one that needed cheering up.

"A Divorce! Why Lillian, I thought you two were getting on real well. I'll be damned. You're about worse off than me." He didn't know what else to say and they all sat, eating in silence. Finally, he spoke again: "What'll *you* do?"

"I don't know. But I'm not giving up and I don't think you should either."

They were eating in Able's kitchen. Able was a big eater and Lillian hadn't seen such a spread since she was a girl. John was a quiet boy and had said little during their discussion. But he could eat like his father. Able had got used to cooking during Lena's long illness and could make a passable breakfast. He'd prepared pancakes and had put a foot-high stack on the table. There was a platter with a dozen fried eggs and another platter heaped with sausage and head cheese and slab bacon. Lillian had brought over two loaves of fresh baked bread and some fresh churned butter. the boys were enjoying the feast and since milking was over and it was a Saturday, they were in no hurry. But after wolfing down several eggs, a half-dozen pancakes and probably two pounds of sausage, John declared he had to finish cleaning the barn and invited Bobby to go with him.

"Lillian, for all the times you've been over here, you ain't seen the barn yet, have you? " Able asked, after the boys had left.

She shook her head.

"Well knowing how you appreciate a good barn, I think you should see mine, just in case this place sells fast. Would you like a tour?" and he laughed.

They finished eating and walked down the wagon path to the barn. It was a nice day, with a cool breeze rustling the new leaves in the big maples around the house. She had only seen the big red barn from the road or his house. It was quite a distance off which belied its size. As they neared it, she could see it was made up of two sections and was a giant of a barn compared to hers. Also, there was a second smaller barn behind it, not visible from the road.

"Two barns, Able? Not many farms can lay claim to that." she said.

He laughed. "Well, that little one right there is real interesting." He pointed to the small barn. "That's the barn that was built by my grandfather. Best we can recollect, that barn was built about 1890. Leastwise, that's what's carved on one a them beams. Let me show you that one first."

As she approached the barn, she was impressed by the architectural charm, given to it mostly by the unusual roof. Sweeping down gracefully from a sharp peak, the steep roof towered three levels high. It was an impressive height for a "little" barn. The eaves came down to within a door's height of the ground. The roof overhangs gave the barn the look of a mountain chalet. Wooden shingles covered the roof.

"Your grandfather had a good eye for design."

"That's why she's still standing. Would a been tore down years ago. But she's an aging beauty that just wants some care now and then. I just keep equipment and stuff stored in there now." He stared up at the wind vane sitting on the front peak. "She's probably doomed if I sell this place. Let me show you the inside."

He took her in through one of the small side doors and slid open the big barn door to let in light. The inside was just as interesting as the outside.

"Just look at these posts and beams," he said, as he swept his arm around the perimeter of the beams supporting the hayloft. "They're all hewn by hand. and they're mortised and tenoned together and fixed with wooden pegs. I don't think there was a nail or metal bolt used in the original construction of these frames."

He explained that everything in the barn had been carefully hewn of wood. There were calf pens made with poles and rails, and hay racks, and horse stables with hay mangers, and cow stalls with stanchions, all made the same way, all still in working shape. They were all skillfully shaped and carefully placed to fit into the whole design perfectly.

"You can't sell this place. It has so much meaning." She was enchanted by the little barn.

"And you know, Lillian? Every time I come out here and look

around, I find something new. Some carved initials or a full name. I found "Andrew G.- 1890" carved on that main beam." he pointed to the beam above her head. "Here. Let me show you something else."

He led her to a small room in the back of the barn. Pieces of old, dried-out harness hung around the room on wooden pegs. At one end, a little window with four dusty panes filtered a pale yellow light into the room. An old cheesebox filled with rusty nails and other bits and pieces left over from some past, unknown activity, rested on the cobwebbed sill beneath the window. "Look at that carving over there," he said, pointing to a shelf mounted between the walls in the corner of the room. A crucifixion, with figures standing or kneeling around the base of the cross, had been carved into the face of a board standing upright on the shelf. It was dark and covered with the dust and grime of age, but was handsomely done in a rugged sort of way. Able took the board down from the shelf. "I found this buried under some trash at the back of the barn," he said. "I always wondered what that shelf was for. As soon as I found this, I knew I had the answer." He handed it to her. "You see, this edge fits perfectly between the two rails on that shelf."

She looked closely at the carving. "Do you know who made it?" she asked, as she handed the carving back to him.

"Naw. No markings on it that I can see. But it must a been done by a catholic, don't you think? We think some of our people were catholic at one time."

"Why do you say that?"

"Well, here, you can see here on this carving." He pointed to one of the kneeling figures. "Looks like the Virgin Mary. Got a halo carved around the head. You see that?"

She nodded.

He put the carving back on the shelf. "I think it belongs here. Maybe I should take it in the house and clean it up. But I kind of like having it here in this old barn." He looked around the small room. "Someday I'll see what's in all these little cheese boxes. Here, now let me show you the big barn."

They crossed the small opening between the barns. The big

barn was a three-level building with a gambrel tin roof. It had lots of windows down the side and in the front, the big bay doors under the peak of the roof for entry into the hayloft.

When they went inside, it seemed even larger. Able showed her the milking floor set up to hold twenty cows on each side of the wagon run. Then he showed her his wonderful milking machines. "Couldn't operate now without these," he said. He looked around the empty barn. "Boy's finished cleanin' up, it seems." The cows had been let out to grazing. It was a good, strong, efficient barn, with lots of light and fresh air.

"I got lots of room in this barn now that we're down to twenty head," he said. "It's been a good barn. Easy to feed in and easy to clean. Good protection from the bad weather. It's been a real good barn for me."

When they got back to the house, he showed her around the rooms she hadn't seen. "How old is this house, Able?" she asked.

"Not very old, Lillian. Not as old as yours."

Then she noticed a floor console TV he'd put in. She hadn't seen it before.

"Wasted my money," he said, when he showed it to her. "Can't get no stations clear. Nearest one is from Schenectady." He laughed. "The TV man said he didn't think I could get anything, cause this house sits behind so many hills. He offered to give me my money back. But I kinda' got fond of it sittin' here in this room."

"Well, that's too bad," she said. "But I wouldn't think you'd have much time to watch TV, anyway."

"That's right Lillian. But I got it when Paul went over to the war. I got it for the news. I got tired of askin' Maynard what was going on."

" I'm sorry, Able. I wasn't thinking."

"Say no more. I know what you meant."

She was about to leave when he said: "Lillian. Bobby asked if he could come over Sunday night to play monotony with me and John. Is that alright.?"

“I think that's fine, once the chores are done.” she said.

“How about you Lillian? Wouldn't you like to come over and join us too?” His eyes twinkled and there was a note of hope in his voice.

She thought for a minute and sighed. “Lord knows, I'm not good at that game, Able. But I just might come over to watch and maybe, to be the banker? Would that do?”

CHAPTER 16

After returning home, she couldn't shake the vision of Able's old barn. It fit in with her ideals, her dreams about this place. That barn had the same sense of belonging; the same commanding presence as a Swiss chalet had in the Alps. And there too was a tremendous history behind it, something she had always treasured. Able believed that it had been built on the original foundation of the house of the first settler there.

When she slept, other, less pleasant thoughts took over her mind. There was Matt and Joyce Hutchins, now competing with Harold and Rosemary for her undivided disgust. But Rosemary's loss had been the most bitter for her. It gave her nightmares that made her feel weak and incapable of love of any sort. But then the nightmares were pushed aside by Able's barn. Able was now becoming important to her in a new sort of way. She was in danger of losing her place, too. In her new dream, she was living at Able's place, and she was telling him what a wonderful place it was. Able was cooking a bountiful breakfast for her. When she woke up, she thought of many new possibilities.

The next day Able came over. When he knocked on the door she was surprised; he was wearing dress pants and a sport shirt. He looked very different without the usual work clothes. In fact, he had managed to plaster down his unruly short hair. She had to stifle a laugh.

"Lillian, after you left yesterday, why I got to thinking. Now I know you're going to think I'm plumb crazy, but just hear me out." He was standing with his hands joined in front of him as if he were in church. "First off, I want to make a proposal to you."

"Proposal? Able what are you up to?" she asked, afraid she already knew.

"Yup. Now, I know I ain't much to look at. And it's a fact that

I'm as ignorant as a brick. But, by golly, we both love farmin' and these hills and that gives us a lot more in common than not. And for those reasons and many more, I would like to ask you to marry me... six months from today." He swallowed hard, trying to clear his dry throat. He was losing his voice. All Lillian could do was stare at him with her mouth opened. "I think six months would do honor to Lena's memory," he continued. "And it would give you time to get your divorce settled. And you'd have time to get used to the idea of marryin' a poor, ugly farmer like me."

"Able, I--"

"Don't say nothing yet, Lillian." He sighed. "L... Let me finish, before I collapse. I'll probably lose everything if I don't do something like this. If we combine our herds and you move over to my place, I think we both can make it. So, I have a selfish motive. But It'll work for you, too. We can both get to keep our places. You wouldn't have to give up this place at all." He stopped and took a deep breath. "I'd be the happiest man on earth if you'd say yes, Lillian, with all due respect to my Lena." He took another deep breath.

Lillian was dumbfounded, dazed by Able's bold proposal. Even though her thoughts and dreams the night before had grazed the periphery of this idea, she had never brought them to the surface or dared to really think about it. He had stood at the door, saying all these things with great courage, punctuated by sighs and deep breathing. Now it was her turn.

"I... I don't know Able. I don't know what to say. I never expected you to make a proposal."

"I know you need to think about it, Lillian. I don't want you to answer now. I got something to add. I've been fighting this family thing and you're lookin' for help too and I think I might have a solution."

"Able, come on in and sit down. Let me close the door and keep the flies out." He came in and they sat down at the kitchen table. Linda and Bobby were there eating breakfast and were very curious about what was happening.

He continued his idea: "I think we need to give the kids, including Junior, an interest in the farm. Give 'em a real share of the place today so's they can feel its theirs. Junior can earn himself a share of the herd, besides his pay. Course, they got to take the losses as well as the gains."

They all sat quiet for a while. She poured him a cup of coffee. "Now that idea has a lot of merit, Able. I think it would be worth trying."

She thought about his proposal that whole day. She had a lot of help.

"Is he crazy?" Linda said. "How could you ever marry a backward person like him? I mean, Harold was bad enough, but at least he was good-looking."

Lillian was weighing off things against her happiness. The "if I do this, then that" sort of weighing off, until she was weary with all the possibilities that come under the category of "yes, but." And when the day was finally done and she crawled into the privacy of her own bed, she realized that it was logically impossible to make some sort of rational decision, so she stopped thinking about all the possibilities. She knew the decision would have to come from some gut feeling.

CHAPTER 17

At the end of the week she called on Able. She'd stayed away for the whole week, to give things time to settle in.

"Well, I don't have an answer for you," she said. "But I'm not saying no, either. We hardly know each other. I think we need to get to know each other better, don't you agree?"

He lowered his head and then stroked his chin. "Yes, Lillian. I know what you mean. But I don't have much time, you see," he said. "You see, I've got some pretty big payments to make to the bank. I had to borrow the money to buy my brother out. And then there's this other thing with my sister Edith. I was going to tell you all this before you went makin' commitments, you understand." He looked at her to see if she understood. She nodded, surprised by these new revelations, and wondered what else would he reveal. "You see, me and my brother John and sister Edith, why we all inherited a share of this farm from my parents. But let me start at the beginning." He showed her into the parlor. It looked clean and orderly like it did the first time she saw it but with its turn-of-the-century furniture, it now seemed to her to be artificial, like an old movie set.

"We all lived here together," he continued, "when my Ma and Pa were alive. When my Pa died and then Ma died, they left this place to us. Edith, she's the oldest, and she kinda' took charge, especially since Ma left her everything inside the house. John decided to sell his share and move out. Edith asked me if I wouldn't buy John's share. She herself wanted to eventually move off the farm and into town." He stopped speaking, trying to collect his thoughts.

"Let's see, then, after John moved, Edith met George Grubbs, a widower. They courted about a year and then finally got married. She moved into his house in town and left most of her furniture here, sayin' she would get it sometime later. She knew I couldn't buy her out, so she takes one fourth the income I make from this place as rent. Between paying off the loan I made to buy John out and paying Edith one fourth, I've been pretty well strapped."

She could see the concern in his face. "That's a lot of pressure. Won't she agree to take less?"

"Hmm... well," he shrugged, "It's even worse than that. You see, she wants me to buy her out. She says I can't run this place no how with them two boys gone and that I'd better sell it before it goes belly up and give her, her share."

Lillian sat back in the old-fashioned parlor chair and folded her arms over her chest. She wondered what she was getting into. "That *is* bad. So that's why you proposed to combine our operations?" she asked. "Do you really think that'll work?"

He looked down and shook his head. "Can't be sure. But, with John and Junior and Bobby and me, and maybe you sometimes, I figure we can handle thirty head. Now if Edith will give me a little more time to get going again, the bank will probably loan me enough to buy her out."

"I don't know," she responded. "Milking machines. Thirty head. All that makes me uneasy; you know what my philosophy is. And my cows have been pampered with hand milking," she said. "I don't even know if they'll let down for those machines."

"Oh, Lillian, that's not something to worry about. These new machines are as gentle as hand milking. Only takes 'em a few days to get used to it. In fact, I think the cows like it better."

They sat silent for a few moments, each trying to sort out what they'd said. "Well, you know, this puts everything in a whole new light," she said, wondering if she had really understood everything correctly. "I'm glad you told me this now. Let me think about it for a while." He wasn't sure that he'd said the right things.

She returned the next morning, which he took as a good sign. "Able, I have a plan she said," her tone more business-like than the day before. "See what you think."

He nodded. "Ok, let's hear it," he responded.

"Remember, I said yesterday that we need to get to know each other better? Well, I still believe that." He sighed in anticipation of bad news. "But, in the meanwhile," she continued, "I'll agree to move my cows over here. That way we can see if we can really work together and if your plan will really work. And if not, I can always move them back." She went silent and watched his face.

"Hmm... well let's see. You mean Junior and Bobby can work over here?" She nodded. "Then, by God, it just might work. Depending of course, on my sister."

"Do you think she'll give you the time you need?" Lillian asked.

"I don't know. But, if you move your herd over and we can show her it'll work, I think that may convince her to keep taking rent until I can get the milk production back up."

Over the next two days, they made the move. She was concerned and sad about moving her cattle, but she thought it was better than losing everything. Lillian left the chickens and three calves in her barn, just to keep it working. She and Bobby walked the cows over to Able's, two at a time.

From then on, they ate breakfast and supper mostly at Able's place. Bobby and Linda seemed extremely happy; the electric lights and the bathroom with sinks with running water and a real flush toilet and a wash machine were like new wonders. They were so happy, they were reluctant to return home at night. And spending evenings with Able allowed Lillian to get to know him much better. She found he had a keen and inquiring mind and even questioned her about her teaching and was resolved to learn something more about geography from her books.

Able told his sister what they had done, and she was unhappily surprised.

"You should have asked me before you start making drastic changes in our plans," she said. She knew about Lillian Sims, but had never met her directly. She didn't remember meeting her at Paul's funeral. "I'd like to meet this lady farmer-teacher, this miracle worker," she said. "I can't believe that you now think that she can save the farm. I think your plan has lots of holes in it, brother. Lots of holes."

Able didn't tell her that he had proposed marriage to the lady, but Edith suspected something of the sort was brewing beneath it all.

After things had gone according to plan for several months, and Lillian seemed satisfied with the way things were going, Able arranged for a Sunday dinner at the farm, inviting his sister and Mr. Grubbs, and everyone from Lillian's family. He hoped his sister would see the merit of their plans and get to know how wonderful Lillian was.

CHAPTER 18

THE DINNER PARTY

The Grubbs arrived that Sunday in a nice shiny antique auto, a Willys Knight, and George Grubbs took great pleasure in sounding the peculiar horn when they pulled up to the front of the house. The car was one of several he kept for pleasure; he was a small time restorer-collector. Lillian watched them get out of the car from the window and saw two rather rotund porcelain figures, somber-faced, in conservative, almost Victorian, dress, ambling up the path to the house. They were accompanied by a third, smaller person. Able went out to greet them and escorted them into the house.

"I'm glad to meet you, Mrs. Sims," Edith said coldly, and shook Lillian's hand. Lillian felt the warm, wet flesh of Able's sister and she felt repulsed and immediately knew from the tone of voice that the greeting was insincere. Edith looked heavier than when she had first seen her on the day of the funeral; her cheeks seemed more jowly. She had two little pig eyes and a large nose, and the effect was remarkable, because all Lillian could think of was *that* very same animal. Edith glared suspiciously at Lillian's pearl necklace and the fine and expensive suit of clothes she was wearing. Edith wore a dark blue polka dot dress with a tight lace collar around her thick neck. Heavy brown stockings with thick-heeled black leather shoes completed her outfit.

Mr. Grubbs was somewhat taller than Edith but looked remarkably like her. His eyes were bigger and had a "sleepy" curl in the lids, but they were still pig eyes set deep in his round face. A checkered sport jacket over a white shirt and a pair of brown pants completed his display. "Nice to meet you," he said, and again she felt the insincerity of the greeting. "Able's told us a lot about you," and he squeezed her hand too tight when he shook it. There was something about him that made her very uncomfortable. "This is my daughter, Gladys," he said, while pointing to the young girl who accompanied him. "Gladys, say hello to Mrs. Sims." Lillian was surprised to meet the pretty girl. Gladys was a slender built thirteen-year-old with dark red hair, the child of his first marriage.

They gathered around the big table in the parlor which was just big enough to accommodate everyone. Lillian thought it would have been presumptuous for her to prepare a meal at Able's house. Instead, she brought over a large roast beef she'd prepared in her own kitchen with baked potatoes, fresh bread and butter from her cows, and two blackberry pies.

"So, you're a teacher, Mrs. Sims?" Edith asked, after shifting and rolling her ponderous bulk to accommodate it to the dining chair. Thick slices of the succulent roast had already been served on big platters and placed on the table. Her hand flew in an arc towards the serving fork.

"Yes. I teach at Hillsdale elementary. The middle graders," Lillian answered.

"Well, I hope it's better than the school we had here. *WE* had to shut that school down, you know." She slid a large slice of the roast onto her plate. "Never heard of such goings' on. You do remember that, don't you Mrs. Sims?" Mrs. Grubbs looked at Bobby, but Bobby was busy looking at Gladys.

"Yes, I certainly remember," Lillian said. "We don't have any problems like that at Hillside, I can assure you." Lillian didn't know whether to call her Edith or Mrs. Grubbs.

"Well, that's what that teacher, what was her name? Mrs. Ellis? That's what she said, and look at the mess that little school was in." She shook her head in apparent disgust as she moved a forkful of meat towards her mouth. "I blame her for that too. It's the teacher's job to keep the kids under control. Don't you think that's true, Mrs. Sims?"

Lillian wondered where her confidence on such a complex issue came from. "What you say has some merit," she replied cautiously, buttering a thick slice of bread. "But it's the parent's job to keep their kids in line. They need to know what they're up to."

"That's right," George Grubbs interjected, adding some weight to Lillian's remarks. "I always know what my Gladys is doing. More to the point, I know what's in her heart." Gladys had been seizing up her new acquaintances, John and Bobby. She squirmed when she heard her name mentioned.

"Well, I still say it's mostly the teacher's responsibility," Edith said with firm conviction. "Especially at school. Mr. Grubbs, tell me how are parents going to know what's going on at school, especially in the school yard? Do you really know what Gladys does at school?" Edith helped herself to another mouthful of roast beef. She hadn't tackled the potatoes yet.

Mr. Grubbs already had his plate overflowing with meat and potatoes. He was about to jam another forkful of meat into his mouth, when she asked *that* question. "What I mean, Mrs. Grubbs," he said, as the fork remained suspended in mid-flight, "is that if you know what's in their hearts, you don't have to know what they're doing in the schoolyard." Then he stuck the loaded fork in his mouth.

John and Bobby and Gladys and Linda were trying their best to ignore this conversation, and had been chatting amongst themselves. Both John and Bobby were intrigued by the pretty girl sitting next to them. Bobby was trying to think of something to say.

"Where do you go to school?" Bobby asked, having more courage than John to speak up. He wanted to shut out the other conversation going on at the table. The voice of Mrs. Grubbs made him uneasy.

"Gloversville Junior High," she said. "And I don't like it."

Bobby had some time to go to get into Junior High; and someone in Junior High was so much more mature and superior to the gawky kids in grammar school.

"Well John here, he goes to Johnstown High," Bobby said. John looked up, surprised. He just nodded his head and went on eating. He seemed afraid of the red-headed beauty sitting next to him.

"Oh, that's a nice school, isn't it, John," Gladys said almost in a whisper, leaning over towards him; looking into his eyes and smiling. Then she whispered something in his ear. He blushed at her nearness and the smell of her perfume and at what she said. She looked around the table and smiled again. Her parents were still engaged in that awful conversation with Mrs. Sims. Linda seemed to be examining her food and thinking of something else. Bobby was looking at Mrs. Grubbs as if he 'd seen a ghost. John almost choked when he felt Gladys's hand slide onto his leg under the table.

"Whatever possessed you to move into that old Morrison place?" Edith Grubbs addressed Lillian with the same air of superiority she had used in the previous round of questions. This question was phrased as if she expected some heroic response; like her decision was made because of economic necessity or failing health.

Lillian took the question as a challenge. "Mrs. Grubbs, I liked the place the first time I saw it," she said, trying to preserve her calm and answer with strength, without affronting the fat lady. "I bought it because it pleased me."

"She's done wonders with that place, Edith," Able said timidly, finally joining the conversation. "It's much better now than when the Morrisons lived there."

Edith twisted her mouth in a smirk. "We just passed by there," she said, turning to look at Mr. Grubbs, "and that house looks the same as ever, doesn't it, Mr. Grubbs. Still in need of many repairs, wouldn't you say, Mrs. Sims? Or maybe ready to collapse is more like it."

Lillian flushed with embarrassment. She knew she should have rebuilt her house long ago. The patchwork repairs she had done just made the old place look worse.

"Really, Edith, I think--" said Mr. Grubbs.

"I'm afraid Mrs. Grubbs is right," Lillian interrupted, to avoid a confrontation on this subject. "I've been perhaps, too concerned about the barn and the fields and my livestock and have neglected the house."

Edith looked at her brother with a widening smirk.

"Did that place come with furniture?" Mr. Grubbs asked Lillian, with a mouthful of potatoes. He hoped to change the direction of the conversation to something he could warm up to. "I ask that, not as a busybody," he continued, "although that I sometimes have to be; but because I'm a dealer in antiques." His nose seemed to elevate as he finished the last statement.

"Oh, indeed he is," exclaimed Mrs. Grubbs, with a noticeable change in her tone. "Mr. Grubbs is a dealer in antiques." She placed emphasis on "dealer in antiques" as if it were some important title.

Lillian looked at the pudgy man again. There were no antique shops around that she knew of and the announcement of his profession puzzled her. "No. There was no furniture," she answered, "except the stoves, and some farm machinery. Do you have an antique shop?" she asked, trying to solve the puzzle.

"Shop? Oh no. Ha ha. antique shop? In Gloversville? Ha ha. Oh no. I travel about and buy old country pieces from places like yours, Mrs. Sims. Then, when I get enough, I take it to New York and sell it there to the retailers. They have the shops. Ha ha."

"That must be fun," Linda interjected. She had taken an interest in the conversation when New York was mentioned.

"It's a great profession my dear," he said, much affected by her faint praise. "I get to meet so many people, and the things I get to own, even if it's just for a little while, why you'd never believe it. They give me great satisfaction. Like the civil war sword I found hanging in a barn, just a while back." His eyes expressed great enthusiasm as he opened his mouth to start the story.

"Oh, don't start with that damn sword story, Mr. Grubbs," Edith said severely. "It just takes too long." She turned her attention to Lillian again. "I understand you've moved your cattle onto our farm," she said, in a disagreeable tone, leaving Mr. Grubbs with his mouth still open.

Lillian looked directly at Edith Grubbs, who was staring back at her. Beneath the jowls and pig eyes, she sensed a self-centered and very clever woman. She knew she was up against a formidable adversary.

"It was by mutual agreement, between Able and myself," she

said calmly. "We feel it will allow us to operate more efficiently. We need to compete in a tight and highly controlled market. Sometimes it takes pooled resources to survive."

"I *would* think so," Edith responded. "There are so many farms, and most of them failing. But tell me Mrs. Sims, how is it you have time to run a farm and teach our youngsters at the same time?" Her voice was now on the edge of anger.

"Now dear, don't get upset," said Mr. Grubbs, waving his chubby hands in front of him, as if speaking to a large audience. "We must remember, just not to get upset. I'm sure Mrs. Sims knows what she can do."

"It keeps me very busy, no doubt, Mrs. Grubbs," Lillian said, flushed by the woman's words, "but I do find the time."

"Well I personally don't think you can share the *important* time you need for teaching with any other activity. And *farming*... a woman... for God's sake... I just don't understand that. She put her fork down firmly as if to accentuate her last statement. Her piercing gaze invited Lillian to do battle.

Lillian knew she would have to counter this attack from this very offensive woman. She had expected some questions, some apprehensiveness, but nothing like this.

"Mrs. Grubbs, I take great pride in my farm, and there is nothing, absolutely nothing unseemly about a woman running a farm. It is an old-fashioned notion to assume that only men can run things. And though my farm is small, it is successful." she was warming up to her defense. "And about teaching, Mrs. Grubbs? *May I ask you,* on what grounds do you base your statements about teaching? Have you been a teacher?"

"Teacher? Me?" she grunted. "Oh, no, Mrs. Sims, I've never been a *teacher,*" she said, while shaking her jowls emphatically. "I leave that to people like you. But you see, I have been a member of the local schoolboard for, what is it now? Seven years I believe?" Her lips parted in a toothy smile as she watched Lillian take a deep breath. "We are charged with oversight of the system, including teachers, as you well know," she said, licking her lips.

"Oh, I didn't know," Lillian said in mock surprise. She felt indignation gripping her. The churlish woman seemed to be winning against her on every front. But she really was surprised because she couldn't recall seeing her during the troubles at school. "And we teachers owe so much to those who sit on the board," she continued, her voice now dripping with sarcasm.

Edith frowned. "Well, I'll not play games with you, Mrs. Sims." Everyone left at the table stopped eating to see what she would say next. John and Gladys had already finished and were outside, exploring. "I believe you and Able have some notion about getting together," she continued, "and maybe keeping this place for yourselves. I want *you* to *understand* that I have a **full** share in this place," she said and her face began to twist and turn red, "and I don't approve of you coming over here." Her lips started to tremble and her body began to shake.

"Now sister, please be calm," Able said. "let's not, and I'm sure you didn't intend to, but let's not say anything that may offend our guests."

"Yes, dear, please don't get upset," Mr. Grubbs said, in a weak voice. But it was too late. Her face twisted and now turned blue and her eyes grew big and round and were bulging from their sockets. The food she had been chewing came oozing out and it became clear that she was sinking under a seizure.

Bobby had been serving gravy from the large gravy boat which he found very unwieldy for his small hands, when she turned her twisted visage and enormous eyes on him. He went back with a start and dropped the heavy server in his lap, which made him, in turn, jump up with a yell. The spilled gravy covered his lap and the server fell to the floor in a splintering crash.

Mr. Grubbs and Able eased the sick woman to the floor. She was wracked with uncontrollable shaking and her body twisted violently. Lillian and Mr. Grubbs tried to calm her while Able ran off to the kitchen to get a wooden spoon. They forced her mouth open and put the handle between her teeth, to keep her from biting her tongue. During all this commotion, Linda had taken Bobby into the kitchen to calm him down and clean him up. Tears welled up; he was scared by everything that had happened. "I'm afraid of that lady," he said. Linda embraced him and told him not to be afraid.

"Oh dear," Able said, "I was afraid this was going to happen. Whenever she gets upset or excited. Always happens." They carried her into the bedroom and Mr. Grubbs asked Able to get some sedatives from her purse. Lillian left the room with him.

"I'm sorry, Lillian," Able said, with fear and sadness coloring his voice. "I had no idea when I talked to her that she was so upset by our getting together." He shook his head in disgust. "I hope you won't think too badly of her; or of me, for putting you through this." He was afraid he had lost Lillian.

"No, I understand," she said as Able struggled to get the medicine from Edith's purse. "But it's clear that we've got to talk," and she left him to see about Bobby.

Lillian left for home as soon as they were sure that Edith Grubbs was recovering from her seizure and in no need of further help.

"Bobby, do you remember Mrs. Grubbs?" Lillian asked, after they got home. "Did you see her during that Sally Rigger incident?"

"Oh, well, maybe... I think so. Yes, yes, I did. At first, I didn't remember her, but then, when she started gettin' red and mad, I remembered her. She was always mad like that with me, when I was there with Miss Ellison. She said I deserved to be punished and expelled. I was afraid... because of her."

"Wonder why I didn't see her during the hearing when they suspended you?" she asked herself, more than Bobby.

"Oh, Miss Ellison told me," he said. "She said, I didn't have to be afraid of Mrs. Grubbs. Mrs. Grubbs was out with her sickness."

CHAPTER 19

The day after meeting Julia, Linda pawned her wedding rings to get the needed money. Julia had been grateful, but that only solved the immediate crisis. More was needed and some weeks later Linda planned an approach to borrow from her mother. Asking for money was always a big thing. She had no friends she could ask. Confiding in Rosemary was considered; she had always seemed like a best friend to her mother. But lately, Rosemary had been acting squirrely. After the last visit with her, Linda sensed there was something very wrong in their relationship. Rosemary had seemed distant, almost cold and she was doing strange things. Her cousin Ed, there at the time, bragged about her taking up hunting: he was teaching her how to shoot. Linda came away with the feeling that Rosemary was losing it and that she would rather not see her or her mother again. Linda saw something dark in Rosemary's face. With her mother left as the only source, she decided to take the bold approach:

"Mom, could you loan me three hundred dollars?" she asked.

"What?" Lillian said, surprised. Linda had never asked for such a large amount. "Did you say three hundred?"

"Yes. I know it's a lot but I really need it. I'll pay you back at fifteen a week." She had already made her calculations.

"Can I ask why you need it?" Lillian asked. Linda had hoped that she wouldn't ask. But she had already planned her story.

"It's a good friend, Ma. She needs help. Her old man ran off on her and left her with no money and a baby. She's trying to get a job, but right now she's having a hard time. I'd even give her more if I could. I'm sure she'll pay it back when she can."

"Who is it, Linda?" she asked, with mounting interest. A woman abandoned by her husband always got her interest.

"I can't say. I promised this person I wouldn't tell anyone about her troubles. Please don't make me break that promise."

Lillian said, "Well, then I won't ask you. But you'll have to wait a week. I need to cash in some bonds for that kind of money."

Linda drummed on the table, thinking.

"Linda?"

"Oh, yes, well, I'm really sorry to have to ask you to do this. But do you think you could loan me something, anything, before Friday? This girl will be thrown out of her apartment if she doesn't come up with thirty bucks by Friday."

"Thrown out! That's horrible, and with a baby? Who would do such a... ."

"Can you Loan me the money?"

"Loan you... the money... let's see... yes, let me check, but I think I can give you thirty now." She went to the bedroom to get the money from the drawer where she kept small amounts of cash.

Linda sighed when her mother left the kitchen. It was hard to keep *that* secret; she really wanted to tell her about Julia and the child, but some immediate problems needed attention first. If she rushed things, the fragile structure of intertwining egos would crumple and she could lose Julia all over again.

That day after work she gave Julia the money she'd borrowed plus a little out of her rock bottom savings account. "God, Linda, I don't know... thanks... thanks, so much. Did you borrow from Ma?"

"Yes, I did. Told her it was for a friend. She didn't question me at all once she knew I needed the money for that."

Julia had taken Linda's advice about her job. That day after their first meeting, she told Mary on the way to work that she was going to quit.

"Why?" Mary asked.

"Mary, my hands are burned so bad, I just can't work those irons any more. I guess I'm just too clumsy." She showed Mary her left hand.

"My God." She was shocked and pulled over to the side of the street. "Let me see the other hand," she said.

Linda showed her the other hand. “God, Julia, why didn't you say something? They look like they're infected.”

Julia shook her head. “I thought I'd get over it; thought I'd learn how to work those irons. I don't have much skill with my hands.”

Mary pulled out into the street again and drove on in deep thought. “Look,” she said, “I've got a little pull in that section. I'll talk to Mike and see if he won't put you someplace else. I heard they need some help down in the wool room. I think it's less money, though. Would that be Ok?”

“It's a job. Sure.”

That evening, Julia told Linda That she’d been transferred off the Irons.

“That's good,” Linda said. “That I'll give us some time to find you something better.” She'd checked with personnel at Ideal that day. “They said they had no openings. But Jerry, the personnel supervisor, told me they were planning on opening a new canvas line in about two months. They'll need pattern cutters and stitchers.”

“Is it mostly straight time?” Julia asked. “I can't work much overtime with Andy.”

“I don't know. But we haven't been working any overtime lately. Our first problem would be to get you trained. Do you know anything about canvas work?”

“Are you kidding? “ she said, shaking her head.

“Would you want to try this?” Linda asked.

“I don't know. How would I learn?”

* * *

“Do you know how to use a sewing machine? “ she asked Julia when she returned from work that day

“No,” she said, “never did it. Besides I don't think I can trust these hands. I'd probably sew my fingers together.” They both laughed, but Julia said she was serious about not being good at jobs that required lots of hand skills. "I've always been clumsy, " she said.

"Well, then you better not take this job. You need to do something like clerking," Linda said. "That's what I do. Can you type?" Julia shook her head.

"Maybe I better ask you what you can do. Or what you like to do?"

"Let's see, when I worked at Erhardts, I was in charge of the cooking machines. I checked food temperatures, cooking times and adjusted the heating levels on the boilers. I was in charge of seven cookers. I kept records, too, for each batch we cooked."

"I knew about that and checked with Knox Gelatin, but they're not hiring. And that experience doesn't help for this kind of work. There are no other food factories around here. Anything else?"

"I like farming," Julia said. "That doesn't help much, does it?"

"*You* like farming?" Linda said in surprise.

Julia nodded her head. "Yes, sounds crazy, doesn't it? But Duane's parents were farmers; they had a dairy farm. When I first went out there, I liked everything about the place. I liked the smells, the cows, the barn, the fields, just everything. When we went there on weekends, I'd help wherever they'd let me. Old Mr. Lippers used to say I was a natural farmer like him; had it in my blood. You know, I think he was right? Do you think I can get a job as a farmer?" and she laughed.

"No," Linda replied. "Just exploring all possibilities. Never know what we'll find if we just look."

But Linda was very interested. Here was Julia, of all people, with a surprise showing of all the traits of her mother. She resolved to start her second mission: to educate Julia about what her mother was really like; to show her that her father's death was not her mother's fault. She knew where to find the common ground. A few days later she started laying the foundation.

"Did you know that Mom has a small farm?" she told Julia.

"What? A farm?" She laughed cynically. "I don't think she knows a cow from a goat," she said. "Mom? Her and her social buddies? Do they all come over to help her? Be serious, Linda."

"You've missed a great deal, Julia," Linda said. "Your mother is really one of the best small dairy farmers around."

Julia looked puzzled. She could see that Linda was serious. "But... but how did this great mover of society become a... ", and she left the sentence unfinished.

Linda related the story of the Sand Creek farm, as they all called the place now. As she described the events, she could see that Julia was taking interest and asking lots of questions. When she finished, Julia shook her head in disbelief. The story had shaken her arrogant confidence in the image she held of her mother.

"It's hard to believe," she said. "This sounds like another person, not my mother. I don't know what to say."

"Don't say anything," Linda said. "Just think about what I told you." It was obvious that she had made an impression.

She saw that it worked. Julia's words now took on a much softer tone when speaking of her mother. The harsh and bitter words were no longer used. Anxiety and mistrust were still there and colored her thoughts, but the deep bitterness was gone. In its place had come a curiosity, a desire to finally know this new woman who was so much like her.

A few weeks later, Linda decided to tell her mother about Julia. Linda's relationship with Julia had strengthened beyond what she ever thought was possible, but she still was cautious. One wrong move and the whole thing could collapse.

"Mom, remember that money I borrowed for a friend?" she asked, one day before leaving for work.

"Sure. Is she getting on now?" Lillian asked. She was removing her barn boots getting ready for school. "Did the money help?"

"Oh, yes. She's much better, thanks to you. And I can tell you who it is now." Linda waited for a response.

"Well?" Lillian said, when no further words came from Linda. "Who is your friend?" She stopped working with the boots and looked at Linda. Her curiosity was aroused.

"Mom, I would have told you sooner, but for good reasons, I couldn't. The girl is... my sister, Julia."

Lillian let the boot she was holding fall to the floor. Her mouth dropped open. Silence reigned for what seemed like an eternity as the two women stared at each other.

"You mean ... my... Julia?" she asked, with a trembling voice.

"Yes, your Julia. And she's a changed person from the one that left you so long ago."

"But... how?" Lillian was almost speechless.

"It's a long story, Ma. But I have even better news for you. You have a new grandson, Andy."

Her words passed through Lillian like an electric shock. She stood up. "A grandson? Andy? Oh, God, I don't believe it. Are you sure?" She felt dizzy.

"Yes, I'm sure. He's a little over a year old. Beautiful boy with curly hair. I think he looks like you."

"Oh God. I still can't believe it. Are you sure? Is Julia... is she Ok?"

Linda explained everything that had passed between her and Julia and Andy. As she talked, Lillian's excitement grew until she was pacing around like a caged tiger.

"I'm really sorry for Julia," she said. "But the truth is I'm really glad that damn Duane Lippers left her... I mean, we never did like him."

Linda continued cleaning up the table. They had just finished breakfast. "I'd like to bring Julia and Andy out here for a visit, but you'd better leave it to me to set it up. Please don't go to see her first and I think it's best to start over and forget the past entirely."

"Linda, Linda. How lucky that... you... you're so good. Yes, of course, I'll leave everything up to you, but please, please, as soon as possible."

It was the next Saturday that Julia agreed to come out to the farm. Her curiosity about the farm and her "new" mother had been keenly honed by Linda. She was eager, although anxiety gripped her heart.

When Linda parked the car, Julia got out with trembling hands. She lifted the child in her arms. When she looked around, she saw the bubbling waters of the little creek and heard them sounding against the enormous silence of the green world she had entered. The tamarack trees stood tall and pristine, now in their most lovely greens. Lillian was on the porch dreading this upcoming meeting, now unsure of how she would react. But when she saw the figure walking up the path, her heart flew out. She couldn't help herself; she started down the path crying silently: “Julia! Andy! Julia! Andy! Oh God, it's so good to see you!”, but the words never came out.

Julia stopped on the path, looking grim. When she saw her mother coming towards her, looking different than she had ever remembered, she felt confused and scared. Lillian was letting gray hair show and she wore a farm dress with a full apron. Julia had never seen her looking like that. Lillian stopped, and as she saw the boy, a big smile spread on her face. The two women stood looking at each other, unearthing their strange feelings. Then the boy saved the moment by extending his hand towards Lillian.

“Andy. This is your Grandma,” Julia said softly, as he leaned towards Lillian.

She gently took him from her daughter's arms. She felt the warmth of his trembling flesh under her grasp. After she kissed him, she looked at Julia again. Do *I have a new daughter?* she thought. *What should I say to her?* But she said nothing and forced a smile instead.

She took the boy and walked up to the porch. She turned and called back: “Julia--- Julia, please... come on in.”

Linda's strategy worked and after the second visit, she stepped out of her role as mediator and let the tense relationship develop on its own. The great wounds seemed to be healing. Julia was almost back in the family again and Andy was a new star. Lillian felt that if all went well, and she was far from sure that it would, she was ready to help them both start a new life whenever Julia was ready to accept it.

CHAPTER 20

After Rosemary's unexpected and scary visit, Harold had been more unsure of himself than ever. He couldn't understand why his thoughts kept turning back to Lillian; why he now felt he wanted to be only with her. But it would be useless he knew, to try to gain her good will again. Lillian should have never left him alone on that farm.

His money was running low. His savings account had less than a few hundred dollars and there was less than a hundred in the coffee can. He had been mailing his mother a money order every month, but now found it was not possible.

He went to the sawmills looking for work but they had nothing for him. He got a few contracts for cutting firewood and a barn repair job in Elmwood Village. Both provided only a small income; he would have to stop the money orders to his mother until he could pick himself up again.

He drove over to Fonda to tell her about the money problem. He hadn't seen her since he'd announced his wedding; a visit was past due. When he passed the bridge spanning the canal, he thought of Rosemary's place just on the other side.

Rosemary! Now she's threatening to kill me!

She had raised his passions and then killed them with all her crazy demands. He was convinced that he just didn't understand women.

Stanley King greeted him at the door. "What a nice surprise," he said, a big smile spreading across his weathered face as he shook Harold's hand. "Your mother will be happy to see you."

Harold thought his mother had aged considerably since he had seen her last. Her face looked cadaverous; her eyes sunken in deep shadowed wells. She seemed as white as the walls of her house, as if no blood coursed through her veins. Gray hair slipped out in long thin strings from under the frilly dust cap she wore. Her left leg was wrapped in heavy brown bandages covered with a brown stocking and her foot rested on a heated flatstone.

"Harold. It's so good to see you," she said, in a surprisingly strong voice. "I'm happy you've come again. You stay away too long." He took her hand and was sure he felt the streams of pain pouring through her leg. He kissed her on the cheek.

"Oh, Ma, I didn't know you were sick," he said, looking into her watery eyes.

She looked up at him. "Sick? Me? Oh, no Harold, I'm not sick," she said. "What on earth... ? But yes. I know... sometimes I forget how old I am. I know I'm not much to look at anymore and wrapped up like this in these infernal rags." She tapped the wrappings on her leg. "But Harold, I'm just getting on in years." She squeezed his hand.

Stanley went into the kitchen and asked Harold to come in with him. "She seems exhausted now, Harold," he said. "I'd not talk about your situation, at least for a while. I'm sure she's going to want to talk to you about it later. She has something to tell you. But not now." Harold nodded. "It's lunch time," and Stanley turned towards making some sandwiches.

"She looks awful sick," Harold said.

"Well, you caught her by surprise. But really, she's just pale. Doesn't get outside much, because of her gout. And she's got diabetes too, remember. Gets her to feeling bad sometimes. But I wouldn't worry Harold. She's got a strong constitution. Now you ought to go back in there and keep her company, while I rustle up these sandwiches."

Stanley came in later with the tray of sandwiches. He placed the tray on the dining table in the sitting room.

"What would you like to drink, Harold? I have some good cider from Coopers' farm. Remember?" Stanley had a pleasant smile and always seemed to want to please. His dark-tanned face and mop of white hair made his smile more luminous. He had a healthy, robust look in spite of his years.

Harold liked the cider from Coopers. And the chicken sandwiches were delicious. As he ate, he looked around the room of bad memories, and for the very first time, he didn't feel like fleeing. For once, he was really there just to visit his mother and not just to ask for something.

Something else occurred to him. Something he had never felt before. He had been lonely in the cabin. He had never felt loneliness before and now it felt good to be in company.

He asked Mr. King if he would take a walk with him after they ate. He wanted to see his old home as perhaps, he'd never seen it before. And he wanted to bury the feelings of the presence here of something dark and evil he had always carried with him.

Just above the house was a shed where the gardening equipment was kept. Mr. King kept a quarter acre under cultivation. It was a daunting task, but one that he thoroughly enjoyed and he conveyed that to Harold.

"Some of the richest soil around, Harold," he said, when showing him the plot of dark earth. Many small plants poked out their unruly heads from every part of the plot.

As they walked up the hill, Harold saw that everything seemed neat and planned. Mr. King seemed to revel in orderliness; the shed was stacked with supplies and tools and feeds ever so neatly as if that were all Mr. King had to do.

They walked up further; all the way to the edge of the woods where crows kept guard at the perimeter. "I figure she's got about a hundred acres there," Mr. King said. "Hasn't been cut over in a long while. Lots of valuable wood in there." A quick glance told Harold that it was probably true.

When they turned to go back, Mr. King remarked: "You really have been staying away too long, Harold. Your mother grieves when you don't come to visit."

"I guess I didn't think," Harold replied.

Mr. King stopped walking. "I tell you what Harold. You'd make your mother very happy if you'd spend the night here, with her," he said. "She's always alone at night, you know. It would make her very happy, really."

"Stay here?" He wasn't ready to go that far. He would need more time before he could do that. "I would like to please my mother. But I can't stay, really. Maybe some time when I've planned it... maybe then."

"I wish you'd think it over, Harold," he said. "She really needs to talk to you. You know, we've been hoping you would come. It's difficult for us to drive out to your place."

"She needs to talk with me? Is something wrong?"

"You know, I'd rather not interfere. I won't say that something is wrong, but I will say that something is not right."

"Well, that's not sayin' much, is it, Mr. King? Anyway, where would I sleep? We can't go cleaning out that old bedroom of mine." Harold knew he could never sleep where he'd been beaten by his father.

"Oh, you can sleep on the couch," he said. "I take naps there sometimes. It's quite comfortable. And please. Call me Stanley?"

"Oh," Harold exclaimed, and then ran out of words. He had always called him Mr. King, from the time he was a boy. And he felt trapped by the sudden invitation. But the fact that his mother wanted to talk to him made the difference. He agreed to stay.

Harold passed the afternoon helping Stanley gather eggs, clean the hen house yard and cultivate a few rows in the vegetable garden. After supper, the dishes were washed by Stanley and dried by Harold and his mother, who felt good enough to stand for a short time. She looked much better now than when he had first seen her that morning; she seemed to have some color in her cheeks. Stanley said he would leave earlier than usual, since Harold was there and he had a number of things to do at home.

"Now Harold," she said, after Stanley had left, "the first thing I have to talk to you about is my Will." She said. "I've made some changes since I talked to you last."

"Ma, you don't have to worry about that," he said. He was always embarrassed when she brought up the Will. He had always said that he wanted nothing that had belonged to his father.

"Oh, but I do," she said. "What I want you to know is that I've left that back woodlot to Stanley. I owe him so much; it'll only cover very little for what he's done for me. I've had a deed drawn up in his name to become active on my death. And I've left him that car, that Model A, and the tools in the stable that used to belong to your father." Harold shrugged. "Everything else still goes to you. I hope you don't mind?"

"'Course not, he's been a big help to you."

"'Course, if he should die first, why then you'd get all that anyway. I just didn't want you having no bad surprises if I died. I want you to remember your Ma as someone who always loved you."

"I know that," he said, feeling closer to his mother than ever before. "And It's fine with me that Stanley is in your Will. Don't fret about it at all."

She looked satisfied. "Harold, would you fetch that flatstone for me?" she said, suddenly wincing and rubbing her leg. "Stanley left it heating in the oven. My leg's acting up again."

Harold brought the stone wrapped in cloth and placed it on the short stool. She moved her leg to rest on top of the warm stone.

"Now. I want to talk to you about Lillian. Let's see if I can keep all this straight." He was surprised to hear Lillian's name. "Lillian came over here, right after you two broke up. She told me what happened and said she was sorry about it. That's how I knew what you were talking about this morning."

"Well, I'll be damned," Harold said, taken completely by surprise. "I didn't know that Lillian and you were talkin' to each other."

"Well, I really got to liking Lillian after you married her. She's too old for you; you'll never have kids, you know. But she's a good woman."

"I know she's good. But what did she tell you?" he asked.

"She said she was sorry, but she had thrown you out because you had taken up with another woman. She didn't mention any names. She didn't know I already knew about Rosemary, but I didn't say anything." Now Harold was wondering again about how Lillian and now, his mother, had found out about Rosemary in the first place. "She wasn't really mad," she continued. "She said maybe it was for the best."

"Is that all?" he asked.

"Well, she brought your things over here. They're in the store room... your old bedroom. I thought you might need them."

"Uh, yes," he said.

"Well?" his mother asked.

"Well what?"

"Is there anything to add to that story?"

"No, not really. You heard it all." He wasn't going to bring up Linda. He didn't think Lillian would have either.

"Well, I'm sorry about all that Harold. Are you going to get a divorce? Are you and Rosemary going to get married?"

He stroked his beard. "Don't know Ma. I don't know what's going to happen." He was afraid to tell her about his troubles with Rosemary.

She shifted her leg on the stone. "Well, I have another tale to tell about Lillian," she said.

"Another... tale?" He was dumbfounded that she seemed to know so much about his affairs. "What kind of tale?" he asked.

"Well, right after Lillian came over, two days later, I believe, a young gentleman come to see me. He was William Svenson Junior from that Creamery over there on Harlan road?" She frowned and stopped to move her foot on the stone. " He wasn't very pleasant at all."

"What did he want?"

"It was about Lillian."

"Lillian?"

"Yes, Lillian," she said, "and mind you, I don't know how much of this is true, so don't go getting' too upset. It may be over nothing. But he said that Lillian had been having an affair with his father."

"What?" Harold blurted, "Lillian having an affair?" He had a wild look in his eyes.

"Yes. Yes. He said it was Lillian. It seems that she had pledged to marry this man's father; his name was William too, when they were teenagers. But Lillian was sent off to school before they could get married."

"Oh, God. And I thought I was the only one." Harold couldn't believe that Lillian was capable of cheating on him. "Why did he come to you, Ma. Did he have a reason for telling you this?"

"He was angry. Said that this affair with Lillian drove his mother off and eventually killed his father. Said he wanted the whole family to know how awful Lillian was. He said that you should know. I guess you didn't know anything about it, did you?"

"No. Nothing. All I knew was that Lillian was seeing old Bill Svenson on a business basis. She had a contract with his creamery. He came out to the house a couple of times to see her cows."

Harold didn't want to believe the story. "But why would he say this if it wasn't true?" he asked his mother. "What has he got to gain?"

"I asked myself that very thing," she said. "It's hard to believe, but why say these things if they aren't true?"

"God, I just can't believe it. Lillian just isn't that kind." He shook his head to emphasize his disbelief.

"Well, Harold, there's lots a' things about a person we might find hard to believe." She twitched her shoulders and her lips parted while she gritted her teeth. She was staring at Harold's old bedroom. "I hope it isn't true. But I had to tell you."

"I know. Sorry you're being dragged into these things."

They sat quiet for a while. Then she said: "Harold, I'm tired now. All this talk has wore me out. I hope I'm right in tellin' you all this." He nodded, to show it was Ok, but he was deep in thought. "Stanley left some bedding on the couch for you. I think I'll go to bed, son." He kissed her goodnight and offered to help her to her room. She said she could manage with her crutch alone, but if he wanted to help, it would be OK.

The couch was plenty big enough for Harold to sleep on. But he didn't sleep at all, and not because of thinking about his father. He felt that something bad was happening, something out of control, and he had a central part in it.

CHAPTER 21

Shortly after the reconciliation with Julia, Lillian received a letter containing a strange request. The return address on the envelope showed it was from Mrs. Baumann. The letter read:

"Dear Mrs. Sims,

"I'm writing to you to request that you allow me to explain some important facts about the incident at Wickersville school. Allow me please to ask once again your forgiveness and to ask a favor. I know maybe you think this is a ridiculous request, since my niece caused you too much trouble. But I think I can tell you something in her favor and show you she is not a wicked person.

To make this explanation, can I come to make a visit? I have an urgent need to explain this to you. Please allow me this.

Sincerely

Mrs. Baumann

Lillian read the letter several times, noting its curious request. She had really liked the Baumanns and felt bad that they suffered so much for the errors of their niece. She even felt sorry for Sarah and Hannah because they both seemed naive and simple minded to have believed in Sally Rigger. The Baumanns had left their home because of the reaction by their neighbors to Hannah's role in the bizarre episode at the school. It had been a good excuse for the locals to vindicate their beliefs in the dark purposes they attributed to the Baumanns: it gave them a reason to exercise their hostility.

She sent off a letter agreeing to a meeting at her place on a Saturday or Sunday two weeks later. But before she sent it off, she asked Bobby if he would agree to see Hannah once more.

"That witch?" he said. "No, I don't want to see her again."

"Why Bobby? It's important for me to know." She wanted to be sure of everything before she forgave anybody.

"It's because I don't like witches. I'm scared of them."

"But she isn't a witch, Bobby," explained Lillian. "You shouldn't think of her that way."

"I told you---they said themselves they were witches."

"Well, it turns out Bobby, that's not true. They did awful things, but they aren't witches."

"Aunt Lilly? How do you know that it's not true? I believed them when they said that. They seemed to know all about being witches."

Lillian stopped her rote answers. Bobby was always coming up with challenges to conventional adult wisdom. How did she know, indeed? Wasn't Sally's mother a real witch? If not, what did it take to be a *real* witch? Lillian didn't know. But she decided to go ahead with her invitation anyway.

"Look, Bobby. I've invited the Baumanns to come here. They'll probably come next Saturday, as they said in their postcard. Why don't you go over to Able's? You can help John with all the things they have to do."

"Oh, yes. That's Ok with me," Bobby replied. "I don't want to see that Hannah Green again."

Then she told Linda about who was coming and what their purpose was. Linda thought it was a good thing; she had also felt sorry for the Baumanns.

"They should be gone by noon," Lillian said. " Maybe it's best if Julia and Andy come in the afternoon." Julia had been helping her mother on the farm on weekends.

"I'll tell her, Ma. We got plenty to do at her place in the morning, anyway."

The Baumanns arrived in the morning of the Saturday stated. They had brought Hannah with them. She was now developing into a pretty young girl.

"Oh, Mrs. Sims, thank you so much for seeing us," Mrs. Baumann said, as they settled in the parlor. Mr. Baumann smiled and shook Lillian's hand. "Thank you. Thank you very much," Mr. Baumann said. Hannah smiled too, and said: "Hello, Mrs. Sims. It's nice to see you again." She seemed very nervous.

"First, let me tell you something about Hannah," said Mrs. Baumann. "Since we left here, Hannah has been going to Catholic school in Amsterdam. It's Saint Ann's Preparatory school. Here she learns her religion and good behavior, don't you Hannah?"

Hannah nodded. "I'm very thankful to my aunt and uncle," Hannah said, a little mechanically. "That is a nice school."

"Let me say," said Mrs. Baumann, "that Hannah was never really a bad girl. She was under the control of that Sally Rigger. But did you know Mrs. Sims, that Hannah was the first girl to tell the truth? After Hannah told the truth, only then did Sarah tell too. That's how your poor Bobby got free from the blame." She shifted her position in the chair and smoothed out her dress. "Now I don't say that Hannah has no blame," she continued, looking at her shoes, "But I think she helped redeem herself when she said the truth."

Lillian didn't know who had told first. But she believed Mrs. Baumann."Well, we can all make mistakes," she said, "but that was a big mistake. All those lies that were told blaming the boys and especially Bobby. It's hard to forget that Hannah helped to produce those lies." Lillian looked at Hannah. "Are you really sorry for what you did?" she asked.

"Oh yes ma'am," Hannah replied, nervously. "I was really not acting normal. I was not thinking about what bad things I was doing. Sally said we were doing good."

Lillian smiled at Hannah as if to confirm that she was somewhat forgiven. "But what brings you to me, Mrs. Baumann? Lillian asked. "Surely it was not just to apologize again?"

"Ah, yes. Well you see Mrs. Sims, when we left here, we moved to Amsterdam. Hannah needed a school, and Amsterdam was far enough away to put the terrible business behind us. But we really were not wanting to leave. We really love it around this place. And we own that nice house. We tried to sell it when we left, but we had to rent. And now the nice couple renting it has moved away. We tried to rent it again, but no luck. This is causing much strain on my husband. He even had to sell his nice car. So, you see we want to move back to our house." She looked at her husband as if to confirm this and he nodded.

"Yes," he said. "It is very hard for us now." There was a sad note in his voice. " We can no longer afford to live in Amsterdam."

"And the thing is," Mrs. Baumann continued, "We must get Hannah back in school. We cannot move back here unless she can get back into school. I fear they will not let her back in. Can you help us with that, Mrs. Sims? I ask you because I know you are a just person. We have a right to live in our own home. Hannah is no harm to anyone."

Hannah had been suspended indefinitely. They would have to review her case to let her back in, Lillian knew. It would be up to the principals of the schools.

"The old Wickersville school is closed, as you must know," Lillian said. "There are two other schools you could apply to. They both have bus service to your area."

"Oh, any school is alright. We are happy with any school," said Mrs. Baumann.

"I'll try, Mrs. Baumann," said Lillian. "God knows, you're asking a lot from me. But I'll try."

"That makes us very happy, Mrs. Sims. You are a generous person." She started to get up to leave. "Oh. I almost forget. I have sent a letter to one of the, what you call them? Board members? To ask for her forgiveness, too. She was the one that convinced others to suspend Hannah. But I received no answer from her. Could you maybe talk to her too? I think she may try to stop Hannah from getting back in school."

"I don't think she can do that," Lillian said. "What is her name?"

"Mrs. Grubbs is her name. Very strong lady."

Lillian's heart dropped. "You wrote her a letter?"

"Yes. I sent it same time I sent the letter to you. But no answer yet."

"I would advise you not to communicate with Mrs. Grubbs anymore," Lillian said. "I'm sure, she'll not change her mind on that subject."

"Oh? I just thought it would help if I... ", she noticed Lillian's frown. "But no. Of course, we will do as you say, Mrs. Sims."

Hannah was becoming restless and fidgeted in her seat. She vaguely remembered the cruel threats she'd made to Bobby and wondered if he were there. Would he try to get back at her?

"Can we go now?" she said.

After they left, Lillian pondered what she was doing and concluded it was the right thing to do. She reasoned that Sarah was back in school and her parents hadn't been forced to move. Sally Rigger and her mother were gone and that was a good thing. But the Baumanns she had always felt, were victims of prejudice: they were foreigners who acted and sounded very different from the native folk. Helping them was fully justified.

The following week, she made arrangements to visit Mrs. Fallbridge, the principle and a teacher at the new Wickersville Elementary. The new school building, located four miles away from the old school site, had eight grades spread between three rooms. Mrs. Fallbridge, a big thick set woman, with solid gray hair tied in a severe bun, taught the seventh and eighth grades in room 103. Lillian knew Mrs. Fallbridge on a professional level, but could still feel the frost in the air when she greeted her.

"I'm here to give a personal reference for Hannah Green," Lillian said. "She will be making an application to get into your school. She's an eighth grader, but she has been held back a term."

"I see," said the stern-faced woman. "And why are *you* making this personal recommendation? Is she a relative of yours?"

"No. It's just that she was suspended from the old Wickersville school. I feel the suspension wasn't fully justified. I also feel the girl has made amends and is ready to join her classmates once again. Do you, by chance, remember that incident?"

"I certainly do," replied Mrs. Fallbridge. "And I must tell you that the admission of that girl to this school is very improbable."

"Why do you say that, Mrs. Fallbridge? Do you disagree with my assessment of the girl?"

"A certain school board member," replied Mrs. Fallbridge, "who is intimately familiar with the Wickersville incident, has informed me about this girl. She's a trouble maker Mrs. Sims, of that you can be sure. Our children do not need that kind of problem again."

Lillian knew that the "certain school board member" had to be Edith Grubbs. She was angry that she had beat her to the schools. "I'm just as familiar with the problem as Mrs. Grubbs," replied Lillian. She watched the woman's eyebrows shoot up in surprise at the mention of Mrs. Grubbs. "I can only tell you Mrs. Fallbridge," she continued, "that this girl was led astray by others. Her aunt and uncle, with whom she lives, are very respectable and have, I believe, completely reversed that bad influence. She deserves another chance." Lillian sat back hoping her argument would have some impact.

Mrs. Fallbridge looked sharply at Lillian. "I'll consider what you have said, Mrs. Sims," she replied with a dismissive air. Lillian knew the answer was really "no", and left feeling badly that she had once again been subdued by Edith Grubbs.

The next day she went in the opposite direction to the North Park school. Mr. Elroy Leep was the principal there. Lillian had met him when North Park put on a travelling minstrel show, visiting all the local schools. That was the previous fall and she had found him likeable but difficult to understand. He was always making grand pronouncements about coming changes in the educational system based on the latest theories. He was a futurist and seemed ill-suited for his role in rural schools. Yet he was also a child of the soil and proud of it. He made use of his farm upbringing at every opportunity and seemed to have a good understanding of the special problems farm kids brought to school. Lillian sensed that he was an opportunist and would jump at a chance to make a name for himself.

Mostly bald, he was tall and thin and wore heavy owlish glasses that constantly slipped down his nose. His hand felt limp and cold when she shook it.

"Miss Sims. It's so nice to see you again," he said and put on a big smile revealing his crooked teeth. He had the habit of addressing all female teachers by "Miss"; it fit his educational theories. The title "Mrs." implied that other worlds, other responsibilities existed beyond the school, and he refused to recognize that. "To what do I owe the pleasure of this visit?"

"I'm here on behalf of a student who will be applying for admission to your eighth grade," she said.

"Oh? this must be an outstanding student to have the benefit of your recommendation!" His glasses slipped down and he pushed them back up.

"Oh, she's very capable, I'm sure. But I'm here to recommend her in spite of recommendations you may have received to the contrary."

"Hmm," he replied doodling with a pencil he had been holding. "Do I understand then, that this is a problem student?"

"I don't think that she will be any problem at all," Lillian replied. "But, yes, she did have some problems some time ago. And she's been held back a grade." Lillian had to be honest, but she wanted him to ask some questions first.

He pushed his glasses back up. "What kind of problems?" he asked.

"She was suspended from the old Wickersville school. Have you heard about that?"

"Oh, that. Why, yes indeed. Just last week there was a board member here, a Miss Gruber, I believe. She mentioned a student by name, ah, let me see. I wrote down the name." He pushed up his glasses and started searching through the pile of papers scattered over his desk.

"Hannah Green?" Lillian asked.

"Ah, yes, that's it. Hannah Green. She made a bad case of her, you know." He started doodling again.

"Wasn't that Mrs. Grubbs? The board member, I mean."

"Ah, yes. Miss Grubbs. Excellent person. Excellent," he said, while rolling his eyes and raising his eyebrows. "But she needs to be better informed about our educational problems, I believe. But otherwise, excellent, excellent."

Lillian seized on this opening. "Yes, I quite agree. Our rural students pose a special challenge that many non-professionals fail to understand. And this girl is one of those special challenges. As you know, rural children are very susceptible to the influence of their schoolmates." She recalled this from a report she had read, or at least, she thought she had read it.

"Yes, yes," he replied enthusiastically. Wasn't it Peterson and Morley? That study in, I believe, in Ohio? Yes. They clearly showed the correlation between population density and conformance to peer attitudes? 1951, I believe?"

Lillian nodded even though she was not familiar with the study. "I believe you're right," she said. She was not patronizing him; she felt reasonably sure that he knew what he was talking about. "And I think there are special problems for farm kids. We, that is, I at least, was so tuned in to life on the farm; it was so different from anything I would experience at school. Didn't you once say you had similar experiences?"

"Oh yes, my yes. We had a particularly tough time getting on with some of the other non-farm kids. My, but I do remember."

"Well that's Hannah Green's case in a way," Lillian said. "She came easily under the influence of two of her peers, both a little older. It was a mistake any of us could have made."

"Yes. I quite agree," he said, pushing up his glasses. "I'm glad we see eye to eye on this Miss Sims. You see, I don't agree with Miss Gruber at all. She seems to know little about our special problems."

When Lillian left, Mr. Leep was doing further research on studies done related to that topic. He would find as many studies as possible to confirm his opinions. She felt that Hannah would get her enrollment here.

But Edith Grubbs was not so easily put off. In a follow-up visit, she learned of Elroy Leep's intentions for Hannah Green.

"You cannot admit this girl, Mr. Leep," she said. "She is a menace to the other children. Just look at what she did at Wickersville. You cannot forget that." Her face flushed with anger. She felt this inept little man was challenging her authority.

"My dear Miss Gruber," he said, pushing up his glasses, "I quite disagree. I think rural children get caught up in these strange incidents by mere chance or fate, if you will. There is no premeditation; things like this just happen. This is in accordance with a study by Jenkins and Brown, I believe----"

"Oh, damn your studies anyway," she interrupted. He had cited several studies to her already.

"1949, I believe," he continued, unabashed. "Pennsylvania, I think?"

"Now see here, Leep," she said with mounting anger, "if you admit that girl, I'm going to recommend that charges of incompetence be brought against you. I still have some influence, you know."

Elroy Leep became incensed by Edith Grubb's posturing. She represented those he disliked; the one's that always wanted to be in charge.

"Do what you have to, Miss Gruning. I will abide by my informed findings."

"That's Mrs. Grubbs, if *you* please!"

"Yes. Miss Grubbs. But I will abide, as I have already said, by my findings. And there are others who support me; Miss Sims for example."

At the mention of "Miss Sims" Edith Grubbs became very agitated. Fearing another attack of epilepsy, she left immediately. "You'll regret this bad decision, Mr. Leep," she threw over her shoulder as she walked out. "You'll regret it!" came echoing back from the empty hallway.

Elroy Leep did in fact, try to admit Hannah Green. When Edith Grubbs objected to the admission and brought charges against him, he had so many studies confirming that his actions were correct that he felt sure the board would agree with his decision, but they didn't and that satisfied the infuriated Mrs. Grubbs. The Baumanns never moved back into their old home.

Before all that took place, Lillian had made one more stop on behalf of the Baumanns. She went to Maynard Peck's store.

"I need a half pound of ham for my lunches," she told Maynard. "And I do prefer it without kerosene," and she laughed. Maynard had a keen sense of humor, she knew, and thrived on people making a pun or joke about him.

"Oh, I don't know, Miss Lillian. Most folks around here prefer their ham with gasoline," and he chuckled. The three men in the store guffawed.

While he was slicing the meat, she said: "By the way, remember the Baumanns? They're moving back here again."

Suddenly there was silence. Maynard stopped slicing the ham and looked at her over the counter with raised eyebrows. "They shouldn't be coming back here Miss Lillian. We don't want them here. And you above all, ought not to want them here."

Chuck Avery, a hefty farmer with a red face, piped in: "Tha's right. Don't need no damn spies and child criminals 'round here, Miss Sims. You want us to keep them out?"

"No, not at all," she replied. "I'm the one that was hurt the most and yet I think they deserve another chance. Their niece, Hannah, is a changed girl. We have to give them another chance."

"Still think old Baumann was spyin' for the Nazi's. they're just a bunch of spies," old man Smith said.

"Mr. Baumann is not a spy, and you can believe that, Mr. Smith, " Lillian said. "And little Hannah is not a criminal. But they are up against hard times and need to live in their old house. You all must be decent Christians and give them a chance. Remember, it was really the Riggers that caused all that trouble at school." She launched into a spirited debate with the four men. They admired Lillian and respected her opinion on most things except farming, and finally gave into her opinion on this.

When she left the store, Chuck was trying to figure some way to make the Baumanns feel welcome without giving up his hostile opinions.

"I'll be damned if I don't believe Baumann isn't up to somethin'," he said. "Course, no one has ever proved it and I ain't one to convict a man without real proof. But I'll be damned if I still don't believe it," and the others nodded in agreement.

"But it's best," Maynard said, "if we're wanting proof like we are, to just let it lie, like Miss Lillian says. Let's give Miss Lillian's way a chance," and they all agreed to do that, too.

Later they found out that all their new-found kindness towards the Baumann's was unnecessary and they happily returned to their former state of affairs claiming Baumann to be a Nazi spy.

CHAPTER 22

After the battle to get Hannah back in school failed, Lillian realized that she couldn't abide Able's sister and that indeed, they were fast becoming enemies. Edith Grubbs was powerful in her own vicious way and was quite capable of inflicting great emotional pain on anyone who got in her way. Lillian felt it best if she could avoid further confrontation with this woman.

Finishing an early breakfast before going to Able's to milk, she resolved to tell him that morning that they would have to bring their new association to an end. It bothered her to do so, because everything seemed to be working even better than planned. Her cows were thriving in the new environment and she was surprised to see that after only a few days, their production actually went up, to a point where they were giving more milk than ever before. But after that fateful Sunday dinner at Able's house, she was certain he would never be able to control his sister.

But Able came to her door first. "Lillian. Good morning, I wish." He seemed agitated. His usual homely smile was buried by a frown.

"Good morning, " she said. "What brings you here so early?" Dawn was just beginning to streak the dark clouds with pink.

"Lillian, I've got your cows here. John and I drove them over and we're taking them up to the barn." He sighed when he saw the surprised expression on her face. "I'll explain when we get them up there."

She left her breakfast and joined them. Bobby and Linda were up, but weren't dressed yet. Able and John and Lillian herded the cows up the hill and into the barnyard.

"It's my sister," Able said, puffing as they struggled to keep up with the cows. "I went over to see her yesterday, trying to get her to go along with our plan. But she turned on me like a tiger; said she wants her share now." He unlatched the barnyard gate and the cows went in without prompting. Lillian remained silent; Edith Grubbs was at work again.

"She's sending some lawyers and appraisers out here today," he continued. "She said if your cows were still on our property, she'd legally have them counted as part of the property. I'm not sure she can do that, but just in case, that's why I'm bringing them back." The cows were in the yard and he closed the gate. "John's going back for that bull. I want you to have him. We'll put him in the upper pasture for now. You can make a place for him in those old horse stalls, if you want." He shook his head in disgust. "I'm real sorry, Lillian. Didn't know she'd act like this. Don't know *what's* come over her."

"I don't know, " Lillian said. "I just don't think I can get on with your sister. Now I'm having trouble with her over a student from that Wickersville school incident."

"Maybe that's what set her off then," Able said.

"Well I certainly hope not," she said with a frown. "That affair is long settled and she shouldn't be so vindictive. We should all put aside the bitter feelings."

"I'm sure that's the right thing to do, " Able said. "But Edith, well sometimes she gets an idea in her head and you just can't shake it, right or wrong. Right now, she's thinking I'm going to ruin the farm and cause her to lose her share. At least, that's what she's been saying. Anyways, that's why she won't wait any longer."

"I'm really sorry," Lillian said, "I wish I knew how I could help you. Will you have to sell now?"

"Can't think of nothin' else. I can't raise enough cash now to buy her out." They started walking back to the house. "We milked them before bringing them over," he said.

She invited John and Able down to breakfast. "Can't stay Lillian," he said. "We got to milk the rest and I got to be ready for them damn lawyers. I'll talk to you later."

She watched John and Able walk slowly back down the road. It was a beautiful morning made sad by that hateful woman. Lillian felt like murder was justified... murder... murder, but she forced the strangely satisfying evil thought out of her mind.

"We've moved the cows back," she told Bobby and Linda, when she returned to the house. "We won't be going over to Able's to milk anymore." She explained what happened.

"Wow," Linda said, disappointed, "his sister has ruined everything."

"Comes close to that, doesn't it," Lillian said. "Able said we can put our milk cans out with his until he sells the rest of his herd. I guess I'll have to join the co-op after that. I guess we're in trouble too." She sat down to finish her breakfast.

"Why are we in trouble, Ma?" Linda asked.

"Well, for one thing, I let Junior go to help Harold with some of his contracts. Harold didn't ask for him, Junior just likes Harold and has been itching to go work for him ever since he left. I'm not going to try to force Junior to stay here. But we just aren't enough to run even this little farm. The other thing is we just don't make enough through the co-op to really hire more hands."

"How about if we had some of them milk machines," Bobby said. Wouldn't that help a lot?"

Lillian was pleased by Bobby's growing interest in dairy farming. He was quick to find solutions for everyday problems. They both had discovered during their stay at Able's farm that the machines worked very well. She was amazed at how quickly the milking was done. And her sensitive taste buds told her that there was no difference in the flavor or other qualities of the milk.

"Yes Bobby, I'll have to admit they work very well," she said. But... remember? We still don't have power, thanks to me."

"Can't they get it here sooner?" Linda asked.

"I don't think so," Lillian said. "And frankly, I'd feel like a fool going down there and asking them to come out sooner."

Linda laughed. Then they all went up to the barn to finish putting down feed for the cows.

During lunch that day, Linda went to the Rural Electrification

Program office, now with only a few people remaining. She'd dressed in her tightest slacks that morning, and now, using her best charms, she asked the new supervisor if the hook-up couldn't be done sooner.

"We're just poor farmers," she told him. "We can't make it without the help of power. We've been waiting a long time now."

"Well that's strange," the man said. He'd been looking Linda over very carefully, since she seemed to be inviting that type of scrutiny. And Linda was doing her own survey. He wore no wedding ring and except for the large ears surrounding his black hair, he was good-looking. "I thought that area was completed long ago," he continued. "Let me check the records."

He examined the records at his desk. "You were scheduled for hook-up more than a year ago," he said. "For some reason they rescheduled you." None of the paper work concerning Lillian's by-pass request had been preserved in the ever-shrinking files. "Well look here," he said. "The poles are already up across from your place if these records are right. All we need to do is drop a service line. Is your barn close to the road?"

"No, it's way up on the hill," Linda said.

"Well, we'll probably have to put up another pole to get up to the barn. You do want the barn hooked up, don't you?"

"Yes, that's very important," Linda said.

"Well, let's see," he said and examined some work schedules. "I can't say exactly, but how about next week? If not, no later than the following week. I assume someone will be home during the day?"

"That's great," Linda said. "We may not be there, though. We all work. But we'll leave the door unlocked, anyway. You can just go in. Will that be ok?"

The man thought for a moment. "That'll do," he said. "Just leave us a note on the kitchen table authorizing us to enter your house to hook-up the power. Make sure it's signed by the head of the household. We'll have to locate the outlets where we think best.

Ok?"

"I'm sure that's Ok," she said.

"You're sure you won't be there?" he asked.

"Yes. I'm sure. But if you need to contact us, I work at Ideal. You can call me right at 12:45, that's during lunch hour; but please, no other time."

"What's the number?" he said with growing enthusiasm.

"Prospect 5-7134," she replied, offering a big smile. She left feeling very good about the chance of getting power and about other, new possibilities.

That evening she told Lillian what she had done. "Isn't that great!" she said. "Now we can get those milk machines and all the other things needed to civilize this house."

Lillian had mixed feelings again, but this time she would not interfere. But she couldn't resist some cautionary advice. "Well, if it makes you and Bobby happy and helps us keep the farm, I guess it's Ok," she said, "but Linda, just don't be so anxious to change everything. There's a lot to be said for things the way they are." She looked at Fred's hat. It was still there. "Don't you feel that 'all those things needed to civilize this house', as you say, the same things we had in Johnstown, obscure the real meaning of things?"

Linda looked at her and smiled. "the *real* meaning of things? No. Not at all. Nothing was ever obscured in my mind."

Lillian shrugged. "Well, I guess it's all relative," she said. "We all look at things differently. I'm ready for the changes again."

Because of the mounting pressure brought by his sister to settle her share, which had now been pre-determined by the survey of the lawyers and appraisers, Able was forced to sell out at a reduced price. He did however, manage to salvage something. He had a strip of land surveyed, bounded by a small brook on one side and Lillian's property on the other, amounting to 43 acres. He made arrangements with the buyer to repurchase this land after the sale was completed. His idea was to simply keep part of his ancestral lands. He didn't know what he would do with it.

CHAPTER 23

The next day she went over to Able's, for what she figured would be the last time. The new owners were moving in at the end of the week. She found him in the kitchen, sitting in a state of depression. His face was lead-colored and his eyes reflected a blackness, showing his inner thoughts. He greeted her as if he wanted to be alone. He didn't want to talk about losing his place anymore. The full meaning had finally settled on him and weighed like a rock on his mind.

"Able, I have a proposal for you," she said. He looked at her surprised. His eyes seemed to shed some of the blackness; to light up a bit. "Able, we both have needs," she continued, not waiting for him to speak. "Why don't you and John come over and live in that cottage I built. It's just sitting there, wasting away, wanting someone to take care of it. And if you're interested, you can buy half share in my herd. And we can bring up the herd by another ten head or so; but we'd need to put an extension on the old barn. In return, you could do all the things I need to hire done now. Someone's got to cut the firewood and do the haying and harvesting. And the house needs rebuilding and the milk needs to be hauled. there are just so many things that need to be done."

He leaned back and crossed his arms and looked at her, puzzled. It was the last thing he'd expected.

"And John," she continued, for Able seemed speechless, "could help Bobby manage the herd; help with the milking. Such a small farm, and yet there's so much work to it. I guess what I'm saying is that we could run this place together, that is, if you're interested?"

He looked at her, his eyes big and round, with no trace of blackness left in them. "Lillian," he said, recovering his wits, "I think heaven sent you here. Oh yes, I'm interested. I was just sitting here thinking. What kind of job could I get? What would I do? I only know farming; that's what I've done all my life. No one needs a farmer for nothing but labor. I'd just be somebody's dumb shovel-man, wouldn't I? And leaving my own place, this beautiful country, is more than I care to think about." He stood up and looked out the window. "Edith is coming to get her furniture tomorrow. Do you think we can get that little house fixed up by tomorrow or the day after?"

She nodded. "I think so. There really isn't much to do. You can start moving some of your things there today, if you like. And as for you not being able to do anything but farming, that's sheer nonsense and you know it."

"Thank you, Lillian," he said. "I guess I'm feeling pretty sorry for myself. But I'll tell you why I'm mostly doing this. It's really for John. The boy is just about as sad as he can be, not knowing what's coming next. I think knowing that he'll be staying amongst friends will greatly comfort him."

Lillian knew they had an agreement. Not marriage, not yet, maybe never, but she was glad that they had had a meeting of the minds.

CHAPTER 24

Rosemary could no longer stand the thought of Harold and Lillian together. Something in her brain snapped when that vision intruded on her saner thoughts. She planned to kill them both. She no longer had any choice.

The first hurdle to her plan was that Harold and Lillian must be home at the same time. The second hurdle was that they must be alone; Bobby must be at school and Linda at work.

She picked a Monday; that was the day when Lillian went in to teach an hour later. She planned to be there at 8 in the morning. If she got lucky, they both would be home alone. If not, there was always the possibility of trying again.

She planned to shoot them both. This was the biggest hurdle by far, since she knew nothing about shooting and was actually afraid of guns. But the thought had occurred to her after her last visit to Harold's place; when he'd infuriated her by refusing to see her. In the brief instant that he had held the door open, her eyes fell on the rifle and shotgun over the fireplace. Suddenly she'd remembered that she still had Matt's shotgun. She had forgotten about it for years and had never seemed able to get rid of it. But after seeing Harold's guns, and thinking about it and deciding that shooting was the surest method of killing them, the gun was taken out of the closet where she had stored it. What does it really look like, she wondered; how does it feel to the touch? And while it was frightening at first and she held it gingerly, her fears were gradually overcome. The gun was, she knew, already a certified killer; it would serve her purpose well. Besides she had the convenient idea that she was just returning it to Lillian. That way she could carry it right into the house without raising suspicion.

Working up the courage to clean the heavy grime and brownish stains from the surface of the Browning, she did it without understanding what she was doing, washing it in the tub, using dish detergent and drying it with a towel. It gleamed, almost like new, only some slight discoloration remained where the blood had been.

But, unlike Lillian, she had never learned to use a gun. She knew she could do it; she was determined to learn how to shoot. Her cousin, Ed Giles, the supervisor at the factory, he could help her. He hunted and he had always tried to get her into bed. She didn't like Ed because he had a porno mind and a filthy mouth. Once he'd shown her some dirty sex comics he'd picked up in New York, and playing cards and other things. But she could use that weakness to get him to show her how to shoot. After committing herself to this plan, she called him on the phone.

"Ed. I need to take up some sport and I think hunting would be good. Harry always hunted," she lied, "and I always kind of liked it." She was lying again, she had never liked it. "Would you teach me how to handle a gun?"

"I can't believe it Rosemary. You? You want to take up hunting?" he said.

"Well, yes, Ed. It's too lonely staying at home all the time. I really would like to try it."

"Well, it's a real good idea, Rosemary. Sure, I'll teach you. You got a gun?"

"Uh, yes, I have one of Harry's guns."

He said he had to go to New York that coming weekend. But he made an appointment to start her that next Saturday.

Ed, even with his difficulty in keeping his hands off her, was a good teacher. "We'll start with a .22 rifle," he said when they met the first time in the fields behind Fletcher's round barn. The property was still for sale. He handed her the small rifle and she took it with apprehension.

"This is so light," she said.

"Yes. Good to learn with. Look, here's the bolt," he said, showing how to cock it open and pull it back. "And this is how the bullet goes in." She watched him insert the tiny shell in the chamber. He closed the bolt and showed her how to operate the safety latch. Then he placed the rifle butt on her shoulder and showed her how to aim.

"It's real important that you learn to keep that goddam rifle butt snug up against your shoulder," he said. "This little gun won't hurt you but the 12 gauge can kick your ass."

She loaded and fired several rounds, amazed at how easy it was, but always missing the cans he'd put on a fence post at about twenty paces.

"Here. Look Rosemary." He took the gun from her and aimed it at the target. "You see. You're using the wrong eye to aim. Use your other eye."

After that she quickly learned how to load, how to aim, how to squeeze off a shot, and all the safety rules. He let her shoot a box of shells that day, to get used to the operation.

Later, he made her buy a hunting license, so carrying a gun in the field would be legal. He was impressed with her ability to learn; he knew of very few women who knew how to handle a gun. He liked teaching her; liked getting close to her; smelling her; feeling her heat. She learned quickly and was skillful as well in putting him off.

When she showed him the Browning, he was impressed.

"It was Harry's," she lied. "I've had it all these years, but didn't know anything about using it."

"That's a fucking beauty of a gun," he said, eyeing the Browning enviously. "You're starting where other people leave off."

Once she knew the basics of handling the small rifle, he started her with a .410 shotgun. The size of the shell disturbed her at first, but she gradually got used to the louder noise and more powerful recoil. He took her to a skeet range, operated by the local gun club. She learned how to track and lead a moving target. She started to enjoy the shooting sessions and began to feel a surge of power and command. It wasn't long before she felt confident enough to move up to the 12 Gauge.

Ed used his own 12 Gauge the first time out, using skeet loads.

"I'll shoot a couple of rounds first," he said. "You watch how I hold the gun tight to my shoulder."

He fired the first round and the roar and kick of the 12 gauge frightened her. But he shot off a box at the flying clays and she gradually got used to the noise and seeing the violent kick.

When he finally let her shoot, she pulled off the first shot with every muscle tensed like a steel spring and her eyes closed in fear. The exploding shell sounded like someone hitting a metal drum inside her head and the recoil sent arrows of pain through her shoulder. For a while, she couldn't hear what he was saying. She was afraid to shoot anymore.

"That's Ok," he said. "Shock and fear are completely normal." And after some time, she bravely got off four more rounds, all misses.

They continued shooting in the afternoons, after Ed got off from work. The days were still not yet very cold and he waited his opportunity with Rosemary, but she gave him no chance. Once she got used to the bigger gun and started hitting targets, he switched her to the Browning.

"Now you'll be shooting in style," he said, as he handled the Browning. "Let me shoot it first to check the sighting."

Several club members were around and he enjoyed showing off with the gun. When he told them it was Rosemary's gun they told him how lucky he was to have such rich relatives.

"Rosemary, this gun's got a hair trigger," he said, after pulling off several accidental shots. "You just got to be careful, it's a lot different than mine." He showed her how to ease into the trigger pull, "you just gently squeeze it," he said, laughing

Rosemary shot the Browning and was shocked when it went off so fast and kicked more violently than Ed's gun. At first, she couldn't hit any targets.

"You're too tense," he said, when he saw her choking up on each shot. "This Browning is just a little lighter than my gun. You'll get used to the kick and the hair trigger. Why are you so afraid of it?"

She continued shooting until she finally hit a clay. But she was glad when they finished. The gun seemed temperamental; ready to go off by just thinking about it.

After a few more sessions, Ed said rabbit season just opened and it was time to go hunting. "I've got to go to New York for a while," he said. "We better go out this weekend. Might be too late when I get back."

The woods around Fletcher's place were posted NO TRESPASSING, but were loaded with cottontails and that's where Ed took her. "Now, killing an animal is different from shooting those clays," he said, when they arrived "And the gun's going to kick some more with these rabbit loads, so don't let it put you off."

They were in a small clearing deep in the woods; the afternoon sun warmed the chilled air. He gave her a box of Remington # 06's. She hesitated; she had always hated killing animals. But it would be a first step in preparation for her final task.

She got off five shots and, in the excitement, pulled the gun and hurt her shoulder. But she managed to kill two cottontails. She was shocked at how easily the rabbits died. There seemed to be only a few small holes in the fur with only tiny drops of blood. Their limp bodies felt heavy and warm when she stuffed them in the game pocket of Ed's hunting vest.

"That's damn good for a broad," Ed said. "Where'd you learn to shoot like that?" and he laughed.

But the killing had stunned Rosemary's sensibilities. She could see her intended victims in the carcasses of the two unfortunate rabbits. Now she felt she was ready. Waiting longer, she knew, could cause her to lose her nerve. Tomorrow would be the day.

Ed laughed again and patted her generously on her behind. "Oh, sweet piece," he said, "at last," and firmly grabbed her buttocks. "Now, how about my reward?" He started to take off his hunting vest holding the dead rabbits. He had to let go of Rosemary to put his jacket down.

She smiled icily and moved away from him. "Not yet, Ed," she said, her eyes blazing like burnished steel. "But I appreciate your help."

Ed jerked his head back in disagreement. "No way, baby. You owe me."

CHAPTER 25

That evening she tore up the hated hunting license and using a towel, cleaned the stains from the Browning once more. She didn't want Ed's fingerprints on it.

But the next morning her timing was off; she was an hour behind because she felt confused. There was an inattention in her mind, too busy with conflicting ideas such as Ed and dead rabbits, that she had lost her focus on what she was about. After dressing and aimlessly preparing breakfast, she combed her hair and then went to the store to buy more milk and coffee. It was only when she came home from the store and became aware of the manila envelope she had put on the table the night before and saw the gun standing in the corner, that she remembered. The gun jolted her confused mind and became her focus, her reminder about what had to be done. She forgot about the coffee and milk and the timing part of the plan and left the house to go to Lillian's. The gun felt reassuring to her, like her only friend.

When she reached Lillian's, it was already too late: no one was there. Both the car and truck were not there and the house was empty. She decided to go to Harold's cabin; If they were there, she could kill them just as well in his cabin.

When she got close to the cabin, she could see his old International parked up in the yard next to the porch. Although she had prepared for this, her heart was pounding and pumped fear throughout her body. She passed the cabin drive and pulled the car off the road where a logging road joined it. Her hands were sweaty and trembling when she removed the gun from the front seat and covered it with a small blanket. She had carefully loaded both barrels before leaving the house. Now, even with the safety on, she feared getting her hands anywhere near the trigger. She tried to remember what Ed had told her about the trigger and remember how it worked yesterday but everything was blank, nothing, she could remember nothing. She wanted to throw the gun down on the ground and stomp on it, but she just stood still, staring at the open door of the car.

She unfroze and then walked slowly back to the cabin driveway and up the drive to the steps. Wild daisies had grown tall around the porch and along the drive and the humming of insects filled the quiet air. When she found herself standing in front of the door, she dropped the blanket and slipped off the safety. Weakness spread over her body and she felt numb; her hand came up with difficulty to knock on the door. Her legs felt like they were about to give out.

The man inside the cabin was looking through the kitchen cabinet when he heard the footsteps on the porch and saw a woman pass by the window, but couldn't tell who it was. She was carrying something wrapped in a blanket. She looked harmless enough. When she knocked, he hesitated to answer, hoping she would go away. When she knocked a second time, he decided he could handle her if he had to.

Rosemary heard the footsteps of the man approaching the door. The cry "Harold" was on her lips, but her voice just gurgled unintelligibly. As the door started to open, she stepped back and at the same time, raised the gun and felt for the trigger. For an instant, a strange face she didn't recognize, looked back at her in horror from the open doorway. In a frantic attempt to abort the shot, she jerked the gun up as it went off. At the same time, the stranger tried to close the door. In the confusion, the gun came away from her shoulder and the recoil slammed her backward; knocking her over the porch railing.

The man had managed to get the door partially closed before the gun went off, but he was badly wounded in the face and neck. Holding onto the door, he couldn't see. He moaned and started to sink to the floor, pulling the door open as he fell outward onto the porch. Crawling blindly onto the porch, his crimson face left a bloody trail. Reaching the rail of the porch, he struggled into a sitting position and rolled against the rail. All he could do was let out little gasps, trying to cry for help.

Rosemary had fallen over the rail head first onto the exposed face of a buried granite boulder, knocking her unconscious. When she come out of it, the world around her was fuzzy; she couldn't focus. Gradually, things begin to clear, but she didn't know where she was or how she had got there. The man on the porch became visible through the daisies and she could see that his face was full of blood. He seemed to be shaking and heaving. When she tried to move; to get up, nothing happened. She tried over and over again to move, but always her limbs and torso wouldn't respond to her will. But she was able to move her eyes and move her mouth and concluded that she must be alive. Blood flowed from the wound in her head, cut on a sharp corner of the boulder, spilling down the side of her face. She tried to move a third time but failed. Then her eyes rolled up and she saw the sky overhead; nothing but a blank blue space. Insects hummed around her head and started landing on her to gorge on the fresh blood. The wounded man broke the silence at intervals with a groan. Flies and mosquitoes started to crawl around her eyes and she tried to brush them away but her arms wouldn't move.

The day crawled by, painfully, and the slowly moving sun burned her eyes but warmed her chilled body. She had the sensation that her arms and legs were blocks of ice and she fell in and out of consciousness. At one point the man starting to move; he was crawling towards the steps when she blacked out again.

When darkness began to fall, Rosemary was still breathing and able to think but was losing her ability to stay conscious. Mosquitoes and other biting insects now covered her face and were crawling into her opened mouth. But she also gained hope with the arriving darkness; she began to remember what had happened and now remembered that the man she had shot was not Harold. Harold must be out somewhere. He should come home soon and find them. But the darkness thickened and she saw stars beginning to twinkle. The wounded man had stopped groaning.

As the night deepened and the moon moved to its midnight position, from time to time other, more insidious noises came to her when she was conscious. They came from behind her from the dark woods where she couldn't roll her eyes to see. Through the throbbing in her head, she once heard something that sounded like the growling and whining of dogs. She listened, but her head hurt so badly that she fell unconscious again.

Later, when she came to again, she smelled the stinking breath of a huge wild dog exploring her face. He was growling at other nearby dogs and licking around the blood on her face. When she opened her eyes and moved her lips trying to scream, the startled dogs jumped back and moved away, back to the edge of the woods.

Drawn by the blood scent, the dogs had been pacing around a fixed perimeter from Rosemary. She was the first in their path and at times, the bolder dogs went up to within a few feet of her. When they saw no movement from the human on the ground, the leader went up and sniffed and licked around her face. That's when she'd opened her eyes and tried to scream. The dogs fell back; they now knew she was alive. And they stayed wary because they smelled a scent they feared most: the shotgun with the spent shell lay within a few feet of Rosemary's head. But as the night passed and the moon drifted back towards the horizon, the acrid scent of burnt gunpowder dissipated in the light breeze while the blood scent became ever stronger. The dogs continued pacing nervously, waiting for the humans to make a move. Later Rosemary heard moans from the man, he was struggling with the dogs trying to kick them away.

CHAPTER 26

When the sun came up the next day, Rosemary was still alive but unconscious. Her face was grotesquely swollen, almost beyond recognition, with insect bites. With the coming light, the dog pack returned to their lair; they were still wary of the immobile humans, and the faint scent of gunpowder still lingered.

Rosemary's hope for Harold's return had been in vain; he was up in Northville working a woodlot. He and Junior were staying at a motel until the job was completed. He'd left the International at the cabin because it wasn't running.

That afternoon, they finished up and drove back to his cabin. Junior planned to spend that night at Harold's place. When they turned up the drive, it was already dark and they saw the dog pack in the headlights, pulling at something on the ground.

"What the hell is that?" Harold yelled. "It's them damn dogs again." He sounded the horn and the dogs scattered off into the woods. Then he saw something in the headlights, behind the International.

"Looks like someone laying on the ground," Junior said.

"Yeh, it's a man alright," said Harold. "He looks to be hurt real bad. Looks like the dogs got at him." They sat there waiting, the engine running and the headlights shining thru the dust, trying to decide what to do. "Look, Junior. I don't know where the dogs are. But we've got to try to help that fella. I've got some shells there in the dash. Hand them to me."

Junior reached in the dash and pulled out a box of .30-caliber shells. He handed Harold five shells.

"I've got my rifle in the back of the truck," Harold said. "I'm going to get it. You stay in the cab till I tell you. Ok.?" Junior nodded and Harold opened the door. He made his way around to the back, took out the rifle and quickly loaded it. He shined his flashlight where the dogs had disappeared into the woods and fired off two rounds; The gunshots split the silence with a tremendous crack. there was no sign of the dogs.

Their nerves jangled, they stepped cautiously over to the man on the ground. When they saw his bloodied, torn face and found that he was dead, they were shocked.

"Looks like the dogs got to him, don't it?" Junior whispered, as if there were someone about that could hear him.

"Could be," Harold said, also in a low whisper. "But who is he? What's he doing here?" It was difficult to see much in the headlights. Everywhere surrounding them it seemed pitch-black.

"We better take him in the cabin," Harold said, "before those dogs come back."

When they tried to lift him, they found he was already getting stiff with rigor mortis. "He's been dead awhile, I'd say," Harold said as they struggled to get him up the steps.

"My door was open," Harold said, after they laid the body on the floor. "And look here," he called to Junior, shining the flashlight on the floor of the porch. "There's blood out here on the porch."

"Huh," Junior said, now puzzled by everything that had happened.

"Maybe he was trying to get away from the dogs," Harold said, "and ran up here on the porch trying to get in the cabin. Dogs must of dragged him out. We better get the sheriff."

They drove over to Peck's store to call Sheriff Bob Gates. Harold told the sheriff over the phone that he'd found a dead man in his driveway, apparently killed by wild dogs. Gates had been sleeping and was grouchy and yelled at him for moving the body.

"But sheriff, them dogs would be eating on him if I'd left him out there," Harold said.

"Well, Ok, then," the sheriff said, his voice loud and still gruff. "But don't touch or move anything else till I get out there. I just never heard of dogs killing anybody." Sheriff Gates went back to the bedroom and told his wife. She looked at her husband who looked so frail to her in his underwear; so different then the public front made by his official clothes. And he was sixty-five, with white hair and a trim white moustache; he should be retired, she thought. These night calls happened too often. Why he was considering running for office again was beyond her.

When the sheriff arrived at the cabin the puzzle deepened. He was a meticulous investigator and saw the shot holes tore into the door that Harold had missed. He also observed that it seemed the cabin had been ransacked. Then he followed the blood trail out of the cabin on to the porch and down the steps.

"This man's been shot," The sheriff told Harold, after examining the corpse. "And the dogs have been eating on him too. I'll bet a plug nickel he was killed by the shot first and not by the dogs. Appears to be from shotgun pellets."

"Shot? God, now nothing makes sense," Harold replied, nervously. "I sure didn't shoot him, sheriff. Like I said, Junior and I been up in Northville working. We were just coming back when we found him in the driveway, like you see him there."

"You say you've never seen him before?" the sheriff asked Harold.

"Well, with his face messed up as bad as that... but no, I don't think so."

"Sure is strange," the sheriff said. " No identification on him. Dressed kind of like a tramp. You say no one was staying here while you were gone?"

"No sir. No one. And the door was not locked as always. Most of us living up here leave our doors unlocked. We don't mind if someone comes in to get shelter or is in need of some food."

"Is anything missing? Was there anything worth stealing?"

"I don't think so," Harold said. "I took my guns with me. That's all that would have been worth stealing."

The sheriff searched the cabin and the driveway; it was still dark outside. He found nothing.

When he came back into the cabin, Harold said: "Sheriff, I been thinking. Maybe... maybe that dead man is old Charlie Stout. He's not wearing any clothes that I recognize, but that beard... it could be him."

"Charlie Stout? Isn't he that strange fella that lives in the woods?"

"Yes, that's him."

"Well, where exactly does he live?" the sheriff asked.

"No one knows, sheriff. He seems to be a hermit. Some people say he lives in a cave up there by Bear mountain."

"How did you come to know him?"

"He's come around here several times. I saw him about a year ago. Came here looking for salt. He traded me a pair of moccasins he'd made himself for a few pounds of salt and some flour. He hated going into stores."

"But you can't be sure it's him?"

"No sir. But it could be."

"Well, I don't know what they were doing Harold," the sheriff said and shook his head. "But I'd say there was at least two of 'em. Someone had to shoot this fella. Must of shot him right there in the doorway by the looks of the door. We'll make a better search tomorrow." The sheriff looked around at the dark woods. "Sure is quiet out here. I'd like you two to stay in a motel tonight. For your own safety."

It wasn't until early the next morning that a deputy spotted the twisted torso outside, almost hidden in the weeds. Harold was shocked.

"God Sheriff, that's Rosemary Allen," Harold said, choking back tears. "She's a good friend. Look at her face! My God, what's happened here? "

"That's what I'd like to know," said the sheriff, examining the body. "Looks like she's broken her neck. Maybe she fell from the porch. Pushed over the rail, most likely."

Harold told the sheriff what he knew about Rosemary and

about his relationship, leaving out the fact that they had quarreled and broken up. He told him that she had come to his cabin a few times before, but he hadn't expected her now.

"Do you recognize this shotgun?" the sheriff asked Harold, pointing to the Browning they had retrieved, now on the floor.

"No. Never seen it before."

"Well it's been fired," Gates said, narrowing his eyes in suspicion. "It was found lying next to her. Maybe she fired the shot that hit the man. Then again, maybe she didn't. We'll try to confirm that with fingerprints and tests of course. Do you know why she was here Harold? You say you didn't expect her?"

Harold was puzzled. He shook his head. The sheriff sounded as if he suspected something.

"And why the hell did she have that gun with her? " the sheriff said. His crew had found her car and the box of shells in the dash compartment. "Looks like she was going to hunt rabbits? And with a special gun like that?" Sheriff Gates stroked his chin. "Did she ever hunt, do you know "

Again, Harold shook his head. "Not that I know of, sheriff."

"Some damned funny business going on here I tell you," the sheriff said scratching his head. "We'll have to wait for the tests and the coroner's report. But something is damn funny, though. We'll have to do a pretty good investigation to find out what the hell happened here!"

Harold felt the same way about somethin' being "damn funny". He couldn't say anything much about the dead man other than he seemed to be a thief or maybe old Charlie Stout. But Rosemary's death puzzled him. What *was* she doing with that gun? And it was such a special gun, at that. Rosemary disliked guns, he knew. When he'd offered to teach her how to handle a rifle, she had steadfastly refused, saying that it would be better for everyone if all such weapons were destroyed.

As soon as he could free himself from the sheriff's ferrety questioning, he went over to Lillian's. He was afraid; afraid of her wrath and vile contempt; it would be difficult for him to see her again. He especially dreaded giving her this tragic news. Lillian had been best friends with Rosemary and he knew it would be hard on her in spite of their recent problems. He had never been in such a predicament before. Harold sorely grieved for Rosemary himself, yet he had to endure Lillian's wrath and try to calm her grief.

Linda answered his timid knock and was shocked to see Harold standing at the door. "You bastard, what do you want here," she said angrily, ready to slam the door in his face.

"Hold it, Linda," he said putting up his hand to stop the door. "I've got some very bad news. Rosemary... she's been killed."

Linda's expression froze. "What did you say?" She started to move, hesitated to get close to Harold but then stepped out onto the porch.

"Rosemary's dead. An accident maybe. I came over to tell Lillian. Is... she here?"

"Rosemary's dead?" Disbelief set in. Linda never trusted Harold. "Is this some kind of twisted joke?"

"No joke, Linda. It's *no* joke. I need to tell Lillian."

At that moment Lillian came walking down from the barn. She couldn't believe her eyes when she saw Harold and Linda together on the front porch. Her eyes blazed in fury.

"What in God's name --" she started to yell.

"Wait, Ma, wait," Linda yelled. "Harold has bad news... about Rosemary."

"Lillian," Harold said quickly, "Rosemary's... it's that she had an accident... she's dead," He lowered his head rather than look in her furious eyes.

Lillian stood still. She looked stonily at the man she detested. The words swirled in her head between belief and disbelief. This man had no right to be here, no right to be with Linda, no right to tell her such a thing. No right at all. But her fury changed to shock when she saw him standing there with his head down, unmoving: suddenly she knew it was true.

“My God,” she said. “Rosemary... dead?” and fought to hold back a rush of tears. “What happened?”

“Nothing is clear,” Harold said, fighting back tears himself. “But it seems she may have been pushed off my porch. Broke her neck. I was up in Northville when it happened.” Then he related the entire story up to that point.

“God, I can't believe it,” Lillian said. “And you've never seen that man before? Maybe someone you worked with, stopped by to see you?”

“Well, I told the sheriff that maybe it was Charlie Stout. But I didn't recognize his clothes. He usually wore that green hat and that rabbit fur jacket. This man was wearing regular old work clothes. I'm just not sure.”

For a moment Lillian thought about inviting Harold in, where they could share their sorrow. But in the end, she couldn't. The three of them stood silent in front of the house.

“I'd best be getting' on,” Harold said, feeling his knees weak and the silence closing in around him. “The sheriffs tearing my place apart, looking for clues. If I find out anything, I'll let you know.”

When Harold left, the two women on the porch were perplexed and deep in sorrow. Their anger with him seemed greatly defused, but he was emotionally drained. Seeing them both together like that had almost caused his heart to stop. His legs had been shaking as he walked to the truck.

Several days passed in the investigation. Both Harold and Junior were called for official questioning. What seemed like a double murder made headlines at Maynard's store. Everyone was talking about it. There would be an inquest to determine if it were murder.

CHAPTER 27

Shortly thereafter, Lillian came home from school and found the sheriff's car parked in front of her house. He was sitting in the car waiting for her. Bobby and Linda weren't home yet.

"Good afternoon, Mrs. Sims," he said with a smile. "I'd like to ask you a few questions." He was wearing his wide brimmed hat which seemed to give him more authority. "Would that be alright?" Lillian asked him into the house. She thought he needed help.

But the sheriff, after poking around Fultonville and Fonda, had found out something about the relationship between Harold and Rosemary, and other information came his way that caused him to think of Lillian as a prime suspect.

"Mrs. Sims, I hope this isn't too much of a shock to you, but I know your husband was having some kind of an affair with Rosemary Allen. He said he didn't think you knew about it. Is that true?"

She looked at him, surprised. she hadn't expected questions related to her private life. And why had Harold denied that she knew anything? "Yes, it's true. But I'm not surprised. I suspected Harold was seeing another woman; at least he was behaving that way. I won't deny it, we're separated; we've had our problems, but I didn't know he was going to tell everyone."

"Well, he had to tell the truth ma'am. It's best during an investigation to tell the truth. Now, can you tell me what you were doing on the 6th and 7th of October? That was last Monday and Tuesday."

"What I was doing? Why are you asking me that? What... was I doing? What has that got to do with anything related to this?"

"It's just a routine part of the investigation, Ma'am, " he said with no threat implied in his voice. "Now, can you tell me what you were doing?"

"Why, let me think," she said nervously, trying to recall her movements. She had left school during the morning on Monday, because she had a sick cow. The vet was coming out, but she had to wait more than an hour for him to arrive. Able and John were signing papers at the bank. That left her with about two hours she had no alibi for.

"You sure you didn't see anybody during that time?" Gates asked, still maintaining his pleasant air.

"Yes, I'm sure," she replied, wondering what that would mean.

"Well, I'm here today ma'am," he said, his voice now turning more serious, "because we've traced the weapon used in the killing. It belongs to you."

Lillian's mouth opened and she felt a sudden sharp pain in her gut. "Sheriff, that's... that's a big mistake," she said, her voice trembling in disbelief of the implied accusation. "The only gun I own is a rifle, and... and it's right here in this house." She started to get up to get the rifle from the cupboard.

"No ma'am, that's not it," Gates interrupted. "The weapon used in this case is a Browning Special double 12-gauge shotgun, over and under. We traced it to your previous husband, Matthew Barry. Then we traced it to you. Got your signature on a police receipt."

"That gun? Oh. God. Not that gun." The vivid memories of that awful day came reeling back. Matt had been crazy about that gun. Crazy enough to kill himself with it "That was the murder weapon? Oh my God! I thought that gun had been destroyed. I can't believe this!"

"Well it's true, Ma'am," Sheriff Gates said.

"Are you charging me with murder?" she asked, half hysterical with fear.

"Murder? No Ma'am, hasn't been ruled a murder yet. In two days the inquest will be held to determine if a possible crime, murder that is, has been committed. I'm asking you not to leave the area until that ruling has been made. Just routine. Now, what can you tell me about that gun?"

"Well, sheriff, this is so absurd," Lillian said, with fear knotting her throat. "I gave that gun to Rosemary right after my first husband's death. I asked her to destroy it for me."

"Why did you want that gun destroyed?" the sheriff asked.

Lillian told the sheriff the entire story of Matt's suicide. "Surely someone must know that Rosemary had that gun!" she exclaimed.

"Well, we'll check on it, Mrs. Sims. In the meantime, please don't leave the area." He left, leaving her numb with anxiety.

As a policeman, Gates' questioning had strengthened his suspicions with facts. She had a strong motive for killing Rosemary, plenty of opportunity during the two hours she couldn't account for, and she seemed to own the weapon involved. But at the same time, his experience with people who have committed a serious crime led him to believe that she had been telling mostly the truth. But he felt she was hedging, maybe even lying about not knowing about the affair with Rosemary.

The coroner's report showed that Rosemary had a broken neck, a blunt trauma head wound, and a bruised shoulder, all thought to have been received when she fell and struck the large rock. She had died from shock from the concussion. The insect bites and the torn lip thought to have been done by a dog, did not contribute to her death.

It was also confirmed that the unknown man had been shot in the head and neck by the shotgun found at the scene. The only fingerprints on the gun were Rosemary's, which was unusual. Fragments of towel fibers had been found around the receiver; It was suspected that somehow the stock had been wiped clean after the shooting took place.

The sheriff pondered the evidence so far. This latest piece of data suggested that it would have been possible for someone like Lillian to kill the man, wipe the stock clean, and then put the gun in Rosemary's limp hands, to leave some prints. Lillian's motive for killing the man was to make Rosemary's death look like it had occurred in a confrontation with him. But who would she have killed first? The theory broke down at that point. He could not create a clear scenario in his mind to account for both deaths, because the man was a stranger to them all, even if he turned out to be Charlie Stout. How could such a thing have been planned? So, he also continued his search to verify Lillian's claim about Rosemary having had the gun in her possession. Linda had told him that Rosemary was learning how to shoot; her cousin Ed Giles was teaching her. Giles could confirm the story about the gun.

When they searched Rosemary's house, they found nothing related to the gun or anything else that would shed any immediate light on the killings. Hung by the wall phone in the small kitchen, they found a notepad with the name "Ed" written on it followed by a phone number. They tried calling several times, but got no response.

Oddest of all, they found all of Rosemary's personal papers carefully placed in a large manila envelope laying on the kitchen table. In the envelope was a recent hand-written Will leaving everything that Rosemary possessed to Robert Wiggs Jr. No one knew, not even Rosemary herself, that this had been part of the third hurdle in her plan; the part that she really couldn't formulate into rational thought. Down in the deepest recesses of her unravelling mind lay the motive for writing the Will. If she were successful in killing Harold and Lillian, she knew her own life would have been worthless. It was the only part of her plan that she succeeded in fulfilling.

Rosemary's papers lying in full view on the kitchen table puzzled the sheriff. Clearly, a person intending suicide would do this. It was equally clear to him that no one would commit suicide by throwing themselves on a boulder trying to break their neck. The only answer that made sense to him was that someone else had planted those papers, trying to make the police believe that her death was a suicide, and that the killer had struggled with Rosemary and that's why she'd died with a broken neck and not as planned, possibly another shooting. And since Bobby was, as the sheriff knew, Lillian's nephew, and benefited from Rosemary's death, his suspicions concerning Lillian deepened. If they didn't find this Ed

Giles soon and confirm Lillian's statement, he felt he was close to making an arrest.

* * *

The day of Rosemary's funeral was the coldest day of the fall so far that year. A light snow had powdered the earth, giving a softness to the grey-brown edge of the coming winter. Harold drove his pick-up truck, following Lillian and Linda in the Buick up ahead. Able and John followed the hearse, where Rosemary rode alone. Her cousin Ed was not there, he seemed to have disappeared.

Harold, Linda and Lillian stood apart at the funeral. Able and John stood on the opposite side from Harold; they had both liked Rosemary. A few of Rosemary's relatives, including her cousins from New York, attended. Based on the reported facts, the local newspapers had turned Rosemary into a hero. It had been reported that she was killed while trying to defend Harold's cabin from the intruder. Rosemary's heroic reputation throughout the county was such that many strangers were there just out of curiosity. She was given a fine departure speech by the presiding minister, who mustered his best oratory and called her "a brave hero in God's citizen army".

But like the sheriff, although for different reasons, Harold didn't believe the news reports. Now he was sure he knew why she was there and that the unidentified man had been shot by mistake. But he was afraid to tell the sheriff that they had broken up and that she had threatened to kill him; afraid that he might come under suspicion for her death. There was too much confusion for him to throw himself into this mess.

CHAPTER 28

The deaths were ruled non-accidental and Lillian was arrested the next day, charged with suspicion of murder. The prosecutor decided to build a case around the murder of Rosemary Allen. The sheriff had presented his version of the double killing to the county district attorney. He agreed there was sufficient circumstantial evidence and motive to make an arrest. Lillian was taken away and jailed. No one had enough money to bail her out.

Everyone was shocked. No one, except for the sheriff and the county attorney, believed she was guilty. They all had known Rosemary as her best friend.

The day after she was arrested, Linda visited her in the morning at the county jail. Lillian looked old, dazed, vacant. Her hair was stringy and seemed to be turning white. Linda was shocked.

“I can't believe this is happening, Ma. What have you done to deserve this! Is there no justice? “

Lillian just nodded. She was still in shock.

“We must get a lawyer.”

“I called Reed yesterday,” she said wearily. “He can't handle it, but he's looking for someone. Said he'd get back with me today.”

“ I'm goin to look for that Ed Giles. He can clear this whole thing up. I mean it's that gun they're tying to you that's doing all this.”

“I know. I know. That gun... ” and she sighed.

“Don't worry, Ma. I'll find that Giles if it's the last thing I do. He can't just have disappeared! And don't worry about the farm. Able said he'd take care of everything until you get free. Said he'd be in later today to see you, after the chores are done.” She left her mother in tears.

Harold didn't know about Lillian's arrest. Right after the funeral he had gone to see the sheriff to make a request.

"Sheriff, I can't stay in that cabin no more. Too many ghosts, and the dogs seem more vicious now. Maybe it's all in my head, but I'm putting it up for sale. Can I do that now?"

The sheriff shook his head. "Don't think so Harold. You better wait a couple of weeks," he said, shuffling some papers on his desk. "We may need to look around some more. It *is* the scene of a crime. I'll tell you when it's Ok."

"I figgered as much. But I also want to move to Speculator. Got a job up there again. Is that Ok?"

Sheriff Gates looked at Harold and stroked his chin. "Ok? Well, I suppose so. Just give me the address and phone where you'll be stayin. You'll probably be called to testify in this case and you'll have to come back down for that."

Harold was surprised. "Testify? About what? I've already told you everything. And there's no phone where I'll live."

Gates leaned back in his chair and stretched his arms. "I think there's going to be a trial Harold," he said, with great importance. "Probably for murder."

Harold's neck bristled. "Murder? But who... ?" He was afraid he was a suspect.

"Can't tell you Harold. Police business. But I can tell you that the fingerprint report identified the dead man. He was Charlie Stout, just like you said."

"Well, I'll be," Harold said. "That means old Charlie was probably at my cabin just looking for some salt or something. Poor guy."

"Yes, a tough break for Charlie. But I'm not so sure he was shot by accident. Look, Harold. I'll let you do this. You go see Tim McCarthy up there in Speculator. He's the town constable. You tell him where you'll be livin'. I'll call him when I need you."

Harold packed a bag and moved to Speculator, glad to get away from the misery of the double killing. He had to get away from Lillian too; he was thinking about her too much. Maybe he was really in love with her, maybe he just never knew it. He cursed himself for letting things get into the state they were in.

When he left the cabin for the last time, he was sad. But he couldn't seem to get Charlie's bloodstains off the porch and door and the boulder kept reminding him of Rosemary's twisted neck. The dogs were now driving him crazy. He just had to get away.

CHAPTER 29

Linda started her search for Ed Giles, leaving Able and John and Bobby to run the farm. Bobby had been angered and frightened by his aunt's arrest and Able did what he could to comfort the boy. Julia also spent as much time with Bobby as she could to help him through the trauma. But they were all confused and hurt; their world had been shaken.

Linda knew where Giles worked and she went out to see his boss.

"We don't know where he is," he said. He was a fat, bald, middle-aged man. He seemed to be sweating all the time, even though it was cool. "He should of been back a week ago. He only had a few days' vacation coming."

"Well, I need to find him. It's awful important."

"Don't know how I can help. Police have been asking for him too. All we know is where he lived."

"Can you tell me who he worked with? Maybe they know something."

He sighed but then gave her the names of three people he thought might know Ed well enough.

"I can't let you go on the floor now. I'll have Janet give you their address and phone. Call them after work. Ok?"

She called that day after work. Two of them knew nothing, but the third, Johnny Caruso, liked to talk.

"Yeh. Maybe I know him, maybe I don't. What do you need him for? Are you a cop? They already talked to me about him." His voice sounded tough. She knew he was from New York.

"No. I'm not a cop. I'm just a woman. I gotta talk to him. My mother's in trouble. Maybe he can help."

"Is she in a jam with the cops?" he asked.

"Yes."

"How do I know I can trust you?"

"Trust me about what?" she asked. "What are you talking about?"

"Nothing. I just can smell cop."

"Look. I'd be glad to meet you Johnny. Would you do that for me?" Linda wondered what Johnny and Ed had been up to.

He agreed and they met at Cherry's Bar and Grill, close to where he lived.

Johnny Caruso was dark skinned and had a mean face, although she couldn't see him too well in the smoky bar. She thought he reminded her of her ex, Frank. But she also thought he had sounded too simple-minded on the phone. Now, he couldn't take his eyes off her.

"What's a chick like you want with Ed Giles?" he asked her. They both had ordered a beer.

"I need to talk with him. He knows something that could help my mother. Do you know where he is?"

"Depends on who's asking."

She was catching on to his game. Johnny liked to be mysterious. "I understand," she said. "you have to be careful... I won't tell anyone else."

"You wanna' go out with me?" he said suddenly, flashing a slick smile. "You ain't got no wedding ring or nothing."

She wanted his help, so she returned his smile. "You're not from here, are you," she said, to change the subject.

"Naw. I'm from Brooklyn, second avenue, close to Red Hook. Ed got me a job up here. Ed, he's crazy, with all that porno stuff... " Then he stopped and shook his head and shot a hard look at her. He didn't seem to like what he saw on her face and at that moment, she knew the game was over. Now she was sure he was suspicious.

He was short and muscular and when he stood up, he looked menacing in the military style jacket he wore. He leaned low over the table and pointed his finger in her face. "You fucking bitch, you better not be working for the cops, " he hissed. "Don't you call me again or you're really gonna get your ass kicked." He left her there to pay the bill.

Unafraid, and now convinced that Ed was up to something, she hired a detective in New York to look for him. She told him where Caruso had said he was from. In two days, he called Linda back.

"Yeh, I found him," he said. "He worked with the Caruso's. He's dead."

"What? It can't be!"

"Yeh it can. Stabbed to death. Did you know he was mixed up with those small-time crooks?" She could detect a tone of amusement in his voice.

"No, No I didn't." She felt herself sinking.

"Yeh, he was running porno junk; cards, key chains, comics, small junk like that. Selling it in your area, up there."

"I didn't know."

"It's nothing really. The cops don't even go after guys like him unless they do something else. He was killed over a broad."

"What?"

"Yeh. He came down here to pick up some of that junk, but couldn't keep his hands off some guy's dame. They got in a fight and he got stabbed. DOA at the hospital. Sorry."

Linda was devastated. With Giles dead, who would tell the truth now about that gun? Who would help her mother?

She told the sheriff about Giles, hoping he could find something further. But nothing came of it so she continued the search for some proof on her own. She tried to reconstruct Ed Giles last few weeks. Find out what he was doing; where he had been.

CHAPTER 30

THE TRIAL

A week later, Lillian was formally charged and jury selection began. Finally, the trial went ahead in the old Fulton County Courthouse.

The county prosecutor, a tall man with a beaky nose and iron-grey hair, wove a tight story about how Lillian had left school that day to do her murderous deed. He said her plan had been to kill Harold Sims and Rosemary Allen; they were making love behind her back and when she found out, she went into a jealous rage. When she got to Harold's cabin that day, she found Rosemary with the hermit, Charlie Stout instead. When she tried to kill Rosemary, Charlie somehow got in the way and she shot him. Then she struggled with Rosemary and pushed her over the rail. Convinced that Rosemary was dead, she saw her opportunity to make it look like Rosemary had killed Charlie. She cleaned her prints off the gun with a towel and put rosemary's hands on the stock. Then she planted the gun next to rosemary's body. She put a box of shotgun shells in her car, to further strengthen the deception and throw off suspicion.

He displayed the Browning as exhibit number 1 to the entranced jury. "This is a *very* special gun," he explained, as he held the Browning under their noses. "Cost well over a thousand dollars. Lillian Sim's first husband owned it. He actually killed himself with it." With his dark looks and words and the way he held it, the Browning looked menacing in his hands. The front row of jurors shrunk back as he extended it towards them.

Lillian's lawyer objected.

The prosecutor changed his approach. "When her first husband died, this gun then belonged to Mrs. Sims," he continued, to thwart off more objections. "The police have a hand receipt from her; they got it when they returned it. This gun never belonged to

Rosemary Allen. We will show later that she didn't even know how to use this gun."

Lillian shuddered as she heard these words. They frightened her, shattered her faith in the truth. Dilbert Telly, the lawyer Reed had recommended, told her to ignore the words, but she couldn't.

As the prosecutor continued, he turned fiercely on any hostile witness attempting to defend Lillian's character. He turned his attacks on her family problems with Matt and her children, as far as he had unearthed them.

Lillian squeezed her hands in dread. *What did he know?*

The prosecutor became so convinced of the truth of his made-up story, that he actually believed it. He felt the jury was beginning to believe it, too. To ensure that belief, he called his special witness.

"Your honor, I would like to call Anna Graham to the stand," he said.

Lillian tensed. *Anna Graham?* She had never heard of her. She turned to look as this new witness entered the courtroom. As she approached her, Lillian felt she was vaguely familiar, but didn't recognize her. Another woman followed the new witness into the courtroom and took a seat in the back with the court spectators. Lillian hadn't been able to see her very well through the crowd.

When the woman took the stand and removed her hat, Lillian put her hand over her mouth and gasped; *It was that woman; It was Joyce Hutchins' secretary!*

After a few introductory remarks, to establish the witness's identity and credibility, the prosecutor launched his attack:

"Now, Miss Graham," he said, with discernable glee, "Can you tell us, in your own words, about your meeting, in Albany, with Lillian Sims, formerly known as Lillian Barry?"

The woman nervously described the meeting that had taken place, placing great emphasis on the gun in Lillian's purse and her threat to kill Joyce Hutchins. "She was actin' kinda' crazy. Kept talking about killing miss Hutchins and talkin' about dogs and cats and such. I really think she was crazy. Miss Hutchins was lucky not to be there!"

The defense objected.

The Prosecutor changed direction. "And is that woman you met and knew as Lillian Barry in this courtroom?" he asked.

"Yes, sir, she is. That's her, right there." She pointed to Lillian.

There was a loud uproar in the courtroom and the judge called for order.

"So, you see, ladies and gentlemen," the prosecutor said, "this witness has shown that Lillian Sims is quite capable of killing someone. We can easily believe that Lillian Sims would have killed Joyce Hutchins had she been there that evening, just like she killed Rosemary Allen."

The defense objected again, but the image the prosecutor wanted to instill in the jury's mind had been established.

The defense asked for a short recess. Lillian saw Joyce Hutchins leaving the courtroom. She was smiling.

"Lillian, is what this woman says, is it true?" Dilbert Telly asked her.

"I'm afraid it is." she replied. "I didn't think I'd ever see her again."

"Why didn't you tell me?"

"It was a long time ago, Mr. Telly. I didn't even think about it."

"Is there anything more you can tell me?" he asked.

"No, she told it like it happened, I think. But I don't want this testimony to go any further. She's already brought out too much about Matt."

"But that's our defense of your character! Matt's cheating is what motivated you, made you angry enough to go to Albany and confront Hutchins… "

"I'd rather drop it."

"Lillian, you're on trial for murder… "

"But I didn't do it! You've got to prove that without dragging

Matt's horrid behavior through this."

"Ok. But do me a favor," he said, "and tell me your version of the story. Try to remember everything; exact words and exact actions."

When the trial resumed, Dilbert cross-examined Anna Graham without mentioning Matt.

"did you say that Lillian Barry, now known as Sims, threatened to kill your boss, Joyce Hutchins?" he asked.

"Yes sir. that was her very words."

"Didn't she really say that she had come there to kill Joyce Hutchins? And that as far as she was concerned, she was dead? And that she wouldn't come back? Isn't that what she really said?"

"I... I'm not sure."

But even with this weakening of Graham's testimony, Lillian sensed that the jury had changed feelings; she believed by their looks that they now thought she was guilty.

But after two more days of testimony, from people that had known Lillian and Matt, the prosecutor managed to drag the Joyce Hutchins affair into full light. Lillian relived the pain all over again. And then he got people who had known Rosemary, to testify that she had never owned a gun and hated hunting.

* * *

Glenda Ellison sat in the rear of the old Fulton County courthouse, trying to sort out what had happened to Lillian. When they'd investigated the Wickersville school scandal, they had become close friends. She was certain of Lillian's innocence and was shocked by the array of cruel charges. Day after day, as more and more of the bazaar incidents of her life were revealed, she saw Lillian slipping further into the abyss of shame, where victims feel like wrapping themselves in the covering silence of death. She was being tried for murder, after all, less than a mile from her former home. The old courthouse was packed with curious spectators, many of whom were her former neighbors.

After a few days, Glenda was allowed to visit Lillian in her cell, a bare, small room with a tiny window high up, a small bunkbed and a little wobbly end table. The toilet facilities were down the hall.

The barred door was locked behind her. They embraced and then sat on the grey prison blanket and when she took Lillian's hand, it felt ice-cold, Like the hand of a dead person, and she squeezed it with sympathy.

"God, Lillian," she sobbed, "How can this be happening? Why can't they see that you're innocent!"

Lillian sighed and slowly shook her head. "I keep asking myself that same question. Yes... yes, I think... " She went silent.

"What Lillian. What do you think?"

"I think... maybe it's because there is no other explanation for those two deaths. Maybe I really did it... maybe... "

"Don't say that. You know you're innocent! There has to be some way to prove it!"

"That shotgun... If only I had destroyed it... "

"We must prove your innocence."

"I don't see how. The only witnesses are dead. Who can help me? No one. I can't take listening to them dragging me and Matt through the mud. That's what Hutchins's doing and everyday it gets worse. I could kill her!"

"God, don't even think that! That prosecutor is like a demon, a witch, he can understand what people are thinking."

"I don't care... I've made out my Will."

"Your Will! But why, for God's sake?"

Lillian put her face in her hands and slowly shook her head. she turned slowly and stared at Glenda, her eyes vacant and tearless, as if she could no longer perceive the world.

* * *

Glenda then met Harold in the courthouse the day before he testified.

"Is there any way we can get these charges dropped?" she pleaded with a trembling voice.

"Don't know, Glenda. This is about the worse thing I could ever imagine. I believe completely that she's innocent. I know it! I know it was Rosemary who did it all. Everything points to her."

"No one seems to agree with you."

"I know... but I've gone over this thing in my mind and the only thing that may save Lillian is the truth. I'm gonna tell the judge everything that happened between me and Rosemary and Lillian... it will be the truth at all costs... I just hope I can do it."

Glenda liked Harold from the first day she'd met him when they talked about Bobby missing school. After spending that afternoon with him, there was something deep inside her that regretted his marriage, and although this tiny thought pinged around inside her, she would never let it emerge into consciousness.

The next day, the prosecutor called Harold to the witness stand. The Sheriff had called him earlier in Speculator to come down. Harold couldn't believe when the sheriff told him that Lillian had been charged with murder and jailed. He wanted desperately to talk with her, to tell her he knew she was innocent, but she wouldn't see him.

"Weren't you and Rosemary Allen lovers?" the prosecutor shot at Harold. He was sure he could get Harold's testimony to lock the case up against Lillian.

"Yes, we were," he said in a low voice.

"And didn't you and Rosemary have a meeting planned on the day of the murder?"

"No, we didn't," he said, his nervousness increased by the sight of the large courtroom crowd. They all seemed to be hanging on his every word.

"But she came over to see you real regular, didn't she?"

No, she didn't." Harold tried to catch Lillian's eye, but she was looking away from him.

"We have witnesses that saw her on the road to your cabin several times."

"I can't deny that. I don't know."

"Well, isn't it probable then, that on the day of the murder she came over to see you? Who else would she come over to see?"

"No, I don't believe that. She wouldn't have come over to see me."

"What? Would you repeat that." The prosecutor thought he had him; that he could now trip Harold up in a lie.

"She didn't come over to see me." Harold looked straight at the prosecutor for the first time.

"I submit that you are contradicting yourself. How can you say that when it is well known, as you admit, that you two were lovers?" The prosecutor said.

Harold squirmed in the chair. He looked at the judge. He wished Lillian would look at him.

"Answer the question," the judge told him.

"We broke up," he said in a voice so low he was difficult to hear.

"You what?" the prosecutor asked.

"Yes sir, " Harold said, now annoyed and angry that he and Lillian were being put through this ordeal. He spoke louder now. "Me and Rosemary broke up. Several weeks before this shooting happened. You see, Rosemary didn't come that day to see me. She came over that day to kill me! She must of killed poor Charlie by accident instead."

Silence filled the courtroom for a moment. Everyone seemed stunned. Then an uproar broke out. The judge pounded his gavel to restore order. "Order," he shouted, "order!"

Lillian looked at Harold for the first time. He was looking back at her; a hint of a smile crossed his face.

When the uproar settled down, the prosecutor made a show of trying to dismiss Harold's testimony.

"That's only an opinion, isn't it, Mr. Sims!"

But the judge ordered Harold to make a full statement.

Harold started off slowly: "Rosemary and me, we got mixed up together and we shouldn't of. It just happened; happened when Lillian was off on a trip. Neither one of us wanted it to happen. I... wanted to stop seeing her, 'cause I knew it was wrong. I felt bad about it, being married to Lillian." He looked in Lillian's direction again. Now her head was bowed.

"Go on," the judge said.

" Yes sir. I'm... .well, I don't know much about how to deal with women. Then Rosemary, well she got too serious and when I wouldn't see her no more, she got real jealous. She wanted me to break up with Lillian, but I wouldn't."

He stopped and looked up at the ceiling. His neck was beginning to knot. "Lillian didn't know what was going on. She never did." He stopped again and looked down at his clenched hands. They were white.

"Is that all?" the judge asked.

Harold looked back at the Judge. "No sir. It's just hard for me to say these things... Anyway, as I said, Rosemary got real jealous. When I refused to see her anymore, she threatened to kill me and Lillian both. I heard her scream it! She said: 'I'll kill you both!' You see, she came out that day to kill me, that's for sure.! And to kill Lillian too. Lillian never killed no one. And that's the truth."

The courtroom went into a second uproar and the judge called for a recess. The prosecutor was shaken. His story had been blown full of holes. As he fumbled to put together a new one based on Harold not being a credible witness, the judge told him he was close to dismissing the case.

"What about that gun your Honor? She can't deny that it was hers."

"Well, I don't know how important it is, when there's no motive." the judge replied. "If Lillian Sims didn't know... you can't have a crime of passion when there's no motive! Besides, you have no credible evidence that Lillian Sims was at the scene of the crime."

The prosecutor was sure he could deflate Harold's testimony but Before he could reply, sheriff Gates came into the judge's chambers with Linda. He was unsmiling; he looked upset.

"You honor, well sir, Linda Boyle here, she's Lillian Sims' daughter, she's found some evidence about that gun. Seems like Rosemary Allen did have it in her possession after all. Show him Linda."

She handed the judge two signed statements from gun club members who had seen Ed and Rosemary using the Browning at the skeet range.

"I verified the statements, judge. No chance of there bein' two guns around like that," the sheriff said. "And I also found that..." he looked sideways, away from the judge, "found that the deceased, Miss Allen, that is, did have a hunting license."

The prosecutor looked at the sheriff, disgusted.

"Is that all?" the judge asked.

"No, sir, it ain't. One of the club members, a friend of Giles, told us Giles had been takin' Rosemary rabbit hunting out at the Fletcher place. I decided to check it out to see if we could find anything relevant to this case and, well, I did." He looked straight at the judge.

"Well, what did you find?"

"We found Ed Giles. Found his body, that is. He'd been shot twice in the chest with a shotgun."

The judge looked shocked. "But... but you said he'd been killed in New York... "

"We got bad information, judge. I can assure you that Ed Giles is now in the county morgue. It seems he was killed by the same shotgun that killed old Charlie Stout, and now we know... it was Rosemary Allen that had possession of that gun. We found a bloody towel in Rosemary Allen's garbage and the fibers match the fibers found on the gun." The sheriff looked grim. "I guess we were wrong."

The judge called for a re-examination of all evidence. All charges against Lillian were dismissed.

CHAPTER 31

When she finished signing the receipts, the county jail clerk returned her watch and purse and the small jade ring Linda had given her. Then Linda brought Lillian home again. The trauma of the trial had taken its toll; she was weary, defeated; white hair covered much of her head; an old pain was clawing at her insides. A deathly pallor had replaced her usual rosy hue. It didn't help things to see her house again and she walked up the front path with slow, measured steps. With each step, some lesser pain pulled at her insides.

Able greeted her warmly at the door. He wanted to embrace her, to kiss her, but was, as usual, too timid. Inside Bobby and John waited with Julia and Andy.

"Aunty," Bobby yelled and ran to embrace her. She was hugged and kissed by everyone and their tears flowed but she remained dry-eyed and although her spirits revived a bit, she felt annoyed by all these happy people. But after these enthusiastic greetings and the little welcoming speeches that seemed interminable, an awkward silence settled over the little group in the kitchen. No one wanted to ask any questions or to revive anything that had taken place at the now infamous trial. Lillian felt strange, like she had no right to be there, no right to their forgiveness.

"Are you hungry Ma?" Julia asked, trying to get the conversation going in the right direction. "We put together a real nice meal for you."

"Yes, " Bobby said, "And I helped Mr. G. and Junior butcher the chickens."

"Well, that's nice," she said and put on a faked smile.

She had eaten little during her stay in jail and had lost twenty pounds. It showed mostly in her sunken chest and cheeks.

They served her a full plate and everyone crowded around the little table, using the rite of supper to scrutinize and evaluate their returned member. For some reason, she found the food repulsive.

"The cows are doing good, " Able said, hoping to somehow revive her; make her look or feel better. "And I think I've got good news. Remember Dexter's in Ft. Plain? Dexter's ice cream? I think they may want to buy straight from your herd. Leastwise, that's what they were sayin' when I met them last week. I'll meet with them again next week."

"That's good, that's good," she said. The mention of her beloved herd should have perked her up, but the depression she'd brought with her was persistent. Her mind wandered to the courtroom; she was still in the jailhouse; her strength sapped. But she smiled for Able.

"Ma, Junior's come back to work for you," Linda said cheerfully. "Said he'll most likely stay with us from now on. Said Harold told him to come back."

"I wonder why? " she said, her eyes radiating unhappiness.

"And you, Able?" she asked, unsmiling. "Are you leaving?"

Able and John had moved out of the little cottage to an old house nearby, just before Lillian had been arrested. She had chided Able because he'd said that the little cottage was haunted.

"I tell you Lillian," he said, "We're doin' fair in that old Benson place. And there was a real scary presence there in that cottage of yours." He smiled because he knew it had become a joke with everyone. "Like someone was roamin' around in those rooms. Now I know there ain't nobody ever lived there, but, by God, I tell you it's true. Me and John couldn't stay there more than one night."

Lillian offered a tiny smile, but after eating one or two bites, exhaustion overtook her. "I'm sorry," she said, the reunion now weighing on her. "But I'm tired. I can't talk... I need to get some sleep." They quickly left, with more tears and congratulations and she was taken to her bedroom by Linda. The bed enveloped her; it was so different from the jail cots and she felt the softness but couldn't sleep.

She had moved from the edge of sanity and her wakefulness gave her time; time free from the pressures of people, to think about what had happened. Now that the threat of execution was over, a threat so palpable that she had felt her brain being squeezed with fear every time the prosecutor bristled with lies, It came to her that her whole life had been put on trial, that she had been a spectator watching the sordid events of her life played out by cruel jesters, insane apes dressed in judicial robes and business suits, cavorting with monkeys in the jury box. Like a stage play, it had been divided into acts. The first terrible act was Matthew, the cruel and unfaithful; the second was Hutchins the wicked whore and tormentor; the third was the act of Harold the fool; the fourth the act of the witch, Rosemary; Rosemary! She was crazy about playing Hecate or Lady Macbeth when helping with the rehearsals for the High School Plays! She had finally absorbed the witches poison. The fifth was the act of blood and murder, the act they had blamed on her! They spared her the evil act of Linda. She had watched this parade of acts, each one causing more pain as it passed, more hatred in her heart for herself and all the participants and those associated with them until she had just wanted to scream and make them all go away.

The bed was soft and she hated it and couldn't sleep.

* * *

But after all, she thought, *they were all wrong; she had really made the right decisions; her farm really had been the foundation she had needed to renew her life. And it was much more than the sum of its buildings and fields and livestock; it had provided the sustenance and meaning in her life that Matt had taken away.* She loved it and everything about it and the life it had given to others like Bobby and the rest.

As the night drifted away, she still couldn't sleep, because the jesters, apes and monkeys would return to perform the parade of acts once more. She tossed and turned and seemed to have a fever. Even though the room was cold, there were beads of sweat on her forehead.

But after all, she thought, t*he fools were after me because, well maybe it's true that I, I am the cause of all that evil. Was it I, I, I who caused all those acts that paraded so arrogantly before me? I didn't* *commit the murders! But I... could I have caused them? Had I... no love... to give?... Who am I?*

She had to get up.

Through the kitchen window, she saw the moonlight falling on the soft, furry needles of the tamarack trees. Dusted with snow, the graceful branches looked as if they were getting ready for Christmas. She remembered how she'd loved those trees when she first saw them and the animals and birds that made them living worlds within themselves. Then she sat in the rocker racked with terrible visions and after some time, fell into a troubled sleep.

Later she awoke and saw the strange eerie light of pre- dawn tinting the snow on the tamaracks with pin-points of blueish pink. She got up, feeling lighter now and more determined, and left the house with the rifle and walked up the hill to the barn. No one was up yet. Her labor was great; the pain kept coming and going.

Slipping on small stones covered with snow, she hurried up the hill. She wanted to see her fields, the woods, the barn, her Jersey cattle; to feel the timelessness of her Adirondack home.

The bench was lumpy with snow; she brushed it away before sitting to view her domain. It was difficult to lean over or move; the bench was now slippery with ice, and the rifle butt kept sliding on the icy patches around her feet. The freezing air enveloped her and after a while, it seemed like sleep would overcome her. She fought this numbing world; she didn't want to freeze to death, it would seem too stupid.

The cloying smell of burning wood came up to her, up from the house; someone was now stirring; starting the fire in the Merrimac. *It would be good for them to have breakfast in the old kitchen on this beautiful morning. Pancakes and coffee and bacon and eggs with the fresh maple syrup I've drawn from the trees around the cottage before all this... and... and...*

Through the chilled air, the dawn broke bold and beautiful, the rays of light slipping through and over the towering trees, disturbed only by the muffled crack of the rifle shot.

CHAPTER 32

Much to the Sheriff's disappointment, the coroner stated that he believed the death an accident. He would make a final ruling after the autopsy. The bullet had deeply grazed Lillian's right temple, and unconscious, it seemed she had died from hypothermia during the estimated two hours she had lain there. The coroner said he believed she had slipped and fell when she tried to sit on the bench and the rifle, which also had a light trigger, went off accidentally, grazing her head, knocking her unconscious. The freezing, killing air did the rest.

"Do you know why she was carrying that rifle?" the sheriff asked Linda, clearly not satisfied with the coroner's explanation.

"Sometimes she carried it for protection… especially early in the morning, if it was still dark," Linda said, while stifling sobs.

"Protection… from what?" The sheriff asked brusquely.

"Well… bears… mostly. Once she went to do chores and saw a bear on the path above the barn. That's when she started carrying the gun. She told us to do the same if we were alone. She said to shoot just to scare the bear off, unless it charged."

"Do you all know how to use that rifle?" he asked.

"Yes, sheriff. She had Harold teach us how to shoot."

"Have you ever had troubles with wild dogs?"

"None that I ever heard of." The others confirmed her statement.

"It seems that your mother had been layin' up there for onto two hours before bein' found. Why did it take you so long to find her?"

"She must 'a got up much earlier than we did, sheriff. When I got up, no one else was up and I thought she was still sleeping. The door to her room was closed. We cooked breakfast and then knocked on the door to wake her up… and when… when there was no sound, I opened the door and saw the bed was empty. That's when I dressed and went up to see if she had started with the chores. I found her up by the bench… " Linda cried out of control. Bobby and Julia were crying with her.

Although the sheriff was still investigating, he was touched by their sorrow and halted the questioning. He was not a hard man and felt he owed Lillian for the ordeal she had been put through.

When the sheriff's investigators went through her bedroom trying to confirm the coroner's opinion, they found that she had made a Will during the trial. When asked, the sheriff said because of the Will, he believed it was suicide, that she'd tried to shoot herself and the rifle butt slid on the ice when she pressed the trigger, but he didn't want to make yet another mistake, seeming old and foolish, so he accepted the coroner's opinion.

EPILOGUE

After Harold's testimony, helping with Lillian's release, Glenda's admiration and feelings for him escalated. A few months after Lillian's death, Harold asked her to marry him because he finally found a woman he could love and they moved into Harold's old cabin. Harold didn't want to move back to the cabin, but Glenda loved it and convinced him that he would get over his fears and the bad memories.

But some days, Harold sees old Charlie Stout lying bloodied in the driveway and on others, Rosemary, well… she actually looks up at him from the weeds with her bloated face and smiles.

Harold anxiously explained to Glenda that they must leave, that the spirits are still active and because of that the wild dogs, being sensitive to lively spirits, have never returned. Since she has never seen the spirits nor the wild dogs, she tries her best to comfort Harold, but refuses to leave.

* * *

The old Sand Creek farm is for sale again.

The End

ABOUT THE AUTHOR

Joseph was born in Brooklyn, NY, and grew up in both Brooklyn and the Adirondacks, one of his favorite places. After a tour in the Army, he took up a career in electronic engineering in New York where he stayed for several years. But he was the restless sort and took jobs that led him around the world.

He has a keen interest in literature and started writing short stories and articles for small magazines early in his career. His world travels, especially over much of Europe, gave him much to write about, including his latest novel about the Viking era. He studied medieval history; German at Bonn University; holds a BA/MA from the University of Texas and published a previous historical novel, OF ARMS I SING, with excellent reviews from Booklist and others.

Serious historical fiction is one of his favorite genres because it is a powerful way to get at the truth and, if balanced and well done, can bring a better understanding between cultures.

He lives in the American Southwest with his wife and continues his research and writing. He remains indebted to his wife for supporting his writing endeavors.